Bell

hidden talent rediscovered

Bello is a digital-only imprint of Pan Macmillan,
established to breathe new life into previously published,
classic books.

At Bello we believe in the timeless power of the imagination,
of a good story, narrative and entertainment, and we want to
use digital technology to ensure that many more readers
can enjoy these books into the future.

We publish in ebook and print-on-demand formats
to bring these wonderful books to new audiences.

www.panmacmillan.com/imprint-publishers/bello

Richmal Crompton

Richmal Crompton (1890–1969) is best known for her thirty-eight books featuring William Brown, which were published between 1922 and 1970. Born in Lancashire, Crompton won a scholarship to Royal Holloway in London, where she trained as a schoolteacher, graduating in 1914, before turning to writing full-time. Alongside the William novels, Crompton wrote forty-one novels for adults, as well as nine collections of short stories.

Richmal Crompton

FROST AT MORNING

BELLO

First published in 1950 by Hutchinson & Co.

This edition published 2017 by Bello
an imprint of Pan Macmillan
20 New Wharf Road, London N1 9RR
Associated companies throughout the world

www.panmacmillan.com/imprint-publishers/bello

ISBN 978-1-5098-5955-9 EPUB
ISBN 978-1-5098-5953-5 HB
ISBN 978-1-5098-5954-2 PB

Copyright © Richmal Crompton, 1950

This book remains true to the original in every way. Some aspects may appear
out-of-date to modern-day readers. Bello makes no apology for this, as to retrospectively
change any content would be anachronistic and undermine the authenticity of the original.

Pan Macmillan does not have any control over, or any responsibility for,
any author or third party websites referred to in or on this book.

A CIP catalogue record for this book is available from the British Library.

Typeset by Ellipsis Digital Limited, Glasgow

Visit www.panmacmillan.com to read more about all our books
and to buy them. You will also find features, author interviews and
news of any author events, and you can sign up for e-newsletters
so that you're always first to hear about our new releases.

FROST AT MORNING

Chapter One

Four children sat round a wooden table under the shade of a copper beech in the Vicarage garden. They were modelling figures from coloured plasticine—red, blue, green and yellow.

Geraldine worked with earnest concentration. She was a plump little girl, with crisp brown hair, large brown eyes, and lips that were thick but beautifully chiselled. Her short fat fingers crushed the plasticine into shapeless pieces, which she joined together slowly and clumsily.

"Look, Philip," she said, "I'm making a train."

The boy turned his dark narrow face to her, drawing his brows together in a quick impatient frown, pushing back the strand of hair that fell across his delicate blue-veined temple.

"It isn't like a train," he said shortly; "it hasn't got wheels."

"I'm going to make wheels," she said. She spoke eagerly, trying to hold his attention. "Look, Philip, I'm going to make wheels of this piece. I'm—"

But he had lost interest in her, moving his slender sensitive fingers over the curving horns of his red antelope, bending over it with passionate absorption.

Angela leant across the table, her blue eyes bright with mischief, her curls a mesh of gold in the sunlight. Suddenly her hand shot out, and she snatched one of the pieces of red plasticine that lay by Philip's elbow.

He stared at her, his face tight with anger.

"Give it me back," he said.

She laughed—a gay mocking laugh, clear as the trill of a bird.

"I want it," she said. "I want it to make a red fire-engine."

Geraldine thrust out her underlip.

"It's his," she said. "You shan't have it."

She seized Angela's hand and forced it open.

"There you are, Philip," she said, placing the red lump at his elbow. "I got it back for you."

He gave her a long, unsmiling look and pushed the piece across to Angela.

"You can have it," he said.

Angela leant back in her chair, rolling the piece between her hands, smiling to herself . . . She didn't really want the red wax. She only wanted to relieve her boredom by teasing Philip.

"I'm not going to make a fire-engine," she said. "I'm going to make a funny face." She glanced at the child next her. "You've not started making anything with yours yet, Monica."

Monica awoke from her day-dreams with a guilty start and bent over the stick of wax, twisting it this way and that, pretending to give it her whole attention, jerking her head so that her dark hair fell over her shoulders to shade her face. It was all unreal to her—the garden, the children, the brightly coloured sticks of modelling wax, but she had to pretend that it was real, had to pretend to be a child with other children. Her mother had said: "Honestly, darling, I can't have you here any longer. I've had you for my six months and daddy's not quite ready for you yet, so I must make some other arrangement till he is."

Seeing the other children intent on their work, she raised her head and looked round the pleasant sunny garden. At the further end of the lawn stood the Vicarage—a long, low building, vaguely ecclesiastic in design, half hidden by climbing roses and jasmine. A photograph taken from where she sat formed the front page of the prospectus that had been sent in answer to her mother's enquiries. Her mother had seen the advertisement in the newspaper: "Vicar's wife offers home to one or two children under seven as companions to own child. Happy home life. Country surroundings. Resident governess," and had said, "I believe this would do." Monica had felt little interest or curiosity. She knew exactly what it would be like. During her short life she had been sent to many such places.

Her eye wandered to the gate at the end of the drive, a narrow drive like a tunnel, between trees whose branches met overhead, and she thought: Suppose the postman comes in now and there's a letter from daddy to say he's ready for me. Her heart leapt at the thought and her mind flew off to the cottage in Yorkshire, and to the untidy little room littered up with daddy's manuscripts and books and fishing-rods. She would tidy it up as she always did. She would sew the buttons on to his shirts and old tweed coat. She would go fishing with him, and they would have long walks together over the wind-swept moors. When they came in she would make the toast while he boiled the eggs and got the tea ready. Perhaps after tea they would put on her favourite gramophone record, the "March of the Tin Soldiers".

Her friendship with her father was the only friendship that life had as yet given her. They shared an accumulation of small private jokes to which no one else held the key. Shy and silent with other people, she would chatter to him unrestrainedly of everything that came into her head. Everything but one thing. She mustn't mention her mother to him. When she was with her father she had to close her mind on the months she spent with her mother, and when she went to her mother she had to close her mind on her father. Her mind was full of closed doors . . . She knew things that children should not know, that she must not mention to other children, things that lay like a fog over her spirit, giving her a sense of fear and, strangely, of guilt.

"What are you making?" said Angela.

"An apple," said Monica at random, moving her fingers ineffectively over the plasticine, struggling against the feeling of unreality that invested the three other children, the sunlit garden and the ridiculous pieces of coloured wax.

"There's daddy!" cried Angela suddenly.

They turned to see the Vicar entering the garden, glancing at his watch as he closed the gate. The quick movement with which he pulled the watch from his pocket and replaced it was his most characteristic gesture. His life was an ordered progress from one appointment to another. He was never late and never early. He never hurried and never dawdled. Every minute of every day was fully occupied with its appointed task, and it all fitted together as neatly as the pieces of a jigsaw puzzle. Even now as he stood—a handsome, middle-aged, dignified man, holding out his arms to the little daughter who was running across the lawn to him—he seemed to be reckoning up the exact amount of time that he could spare to the encounter.

"Hello, daddy!" she called gaily.

He lifted her up and she clung to him, putting her arms round his neck, kissing his cheek, turning her head for a moment to make sure that the others were watching. There was triumph and a faint unconscious cruelty in the laughing glance she sent them.

They watched her sombrely, in silence, forgetting the coloured models that lay before them on the table, forgetting their usual quarrels and differences, united by a common sense of exclusion. With the quick sensitiveness of childhood they realized all the implications of the little scene. It was Angela's father, Angela's home. She was here by right. They were here because, for the time, at any rate, their own parents did not want them.

The Vicar set his daughter down and waved to the other children.

"Hello, children!" he called with the impersonal heartiness that was part of his professional equipment, then, purposeful, unhurried, his mind already occupied with the next item on his programme, he turned to go indoors.

Angela danced back across the lawn and sat down at the table, spreading her dainty smocked frock over her knees. They watched her, still in silence, then Philip spoke in a high-pitched unsteady voice.

"My father's bigger than him. He's braver, too. He's shot lions. He rides horses. He climbs mountains. He's teaching me to do things, too. I can catch cricket balls. I can nearly dive—"

"You're frightened of the dark," said Angela.

He ignored her.

"He comes to see me in bed every night. When I had bronchitis, he sat up with me in the room all night."

"Why didn't your mother do that?"

"I haven't got a mother. I'm glad I haven't. I don't like them. We don't either of us want a mother. We like being alone together."

"Why did he send you here then?" said Angela.

"He had to go away," he said, his voice rising shrilly. "On some business. Where he couldn't take me. He's going to come back as soon as he can. He said so."

"I'm a princess," said Geraldine suddenly.

She spoke uncertainly, with an undernote of aggressiveness, as if challenging the others to contradict her. But no one took any notice, and in the silence her mind went back to that talk her parents had had with her the week before she came away. She remembered every word and look, remembered them with a turmoil of spirit in which bewilderment, desolation and excitement were equally mingled.

They had sat on her bed, one on each side of her, speaking in a sort of antiphon.

"So, you see, darling, though you aren't really our own little girl . . ."

"We love you just as much as if you were . . ."

"Even more, darling . . ."

"We didn't tell you before because we wanted you to feel just as if you were our own little girl before we told you . . ."

"You see, it doesn't make any difference . . ."

"No difference at all, sweetheart . . ."

Slowly Geraldine had collected her scattered forces. Those rather surprising facts that she had recently learnt about babies . . . What exactly did they mean in her case?

"Then I wasn't ever inside you?" she had said.

"Well, no, darling," admitted Mrs. Mortimer.

"But I was inside somebody?"

"Yes, darling."

"Then—then that person was my real mummy?"

"In a way, darling."

5

"Let's not think about that," said Mr. Mortimer briskly.

But Geraldine wanted to think about it.

"Why didn't I stay with her? Why did I come to you?"

"She didn't want you, darling, and we did . . ."

"We wanted you very badly indeed . . ."

"So now, Gerry darling, go to sleep and forget all about it."

But she didn't forget all about it. Sometimes she tried to. Sometimes—for neither of her parents had ever referred to it again—she almost managed to persuade herself that the strange conversation had never taken place, and that the two whom she knew as mummy and daddy were her real father and mother just like other little girls' fathers and mothers. But at other times the words, "She didn't want you, darling," lay like a weight at the bottom of her heart. Her real father and mother didn't belong to her. And the ones she called mummy and daddy didn't belong to her either. Not really. Not in the way that other children's parents did. It was as if her most precious possession had been suddenly snatched from her and she was left utterly terrifyingly bereft. And then she would take refuge in vague dreams of self-importance. She was a princess sent as a baby to foster-parents to be safe from the plots of her enemies. One day her royal father would send for her and she would go to her own kingdom where she would reign as a queen—fêted, courted, obeyed.

"I'm a princess," she said again.

Angela turned to look at her.

"You can't be a princess," she said. "Your mother isn't a queen."

"My real one is," said Geraldine, and repeated, "My real one . . . She lives a long way off, and she sent me away because of enemies . . ."

Her voice trailed away. The story failed to convince even herself.

"You're making it all up," said Angela. "I know where your mother and father live. They live at Maybridge and it's not far from here, and you're going back there quite soon now."

"I know," said Geraldine flatly. Then the note of aggressiveness crept again into her voice as she added: "They've got a surprise for me when I get back. They said so. It might be a pony. I think it is a pony."

But they weren't listening to her any longer. Philip was twisting the thin spiral tips of his antelope's horns. Angela was fashioning her wax into a face with a long nose and spikes of hair. Monica was sitting there, her pale face shrouded by her long dark hair.

"Where do your mother and father live, Monica?" said Angela suddenly.

Monica did not answer for a few moments, then she said slowly: "My father lives in Yorkshire and my mother lives in London."

"Why don't they live in the same place?"

There was a silence as they waited for her answer. Even Philip had lifted his head from his red antelope and was watching her.

Then a clear incisive voice cut through the silence, and Miss Rossiter, the nursery governess, came across the lawn from the house.

"Well, children, how are you getting on?" she said.

But even that didn't break the spell. They still waited for Monica's answer.

"Why don't they live in the same place?" said Angela again.

"Because they're divorced," said Monica.

She looked at Miss Rossiter as she spoke, and Miss Rossiter averted her eyes. Something about the child always made her feel uncomfortable.

"Hush, dear," she said. "Don't talk about it."

"I wasn't going to," said Monica. She spoke gently, reassuringly. "I wasn't going to talk about it."

"And now let me see what you've all done," said Miss Rossiter, speaking with an intensification of her usual briskness as if to shut out the memory of the unfortunate word. "What about you, Geraldine, dear?"

"It's a train," said Geraldine.

"It's not very like a train, dear," said Miss Rossiter.

"I haven't finished it yet," said Geraldine earnestly. "I haven't had time. I'm going to finish it. It'll be like a train when I've finished it."

7

"Well, you must try to work more quickly, dear."

Miss Rossiter put out her hand to take the shapeless object, but Geraldine snatched it up and held it closely to her. Her face was flushed, her childish brow lowering.

"It's mine," she said. "It's mine. I made it."

"You can have some more wax to-morrow, dear, but—"

"It's mine. You can't take it from me. It's mine."

Miss Rossiter smiled uncertainly. She was a tall, fair girl of about twenty-two, with fresh colouring, regular features and blue eyes. Her expression held an earnestness that left little room for humour but that was genuinely kind and sincere.

"Well, dear . . ." she said inconclusively and turned to Angela. "And what have you made, Angela?"

Angela leant back in her chair and moved the long yellow nose of her "funny face" to and fro.

"Oh, Angela!" said Miss Rossiter, smiling despite herself.

Angela began to laugh—gay little drifts of laughter that seemed to float away through the summer air like bubbles.

"It's funny," she said. "It made you laugh."

"But you've not really been working, have you, dear?"

"Oh, no," said Angela, and laughed again.

Miss Rossiter moved down the table to Monica's chair. She moved slowly, reluctantly. This child with the pale composed face and withdrawn manner had her somehow—she didn't quite know how—at a disadvantage. She had remonstrated with Mrs. Sanders about taking her.

"Don't you remember the case?" she had said. "It was in all the papers. A shocking case. And the child was brought into it. I don't think we ought to have her. There are the other children to consider."

"Children are safe from that sort of thing," Mrs. Sanders had said carelessly. "To the pure all things are pure, you know."

But Miss Rossiter wasn't so sure that to the pure all things were pure.

Monica rolled her pieces of modelling wax into a ball and handed it to Miss Rossiter.

"I began to make an apple," she said, "but I didn't do much of it, I'm sorry."

"That's all right, dear," said Miss Rossiter, turning with relief to Philip and looking at the graceful red antelope that stood on the table—spindly legs, tiny hooves, long curving antlers. "Oh, Philip, that's lovely!"

But Philip was gazing at it with a tautening of his thin nervous face, seeing it suddenly as a travesty of his vision. The thing his mind had seen had been exquisite. This thing he had made seemed to mock him in its clumsiness and shapelessness.

"It's not," he said stormily. "It's horrible . . ."

He crushed it savagely in his hand, then, lips trembling, turned and ran across the lawn, plunging into the shelter of a weeping willow whose branches swept the ground. Geraldine dropped the "train" she had been holding and ran after him.

"Oh, dear!" said Miss Rossiter.

These unwanted children who came to share the happy home life of the Vicarage were always a little difficult.

She addressed the remaining two children in her clear ringing voice,

"Now, children, we're going to take a picnic tea into the woods. I'll go in and get the things ready and will you tell the others that I want you all to come when I blow the whistle? And don't make a noise on the lawn. Remember that Mrs. Sanders is working."

She glanced in the direction of the house. At an open window on the ground floor the Vicar's wife could be seen seated at a desk, surrounded by a wild confusion of papers, her hair disordered, a streak of ink across her brow.

Chapter Two

The wood was cool and dim, chequered by green shadows, alive with the whispers of insects and the song of the birds, heavy with the acrid sweetness of leafy growth. A tiny stream ran through it, rippling, clear as air, over its bed of pebbles. Beneath the trees bracken thrust up tall graceful fronds. In the clearings drifts of willow herb were gay and heartlifting as a sudden burst of music.

The children often brought their tea here on fine afternoons, and to-day the party had been increased by the addition of Patsy Gosport, a fat little girl with gingery curls, a tilted nose and a soft round mouth, who lived at The Limes next door to the Vicarage. She had been swinging on the gate as they passed and had joined them on a casual invitation from Miss Rossiter. The children had played in the wood and had had tea in an open space beneath a large beech tree. After tea Miss Rossiter had read aloud to them, choosing "Little Thumb" from her book of Hans Andersen's Fairy Tales.

Philip, sitting apart from the others, had listened with barely concealed impatience, taking up pieces of earth and crumbling them between his fingers, drawing his brows together in his quick nervous frown. The words were beautiful, but Miss Rossiter spoilt them . . . She had a penetrating voice, and she read in an over-dramatic fashion that made him feel hotly uncomfortable. As soon as she had finished, he slipped away from the rest and wandered down a little path that wound among the trees. He wanted to be alone, but, glancing round, he saw that Geraldine, too, had left the group and was following him. His lips tightened and his brows shot together again. He wanted to avoid Geraldine . . . This morning she had found him crying under the willow tree, heartbroken by his failure to create his dream antelope, and she had put her arms round him, murmuring words of sympathy.

"Don't . . . Philip, darling, don't . . . It doesn't matter . . . It's all right."

He had clung to her blindly for comfort, but now the memory sent flames of humiliation through him. He hated her because she had seen his tears and because he had turned to her for consolation. He quickened his footsteps, but, slowly, relentlessly, she gained on him, till she was walking by his side.

"Hello, Philip," she said.

The timidity of her tone increased his anger. He thrust his hands into his pockets and walked on scowling, without answering or looking at her.

"Philip . . ."

Still he said nothing, and together they passed under the green arches of the hazels. A dragon-fly darted across the path just in front of them; a jay rose with a flash of colour from a tall blackberry bush nearby. Philip walked with face averted, trying to pretend that she was not there.

"Philip . . ."

He gave a grunt.

"I want to ask you something . . . My mother and father call me Gerry. It's their pet name for me. Will you call me Gerry too? I do so want you to."

He searched for words to express his sense of outrage.

"You don't call people names like that because they ask you to," he said at last. "It makes you want not to . . . You don't understand . . . You don't understand anything."

"But, Philip"—she was puzzled—"I thought you loved me. I thought we were friends. We were friends this morning under the willow tree when you—"

He cut her short, his face flaming, his heart beating unevenly.

"I don't love you," he said savagely. "I don't I don't."

The path had reached a narrow plank bridge that spanned the stream. Beneath it the stream formed a little waterfall, lying smooth as silk over the boulders, then sparkling in the sunshine as it splashed again into its clear pebbly bed. Philip had wanted to come here to watch it, but the joy it should have given him was absent because Geraldine stood beside him, plump and ungainly, sending out waves of sticky affection that seemed to clog his spirit.

"Go away," he said, without turning his head. "I don't want you here."

Even at that she did not take offence. Her soft brown eyes held bewilderment, hurt, solicitude, but no resentment.

"You shouldn't say things like that, Philip," she said gently. "It's rude. It doesn't matter to me because I love you, but"—she hesitated, then continued, slowly, conscientiously—"when you're rude to other people, like you are sometimes to Mrs. Sanders and Miss Rossiter, it worries me terribly because—because they don't know how nice you are really. I think you ought to try to be more polite to people."

He was stifled by a sudden rush of fear and anger. He felt as though she were holding him in her hot moist hands . . . fingering him . . .

"Leave me alone," he said in a high choking voice. "I hate you. I hate you more than anyone else in the world. I shall always hate you."

She turned at that and walked away—a squat, disconsolate figure, treading awkwardly along the narrow winding path.

Philip drew a long tremulous breath of relief and sat on the bank of the stream, gazing down at the water, taking comfort from the silence and solitude. Next him was a large stone. He put his hand on it. It was firm, smooth-textured, warmed by the sun, the small dents in it soft with lichen. He touched the lichen gently . . . tiny feathers of gold and green, delicately fashioned and lovely as gossamer. A deep stillness seemed to hold the wood. Overhead the beech leaves were like cups, catching the sunshine and spilling it on to the ground beneath . . . And suddenly all the unrest of his spirit was stilled, and happiness welled up in his heart. He sat there, hardly daring to breathe lest it should break the tenuous spell. These flashes of happiness visited him at rare intervals, seeming

12

to catch him up into a world where everything was fine-drawn and exquisite, intensifying and heightening the beauty of the ordinary world around him, so that stream, moss, trees and grass were drenched in magic and mystery. And with the happiness came a strange sense of power, making him exultantly aware of secret forces within him that belonged to him alone, that he shared with no one.

He didn't know how long he had sat there when Angela came down the path, but she came so lightly and silently, like a leaf blown by the wind, that her coming did not seem to break the shining brittle world that held him.

"There you are, Philip," she said. "Will you play hide-and-seek with me?"

He shook his head.

"No. I don't want to."

She sat down by him.

"What are you thinking about?"

"I don't know."

"You must know what you were thinking about. Were you thinking about what you're going to do when you're grown-up? I often think of that."

"No."

"What are you going to do when you're grown-up?"

"I don't know."

"I do. I'm going to have lovely clothes and go to parties." Her small face was alight with eagerness. "I'm going to have my photograph in the newspapers. What are you going to do, Philip? What do you want to do?"

"I want to be like my father."

"What's he like?"

"He's very brave and very strong. He's been out to Africa shooting big game. Once he went on an exploring expedition."

He didn't know why he told her all this. When Geraldine wanted you to tell her things, it made you want not to. Angela didn't care whether you told her things or not, and it made you want to tell her.

"You felt sick when you looked down from the church tower. You could never be like him."

"He once won a championship at the winter sports," he went on, as if he had not heard her. "He's climbed some of the highest mountains in the world."

She leapt to her feet. She was bored and irritated. She'd wanted to play hide-and-seek and he wouldn't play. He would only talk about his father. He hadn't been interested in what she was going to do when she was grown-up. He was a stupid, silly little boy.

"You're a baby," she taunted him. "You cried this morning because you couldn't make that plasticine thing properly. You cried and let Geraldine comfort you. I saw you . . ."

With that she turned and ran down the path out of his sight.

She had pricked the bubble of his happiness and the hurt she had dealt him could not be solaced by anger. Somehow he could never be angry with Angela as he so often was with Geraldine. And what she had said was true. He set his lips tightly and gave himself a little jerk as if to shake off his dreaminess.

When he came to the Vicarage he had decided to practise being strong and brave every day, so that when he went home his father would notice the change in him and be pleased. Every night he stood at his open window—a thin under-grown child, with bony wrists and fragile blue-veined temples—flinging his match-like arms up and down, to and fro, with frantic energy, pausing every now and then to search for traces of the biceps that he was hoping to develop. That part, of course, was easy. It was the practise of bravery that he found difficult.

His father had tried to teach him boxing, and he had cried at the first blow. The memory of the faint contempt in his father's voice as he said, "All right, old chap, we won't do any more now," still sent a wave of shame through him. And that was not the only shameful memory . . . There were those "catches" his father sent him and that he dropped because the ball stung his hands . . . There was the plunge from the diving-board into the water that he shirked time after time, creeping round ashamedly to the steps at the shallow end . . . He must learn to bear pain and shock . . .

He must do something that hurt him every day . . . He looked down at the stone on which his hand rested. It would hurt if he knocked his head against it hard . . . really hard . . .

Angela ran lightly down the path to where Miss Rossiter sat under the beech tree engaged in picking up a stitch that she had dropped in her knitting several rows back. Miss Rossiter did not usually drop stitches, but ever since tea only half her mind had been on her work. From where she sat she could see Monica and Patsy Gosport sitting on a fallen log behind a thick holly bush talking . . . Miss Rossiter always felt uneasy when Monica was alone with any of the other children, and the strange glance the child had sent her that morning increased her uneasiness. Quite obviously the child knew things, and children who knew things were apt to impart their knowledge to other children. Miss Rossiter had moved her position several times, so that she could keep them in view. Once or twice she had strolled in their direction so that she could hear what they were saying. She had been relieved to find that Patsy was doing most of the talking and that she was talking about such things as scooters and her garden and her kitten. Still—plants and kittens could lead to anything . . . She shifted her position again, so that she could see Monica's small pale face through the bushes. It was as composed and expressionless as ever. Sly. That was the word.

Angela reached the clearing in a series of running leaps.

"Shall I wash up for you, Miss Rossiter?" she said.

Miss Rossiter looked at the remains of the tea, still outspread on the ground in front of her.

"I was only going to rinse them in the stream, dear," she said. "They can be washed properly when we get home."

"I'll do it for you," said Angela.

"That's kind of you, dear," said Miss Rossiter.

She spoke with qualified enthusiasm. She knew Angela's "helping" . . . The whole process would be abruptly abandoned as soon as any fresh interest presented itself. But Angela, having, for the moment, no other means of relieving her boredom, was gathering up cups, plates and milk-jug with an air of bustling activity.

"Don't take more than you can carry, dear."

"I'm all right," said Angela airily. "I can carry heaps of things."

She vanished among the trees, and for some moments there was silence—a silence broken suddenly by the smash of crockery. Miss Rossiter sighed, put down her knitting and went to investigate. Pieces of a broken milk-jug lay on the path, but Angela was nowhere to be seen. Miss Rossiter gathered up the pieces and returned to her post. Soon Angela came back with the tea-things. She looked serene and complacent.

"There!" she said. "I've rinsed them all out for you. I am a help, aren't I?"

"Yes, dear, but I'm sorry you broke the milk-jug."

"What milk-jug?" said Angela.

"The one I found on the path."

"Oh, that!" said Angela. "That was there when I got there. Someone else must have dropped it. I didn't."

"But I heard it break, Angela."

"No, you couldn't have done. I dropped some spoons and picked them up. That's what you must have heard."

"Darling, it doesn't matter about breaking the jug, but you mustn't tell a lie about it. I saw you take the jug away with the other things."

Angela's wide blue eyes met Miss Rossiter's with a look of innocent surprise.

"You couldn't have. I'm not telling a lie. I didn't break it."

"Angela," said Miss Rossiter solemnly, "I'm afraid I must tell your mother that you've told me a lie."

"I haven't. I didn't."

"Oh, Angela!" said Miss Rossiter in deep reproach.

But Angela was already dancing off lightly among the trees. "I didn't. I didn't," came from her in a clear, gay little voice, growing fainter and fainter as she went farther away. "I didn't. I didn't. I didn't. I didn't. I didn't."

Miss Rossiter sighed again as she began to pack the tea-things away into the picnic-basket.

*

"Go on," said Monica eagerly. "Tell me some more."

But Patsy was growing tired of the recital.

"There's nothing more to tell," she said.

"Yes, there is," protested Monica. "There must be. *Do* go on. Look! Here's the last biscuit. Take it."

Miss Rossiter had divided among the children the biscuits left over from tea, and Monica had been doling hers out one by one to Patsy in order to prolong the recital.

Patsy took the biscuit and began to nibble it.

"There's nothing more to tell," she repeated. "I've told you everything."

"Tell me again, then," pleaded Monica. "Please tell me again. Tell me more about the baby. Tell me everything you do all the time."

The family at The Limes had enthralled Monica ever since she came to the Vicarage. She had watched them through the hedge and from the windows, had strained her ears for every sound—the laughter and gurgles of the baby in his pram, the shouts of the schoolboy brother, the father's voice whistling rather untunefully as he worked in the garden, the mother singing to herself as she hung out or took in the washing.

"Does the baby always come into your bed in the morning?" said Monica.

"Most mornings. I play with him and show him his picture book."

"And what happens after that?"

"Mummy takes him and I get up. I go into their bedroom and they help me dress. And then we have breakfast."

"And do you always go down to the gate to see your father off? All of you?"

"Yes. I get his attaché-case and Derek his hat and Jacko—"

"That's the baby, isn't it?"

"Yes. Jacko gets his gloves. Mummy helps Jacko get the gloves, of course. Then we all go down to the gate to see him off."

"And what do you do then?"

"Oh, I'm tired of telling you."

17

"Please, Patsy. I've got some chocolate at the Vicarage. I'll put it through the hedge for you when we get back. Please go on. Who puts the baby to bed?"

"I help mummy bath him and we put him to bed together. Then mummy reads aloud to Derek and me. She's reading *Alice in Wonderland* now. It's lovely. And then it's time for daddy to come home, and Derek and I wait at the gate till we see him coming and then we run down the road to meet him. We race each other. Sometimes I win. I think Derek lets me."

"And after that?"

"We help daddy in the garden and he helps Derek with his homework and I go to bed and mummy tucks me up and daddy comes in to say good night."

Monica was silent, storing up every detail in her memory. She never identified herself with the next-door family. She merely watched and listened, with a curious ache, as of hunger, at her heart, snatching avidly at every crumb of information about them.

"Jacko was crying yesterday morning."

"He fell down. He can't walk very well yet."

"What were you all laughing at yesterday afternoon?"

"I don't remember. Jacko, I expect . . . Oh, I'm tired of telling you things. Let's talk about something else."

"What shall we talk about?"

"Let's choose three wishes . . . Suppose a fairy came and gave you three wishes, what would you choose?"

Monica was silent for some moments, then:

"I'd wish that you'd ask me to tea to your house," she said with a quick intake of breath.

"Oh," said Patsy. She considered. "Well, I think we could. I'll ask mummy. When could you come?"

A faint tinge of colour had crept into Monica's cheeks.

"Can—can I come to-morrow?"

"I think so. I'll ask mummy . . . Now I'll tell you about my three wishes."

Miss Rossiter closed the picnic-basket and gave the blast on the

18

whistle that was the signal for the children to assemble at the clearing. They came back one by one through the trees. Angela carried an armful of willow herb. Geraldine had been crying. There was a faint bruise on Philip's forehead.

"What have you done to your head, Philip?" said Miss Rossiter.

"I fell."

"You ought to bathe it," said Geraldine. "I'll bathe it for you in the stream."

"Leave me alone," he muttered savagely.

Angela ran on ahead to the stile that separated the wood from the road.

"There's Mr. Hassock," she said, standing on the top rung. "Hello, Mr. Hassock."

A man in shabby flannel trousers, a blazer and a clerical collar stopped short in his progress down the road and waited for the picnic party to emerge from the wood. He was tall and powerfully built, with a shaggy, somewhat unkempt look about him. His face—square-cut beneath a thatch of black upstanding hair—was tanned by exposure to sun and wind, and his eyes, beneath thick overhanging brows, held a kindly humorous twinkle.

Miss Rossiter, who disliked the curate, had tried to hang back, so that he should have passed the stile before she emerged from the wood, but the ruse had been unsuccessful.

"Hello, children," he said. "Good afternoon, Miss Rossiter . . . Allow me."

He took the picnic-basket and walked beside her, swinging the basket to and fro, obviously finding a certain difficulty in accommodating his long strides to her shorter steps.

"Had this lot for some time, haven't you?" he said, jerking his head in the direction of the children.

His deep rumbling voice had a hint of laughter in it. The suspicion that he found her—and indeed the whole Vicarage *ménage*—amusing had annoyed Miss Rossiter for some time.

"They're all going soon," she said. "We're expecting some new ones at the end of the month."

"I often wonder how you can stand the life," he said.

She stiffened.

"I love it," she said. "Mrs. Sanders is my greatest friend, and I love helping her. I love children, too."

"I know. I know. I know. That's all very well, but never a day off. You never do have a day off, do you?"

"I don't want a day off. I could have as many as I liked if I wanted them."

"There's something wrong in your not wanting them."

"My work at the Vicarage is my whole life. I help Mrs. Sanders with her writing as well as with the children."

He snorted.

"I know you do."

"Please don't swing the basket like that. You'll be breaking something."

"No, I won't. I'm swinging it carefully . . . How old are you?"

"Twenty-two," she said, answering the question before she realized its impertinence and then wishing she hadn't done.

"There!" he said triumphantly. "I knew you were too young to make a drudge of yourself. You've got your whole life before you. You ought to get out and about. Meet people. Kick over the traces."

"Did you know," she said frigidly, "that my *fiancé* was killed in the Battle of the Marne only a week after our engagement?"

"No, I didn't," he said. His voice was still loud and booming and cheerful. It lacked the note of hushed sympathy that she usually heard in people's voices when she told them the story of her engagement. "But what of it, anyway? The Battle of the Marne was in 1918 and it's 1922 now. How long had you known the chap before you got engaged to him?"

"A fortnight."

"I expect you hardly remember what he looked like."

"I remember perfectly."

"You were just a romantic schoolgirl, and you're a romantic schoolgirl still. You ought to try to grow up. You're wasting your life."

"I'm not wasting my life," she said indignantly. "Olivia's work is of value to humanity."

He shot her an amused glance.

"You don't really believe that, do you?"

Her cheeks flamed with anger.

"You're being extremely impertinent."

"I know I am," he said mildly; "but I don't like to see people wasting their lives for the sake of a bit of play-acting." He paused for a moment, then went on: "Bertie Carstairs was talking to me about you last night. He said he'd asked you to go to the cricket-club dance and you'd refused."

"He's always asking me to go to things with him," she said. "I've told him. I don't go out."

"Yes, but he's a decent chap, you know. I said I'd put in a word for him to you. I thought you might listen to me."

"Why on earth should I?" she said, too much astounded for the moment to be angry.

"Well, people do sometimes," he said modestly. "Now listen. Let's get this straight. Bertie's a splendid chap, and just because this other man—whoever he was—"

She interrupted him.

"I should like you to know," she said, "that the night before he was killed my *fiancé* wrote to me asking me, whatever happened, to be faithful to his memory, and I took a vow then and there that I would be. Don't you think that a person's last wish should be sacred?"

He considered.

"Not more than any other wish," he said. "Less so, in fact, because people generally make their last wishes at a time of mental and physical stress that gives them a distorted view of any situation."

"How *can* you talk like that!" she said heatedly. "He died fighting for me—"

"And himself, you know," he put in.

She ignored the interruption and went on:

"How could I meet him in the next world if—"

Her voice trailed away.

"I think you've got a completely wrong idea of the next world."

The amusement in his voice brought the colour flaming to her cheeks.

"I don't want to discuss it with you," she said. "I've already told you that I'm happy and that my work is my whole life."

"No, it isn't," he said. "It's your drug. You take it to stop yourself living. You're a drug addict of the worst kind—far worse than any poor chap who takes opium or cocaine, because he knows he's doing wrong and you do it in a glow of morbid self-righteousness."

"Can't you understand?" she said. "I give my life to these children because—because I look on them as the children Frank and I might have had."

"All of them?" he said. "They're rather a mixed bag, you know."

Lips compressed, she snatched the basket from him.

"Please go. I've told you I don't want to discuss the matter with you," she said. "You've no sympathy or—or decency."

He took the basket back from her, his eyes twinkling under their bushy brows, and they walked on in silence after the children.

The children had stopped at the gate of The Limes and stood there in a little group. Philip was clutching the armful of willow herb. Angela, tiring of it, had thrown it down in the road, and he had picked it up, not because he wanted the flowers but because he could not bear to see them left in the dust to die.

"Let me carry them," said Geraldine.

"No," he said, scowling at her over the wilting flowers. He felt foolish and ashamed, resentful of the impulse that had made him gather up the blooms, angry that Geraldine should understand it.

Monica's eyes were fixed on Mrs. Gosport, who was talking to Patsy at the front door. There was a worried expression on Mrs. Gosport's kind, pleasant face, and she kept glancing at Monica as they talked.

Miss Rossiter and the curate stopped at the gate.

"Thank you," said Miss Rossiter to the curate in chilly dismissal, taking the basket from him again.

He accepted his dismissal and strode on down the road, swinging his arms, covering the ground with his long, rapid stride so swiftly that he seemed to vanish round the bend of the road as soon as he left them.

Mrs. Gosport came down the path to the gate

"Could I speak to you for a moment, Miss Rossiter?"

The two walked out of earshot of the children, skirting a scooter and the remains of a dolls' tea-party that lay on the lawn.

"I don't know quite what to do, my dear," said Mrs. Gosport. "Patsy wants me to have the little dark girl—Monica, isn't it?—to tea, and I'd love to, of course, but—what's the child like? I mean, what's her background? One has to be so careful."

"I know," said Miss Rossiter. "I do appreciate that . . . It's rather an unhappy story. Her mother's divorced and the case was quite a notorious one. She seems to have been absolutely shameless. The name's Patterson. Do you remember the case? It was about two years ago."

"No. I never read divorce cases. I suppose the child—knows things she shouldn't?"

"I'm afraid she does."

"Then I'd really rather she didn't come. I do try so hard to keep that sort of thing from them while they're little. I know you understand."

"Of course I do," said Miss Rossiter. "I'll tell her quite kindly. I'll say you're too busy."

"Y-yes," said Mrs. Gosport. She still looked rather worried. "But—I hate to disappoint a child. If she seems to mind terribly, I'll have her. I'll try to be with them all the time, though it's not easy with the baby and the tea to get."

"I'm sure it'll be all right," said Miss Rossiter.

She walked down to the gate.

"Now come along, children . . . Oh, Monica dear, one minute!"

The little procession began to move along the road towards the Vicarage.

"I'm afraid that Mrs. Gosport can't have you to tea to-morrow, dear, after all. She's very busy just now. You don't mind, do you?"

"No . . ." said Monica.

The small face was quite expressionless and composed.

23

Miss Rossiter turned to give a reassuring nod and smile to Mrs. Gosport, who still lingered at the gate.

Obviously the child didn't mind at all.

Chapter Three

"May I come in, Olivia?" said Miss Rossiter, opening the study door.

"That you, Greta?" said Mrs. Sanders, raising her head from her desk. "Yes, dear. Come in . . . The little ones safely in bed?"

"They're in bed," said Miss Rossiter, entering the room, "and, I hope, safely. How are you getting on?"

She steered her way as she spoke over the sea of manuscript that covered the floor.

Mrs. Sanders pushed a lock of her untidy hair from her forehead and leant back in her chair.

"On the whole, well," she said. "I've come up against a few difficulties, of course." She turned over some pages of the confused heaps of papers that surrounded her. "I've got Sir Neville and Luella engaged and I'm bringing the real wife back from Paris. I'm not sure whether to bring her back in time to forbid the banns or to interrupt the marriage service. Either would be effective."

"Both have been done before," said Miss Rossiter.

"Everything's been done before," said Mrs. Sanders blandly. "I've played with the idea of letting them actually get married before the real wife turns up, but that's a bit—strong, perhaps."

"Perhaps . . . and she's dying of consumption, anyway."

"No, dear. That's the wife in *Barren Heritage*."

"Oh, yes."

Mrs. Sanders always worked on two or three novels at the same time, and sometimes it was difficult to keep them clear in one's mind.

"Sit down, Greta dear. I'm sure you're tired."

25

Miss Rossiter looked round the room. Every chair was occupied. There was an untidy pile of manuscript on one, a welter of books and newspapers on another, a tray of tea on another, a skirt and hat on another. On the long sofa against the wall was a picture, a tin of biscuits, a large old-fashioned mousetrap, a sponge and a bunch of bananas.

"Make room, dear," said Mrs. Sanders vaguely.

Greta made room between the mousetrap and the bananas.

"Do look at that picture," said Mrs. Sanders. "I brought it down from the spare bedroom. I believe she's supposed to be an Early Christian, but she looks exactly as I imagine the adventuress in *Tangled Weds* to look, and I'm going to keep it by me till I get to her description. Just pass me the sponge, dear. My hands get so sticky . . . I think there's another mouse. I've been hearing rustlings again."

Miss Rossiter was studying the picture.

"She looks a bit raffish," she said.

"Raffish!" said Mrs. Sanders. "That's the word I want." She began to burrow among the sheets of manuscript. They flew up around her as if driven by a whirlwind, fluttering down upon the floor. "I want it for Edwin's sister in *Fallen Sheaves*. I simply couldn't think of the right word . . . Oh, here it is."

"It's probably the same mouse you caught last week," said Miss Rossiter. "You let it out again, didn't you?"

"Yes. I can't bear to see an animal suffer . . . I think I'll write a fresh paragraph for 'raffish'."

Her pen made a shrill scratching sound as it flew over the paper. (She disliked fountain-pens because, as she said, they lacked character.) Plunging it into the inkwell, she sent little showers of ink on to the desk all round her.

Mrs. Sanders was a large, untidy woman of quite astounding beauty. Her hair was generally coming down, she wore a strange collection of ill-assorted garments, ink covered her fingers and frequently found its way to her face, but nothing could dim the radiance of her beauty.

When the Vicar first met her she was living in lodgings in Chelsea supporting her father (once a well-known artist, now a peevish invalid) by writing stories for the cheaper women's magazines. The two lived in poverty—if not in actual squalor—but both were supremely indifferent to their surroundings. A friend who had known the artist in his younger and more successful days had introduced the Vicar to them, and the Vicar had fallen in love with her at first sight. He thought of her as a "lily on a dung-heap" and longed to transport her from this sordid existence to a gracious ordered life. Her father was the only obstacle, and her father solved the problem by dying a few weeks after their meeting. So the Vicar and Olivia were married, and the Vicar removed his lily to a more salubrious atmosphere.

He was disconcerted to find that what he had thought of as the dung-heap accompanied her. She continued to be uncompromisingly "Bohemian". The Vicar had taken for granted that after her marriage she would give up writing, but it never occurred to her to do so. She never even realized that he wanted her to give up writing. She was bland, vague, absentminded, sublimely imperturbable and magnificently evasive. It was impossible to join issues with her on any subject, for nothing had any reality to her outside the plots— heart-stirring and sometimes a little daring—of her novelettes. So in the end the Vicar gave it up. Even the gracious ordered life he had planned for her vanished on her approach. Disorder sprang up around her like a magic growth wherever she went. She carried her own world about with her and it was impervious to assault.

And yet the marriage was far from being an unhappy one. The fact that she undertook no duties in the house or in the parish was, on the whole, an advantage. The Vicar's old nurse had managed the house for him ever since he was appointed to the living. There was an army of devoted church workers who ran the parish methodically and with the minimum of friction. Olivia, serenely indifferent to both house and parish, living entirely in the feuilletons that she poured out unceasingly under the pen-names of Gloria Fortescue, Sonia Glendinning and Marcella Montmorency, got in nobody's way, trod on nobody's corns. Her churchgoing was spasmodic. When she attended church, she attended it in regal state, wearing one of those flamboyant garments that conformed to no fashion but that somehow enhanced her Junoesque beauty. However distrait or untidy she might be, her entry into any place suggested a ceremonial procession.

And the novelettes were successful. Money poured into the Vicarage. After every fifth chapter Olivia rested from novel writing and wrote a poem, in order, as she said, to refresh her soul. They were poems of uplift, inculcating by means of rhymed couplets the simple virtues of cheerfulness, helpfulness and unselfishness, and they sold like hot cakes. They appeared on calendars and Christmas cards and little illuminated placards. They were done in poker-work. They were framed in *passe-partout*. They hung in kitchens, sitting-rooms, offices. It was one of these that had made Miss Rossiter known to her. Miss Rossiter, bewildered and desolated by the death of her *fiancé*, had derived much comfort from a poem of Mrs. Sanders' called "Heart's-ease" and had written to the author to tell her so. Mrs. Sanders, whose latest heroine had just lost her *fiancé* in the war and who wanted a little first-hand information on the subject, suggested a meeting. At the meeting it was disclosed that Miss Rossiter was a nursery governess and that Mrs. Sanders wanted a nursery governess for her little daughter, Angela. Within a week Miss Rossiter was installed in the Vicarage, eager to devote her life to her new friend.

Miss Rossiter was simple-minded and full of energy. She wept over the feuilletons, she was inspired by the poems, she constituted herself secretary, attendant and disciple to the authoress as well as governess to Angela. And even that was not enough. Angela, she considered, needed a companion. An advertisement was put into a leading London paper. There were several replies. Three companions were chosen. Miss Rossiter coped with them skilfully and efficiently. The three went in due course and were replaced by three more. A succession of companions for Angela streamed through the Vicarage. They were mostly children whose parents were anxious to dispose of them for a few months and were willing to pay handsomely for the temporary boon of childlessness. Mr.

Sanders found the fees a useful addition to his stipend, for, though money poured into the Vicarage, it poured out again as quickly.

Mrs. Sanders was extravagant as only a vague impractical person can be extravagant. She seldom went shopping, but when she did she bought everything she saw. She loved barbaric jewellery and ornaments. It made little difference whether these things were real or imitation. A few shillings or a few hundred pounds were more or less the same to her. She would buy half a dozen model dresses at the same time, have what she called a "day's dress-making" on them—tear them to pieces, make one out of two, two out of one, turn a dress into a cloak, a cloak into a dressing-gown—then buy half a-dozen more to make good the damage.

She handed an untidy sheaf of papers to Miss Rossiter.

"Darling, will you just go through this and put the flowers right? It's the description of the garden in chapter ten."

Miss Rossiter took the papers and put them into some sort of order.

"What month is it supposed to be?"

"July."

Miss Rossiter forbore to call her employer's attention to the fact that the present month was July and that from the study window she could see the Vicarage garden ablaze with July flowers. Mrs. Sanders seldom saw anything that was before her eyes. Only the week before she had gone into Maybridge to do some shopping and had returned in a taxi filled almost to overflowing with delphiniums that she had bought at a florist's.

"Aren't they a heavenly colour!" she had said. "I simply couldn't resist them."

It was the Vicar who pointed out that the border at the side of the lawn was full of delphiniums of that particular shade.

"So it is!" Mrs. Sanders had said with interest. "I never noticed."

Miss Rossiter drew her pencil through narcissus and chrysanthemum.

"I just put down anything that came into my head," said Mrs. Sanders unnecessarily. "I always find that stopping to think about details chokes the flow of the story."

"I shouldn't have 'periwinkle'," said Miss Rossiter. "It's a weed."

"What a pity!" said Mrs. Sanders. "It's such a nice word, isn't it?"

"Yes," said Miss Rossiter, drawing her pencil through michaelmas daisy. "Have you decided about Julian?"

Mrs. Sanders frowned thoughtfully.

"I think he must marry Mirabel. At present, of course, he's in love with Valerie, but I want Valerie to remain faithful to Cyprian's memory."

The faint depression that had clouded Miss Rossiter's spirit ever since her meeting with Mr. Hassock on the way home from the picnic cleared away . . . She felt safe and happy in this world of Olivia's, in which people remained faithful to other people's memories as a matter of course.

"By the way, dear, someone rang you up this afternoon and wanted to speak to you. It was a man. I've forgotten what he wanted and I've forgotten his name. Reggie something."

"Bertie Carstairs?"

"It might have been," said Mrs. Sanders, appearing to give the matter deep thought. "It's quite possible. I didn't see you in the garden, so I said you were out."

"I was. I didn't want to speak to him, anyway. I took the children into the wood for a picnic tea."

"How nice, dear! I'm thinking of having a picnic in *Barren Heritage*. It brings all the characters together and one can hang a few nature descriptions on to it. Did the children enjoy it?"

"I think so. I was a little worried about Monica—"

"She's the film star's little girl, isn't she?"

"No, dear. That was Petronella. She went home last month. Monica's parents are divorced."

"She gets into those dreadful rages, doesn't she?"

"No. That was Dinah. She's gone to America with her mother. At present we have Monica and Geraldine and Philip."

"Philip! I remember about him. His father's in prison. I was going to use the situation in *Stony Paths*, wasn't I?"

"No, dear. Philip's father isn't in prison. You're thinking of little Leonard who was here in the spring."

Mrs. Sanders looked at her, frowning intently.

"Darling, I must get this right. Tell me about the children we've got with us now. I know you've told me once but I've forgotten. I'm deeply interested in the work we do for these little people, and I must be clear about it."

"I shouldn't bother," said Miss Rossiter soothingly. "They happen to be going quite soon and fresh ones will be coming." She put the papers back on the desk. "Have you finished chapter ten?"

"Nearly. I worked all lunchtime, you know, because I wanted to get on with it."

"Didn't you have any lunch?"

"I had some biscuits and I think I had a banana. Or was it grapes?" She opened a drawer in the desk, full of biscuits, pieces of chocolate, apples, loose dates, paper clips, indiarubbers, pen-nibs and odds and ends of manuscripts, and considered the contents speculatively. "I think it must have been the grapes. They seem to have gone."

Mrs. Sanders, when in good writing vein, dispensed with conventional meals and remained throughout the day seated at her desk, nibbling at intervals the biscuits and fruit that she kept there in readiness. Occasionally Miss Rossiter, seizing her opportunity, would clear out the bits of biscuit and cake, the often mouldy remains of oranges, grapes, peaches and chocolate that accumulated in almost every drawer, but the opportunity seldom occurred.

"Adrian's got someone coming to dinner," went on Mrs. Sanders. "It's someone important—a bishop or churchwarden or something— and I promised to have dinner with them. I've dressed ready for it in good time so as to be sure not to forget."

Ever since she came into the room Miss Rossiter had been throwing sidelong glances at her employer's costume. It was a flowing voluminous dress of red velvet, tightly gathered at the waist, that she had had made about six years ago for a fancy dress dance at which she had appeared as Queen Elizabeth. Altered, renovated, it was still worn by Mrs. Sanders for most formal occasions, though her wardrobe was filled with expensive up-to-date dresses. No one—probably not even Mrs. Sanders herself—knew the reason for this.

"Why didn't you put on the new black one?" said Miss Rossiter.

"Not black, dear," said Mrs. Sanders. "Not while I'm working on chapter ten. I want Rosaline to defy the conventions, and I think that red suggests that much more than black. If I'd worn the black dress I might have been tempted to compromise. I'm so sensitive to atmosphere."

"I know, dear, but you've had that red dress for such a long time. What about the green one—the one you bought last week?"

Mrs. Sanders wrinkled her brow.

"I did something to it. I've forgotten what, but I know I did something to it. I think I made it into cushion covers." She glanced round the room at the armchairs and sofa. "No, it couldn't have been that . . . I believe I used it to brighten up that brown dress. I've never liked that brown dress . . . Anyway, I couldn't have done chapter ten in green. There's something so detached and cynical about green." She collected her manuscripts into an untidy heap and went on, "I'm so glad the children enjoyed the circus."

"Picnic," said Miss Rossiter. "Mr. Hassock came home with us. I don't like him."

"I don't like him much either," said Mrs. Sanders, "but I think he'd do for Sir Jasper in *Fallen Sheaves*. There's something dark and sinister about him."

"I don't think he's sinister, exactly," said Miss Rossiter. "He's merely boorish and ill-bred and completely lacking in understanding. He—"

The door opened and the Vicar came in.

"Well, my dear," he said, removing the tea-tray on to the top of a bookcase and lowering his tall frame into the armchair. "How are you getting on?"

"Quite well, thank you, Adrian," said his wife. "I haven't"—with a touch of pride—"forgotten about dinner."

The Vicar looked round the chaotic room. The sight roused no irritation in him, though his own study—on the other side of the house—was a model of order and efficiency.

Mr. Sanders was essentially a man of business. His business was religion and his god was organization. He regarded the numbers of his congregation as a merchant might regard the profits of his trade. Even his charm and good looks he used deliberately to lure people into his church and enrol them among his parish workers. His sermons were well thought out and well delivered, but it was as a committee man that he excelled. He was on every committee for a radius of ten miles, and he attended every meeting of every committee, guiding its decisions with a nicely adjusted mixture of tact and firmness. In spite of this, not only did his wife's lack of method cause him no annoyance, but he was as much in love with the large beautiful ridiculous creature as he had been when he married her. It was as if his coldness and dryness found solace in her warmth and exuberance, as if something dead in him took life from her vitality. And Mrs. Sanders—as far as she could love a creature of flesh and blood—loved her husband. He conformed in type to her middle-aged heroes. He was tall and "distinguished-looking". His hair was greying at the temples. She put him into every book she wrote. He was diplomat, solicitor, secret service agent, general, aristocrat, and, frequently, guardian of an attractive ward. Sometimes he was just a butler—once he had been a postman—but he was always there.

He turned to Miss Rossiter.

"And how are the children?" he said. "The little boy—Philip, isn't it?—looks very delicate."

"His father isn't in prison, you know," said Mrs. Sanders, as if imparting an interesting piece of news. "It was someone else who was in prison."

"Of course Philip's father isn't in prison," said the Vicar. "He lives at Penbury. Only a few miles away . . . It's rather an odd coincidence that we should have two children from our own locality. Little Philip Shenstone from Penbury and little Geraldine Mortimer from Maybridge."

"Geraldine?" said Mrs. Sanders thoughtfully. "Her people aren't in India, then?"

"No, my dear."

"I just wondered. So many people seem to be. People with children, I mean."

The Vicar joined the tips of his fingers together and leant back in his chair.

"I like to think that our home is an anchorage for these little storm-tossed souls," he said.

He gave voice to this sentiment frequently, preferring to ignore the financial benefit that he reaped from the anchorage.

"He was put in prison for selling shares," said Mrs. Sanders. "I remember I wanted to use the situation in *Stony Paths*, but Greta thought I'd better stick to forgery. She thought I might get confused in shares."

"She was probably right," said the Vicar. He took out his watch and glanced at the clock on the chimney piece. "Your clock is two minutes slow, my dear."

"I don't think it matters," said Mrs. Sanders. "Gargantua wouldn't let the people who lived in his Abbey have any clocks at all. He said that the greatest waste of time was to count the hours, and I think he was right."

A smile flitted over the Vicar's thin, ascetic face.

"I didn't know you'd read Rabelais."

"Oh, yes," said Mrs. Sanders; "I found it rather dull except for the lewd parts, and there were disappointingly few of them. I'd been led to expect there would be more."

The Vicar gave a discreet cough and rose from his chair.

"Well, I'll be going now, my dear. I have one or two letters to write. I'll see you at dinner?"

"Yes," said Mrs. Sanders absently as she turned back to her desk, then, as the door closed on him: "Oh, Greta dear, remind me that I've dressed. I don't want to do it again."

"Olivia . . ."

Mrs. Sanders' pen was already flying over the paper. She gave a grunt that might have been intended to convey either encouragement or discouragement.

"Angela told me a lie this afternoon. It was quite a deliberate lie. She broke a milk-jug then said she hadn't done it. It didn't matter about the milk-jug, of course, but she refused to own that she'd done it. I think you ought to speak to her about it tomorrow."

Mrs. Sanders looked up, her face alight with interest.

"It's quite a coincidence, my dear."

"A coincidence?"

Mrs. Sanders laid down her pen.

"Well, do you remember Flavia in *Tangled Webs*? She must be completely and utterly dishonest, you know. She steals Lady Pembroke's diamonds after the ball at Enderby Towers, you remember, and I've been thinking that it would be a good thing to show her as a child. I want her mother to be a very sweet and good woman, and I want her to do her best to counteract the bad elements in the child's character. The child's evil influence, of course, is her governess, Miss Smythe, who's always hated the mother. I'd meant to start when Flavia was eighteen, but I think a few chapters about her childhood would establish the character, and I don't think it would make the book too long, do you?"

"No," said Greta doubtfully.

"Well, I'd thought of beginning with the child committing some small act of dishonesty—stealing a peach from the conservatory that she'd been told not to touch—and the mother should talk to her about it. That would show the two opposing forces fighting for the young soul, wouldn't it?"

"Yes," said Greta still more doubtfully.

"If I have a little talk with Angela now it will help me a good deal with that scene. The child's reaction. My own feelings. It will take me right into the heart of the atmosphere . . . Will you fetch her, dear?"

"Now?" said Greta.

"Why not? I might have lost the thread by to-morrow. These ideas are apt to come and go."

"But she's in bed."

"She may not be asleep. Don't wake her if she's asleep, of course. But, if she's awake, ask her to put on her dressing-gown and come down to me."

Greta hesitated a few moments then went from the room.

Mrs. Sanders rose from the writing-desk, drew the armchair that her husband had just vacated into the centre of the room and took her seat upon it. Soon the door opened and Greta appeared, leading Angela by the hand. Angela, though wearing her pink woollen dressing-gown and pink bedroom slippers, was bright-eyed, rosy-cheeked and looked far from sleepy. Greta had found her out of bed, pirouetting before the mirror in her nightdress, wearing her bedspread over her shoulders as a cloak and the dressing-table cover over her curls as a head-dress.

"Leave us, Greta," said Mrs. Sanders in a deep voice.

Greta departed, closing the door behind her.

Mrs. Sanders spread out her arms with a grandly maternal gesture.

"Come to mother, my darling," she said.

Angela ran across the room and was gathered on to the capacious lap.

"Darling," said Mrs. Sanders, "you love mother, don't you?"

"Yes," said Angela.

"You always tell her the truth, don't you?"

"Yes," said Angela.

"You did take the peach, darling, didn't you?"

"Yes," said Angela, snuggling down happily in the warm voluptuous embrace.

"Darling, it's Miss Smythe, your governess, who's trying to come between us, isn't it?"

"Yes," said Angela with a long contented sigh, and added, "It's Miss Rossiter who's my governess, you know."

"Oh, yes," said Mrs. Sanders uncertainly.

She gazed in front of her with a frown of perplexity, as her mind strove to disentangle the confused medley of fact and fiction that occupied it. Peaches . . . There weren't any peaches in the Vicarage garden. There never had been.

"I was wrong, darling," she said at last. "It was the milk-jug you broke."

Angela sat up, tense and rigid.

"I didn't," she said. "I didn't. I didn't. I didn't. I didn't. I didn't."

But Mrs. Sanders had suddenly thought of another ending for chapter ten. She drew Angela to her and kissed her.

"Well, never mind, darling," she said. "Mother's busy now and you mustn't disturb her. Run off to bed. Look!"

She put Angela down, went to the writing-desk and, burrowing in a drawer, brought out a half-eaten bar of chocolate.

"There you are, my pet. Now run along. Good night."

Nibbling the chocolate, dancing lightly in small pink slippers, Angela ran off to bed.

When Greta opened the door a few minutes later, Mrs. Sanders was busy writing at her desk.

"Did you speak to her?" she said.

"To whom, dear?" said Mrs. Sanders, without stopping the swift erratic movements of her pen.

"Angela."

"Oh, yes, dear. We had a nice little talk. I think she was really sorry. I don't think she'll steal the fruit again."

Chapter Four

Mrs. Mortimer moved the pram further into the shade, looked into it to make sure that its occupant was still asleep, then tiptoed across the lawn and through the open french window into the little sitting-room, where her husband was tinkering with the wireless.

Mr. Mortimer was always tinkering, and Mrs. Mortimer would have felt that there was something wrong with the house if there had been nothing for her husband to tinker with.

"She's still asleep," she said.

"Good!" said Mr. Mortimer. "What time is her next feed?"

Mrs. Mortimer glanced at the clock.

"Not till three."

"Was she sick after the last one?"

"Only a little. They say at the clinic that it doesn't matter."

She crossed the room and sat down on the sofa—a fair slender woman who would have been pretty had it not been for something vaguely devitalized about her. Her hair and eyes lacked lustre, and there was a suggestion of languor in all her movements.

Her husband packed his tools neatly into his toolcase.

"It should be all right now," he said.

"It seemed all right to me before," said Mrs. Mortimer with a smile.

"The tone was a bit harsh. It's better now."

He sat down by her on the sofa and put his hand on hers.

"Grace . . ."

"Yes?"

"I'm a bit worried about her weight."

"I don't think you need be, dear. She's only an ounce or two under average. They often are."

"What about increasing the feed?"

"I don't think so. She takes as much as she needs. They said she was very fit."

"It's all so new to us, isn't it? Gerry, of course, didn't come to us till after she was weaned."

There was a short silence, then:

"Albert . . ."

"Yes?"

"Are you terribly disappointed that it wasn't a boy?"

"No . . . no, dear. I'm not disappointed at all. It'll be nice for Gerry to have a little sister. Two girls together, you know. It's more convenient in lots of ways. They can share a bedroom and that sort of thing."

"Yes. And clothes. It's easier to dress girls. Anyway, there it is. And we can't have a boy now. Were you disappointed about that?"

"About what, dear?"

"About the doctor saying I couldn't have any more children."

"Of course I wasn't. We've got our little family. Gerry and Elaine. You know, Grace . . ."

"Yes?"

"We must be terribly careful about Gerry. We mustn't let her think for a moment that we don't want her, now that we've got a child of our own."

"Oh, Albert, of course."

"We must show her even more love than we show Elaine. At first, anyway. We must teach her to love Elaine that way."

"Yes, dear."

"I wonder what her first reaction will be."

"She'll probably dislike her. Children are inclined to be jealous."

"We must be very patient."

"Yes. What time did you say you were going over to Appleton to fetch her?"

"I wrote to Mrs. Sanders to say that I'd be at the Vicarage by four. Then we can catch the four-thirty back . . . I think it was a wise move to send her there."

"It was terribly expensive."

"I know, dear, but think of the influence of an atmosphere like that on a child's mind. An atmosphere of culture. I was tremendously impressed by the Vicar. A well-read and very charming man."

"People say she's rather odd."

"One must make allowances for genius." He glanced at a poem called "The Home", done in pokerwork, that hung on the wall over the chimneypiece, and smiled. "When we bought that for our little home we never knew that one day we'd meet the writer of it."

"We didn't actually meet her, you know, dear."

"I know. She was busy writing, but she was there. One felt"— he sank his voice reverently—"the atmosphere of culture in the house all the time . . . You know, dear . . ."

"Yes?"

"I'd like to send the girls to college if we could manage it."

"Y-yes, it would be nice, but it would cost a lot, wouldn't it?"

"We could save up and they might get scholarships. Gerry's intelligent, and—I was looking at Elaine's forehead last night."

"It's bumpy, isn't it?"

"It's very well developed. And she notices things."

"She's only a fortnight old, dear."

"I know . . . Of course, we didn't have Gerry at that age, so we can't compare them, but I think they're both going to be clever."

A wail cut sharply through the air. Mrs. Mortimer had leapt to her feet, but her husband laid his hand on her arm to restrain her.

"Don't go, dear. She'll expect you to take her up if she sees you, and they said we oughtn't to take her up when she cries."

Mrs. Mortimer's eyes, large and anxious in her thin face, were turned in the direction of the garden. The two sat there, listening . . . The wails continued.

"Something might be hurting her," said Mrs. Mortimer. "A strap or a safety-pin or something."

"I'll just go and see," said Mr. Mortimer.

40

She watched him go through the french window and across the lawn. He was a rather plump little man with a round rosy face, dark clipped moustache, and dark shiny hair. The wails died away and he returned on tiptoe.

"I moved the pram to and fro just a little," he admitted, taking his seat beside her again, "and she dropped off . . . One mustn't make a habit of it, of course."

"No," she agreed, leaning against the back of the sofa and closing her eyes.

His glance swept round the room with a mixture of pride and speculation. There was little in it that he had not made himself. The bookshelves, the occasional table, the writing-table, the chair with "PAX 1918" carved on the back, all represented long happy hours of work in his carpentry shed. He was never quite contented unless he had "something on hand". He had even made the folk-weave curtains that hung at the windows. His wife had been prostrated at the time by one of those blinding headaches to which she was subject and which no doctor had been able to cure. He had carefully measured the material, cut it with long competent sweeps of the cutting-out scissors and sat at the kitchen table all Saturday afternoon, working the sewing-machine. The short net curtains he had made by hand. I ought to be the home-maker, she sometimes thought, but I'm not. He's the home-maker, and he does everything so much better than I do . . .

The little suburban house was the mainspring of his life. He spent all his money and energy on it. He was a clerk in a firm of leather manufacturers in Maybridge, a small market town, and every penny of his small salary was carefully budgeted. He kept an eye on the household stores, did a good deal of the shopping and coped with most of those small crises that generally need the help of plumbers or builders. Not infrequently he cooked the Sunday dinner. He was earnest, conscientious, full of energy and devoid of humour. Sometimes his wife wondered why she didn't find him irritating, but she never did. His kindness was inexhaustible, enclosing her in a warm protective mist. She felt vaguely uneasy and afraid when he was away from her.

41

His joy in the birth of their child had touched her deeply. She knew that, though he had done all he could to hide it, their childlessness in the first years of their marriage had been a grievous disappointment to him.

It was the doctor who had suggested that they should adopt a child.

"There's no reason at all why you shouldn't have children of your own, you know," he had said, "but often to adopt a child relieves a sort of psychological tension. You relax and then, with luck, you have one of your own. That is, if you want one of your own when you've adopted one."

"Indeed, indeed we do," Mr. Mortimer had assured him earnestly.

So the doctor had put them in touch with Geraldine and Geraldine had arrived.

"What are you thinking of, dear?" said Mrs. Mortimer suddenly.

"I was wondering . . ." said Mr. Mortimer. "I've got a nice piece of oak left over from the corner cupboard. It might just make another bookcase."

Mrs. Mortimer's eyes roved round the small overcrowded room.

"I don't think there's enough space for it," she said.

"If we moved the writing-table nearer the window . . ."

"I think it would be too much, even if we did that."

"Perhaps you're right," he said a little wistfully. He glanced out of the window. "She's gone off all right . . . You know, dear . . ."

"Yes?"

"I've been wondering if later on we could turn the garage into a playroom for the children. We're never likely to have a car. If we had the doors taken away and a bow-window put in, I think I could manage everything else myself."

"It would cost a lot even so, wouldn't it?"

"We could save up for it. It would be nice for them to have a place of their own." He rose and went to the window and stood looking out at the garden. "We shan't be able to keep the garden as tidy as this when there are two of them running about in it. You know, Grace . . ."

"Yes?"

"Wouldn't it be rather nice to put some flowers in Gerry's bedroom? I want her to feel that we've been looking forward to her coming home. Those first few minutes will be very important. If anything happens to make her feel that we put Elaine first it might turn her right against the child."

Mrs. Mortimer rose from the sofa with an effort.

"Yes."

"Don't you come, dear. I'll see to it."

"No. I'll come too."

Together they went into the garden. It was the usual suburban plot—a small lawn edged by a flower border and enclosed by a privet hedge, the whole showing signs of the most meticulous care. The lawn was closely mown, the edges neatly cut, the soil freshly hoed and weeded, the flowers ranged with perfect symmetry. A pear tree grew in one corner of the lawn, and in the middle was a cement bird-bath that Albert had made last spring.

He stood now, looking about him with the familiar mixture of pride and speculation on his round rosy face.

"There isn't another garden in the road to touch it," he said, lowering his voice so as not to disturb the sleeping occupant of the pram. "I think so every day when I come back from work. And the bird-bath gives it character, especially now it's—mellowed a little. Don't you think so, dear?"

"Yes, it's lovely," said Grace, slipping her arm through his.

"I wonder . . . How do you think a sort of rustic arbour would look in the corner of the path just there? They're quite easy to make."

"I think it's better as it is," said Grace. "A lot of things in a place make it look small."

She had with difficulty restrained him from making a whole army of "garden ornaments" after he had finished the bird-bath.

"Yes," he agreed reluctantly. "I see what you mean. It might take away the—spaciousness. But we can bear it in mind, can't we? It would look very picturesque with some Dorothy Perkins trained over it."

"Yes, we'll bear it in mind," she compromised.

He tiptoed to the pram.

"Do come and look at her," he said.

They stood together, arm in arm, looking at the downy tuft of hair and the curve of a flushed cheek.

"I think she's going to be pretty, don't you?" he said.

She smiled.

"I think she's lovely now."

"Well, I suppose we mustn't waste time . . . Will you cut a few flowers, dear, and I'll go and look at the slug trap. I think there's just time for that."

He handed her the scissors and went round to the small vegetable plot at the back of the house, where peas, beans, spinach, onions and cauliflowers grew in straight narrow ordered lines.

Grace cut the blooms slowly and carefully, taking one here and there from the back of each cluster. It had been a generous gesture on Albert's part to suggest cutting them at all. He liked to have what he called a "show" in the garden, and to cut the flowers diminished the effect.

"It's caught six," he said triumphantly, coming back to the front garden. "I think that will do, dear. I shouldn't cut any more."

They went indoors, put the flowers into a tall green vase and carried them upstairs.

At the top of the stairs was a bookcase that Albert had made to house his Hundred Best Books. He gave half an hour to them every evening, beginning at nine-thirty and stopping at ten. He had ploughed his way in this fashion through *Sartor Resartus*, Hume's *Treatise on Human Nature*, Johnson's *Lives of the Poets*, Macaulay's *Essays* and Ruskin's *Crown of Wild Olive*, and was now in the middle of Mottley's *Rise of the Dutch Republic*. He read with frowning concentration, never made any comment on what he read and stopped always on the first stroke of ten. Sometimes Grace suspected that he stopped in the middle of a sentence. At ten he would take out his Weather and Events diary and make his entry for the day. He had kept a Weather and Events diary for the last ten years. The weather and the chief political event of the day (he never obtruded his private affairs upon it) were entered neatly in his small careful handwriting.

They entered the bedroom at the end of the landing. It was, like all the rooms in the house, fresh and clean and overcrowded with furniture. Albert had made the little bed with "Gerry" carved on the headpiece, as well as the dressing-table and the dressing-stool (also with "Gerry" carved on it) and the bookcase. The books held a selection from a list of Best Books for Children—compiled under the headings 4 to 7, 7 to 10, 10 to 14. Albert had bought all but two of the 4 to 7 section.

"We'll put the flowers on the dressing-table, shall we?" he said. He turned to her with a smile. "This is a great day in our lives, darling—the first day we have our little family all together under our roof. It's a sort of—landmark, isn't it?"

"Yes . . ." she said.

"Well, I mustn't dawdle any more. Time I started for Appleton."

"And I'll give Elaine her bottle," said Grace.

She stood at the window and watched him go down to the gate—a small dapper figure in striped trousers, black coat and the bowler hat that he seldom discarded even in the summer.

"What's the surprise?" said Geraldine.

They were walking up from the station, Albert carrying her suitcase. Though Geraldine was not his child, her short stumpy figure bore a curious resemblance to his.

"Ah, you must wait for that," he said.

They plodded along in silence for some minutes, then he said:

"Did you enjoy being at the Vicarage?"

"Yes . . . I liked Philip, but I didn't like Angela."

"Were there just the two of you?"

"No. There was Monica, too, but she didn't talk to anyone . . . Is it a pony?"

"Is what a pony, dear?"

"The surprise."

"Well, no, dear. Mummy and I couldn't afford a pony, you know. They cost a lot of money."

Her mind turned to the other possibility. Was she a princess who was now to be sent back to her royal parents?

"Am I—" She stopped, unable to tell him what was in her mind. "Am I going away?"

"Why, no, dear," he said, surprised. "Mummy and I couldn't get along without our little Gerry. You've been away, you know, and we missed you all the time. Every night we said to each other, 'So many days and our little Gerry will be back with us.' I expect you missed us too, didn't you?"

"Yes . . . We used to have tapioca pudding for supper."

"Did you? Well, if you liked it, I'm sure mummy could manage to get it for you for supper."

"I didn't like it much. It was sticky . . . Is it a bicycle?"

"No, dear . . . You're too young for a bicycle. And, anyway, bicycles cost a lot of money too; though, when you're a big girl, mummy and I will try to let you have one."

"Is it cheap—what you've got for me for a surprise? I mean, doesn't it cost any money?"

He chuckled.

"Well, in one way it does and in another way it doesn't, but I'm not going to tell you any more about it . . . Here we are!"

He opened the gate for her and they went up to the brightly painted front door.

"Where's mummy?" said Geraldine as they entered.

"We'll see her in a moment. We'll go up to your bedroom first and take your things off."

Geraldine plodded upstairs, followed by Albert. Inside the bedroom she stood and looked around her.

"Is it the flowers?" she said.

"No, no," he smiled. "You won't have to wait long now. Let me take off your coat and hat and tidy your hair."

He took off the coat and hat and hung them in the wardrobe, then with deft gentle movements drew the comb through her thick curly hair.

"Tell me if I hurt you."

"No, you're not hurting me . . . Is it a new paintbox?"

"Ah, we're ready now. You can come and see for yourself what it is."

She took his hand and they crossed the landing to the room opposite. Grace sat by the window. On her knee, gurgling contentedly in its crisp white nightgown, lay the baby.

"There! That's the surprise," said Albert.

Very slowly Geraldine approached the chair. There was something trance-like in her movement. The colour had faded from her cheeks, and her eyes were fixed intently on the tiny face. She stood by the chair, looking down at it. The blue eyes gazed solemnly back at her. The small perfect hands opened and shut.

Geraldine spoke in a whisper, not taking her eyes from the tiny face.

"Is it mine?" she said.

"In a way it is," said Albert, smiling down at them. "You're going to help mummy look after her. You see, she's so little that she can't do anything for herself at all, so there'll be lots of things you'll be able to do for her."

"I'll do *everything*," said Geraldine fiercely.

"She's sweet, isn't she, dear?" said Grace.

Her hair clung limply to her forehead, and there were blue shadows beneath her eyes.

"Let me clear up for you," said Albert, taking the bath and carrying it to the bathroom.

When he returned, Geraldine stood in just the same attitude in front of the baby.

"Can I hold it?" she said.

"I think you might," said Albert. "Look! Sit on this chair like this and I'll take her from mummy's knee and put her on yours . . . There she is . . . Put your arm round her like this . . . Look! If you give her your finger she'll put her little fingers round it . . . There! I said she would . . . She loves you already."

He bustled about the room, clearing away the bath paraphernalia, while his wife prepared the cot. Geraldine sat like a small statue, tense and rigid, holding the baby, gazing down at its face.

"There! Everything's ready," said Grace at last. "Come along, darling. Let me have her now."

But Geraldine clung tightly to the warm fragrant bundle, only raising her eyes to fix them in a hard defiant stare on Grace.

"No," she said. "No . . . It's mine!"

Chapter Five

Barry Shenstone, perched on the stone balustrade, looked down at his wife, who was sitting in a deck-chair on the terrace beside him. He had only been married for a few weeks, and it still gave him intense pleasure to look at her. She was a small graceful woman, with smooth dark hair, wide cheekbones and deep blue eyes.

"You're frowning," he said. "Don't frown, or I shall begin to think that you're regretting it."

"Regretting what?"

"Your marriage."

She smiled.

"Darling! . . . But I am rather worried."

"What about?"

"Philip."

"Why?"

"Well, he's coming home to-day, isn't he?"

"Yes, but there's nothing to worry about in that."

The faint frown had returned to her brow.

"I wish you'd—prepared him; told him about us."

"Oh, he'll take the whole thing in his stride. Kids do. He'll be tickled to death to find a mother and brother here. And *such* a mother and brother . . . Stephen's a grand kid, you know."

She gave a little twisted smile.

"I know . . ."

Though she loved her new husband deeply she had entered upon this second marriage with many misgivings. Her first husband had died of tuberculosis in Switzerland, and after his death she had stayed on in the mountain village that had become dear and familiar to her. It was there that she had met Barry and from there that she had come to England the week before the wedding. Despite her love for Barry, her heart had been heavy with secret doubts . . . How would Stephen reconcile himself to a new home and a new father? And how would Barry take to another man's son, in whose upbringing he had had no hand? The problem had solved itself with almost bewildering simplicity. The two had liked each other from the start. After a few weeks, Stephen might have known no other father, and Barry's whole pride and interest seemed to be centred in the boy. Till now, when he was on his way home, she had given little thought to Barry's own child.

"I hope that he and Stephen will get on," she said.

"Why shouldn't they? They'll get on splendidly. Stephen'll do Philip no end of good. He's inclined to be a bit of a cissie. A brother like Stephen's just what he needs."

"I wonder . . ."

"I don't wonder. I know. It'll toughen him up, and that's what he wants. Cricket, now . . . He muffs the simplest catches and can't hold a bat straight."

"He's only a baby, Barry. You expect too much of him."

"You've got to start young to be any good at games. Stephen's not much older and he's got the makings of a first-class cricketer already. I've never seen a kid of his age handle a bat as he does, and as for bowling"—he chuckled—"he caught me napping yesterday. Got me out first ball."

Idly she watched a robin hop with quick clean movements on the ground near her feet.

"I'm rather sorry you sent him away at all," she said. "He may—resent it."

He laughed.

"My dear girl, he'd hardly expect to tag round with us on our honeymoon."

"No, but I think we ought to have had him back here at once, as soon as we came home, when we had Stephen."

"Nonsense! We talked it all over . . . I wanted to give Steve time to settle down and then have Philip back to find a ready-made mother and a brother waiting for him. Part of the home, as it were.

"How simple you make it sound!"

"It *is* simple."

"Oh, the first part's gone off all right, I admit. Stephen might have lived here all his life. You might be his real father."

"That's how I feel," he said slowly. "I tried to do my stuff with Philip, but I've never been really fond of kids. I never thought I could take to any child as I've taken to Stephen."

"Yes, it's made me so happy," she said. "I suppose that really there's nothing to worry about."

"That's what I keep telling you, my sweet."

"And I keep telling myself, too, but I can't quite convince myself."

"You've just got worked up. Everything will be plain sailing once the kid gets back."

"I suppose so . . . You're fetching him yourself, aren't you?"

"No. I've told Rogers to fetch him; I can't very well go in this get-up"—he looked down at his open-necked shirt and riding breeches—"and I can't be fagged to change."

"When are you going to—tell him?"

He put his hands in his pockets.

"Dunno. Haven't thought about it . . . Won't he just come back and find you here and accept the situation?"

She looked at him with troubled eyes, faint lines etched again on her brow.

"Don't you see, Barry? It might be a shock . . . Listen. When he comes I'll keep out of the way—fortunately Stephen's out, anyway—and you can take him up to his bedroom and tell him there."

"All right," he said easily. "Just as you like. But I bet you anything he'll be as pleased as Punch. It must have been damn' dull for the kid alone here with me. Anyway, he'll be glad to get away from the Vicarage."

"What's wrong with it?"

"It's a madhouse. The woman's completely bats."

"She writes, doesn't she?"

"Yes. Foul little verses, urging people to higher things. And novelettes full of pulsing passion."

She smiled.

"What made you send him there?"

"It was near, and they look after the kids quite well. The mad woman doesn't have much to do with them. A nursery governess seems to run the show. Anyway, it seemed a convenient place to park him for the time being."

"All the same, I wish you'd told him before he went."

"Darling, you attach too much importance to a child's reactions. He probably won't have any at all. Kids take things as they find them. I used to come back from school and find all sorts of changes at home. Cousins I'd never heard of staying there and that sort of thing. It never worried me for a second."

"That's different."

"No, it isn't. I tell you, children don't worry about things. They just take them for granted."

"That rather depends on the child, doesn't it? You've never told me much about Philip, Barry. What's he like?"

"That's his photograph on the library table, you know."

"Yes, I know . . . But what's he like himself?"

"Oh, I dunno. Just a kid like any other kid. As I said, he's a bit of a cissie. That's why it'll be so good for him to be with Stephen."

"Yes, but what does he like doing? What's he interested in?"

Barry considered.

"I've never thought about it. Games, I suppose. Most kids are keen on games . . . but he's not much good at them. We'll have to take him in hand. Inclined to moon about a bit, but I expect he'll lose all that when he's got Stephen to play with. Stephen's going to be the making of him."

"I wish you didn't take it so casually."

"I don't think I do take it casually. Actually I've been morbidly conscientious about the kid. It'll be a relief to hand him over to you and Steve . . . Anyway, darling, let's forget him." He got down from the balustrade and stood looking at her—a tall well-built man, with gingery hair, blue eyes, a long mouth and clean-cut features. "You're lovelier than ever to-day. Did you know?"

The tension of her brow relaxed.

"I know I'm not lovely at all, but go on thinking so."

"I never stop thinking so. I think it every minute of every day." He held out his hands and pulled her to her feet. "Come along. Let's go and see how they're getting on with the bathing pool." They went down the terrace steps to the lawn. Beyond the lawn was a small shrubbery and beyond that, divided from it by a ha-ha, a meadow where workmen were busy excavating a plot of ground.

The two stood watching them. The foreman came up, touching his cap.

"Going to be a nice job, I think, sir," he said.

"Yes," said Barry. "I've always meant to have it done. It was my father's idea originally, but somehow we've never done anything about it till now."

"Yes. I remember 'e spoke to me about it once, sir."

"It'll be popular with the young people."

"That it will, sir! Should be finished before the end of the summer, too, if the weather holds."

"Good!"

The man went back to his work.

Barry turned and let his eyes wander over the garden to the house—a small Queen Anne manor of red brick, mellow and beautiful—and down to where the lawn sloped to the river. A deep sense of peace and well-being possessed him. He had been born here and had spent his childhood here. Not even the tragedy of his first marriage (his wife had died a few days after Philip's birth) had impaired the essential quality of serenity that the place had always held for him. And now his second marriage was bringing him the completion of his inheritance. "It's bigger than I thought it was going to be," said Ann.

"Well, I expect the whole neighbourhood will want to use it, and Stephen will be bringing his friends home for the holidays. He's a pretty good swimmer for a kid, you know. Dives like a fish.

It was watching him swim that made me decide to have the thing done this year."

"Does Philip like swimming?"

"I think so. Funks diving, though. Perhaps Steve will teach him. Boys learn these things from other boys, you know . . . When we were kids we used to swim in the river, but the motor launches have rather spoilt things now. I think I'll get a new boat for next summer. Steve handles an oar pretty well for his age . . . What time will he be back, by the way?"

"I told him to be back for tea. He's only gone over to the Petersons'. The boys were going rabbiting in the woods with their new terrier and they wanted him to go with them. He's taken Major."

Barry's long mouth widened into a grin.

"It'll probably end up as a dog fight instead of a rabbit hunt . . . I promised I'd give him some balls to-night. The little beggar gets furious if he thinks I'm putting him off with anything less than the real thing. Makes me go all out on him."

"I don't know why young males are never happy unless they're half killing each other," said Ann. She glanced at her watch. "Let's go back to the house now. I don't want Philip to see me till you've told him."

He smiled indulgently.

"All right, my dear, but you're worrying yourself quite unnecessarily. He's going to eat out of your hand."

They went to the drawing-room and she wandered restlessly to and fro. It was a long room, with dove-grey panelling, a marble fire-place, and curtains and chair-covers of flowered chintz, fragrant with the scent of the roses and sweet peas that she had cut and arranged this morning. She had given special care and thought to the massing of bloom and colour, with the vague idea of welcoming to his home the small boy whom she had not yet seen.

Barry watched her, an amused smile on his well-cut lips.

"All het up, aren't you?" he said.

She went to one of the windows . . . and drew back quickly. A car was just turning into the entrance gates. By the chauffeur sat a boy in a grey flannel suit.

"He's here," she said urgently. "Go and meet him at the front door, Barry. Don't bring him in here. Take him up to his bedroom and—tell him."

"Right!" said Barry and went with his loose easy stride from the room.

She stood there listening, her head turned in the direction of the door . . . Barry's voice . . . a child's voice, thin and a little high-pitched . . . footsteps going upstairs . . . Barry's laugh and then the closing of the bedroom door.

She looked around her, wondering what changes he would notice. She loved the room and had made so few changes that she hardly knew herself what she had altered. The position of a chair there . . . a table there . . . She had kept little of her own furniture. The Sheraton bureau-bookcase alone belonged to her.

Though beautiful, the room had had a slightly bleak look when first she came here. It was used only on rare occasions. Barry lived chiefly in the library, and Philip had divided his time between that and the old nursery upstairs. Since her coming the room had blossomed into life, gaining colour and poise and vitality, becoming comfortable and, as a room should be, a little haphazard. On an impulse she moved the photograph of Stephen from the writing-table to the window-sill, putting it into the shadow of the curtain. Then she moved her pedestal work-table out of sight behind the lacquered Chinese screen, trying to make the room look as he would remember it. A half-made model of an aeroplane lay on the small card-table, left there by Stephen this morning. She put it with her work-table behind the screen. Then she looked round again, frowning anxiously . . . This room must strike no alien note. It must hold out the welcome of home, loved and familiar, to Philip, as soon as he entered it.

The door opened suddenly and Barry entered.

She swung round.

"Well?"

He closed the door.

"Well, what?"

"How did he take it?"

He met her gaze with his pleasant lazy smile.

"I haven't told him."

"Oh, Barry!"

"Much better let him come down and find out for himself. Get the thing over at once instead of taking two bites at it. He'll take the whole thing for granted as soon as he sees you."

"You funked it."

"No, I didn't; but I thought, why waste time on explanations when the explanation's waiting for him downstairs?"

"I wish you'd told him . . ."

"You're making a mountain out of a molehill, my dear. It's a way women have, even the most sensible and adorable."

"Is that me?"

"Is what you?"

"Sensible and adorable."

"You know it is. Relax, darling."

He put his arms round her and pressed his lips upon hers.

When his father had gone, Philip stood and looked round his bedroom, drawing a deep sigh of relief. It was good to be back here in the life that he and his father had built up together. He wondered if his father had missed him while he was away. There had been something in his manner—a touch almost of tenderness—that had made him think he had been missed and had sent a wave of happiness through him.

He had lain awake most of last night, dreaming of this home-coming, longing for it, counting up to sixty and saying "It's another minute nearer now." . . . Again and again he had summoned the memory of his father's handsome good-natured face, the laughter creases at the side of the blue eyes . . . the pleasant finely moulded lips . . . the tall powerful frame . . . investing the whole, in the passion of his hero-worship, with such glamour that it might have been the form of one of the gods of old returned to earth.

And earnestly, sitting up in bed, his arms clasped round his thin knees, he had taken stock of the situation. His absence from his father had given him a new clarity of vision. With the perception of the lover—keen and unchildlike—he had realized something of the loneliness of his father in the big empty house. Through the years to come he must be his father's companion. It was a position for which he must strain every nerve to fit himself. He must become strong and brave. He must rid himself of all his childish fears . . .

Then sleep had overcome him, and he had fallen into an uneasy dream in which he struggled to reach his father through swelling seas against which he could make no headway.

This morning his mood of high resolve still upheld him, and he had passed the day in a state of trembling exaltation. Not all Miss Rossiter's admonitions could persuade him to eat his breakfast. He had tried to eat, but his throat refused to swallow. And now he was here . . . The joy of home-coming welled up in him as he looked round the small familiar room. The old beloved routine would now establish itself again. He would have tea with his father in the library, and together they would walk round the gardens with Major at their heels . . . They would visit the stables where Bonny, the mare, would eat the sugar he had saved from tea . . . They would go to the kitchen gardens, where pears and nectarines and peaches were ripening against the sun-baked walls . . . the orchard, where small green apples jostled each other on the branches or fell softly on to grass beneath, grass that in spring was starred with golden daffodils . . . the rose garden and herbaceous borders ablaze with colour . . . the conservatories full of heliotropes and lilies and the faintly malevolent faces of orchids. Then they would visit the place where they were making the new bathing pool.

He went to the window and leant out, looking over trees, river and meadow to the hills beyond. Something of his father's love for this small corner of the world stirred in his heart. To-morrow he would ride with his father round the farm . . . down the leafy lanes . . . along the cool glades of the wood . . . He was not afraid of riding. It was the jumping that turned his heart cold with fear. He tightened his lips. From now on his fears must be overcome. In his new exalted mood he felt no doubts or misgivings. His eyes went to the terrace beneath his window and the lawn at the feet of the steps. An air of slumbering quiet seemed to brood over it all. On the lawn a thrush sat, with feathers luxuriantly outspread, motionless, sundrenched . . . The cooing of a wood-pigeon—soft and rhythmic—floated through the air.

The sound of the stable clock striking four roused him from his dreams. He withdrew from the window, washed his face and hands, brushed his hair and turned to the door, intending to go downstairs and along the passage to the library. Then he stopped, remembering that his father had said, "Come to the drawing-room when you're ready." He felt puzzled and—he didn't know why—a little troubled. They never had tea in the drawing-room. On the first day of his home-coming he didn't want to deviate by the smallest detail from their usual routine.

Slowly he made his way down the wide shallow staircase, crossed the hall and entered the drawing-room.

And there he found his father holding in his arms a woman he had never seen before.

Barry was not in any way disconcerted. So much the better, he thought. The kid had the whole thing handed to him now on a plate. No need for a lot of palaver. Barry had always hated palaver . . . But Ann gazed with dismay at the child who had suddenly appeared in the doorway. He stood there, not speaking or moving, his eyes, large and dark in his pale face, fixed on her . . . He looked, somehow, drained and emptied, as if the small still form were only a shell.

"Come along and meet your new mother, Philip," said Barry breezily. "We got married while you were away."

Philip advanced slowly, his eyes still fixed on Ann.

"Well, where are you manners? Say how-d'you-do," said Barry jocularly.

"How-d'you-do," said Philip, holding out his hand.

It was small and fragile and ice-cold in her clasp. The words she had meant to say—"I hope we're going to be friends" . . . "This isn't going to make any difference, you know" . . . "You must try to look on me as a sort of grown-up sister"—died away unspoken. She realized that there was nothing to be said . . .

His eyes roved round the room, and she knew that he noticed every change, however slight, that she had made in it. They came to rest on Stephen's photograph, which the curtains did not quite hide, after all.

"That's your new brother," said Barry.

Philip's eyes grew larger and darker as they devoured the boyish good-looking face of the photograph . . . the straight nose, the smiling lips, the shapely head set gracefully and proudly on the upright neck. It was a "head and shoulders" photograph, but it suggested a sturdy well-built body and a robust physique.

"Is he—here, too?" said Philip.

He seemed to be a long way off, watching himself standing there in the room, listening to himself saying the words.

"Oh, yes," said Barry. "He's out rabbiting now with the Peterson boys, but he'll be back for tea. It'll be nice for you to have a brother, won't it?"

"Yes," said Philip.

He began to back slowly towards the door.

"Come along," said Barry, throwing himself into an armchair and holding out an arm. "Come and talk to us. Tell us all you've been doing while you've been away."

"Yes, do, Philip," said Ann softly. "Perhaps you'd like to go round the garden with your father. I'm afraid it's been a—shock to you."

"No!" said Philip. His quick breathless voice fiercely repudiated the sympathy of her tone and manner. "No! I—I'll go and unpack my things now, shall I?"

"Yes, that's all right, old chap," said Barry. "Run along."

Philip went upstairs to his room and closed the door. Then he sat down on his bed, staring in front of him. His heart was beating unevenly, and gusts of trembling shook him . . . He didn't know how long he had sat there when he heard voices in the garden below. He went to the window and stood in the shadow of the curtain looking out. His father was there on the lawn with his stepmother and—the boy. The boy was the boy of the photograph—well-grown, handsome, with a pleasant smile, blue eyes and fair unruly hair. Major, the fox-terrier, was jumping up at him, still excited by the "rabbiting".

"Well, how did you get on?" Barry was saying.

The boy said something that Philip could not hear and they all laughed.

"Well, come along in to tea," said Ann.

"Oh, one minute," said the boy. "Would you look at my gun, Dad? It seemed to have jammed this morning."

He ran indoors, Major leaping at his heels, and returned with a gun.

It was only an airgun but it was almost as large as a real one. They bent over it together. Philip noticed that the boy handled it knowledgeably and with the air of an expert. Then the boy raised it to his shoulder and fired into the trees.

"That's all right," he said. "That's fixed it."

The three of them began to walk slowly towards the house. His stepmother's arm was linked with his father's. His father's hand rested on the boy's shoulder. They suggested a group that was complete and self-sufficient.

Philip turned back into the room. He wasn't trembling any longer, but there was a cold numbed feeling at his heart. They didn't want him. All right, he wouldn't want them. He tried to whip up his anger against them in order to hide from himself the misery that threatened to engulf his spirit, the black emptiness that lay ahead of him.

His eyes went round the room. From now on this would be his world. The rest of the house belonged to them. He thought of the woman . . . the boy . . . with cold dispassionate hatred. He dared not think of his father because to do that might break down the barrier behind which his wounded pride and childish bitterness were taking refuge. He seemed to be actually building the barrier as he stood there . . . inch by inch, with almost superhuman effort . . . shutting himself away from them . . . cutting off, painfully and relentlessly, that part of him that would have reached out blindly to them for comfort . . . taking an acrid joy in his desolation. From now on he would belong to himself and himself alone. His hands were tightly clenched, his lips set in a tight unchildlike line.

"Philip!" called Barry from the hall.

He made no answer, only stood there, stiffening his resolve, fighting against the weakness that threatened suddenly to overcome him.

"Come along down to tea, Philip," called Barry.

For a few more moments he remained silent, afraid of answering lest his voice should betray him.

Then he called:

"I'll be down in a minute."

To his relief his voice sounded casual and ordinary.

Barry returned to the drawing-room.

"I told you it would be all right," he said to his wife. "I was sure the kid would take it in his stride."

She smiled a little unsteadily.

"I wish I could be as sure," she said.

Chapter Six

Monica looked anxiously out of the window as the train drew into the station. Babs (everyone called Monica's mother Babs, and it had never occurred to Monica to call her anything else) had said she would be there to meet her, but Babs was apt to forget things, especially when they were not particularly interesting.

Miss Rossiter had seen her into the train at Appleton station and had put her in charge of the guard. Whenever the train stopped at a station the guard had come along to have a word with her. He was a large man with a bushy moustache, a gold tooth, and eyes that twinkled in kindly amusement even when he was quite serious. He said that he had a little girl of her age at home called Cherry. He had a brown dog, too, and a little white kitten that slept between the brown dog's paws.

Monica, craning her head from the carriage window, felt uneasy on his account as well as her own in case Babs should not be there. He wouldn't know what to do with her . . . He might leave her at the Left Luggage office, of course, or he might take her about with him on his other journeys till Babs turned up. In any case it would be a nuisance for him. She drew a quick breath of relief as she saw Babs walking on to the platform just as the train stopped. She wore a new hat and a new dress and looked so lovely that— though she always looked lovely and generally wore a new hat and a new dress—sudden shyness possessed Monica, making her hang back from the meeting and stammer a little when she spoke. She always had this feeling of shyness when she met Babs after an absence, however short. There was something about Babs that set her apart from other people's mothers. She was more like a person in a picture book or a story than a real person. Even the guard seemed to feel it as she thanked him with her air of wistful sweetness and slipped the ten-shilling note into his hand. He stood there watching her till she had vanished among the crowd, holding Monica's hand.

"I've got a taxi, darling," she said, as they made their way to the station entrance. "What sort of a journey have you had?"

Monica began to tell her about the guard's little girl and brown dog and white kitten, then stopped when she saw she wasn't listening.

In the taxi Babs put an arm round her and drew her against the scented softness of her breast.

"It's lovely to have you back, darling," she said, but there was a far-away look in her beautiful eyes and a slight frown between her eyes as if her thoughts were elsewhere. That didn't trouble Monica. She never expected to have Babs' undivided attention.

But a faint cloud invaded her happiness when she entered the sitting-room of the flat and found Reggie there, standing on the hearthrug.

Reggie was a tall young man with greying hair, a smooth unlined face and rather close-set eyes who had been a frequent visitor at the flat before Monica went away to the Vicarage. He visited it chiefly at times when Fred, her mother's husband, was not there, holding long telephone conversations with her on the days when they did not meet and sending her sheaves of expensive hothouse flowers.

Monica disliked him, but—so precarious was her foothold in her mother's life, so earnestly did she strive to secure it—was careful to hide her dislike from both Reggie and her mother . . . She was a little bewildered, however, by the situation. She hadn't expected to come back here at all. She'd had her six months with her mother, and she had expected to go to Yorkshire to her father.

After submitting for a few minutes to the mixture of facetiousness and superciliousness with which Reggie always treated her, she looked at her mother enquiringly.

"When am I going to daddy?" she said.

63

"Oh, darling!" said her mother ruefully. "I was going to—"

She glanced from Reggie to the child with an air of wistful appeal and went on, "Come into your bedroom, dear, and I'll help you take off your things."

They went into the little bedroom that was called Monica's bedroom when she was at the flat. It was really anybody's bedroom. There were a few of Monica's books in the bookshelves but most of them were modern novels of the more erotic variety. Ash-trays lay about, full of ash and cigarette ends. Tins of talcum powder, bottles of hairoil stood on the glass shelf. The drawers were always full of other people's things, and Monica kept her clothes in her suitcase under the bed. There was a frowsty smoke-laden air in the room. But to Monica, after the clean hard alien brightness of the Vicarage, it was indescribably dear. She looked round it with an intensity of loving recognition.

"Darling," said Babs, closing the door, "I've got something to tell you."

She stood irresolute for a moment or two, then sat on the bed, drawing Monica down beside her. Something in her manner—affectionate, troubled, nervous—seemed to lay a cold warning finger on the child's heart.

"You see, darling, daddy was ill. That was why you couldn't go to him."

"Ill?"

"Yes. He had to have an operation. He didn't want you to be told."

"But where is he now?"

"Darling . . ."

Babs looked helplessly around. She was a lovely, gentle delicate-looking woman—so lovely, so delicate, so gentle that there was always someone at hand to shield her from the unpleasant things of life. This situation was decidedly unpleasant and there should have been someone at hand to shield her from it. Her eyes rested on the door that divided her from Reggie as if silently asking his help. The room had dissolved in a sort of mist round Monica, then slowly the mist cleared.

"You mean—he's dead?" she said.

Babs drew a quick breath of relief.

"Yes, darling, that's it . . . You'll"—the nervousness returned to her voice—"you'll be brave, darling, won't you?"

At the moment, as if in answer to her unspoken call, there was a knock at the door, and Reggie entered.

"I've made some tea," he said. "Come and have it. Come along, kid."

Mrs. Deverel gave an uncertain little laugh.

"The maid's let me down, Monny darling. She just hasn't turned up, so we're coping as best we can till we can get someone else . . . Come and have some tea, darling."

Monica shook her head.

Babs stood up, trying to conceal her desire to escape. She found emotional scenes wearing, and—though she exerted her charm on them automatically—children bored her.

"You'd rather be left alone for a little, wouldn't you, sweetheart?" she said solicitously. "Just come along and have some tea when you're ready."

Then she drifted—vague, unhappy, heart-stirringly lovely—from the room.

Monica sat on the bed where she had left her. She was so stunned by the news that her mind refused to take it in. And then, through the numbness of her spirit, there penetrated little threads of sound. Reggie and her mother were talking in the next room, and the door was not quite closed.

"But, hang it all, Babs, you're not going to have the kid here permanently, are you? It's going to be a frightful nuisance."

"I know it is, darling, but what can I do? Fred's got up on his hind legs about it. He says we must make a home for her . . . After all, she's no trouble."

"You know what I mean. We can't have her hanging about here. It's not—safe. You must get round Fred to send her away somewhere."

"Hush, darling! Don't talk so loud. She might hear."

"Of course she can't."

But he put out a hand to push the door to as he spoke.

A cold familiar fear closed round Monica's heart, shutting out everything else, even the thought of her father. In her short life she had been buffeted to and fro, "parked out" for a month here, a month there, and she craved for home with a strange unchildlike hunger. She had hated all the places to which she had been sent . . . bare bright rooms, full of little chairs and tables, with stencilled nursery pictures on the walls . . . communal books and toys . . . the brisk impersonal kindliness of the professional trainers of youth . . . sitting in little rows, going out in little groups. She longed for the cosy intimate hugger-mugger life of home . . . her own place . . . her own things . . . sitting on the kitchen table helping weigh the currants, shell the peas . . . curling up on the hearthrug in front of the fire with a book . . . silly little jokes that no one else understood . . . people loving you . . . This flat of her mother's was now the only home she had, and the knowledge that its security was threatened filled her with terror.

Babs had said that she was no trouble, but she must be more than that. She must help. She must help so much that they'd want her to stay.

There were two doors to her bedroom. One opened into the sitting-room, the other into the hall. She went out into the hall and down the passage to the kitchen. And there she set to work, filling the sink with water and piling into it the used crockery that was stacked all round.

In the sitting-room Mrs. Deverel lay back on the settee, smoking a cigarette. Reggie stood on the hearthrug, looking down at her.

"I can't do it, Reggie," she was saying. "It's no good asking me."

"Look here, Babs, you can't let me down," he protested. "It's all fixed up."

"You knew she was coming back to-day."

"I didn't."

"I told you."

"Well, if you did, I'd forgotten. Anyway, I naturally thought you could leave her with the maid or something. After all, you've sent her home to sleep with the maid sometimes."

"Aggie's left me in the lurch. I've told you so."

"Well, surely someone in one of the other flats could take her."

"Don't be a fool, Reggie. We might as well tell Fred the whole thing as do that."

"Now listen, angel. The crowd's coming. It's only an hour's run to Brighton and it's going to be a marvellous dance. They do things well at the Splendide, you know. I booked the room as soon as I heard of it. The whole thing was fixed up at a moment's notice. Bunny's getting up the party and we're all coming back first thing to-morrow."

"I keep telling you. I can't leave Monny."

"And I keep telling you—it's a chance we mayn't get again for months. Fred's away till Tuesday, isn't he?"

"Yes."

"We could stay over till Monday if you could find someone to take the kid."

"Well, I can't. You know I can't."

"I'm not going to let you mess everything up for a crazy notion like that. Think of it, my sweet. Think of it."

She thought of it . . . and her lips curved into a wistful dreamy smile.

"Oh, Reggie, it would be heavenly."

"It's fixed, then."

"No, it isn't. What about Monny?"

"Leave her here by herself."

"Darling, I couldn't. Fred would kill me if he ever found out."

"He won't find out. She's not his kid anyway. Why should he fuss about her so?"

"I don't know, but he does."

"She'll be all right here. She's not an infant in arms. She can feed and dress herself. There's food in the place, isn't there?"

"Yes."

"We'll come back to-morrow."

"I oughtn't to . . ."

There was a note of weakening in the gentle voice. The lovely eyes were still troubled, but there was a starry brightness in them, as if she were already in the ballroom, with the lights, the music, the laughter. He hastened to follow up his advantage.

"It'll do you no end of good. You've had no fun for ages. You'll be able to tackle the whole thing—Fred and the kid and all the rest of it—much better after a little break. And—think of it, darling—I've got one of those front suites overlooking the sea."

"No, Reggie, I couldn't."

But he knew that the battle was over and that he had won.

A few minutes later the two of them went into the kitchen. Monica still stood at the sink, intent on her washing-up. She turned as they entered and gave them an anxious uncertain smile, her heart shrinking from the news they might be bringing her.

"I've done all the knives and forks," she said in eager propitiation. "I'm doing the plates now. It won't take me long. Then I'll clean the spoons and forks. I know where the stuff is."

"Splendid!" said Reggie jovially. "Splendid! Good chars are scarce. They'll be queueing up for you before we know where we are."

She could tell by his manner—over-hearty, ill at ease—that they thought she would not like what they had to say to her.

"Come into the sitting-room a moment, darling," said Babs. "I want to speak to you."

"I'll go on with the good work," said Reggie, seizing an apron that hung behind the door, tying it round his waist and doing a *pas seul* on the kitchen mat. Neither of them laughed.

"Come, darling," said Babs, and led Monica into the sitting-room, shutting the door behind them.

On the settee, enclosed in the fragrant circle of her mother's arm, Monica surrendered, despite herself, to a sudden rush of happiness. But anxiety was still there behind it. People weren't kind to you like this for no reason. Were they going to send her away again—now, at once?

"Darling," said the sweet slow voice, "will you do something for me?"

"Yes."

"You know that sometimes I've gone out in the evenings and left you in bed when we hadn't a maid?"

"Yes."

"And you were all right, weren't you?"

"Yes."

"And often I've left you alone in the flat in the mornings when I've been out shopping, haven't I?"

"Yes."

"Well, listen, sweetheart. I have to go out this evening and I won't be back till to-morrow. I want you to go to bed to-night just as if I were coming back later when you were asleep, and then, when you wake up to-morrow, you'll know that I'll be back soon, and you can see to yourself and get your own breakfast, can't you?"

So they weren't going to send her away . . . Monica's heart leapt in wild relief, refusing to face the thought of the long hours of loneliness.

"Yes," she said breathlessly. "Yes, of course."

"You won't mind?"

"No, of course not. Of *course* I won't."

"You know where all the things are, don't you, sweetheart? There's plenty of milk in the frig. And there's bread. And butter. You can boil yourself an egg for breakfast. That'll be fun, won't it?"

"Yes . . . Yes, it will."

"That's a good girl. I'll bring you a present home . . . And, darling . . ."

"Yes?"

"You—you won't tell anyone, will you?"

"No."

"You—won't mention it to Fred when he comes home, will you?"

"No."

"It'll be our secret, won't it?"

"Yes."

The interview was successfully over, and Babs had lost interest in it. She rose and went towards the kitchen.

"Let's see how Reggie's getting on," she said.

Reggie wasn't getting on at all. He had taken off his apron and was sitting on the kitchen table, smoking a cigarette. He sprang to his feet as they entered.

"Well?" he said.

"Monny doesn't mind," said Babs. "Isn't she a pet!"

"Good for her!" said Reggie heartily.

Babs opened the refrigerator door.

"Look, darling. There's some milk here. And"—vaguely—"you'll find other things about somewhere." She looked at Reggie. "What time ought we to start?"

"How long will it take you to put your things together?"

"Not long. Let's have a drink first."

They went back to the sitting-room, and Monica busied herself again at the sink. She worked with redoubled energy now that she knew she wasn't going to be sent away. She'd sweep the floor when she'd finished washing up. And she'd scrub the table . . . She heard the clink of glasses and the sound of voices from the sitting-room. The wistful note had left her mother's voice. It was clear and confident. Her laughter rang out more and more frequently.

"Just one more," Monica heard her say, and Reggie answered: "No, my pet. You've had more than enough already. You'll be tight before we get there at this rate."

When the taxi came, Monica stood at the door to see them off.

"You'll go to bed soon, won't you, darling?" said Mrs. Deverel.

She had put on a different hat—a gay little hat that perched on her forehead and threw an alluring shadow over her violet-blue eyes. There was a glow and sparkle about her loveliness that made Monica catch her breath. She leaned out of the window of the taxi as it began to move off. "You could make yourself some bread and milk for supper, couldn't you, darling?"

"Yes . . . I'll be all right," said Monica reassuringly.

The taxi disappeared round the corner of the road and Monica returned to the kitchen. She finished the washing-up, swept the floor, scrubbed the table and tidied the chaotic room as best she could. Then she drank some milk, ate some bread and butter, and went to bed.

So full of emotions and incidents had the day been that the strange stunned feeling still persisted. It was only a few hours since Miss Rossiter had put her in charge of the guard on Appleton station, but it seemed now part of another life, so distant that she could scarcely remember it. Kaleidoscopic scenes flitted before her closed eyes . . . The guard's face framed in the carriage window . . . Babs' face looking down at her in the taxi . . . Reggie's small mouth curved into its supercilious grin . . . piles of crockery in the kitchen sink . . . the shadows gathering in the corners of the room when her mother left her . . . She shut away the thought of her father, summoning the other thoughts to form a sort of barrier between her and it . . . The pictures began to fly past her eyes more and more quickly like slides in a magic lantern . . . The guard . . . Babs . . . Reggie . . . Babs . . . Reggie . . . the guard . . . the crockery in the sink grew to a mountain that touched the ceiling . . . The shadows took shape and began to move . . . Reggie . . . Babs . . . the guard . . .

Then exhaustion claimed her and she fell asleep.

She didn't know how long she had been asleep when she was awakened by a sound. She sat up, her heart beating unevenly, and looked about her. A shaft of moonlight fell across the room from between the curtains, giving the well-known objects an unfamiliar and slightly sinister aspect. Slowly her eyes went to the door, and she strained her ears for the small furtive sounds that crept through the silence. Someone was moving about in the flat . . . She sat there motionless, her heart hammering in her thin chest, her face stiff with fear. Footsteps were approaching the door. Slowly it opened and she saw the shadowy form of a man entering the room. She gave a strangled cry of terror . . . then he moved into the shaft of moonlight and she recognized the thick-set burly frame. It was Fred . . .

"Monny?" he said.

71

He came across the room and sat on her bed.

"Where's your mother?" he said.

She gazed at the blunt rough-hewn features, drawing comfort from their kindliness. He took one of her small cold hands and held it in his enormous grasp tightly, reassuringly.

"All right," he said. "Don't tell me . . . I suppose I can guess—more or less. Don't worry, kid. I'm not going to drag you into it."

She spoke in a quick unsteady voice, making the first excuse for her mother that came into her head.

"She didn't know you were coming back to-night."

"I know," he said with a grim twist of his lips. "Oh, it isn't a trap. The man I'd gone to do business with was suddenly taken ill so I got the next train back." He looked round the room, and another idea struck him.

"My God, Monny! She's not left you here all night alone, has she?"

She grew tense and flamelike in her eagerness to shield her mother.

"I don't mind. I don't mind at all. I like it. I wasn't frightened till I heard you. She'll be back to-morrow."

He slipped an arm round her.

"She told you about your father?"

The thought couldn't be kept at bay any longer. She relaxed against his shoulder and began to cry. He held her closely.

"That's right, old lady . . . Have a good cry . . . No, don't try to stop . . . It's only old Fred . . . I'm not your father, kid, but I'm going to have a darn good try to look after you . . . Now listen! Whatever happens, there'll always be old Fred . . . Always remember that.

"It was the hell of a mess that brought us together and we're in a hell of a mess again now, but I'll see you through as if you were my own. See? Don't worry about things. Just say to yourself, 'I've got old Fred and he'll see me through'. There! Feeling better?"

The tempest of her grief had spent itself. He wiped away her tears with his pocket handkerchief, then with clumsy tenderness laid her back in bed, smoothing her pillow, straightening the bedclothes and tucking her in.

"Do you feel like going to sleep ?" he said.

She shook her head. Her face was flushed and swollen by tears.

"Tell you what!" he said with a sudden inspiration. "I'll read to you, shall I? I remember once when I was a kid and had 'flu or something and couldn't sleep, my mother used to read to me. Let's try that now, shall we?"

He switched on the light and went over to the bookcase.

"Look!" he said, taking a book out. "*Water Babies*. That sounds all right, doesn't it?"

She nodded.

Bringing a small upright chair to the bedside, he lowered his enormous bulk into it. He sat for a moment or two, lost in thought, then began to turn the pages.

"Start at the beginning, shall we?" he said.

Again she nodded.

He cleared his throat and began to read aloud in a slow expressionless voice.

" 'Once upon a time there was a little chimney sweep, and his name was Tom . . .' "

Chapter Seven

Mrs. Sanders sat at her desk, reading over the chapter that she had written the night before. She was wrapped in an embroidered Chinese shawl that she had seen in the window of a second-hand clothes shop in Maybridge yesterday and bought on an impulse. Every now and then she raised her hand to wipe away the tears that coursed down her cheeks.

"That you, dear?" she said in a choking voice as the door opened to admit Greta.

"Yes," said Greta, coming in and closing the door.

She was not at all perturbed to find her employer in tears. Mrs. Sanders could seldom read the adventures of her own heroines without being moved to tears by them. And certainly their sufferings merited sympathy. They were perpetually being misunderstood and compromised and jilted and spurned and exposed to almost incredible hazards and temptations. Even the knowledge that everything came right in the end seemed hardly to compensate for all they had to undergo.

"I'm sorry, dear," said Mrs. Sanders. "I was reading that part where Maureen's husband deserts her, and—well, it was just too much for me. There she is, without a penny, with nowhere to turn, deserted by the man she loves . . ." Her voice trailed away.

"I know," said Greta, sitting down on a small chair by the desk. "I remember how I felt when it happened to Mrs. Fordice."

"Who's Mrs. Fordice, dear?" said Mrs. Sanders, trying to disentangle the fringe of the shawl from the handle of one of the drawers of the desk. "I think I'll cut it off. It keeps getting in the way."

"The woman who lived at Rose Cottage," said Greta, freeing the fringe. "Her husband went off and left her with two children and no money at all."

"Oh, yes, I remember," said Mrs. Sanders, settling the shawl about her shoulders again. "She had a bulldog and was very inconsiderate. She kept coming and bothering Adrian at all hours."

"She was in great trouble, you know," said Greta mildly.

She had often noticed that, though Olivia could weep copiously over the sufferings of her own heroines, she remained completely unmoved by the sufferings of the flesh-and-blood people around her.

"Yes, of course," said Mrs. Sanders. "Have you time to type the new chapter now?"

"Not just now, I'm afraid," said Greta. "I've got the children on my hands this morning. I looked in to remind you that it was Angela's birthday."

"Is it really?" said Mrs. Sanders with interest. "How old is she?"

"Seven."

"Are you sure?" said Mrs. Sanders thoughtfully. "I thought she was older."

"No. She's seven."

"We ought to do something about it, oughtn't we?" said Mrs. Sanders, turning round from the desk with a sweeping movement that sent a box of paper clips on to the floor and caught a small letter-balance up in the fringe of the shawl.

Greta picked up the paper clips and extricated the letter-balance. "How do you mean?" she said.

"Let's take them all out for a treat," said Mrs. Sanders. "I'm going to give myself a break before I start the next poem, so I could spare the time. I'll hire a taxi and take them all into Maybridge."

"No, no," said Greta, recoiling at the thought.

She knew these grandly maternal moods of Olivia's, when she would take a taxi-load of children out for the day, bringing them home late at night, pallid, exhausted, fractious and generally with one or two of them missing.

"And, you remember," she went on, "we asked Angela what she wanted and she chose a party. She wanted to have those children who were here last summer. Geraldine and Philip and Monica."

"Can we get them?"

"Yes, as it happens, we can. I did tell you about it at the time, dear. Monica's parents have taken a cottage just outside Maybridge and, of course, Geraldine and Philip live in the neighbourhood anyway."

"But we must have more people than that, Greta," said Mrs. Sanders, flinging out her arms with an expansive gesture that left the fringe of her shawl entangled in her brooch. "We must fill the house. We must ask everyone we know . . . How many people do we know?"

Greta sighed. Olivia's indifference to the affairs of the household was sometimes trying, but much less trying than her occasional interest in them.

"No, dear. It will be quite all right. We've asked the Gosport children and the doctor's children and one or two others. And, of course, there are the children we have with us at present."

"Of course. By the way, who are the children we have with us at present?"

"The twins, you know, whose parents are in India. And Jaqueline, whose parents are on a Mediterranean cruise. And—"

"I don't think I'll try to learn their names, after all," said Mrs. Sanders. "It only confuses me. There's a little boy here, isn't there? Didn't you say he was a Moravian? Such an odd religion, I always think."

"No, dear. Trevor's a Mongolian."

"What do they believe?"

Greta smiled.

"They don't believe anything."

"Oh, atheists," said Mrs. Sanders with mild interest.

"No, no . . . They're a little underdeveloped. He has his own nurse with him. Look! There she is in the garden now."

Mrs. Sanders craned her neck to see a woman leading a small boy by the hand across the lawn.

"Oh, that's his nurse, is it?" she said. "I've met her once or twice on the stairs and wondered who she was . . . By the way, have I given Angela a birthday present?"

"I got one for you, dear. She's delighted with it."

"I'm so glad," said Mrs. Sanders graciously.

She turned again to the desk and began to collect the scattered manuscript, then she stopped, a speculative frown on her face.

"You know, dear . . ."

"Yes?"

"It occurred to me last night. I really ought to use some of the—ecclesiastical atmosphere I live in. I mean bishops and clergymen and organists and people like that. How long have I been here?"

"Eight years."

"Yes . . . Well, I ought to be soaked in it. I *am* soaked in it. Vestry meetings and parish councils and anthems and Women's Institutes."

"But you never go to any of them."

Mrs. Sanders waved the objection aside with a gesture that freed the shawl from her brooch and caught it in the letter-basket.

"That's nothing to do with it," she said, taking a large pair of scissors from the pen-tray and cutting off the fringe where it had caught in the basketwork. "I don't know why they put all these loose threads on it. They're quite unnecessary. The garment's quite complete without them . . . No, dear. It's the *atmosphere* that counts, and I live in the atmosphere, so I must have absorbed it. As an artist, I oughtn't to waste a background like this. I wonder . . ."

She stopped.

"Yes?" said Greta a little apprehensively.

"You remember the plot I thought of for *Barren Heritage* and didn't use?"

"Yes."

"Well, couldn't I adapt it to an ecclesiastical atmosphere? I mean, if the Bishop fell in love with the Vicar's wife . . ."

"I don't think Bishops do fall in love with Vicars' wives," said Greta.

"It would be a good situation," said Mrs. Sanders wistfully, "and I wouldn't put any actual *passion* into it."

But Greta knew that it was impossible for Olivia to tackle any situation without putting passion into it.

"The Bishop might not like it," she said, doubtfully. "The Bishop here, I mean."

"He probably wouldn't read it," said Mrs. Sanders. "I don't think Bishops do read much. They're too busy holding synods and revising the Prayer Book. Still, we can bear it in mind, can't we?"

"Yes," said Greta, "we'll bear it in mind."

"Oh, there was something else I wanted to ask you," said Mrs. Sanders. She burrowed among her manuscript and drew out a page. "Is 'ripping' out of date? As a slang word, I mean."

"I think it is rather," said Greta.

"I wish you'd get me some modern slang, my dear. I'm hung up for it in this chapter. Find some and make a list, will you?"

"Yes, but—what sort of slang? What connection do you want to use it in?"

"Any connection," said Mrs. Sanders vaguely. "Just make a list of slang and I'll fit it in. It's about young people, you see, and I want it to sound up to date."

She collected the papers that covered her desk and handed them to Greta.

"Put these in order, too, will you? I've finished chapter fifteen and I'm going to take a break for a poem."

She leant back in her chair, gathering her shawl about her. Paper clips, pen nibs and a small desk calendar dangled in the fringe. Greta took the papers and began to try to arrange them, reading the beginning and end of each sheet to see where they fitted together. Mrs. Sanders never numbered her pages. To do so, she said, would interrupt the flow of her ideas.

"I thought of writing one on the lines of 'Does the road wind uphill all the way?' and—'I am the captain of my soul'," she went on. "Do they come in the same poem or are they different ones?"

"I think they're different ones," said Greta, puzzling over a word that might have been "hyena" or "hyacinth" or even "hymnal". The rest of the sentence gave little clue.

"You know . . ." said Mrs. Sanders, "I've been wondering whether to get a—dictaphone, they're called, aren't they? They're less soulless than typewriters and shorthand, and I think that if I actually *told* the story instead of writing it, I could work myself up better."

"I think you work yourself up quite well now," said Greta, deciding that the word was "hymen".

"Yes, but it would take away that last small obstruction that mechanical means seem to interpose between the artist and his audience. I should feel that the story was going straight from my heart to the heart of the reader; I could be more intimate, more—more *stark*."

Greta quailed at the thought as she fastened the papers together with a clip.

"And now for the poem," said Mrs. Sanders, closing her eyes. "Something like this, 'Does there seem no end to the weary road?' The next line must end with 'load', of course . . . Then 'light' and 'height' and 'soul' and 'goal' . . . It's coming . . . It will have come completely by to-night." She opened her eyes and, sitting up straight in her chair, continued briskly, "Did you say that it was Angela's birthday to-day or to-morrow?"

"To-day."

"Have I wished her many happy returns of the day?"

"I don't think so."

"I'll do it now, then. Will you fetch her, dear?"

Greta went out into the hall and along the passage. From the closed door of the Vicar's study she heard the subdued sound of voices. She recognized the Vicar's and Mr. Hassock's.

She felt depressed and ill at ease. Somehow—she didn't know why—she was no longer stirred by Olivia's novels, no longer uplifted by her poems. She had struggled for some time against the knowledge, but she couldn't ignore it any longer. A heavy burden of disloyalty weighed on her spirit. The feeling of boredom—and, worse still, of amusement—that seized her when Olivia began to discuss her work was a betrayal of the friendship that had been her solace for so many years. She dated the beginning of this feeling from the day when Mr. Hassock had walked home with her from the picnic. The twinkle in his eye, when she mentioned Olivia's work, had sown, as it were, a seed that, despite all her efforts to crush it, was growing and blossoming. From that day, too, dated the realization that she couldn't remember Frank. She could only think of him as he looked in his photograph, standing stiffly upright, wearing his uniform, staring straight in front of him. She couldn't remember how he had moved and spoken, couldn't even remember how he had smiled.

She had been to the pictures with Bertie Carstairs last week, and, though she had enjoyed the picture, she had found Bertie difficult to talk to. She had nothing to talk about but Olivia's work and the children, and naturally he wasn't interested in either. That didn't really matter very much, because Bertie—an amiable young man with slightly protuberant eyes, a smooth girlish skin and a small golden moustache—was quite content to do most of the talking. He was opinionated and somewhat egotistical, but he made no secret of his admiration. He urged her to join the tennis club, the golf club, to watch the cricket match on Saturday and go to tea to his aunt's on Sunday. He had bought tickets for the Hospital Dance in Maybridge at the end of the month and took for granted that she was going to it as his partner. She should have felt flattered, but she only felt lost and unhappy. It was as if the gates of the only world she knew—the world in which she had been secure and at peace—had been closed on her, and she could not find the key to any other. If Frank had lived, of course . . . but somehow she couldn't imagine Frank dancing and playing tennis, though she knew that he had done those things. She could only imagine him staring woodenly at her out of a leather frame.

Going upstairs she found Angela seated at the nursery table, wearing an expression of extreme hauteur and apparently doing nothing. She could not know, of course, that Angela was a queen presiding over a meeting of her council—a queen of such astounding charm and beauty that suitors flocked to her from every part of the world. Only yesterday her prime minister and the commander-in-chief of her army had fought a duel for her in which both had been killed. She had attended the funeral, looking exquisite in trailing black (being a black petticoat of her mother's, it had trailed considerably) with a table-runner pinned to her shoulders. Glancing down now at her small person, she didn't see a blue-and-white check gingham frock and strap-over shoes. She saw a robe of white velvet, stiff with pearls and embroidery, and gold shoes resting on a footstool of rubies and emeralds.

Before coming up to the nursery she had tried to persuade the children in the garden to join the game, but they had refused. The twins, invited to be privy counsellors, had continued to play "house" under the weeping willow, and Trevor, appointed her page and ordered to kiss her hand, had responded by biting it. So she had come up to the nursery to hold her court in solitary state.

"Why aren't you out with the others, dear?" said Greta, opening the door.

Angela raised a languid hand to straighten her crown.

"I preferred to be alone," she said distantly.

"Well, your mother wants to speak to you, so will you come downstairs a moment?"

Angela inclined her head regally. An embassy from a foreign potentate had arrived and was waiting an audience. Slowly she followed Greta downstairs. Greta was her herald, and the banisters on either hand were ranks of soldiers, standing to attention.

She bowed gracefully from side to side as she descended the steps and stood for a moment in the doorway of her mother's study before making her entrance with a sweep of the white velvet robe.

"Oh, there you are, darling!" said Mrs. Sanders. "Many happy returns of the day."

Angela inclined her head graciously.

"Thank you," she said.

"Thank your mother for her present, dear," said Greta.

"Thank you for my present," said Angela.

"Let me see . . . What did I give you?" said Mrs. Sanders.

Angela saw a beautifully caparisoned, curvetting steed . . . a tiara of sapphires and diamonds . . . an ivory throne . . .

"You gave her a pencil-box," said Greta.

"I hope it was a nice one, dear, and I hope you liked it," said Mrs. Sanders.

"Yes, thank you," said Angela. "It's very beautiful."

She had decided on the ivory throne and mounted it with slow stateliness to the accompaniment of a roll of drums. A page handed her a sceptre and everyone bowed low. She inclined her head again graciously. Somewhere in the background was a large untidy ludicrous figure . . . That figure had lately begun to cause Angela acute humiliation. It was incredible, preposterous, that it should be her mother. She had fought desperately against the fact and had finally won the victory. The figure was that of the faithful old nurse – who had reared her from babyhood and now waited on her patiently, humbly, among the other servants. It no longer struck any discordant note in the harmony of the scene.

"I've got some chocolate somewhere," said Mrs. Sanders, turning back to the desk with a sweeping movement that caught the fringe of the shawl in the waste-paper basket. She flung it off with a gesture of annoyance and threw it lightly to Angela.

"There you are, dear," she said. "I thought it would give me a feeling of poise and serenity, but it doesn't. Make dolls' clothes of it."

"She doesn't play with dolls, do you, Angela?" said Greta, smiling.

Angela didn't answer. She had taken out clips, pen nibs and desk calendar and was draping the shawl over her shoulders. She wasn't a queen any longer. She was a famous dancer. A packed hall awaited her appearance. Thunders of applause broke out as she stepped on to the platform . . . Arms outspread, she pirouetted across the room.

Mrs. Sanders watched her absently.

"Of course it's no use to me now," she said with a note of regret in her voice. "I don't handle children. I've cut out that chapter about Flavia as a child with the peaches. I felt that it didn't do me justice . . . No," still watching the small pirouetting figure, "she'll be more useful to me when she's in her late 'teens. I use that age quite a lot." She took up a sheet of paper from her desk and studied it. " 'Soar' . . . What rhymes with 'soar'? . . . 'boar' . . . That's no good. Greta, dear, will you get me my rhyming dictionary? I think it's in my bedroom. I remember seeing it in my shoe cupboard not long ago. Or it may have been my medicine cupboard . . ."

Greta went out into the passage again. She could still hear the voices of the Vicar and Mr. Hassock coming from the study. She went up to Mrs. Sanders' bedroom and began a systematic search. She did not look in the shoe cupboard or the medicine cupboard because she knew by experience that things never turned out to be where Mrs. Sanders remembered having seen them.

The Vicar sat his desk, his fountain-pen poised over the pad on which he made notes of interviews, however unimportant. On the desk were several files and ledgers, neatly stacked. There was an In-basket and an Out-basket. Everything was scrupulously neat and methodical. A bookcase near the desk was full of more files and ledgers and books of reference, while the other larger bookcases that lined the room held the leather-bound classical and theological books that had formed the Vicar's studies in his younger days. An air of arid culture brooded over the whole. The curtains had a rich dark look. The armchair was upholstered in dark brown hide. An enlarged photograph of the Roman Forum hung over the fireplace and Arundel prints of Jeremiah, Ezekiel and the Delphic Sibyl gazed gloomily down from the walls. On the chimneypiece were two terracotta vases from Athens, a greenish bronze oil-lamp from Pompeii, a crucifix from Oberammergau and a small reproduction of Donatello's St. George from Florence. There were no flowers in the room, because the Vicar disliked their untidy habit of dropping petals about. The carpet, like the curtains, had a rich dark look. Everything in the room was muted, scholarly and correct, and nothing was ever out of its place.

"You'll visit Mrs. Taylor, then?" the Vicar was saying. "Dr Merrivale says it's some time before she'll be about again."

"Yes, I like visiting Mrs. Taylor," said Mr. Hassock cheerfully. He was sitting astride a chair, his arms resting on the back, in an attitude that the Vicar secretly considered to be unclerical and lacking in dignity. "She has a grand sense of humour."

The Vicar looked at him blankly. He had little consciousness of his parishioners as separate individuals. He only saw them as audiences of his sermons or passive recipients of his ministrations.

"She has some wonderful stories of the village as it used to be when she was a child," went on Mr. Hassock. "When her grandmother was expecting her first baby her grandfather fetched the doctor as soon as the labour pains began and locked him in the house. Kept him there for a day and a night. Simply refused to let him go till the child was born."

"Really?" said the Vicar, frowning slightly, not at the story, which did not interest him, but at the way the curate was tilting his chair, which was fragile and Chippendale.

"Yes . . . He must have been a remarkable old man. He had an affair with the youngest Miss Tomlinson in the days when the Misses Tomlinson kept a Select Academy for the Daughters of Gentlemen at the Grange. His daughter by Miss Tomlinson was brought up at the school and married a German count."

"I should discourage gossip, if I were you," said the Vicar dryly.

"I try to," said Mr. Hassock, "but I find it so intensely interesting. Besides, it somehow doesn't seem like gossip when it deals with a past generation."

The Vicar made no comment, glancing at the paper on his desk on which he had made notes for the interview with his curate. The notes consisted of the words: "Sermon. Open-air Service."

"By the way," he said casually, "I'll preach the sermon myself at Evensong next Sunday."

He had arranged that the curate should preach every other Sunday evening, but he had recently noticed an enlarged congregation, with an unusual influx of young people, on the evenings when the curate was expected to preach. The Vicar would not have admitted to himself that this was his reason for making the change, but he generally considered it his duty to discourage any curate who was becoming too popular. The personal element, he held, was always dangerous in religion.

"Very well, sir," said Mr. Hassock.

The faint twinkle in his eyes made the Vicar feel uncomfortable and a little annoyed, but gave him courage to go on to the second item on his notes with more decision than he had intended to show.

"And I think you must discontinue those Saturday night open-air services in Maybridge," he said. "I've spoken to the Rector about! it and he agrees with me."

The Saturday night open-air services had been originated by Mr. Hassock together with one of the Maybridge Parish Church curates with whom he was friendly, and the two had thrown into it their joint and by no means negligible fund of enthusiasm.

"I shall be sorry to do that, sir," he said. "There's been a very good attendance lately. Some of the busmen have been coming from the garage. You made no objection when I first suggested it to you."

"I know," said the Vicar, leaning back in his chair and joining the tips of his fingers. He had made no objection because he thought that the venture was foredoomed to failure and that a little failure would do his curate no harm, "but I've come to the conclusion that the whole thing is rather lacking in dignity."

"Do you think that dignity is necessary in religion?" said Mr. Hassock.

"I certainly do," said the Vicar, feeling himself there, at any rate, on sure ground.

He glanced disapprovingly at his curate's costume—a college blazer over a shapeless pair of flannel trousers. The dog collar that accompanied the costume seemed to be protesting in mute horror against its associates, and a pair of rather bright brown brogues did little, in the Vicar's eyes, to redeem the situation.

Looking down at his own neat grey suit, he wondered whether to speak to the curate on the subject now, but it was not on his notes, and he never liked to introduce a subject before he had thought it over and included it in his notes, so, with the, "Well, I mustn't waste any more of your time . . ." that was his usual dismissal, he turned round again to his desk.

As Mr. Hassock went into the hall he saw Greta coming downstairs. She hung back, but he waited for her.

"Did you go to the pictures with Bertie?" he said in his abrupt unceremonious fashion.

"Yes."

"Did you enjoy it?"

"Yes, thank you."

"He's very anxious for you to join the tennis club."

"I know."

"You will, won't you?"

"Do you belong?"

"Me? No, I've no time for it."

"I haven't either."

"Yes, you have. You can make time."

"So can you."

"I can't . . . I've got the Sunday School treats to organize this month as well as a hundred other things . . . Bertie's coming along with the Sunday School treat to Eastbourne to give us a hand. Why don't you?"

She hesitated.

"Very well . . . I will."

"Good for you! Well, good-bye."

He strode out of the front door and down the drive.

She stood for a moment, surprised by a sudden feeling of happiness. Frank seemed real to her again, her work with Olivia and the children full of interest and excitement. It was as if a weight had dropped from her heart. She was humming to herself as she entered Mrs. Sanders' study.

Angela had gone, and Mrs. Sanders was sitting at her desk, looking out at the children who were playing on the lawn.

"I couldn't find your rhyming dictionary," said Greta.

"No, it's all right, dear," said Mrs. Sanders. "I found it in the tin with the preserved ginger and I decided not to use 'soar', after all. The poem will be quite long enough without it . . . Tell me, dear, which of the children did you say was the little atheist?"

Chapter Eight

Mrs. Mortimer sat down on the Windsor chair by the kitchen window for a moment's rest. Everything was well in train for the midday meal. The potatoes and the greens were simmering under lowered gas-rings, and the fish for Elaine was steaming between two plates over the potatoes. The rabbit and the jam roll were both cooking in the oven. Out in the back garden the washing was hanging on the line, and in the front garden Elaine was asleep in her pram. She glanced at the clock. Albert would now be starting from the office where he worked. She imagined his neat dark squat figure standing in the bus queue in Maybridge Market Square.

After a few minutes she rose from the chair and, taking the tablecloth from the drawer in the dresser, spread it over the table, smoothing out its folds with deliberate, almost caressing, movements, laying on it cutlery, glasses, salt-cellar. A feeling of deep contentment possessed her. The moment seemed so perfect, so fraught with peace and security that she wished it could last for ever . . . Herself pottering slowly, dreamily about the little house . . . Elaine asleep in the garden . . . Albert on his way home to them.

After glancing round the table to assure herself that she had forgotten nothing, she went out into the garden and tiptoed across the lawn to look at Elaine. Elaine lay on her back in the pram— eyes closed, dark lashes sweeping flushed cheeks, lips like a sleeping cherub's. She had had her first birthday last week, and Grace had asked the nurse from the clinic to tea.

"She's the best advertisement we've got," the nurse had said. "She's a credit to you, Mrs. Mortimer."

"And to me," Geraldine had said.

"Yes, and to Gerry," said Albert proudly. "Gerry's a real little mother, isn't she, Grace?"

"Yes," Grace had said quietly

Resolutely she thrust the thought of Gerry from her mind, and went round to the back garden, where a row of tiny garments hung on a line above the cement path.

She remembered the evening when Albert had made the path and how annoyed he had been the next morning to find that a cat had walked down it while it was still damp. Grace rather liked the dainty paw-marks and sometimes imagined a small cat ghost treading its way delicately along the narrow path . . . Albert had made the drying-props, too, setting them firmly in wooden slots in the ground, and devising an ingenious little pulley by which she could lower the line without stretching up to it.

The back of the house faced east and the sun was stronger here—September sunshine with a life-giving tang in it. She began to take the clothes down slowly, holding up her face to the sun, letting her thoughts flow languorously to Albert, to Elaine, to the little home that was her world.

Suddenly a rather owl-like face with prominent nose, plump cheeks and a head tightly encased in a large handkerchief appeared over the fence.

"And how are you these days, Mrs. Mortimer?"

"I'm much better, thank you," said Grace, looking at her neighbour with mild interest.

The last time she had seen her neighbour was yesterday afternoon when Mrs. Shanks had been emerging from her front door to do her shopping in Maybridge; and Mrs. Shanks at the back of her house and Mrs. Shanks at the front of her house were so different that it was almost impossible to believe that they were the same person. At the back of her house Mrs. Shanks wore a shapeless grubby overall, down-at-heel shoes, an unadorned face and hair compressed into unseen curls beneath a tightly bound handkerchief. Between the back door and the front door, however, a mysterious transformation always took place, and Mrs. Shanks would emerge from her front door in high-heeled shoes, silk stockings, rouge, powder, and lipstick, with massed curls beneath a tilted hat. Both voice and manner shared in the transformation. At the back of the house they were slipshod and slightly common. In the front of her house Mrs. Shanks was archly dignified, exquisitely refined.

"Yes, having the baby did you no end of good. It does, you know. Clears everything out. I knew a woman once—" Grace had bent down to pick up a clothes-peg and obviously wasn't listening, Mrs. Shanks' voice trailed away. "But you ought to be careful not to overdo things," she ended, rallying.

"I'm very careful," said Grace.

Grace baffled her neighbours. She was so gentle that they could never take offence, and so remote that, as they said, they "never got any further with her". To Grace her neighbours simply didn't exist.

"Well, you get through a lot of work," said Mrs. Shanks, ignoring the fact that Grace had turned her back on her as if in order to reach the line more easily, "but, then, Gerry's such a help, isn't she?"

"Yes," said Grace, dropping a frock of Elaine's and a petticoat of Geraldine's into the clothes-basket.

"You must miss her now term's started."

"Yes," said Grace again.

"She was chatting away to me last night. Told me you were all going over to Appleton to a party this afternoon."

"Yes," said Grace, moving the clothes-basket further down the path.

"Where she went while you had Elaine, isn't it?" said Mrs. Shanks, following its progress so that her face was again opposite Grace's over the fence.

"Yes," said Grace.

"She's Gloria Fortescue, isn't she? The wife, I mean. I love her stories. I'm reading one now in *Home Moments*. 'Lavender's Quest', it's called, and I can hardly wait for next week. Nothing seems to go right for that poor girl. Makes one's heart bleed. Are you reading it?"

Grace gave her gentle remote smile.

"No . . . I'm afraid I'm not much of a reader. I generally have sewing to do."

"Yes, one does with children. No end to it, that's what I always say. When you aren't washing you're mending, and when you aren't mending you're cooking. Not to speak of clearing up after them and getting them to mind their manners and do as they're told . . . but you miss them when they've gone. You look forward to the peace of it and when you get it you want them back."

"Yes," said Grace vaguely.

"What about Elaine this afternoon? Would you like me to mind her while you're away?"

"Oh . . . No, thank you. Mr. Sykes—that friend of Albert's who's a builder—is going to Appleton on a job, and he says he'll drive us over and bring us back." She sighed and added, almost to herself: "I shall be glad when it's over. It's a nuisance."

"But you'll have Gerry to help you."

"Yes . . . Yes, of course."

"You know, Mrs. Mortimer, you're lucky in that child. As good as gold, she is, and going to be pretty when she thins down. She's fat now, but it's only puppy fat."

Grace took down a vest of Elaine's and examined it anxiously, wondering if it had shrunk.

"You never know how an adopted child's going to turn out when you take it on as a baby," went on Mrs. Shanks. "Might turn out to have thick ankles or a stammer or sticking-out ears. And worse things than that, too. Why, only the other day I heard of a couple who adopted a baby. It seemed all right at first except for a slight squint and then after a few months—"

But Grace had gathered up the basket, and murmuring, "Well, I must get these in . . ." was already on her way to the house.

Mrs. Shanks gazed after her wistfully. Having begun the story of the adopted baby with the squint, she was eager to go on with it. She gazed at the farther fence and wondered whether it would keep till her other neighbour had returned from shopping. Deciding that it wouldn't, she went indoors, changed shoes, stockings, and dress, did up her face, combed out her curls and set off to tell the story to the woman who kept the general shop at the corner.

In the kitchen Grace folded up the clothes ready for ironing and put them back in the basket. She glanced at her watch again. She was well on time. The rabbit smelt lovely. The potatoes were boiling a bit too fast. She turned down the gas-tap. The sense of peace and security still upheld her. Dreamily she moved a vase of nasturtiums from the dresser to the centre of the table. The nasturtiums were doing so well this year that the few she had picked couldn't spoil the "show" in the garden. Then, taking up the clothes-basket, she carried it into the garage to be out of the way. There she stood for a few moments, looking round with a smile that was tender and faintly amused. Albert worked here every night now, and the "playroom" was gradually emerging from the garage. The doors had been taken away and replaced by a bow-window, put in by Mr. Sykes, and Albert was covering the walls with a composition panelling of imitation wood rather violently grained. The general effect was a little dark, but Albert was collecting brightly coloured pictures—animals and nursery-rhyme characters with a judicious admixture of more educational features, such as enlarged photographs of the Duomo at Florence and the Niagara Falls. He had also begun to collect reproductions of famous paintings and sculptures, which he intended to put on the walls when the girls were older.

"It's a pity the nude comes into so many of them," he had said regretfully, "because I think you can't be too careful."

The table in the middle of the room was covered by strips of panelling, and near it, on a sea of shavings, stood the bookcase that he was making to house the children's Hundred Best Books. He was carving "Sapientia Rectum Docet" on the top of it. He knew what it meant but could never remember whether it was Greek or Latin. He had finished "Sapientia" last night and had called Grace in to admire it. He had looked very earnest as he stood there, with his shirt-sleeves rolled up over his elbows, wearing the apron that he always wore when he was doing carpentry.

"I do so want them to be cultured," he had said, "and you can't acquire culture in later life. I know because I've tried. You've got to acquire it unconsciously in childhood. Don't you agree, darling?"

And Grace had agreed, seeing Elaine toddling about the room sitting at the table . . . doing her homework laughing . . . singing . . .

He had made two chairs—one with "Gerry" carved on it and the other with "Elaine"—and had recently set his heart on a piano. You couldn't be cultured, he said, without an appreciation of good music, and you couldn't acquire it in later life. He knew because he'd tried . . .

The whole thing, of course, was turning out more expensive than he had thought it would. He had long ago given up his occasional pipe and glass of beer. He needed a new suit, but he had decided to put it off for a year.

She picked up a strip of panelling that had fallen on to the floor and replaced it on the table . . . and, as she did so, her mind leapt forward into the future. They would be old one day—Albert and she. The girls would have left them. Perhaps there would be grandchildren . . . Elaine's baby sleeping in the pram in the garden, while she and Elaine had tea together, discussing its weight and its feeding and exchanging gossip . . . Albert would retire, and she would have him with her all day. The two of them growing old together, engrossed in the little interests that made their life. The vague contentment that had enwrapped her all day sharpened to happiness.

She returned to the kitchen, and began to sieve the vegetables for Elaine's dinner. It was nearly one o'clock now. Geraldine's school closed at ten to one, and sometimes she reached home before Albert. She might be here any moment now. The thought was like a crack in the walls of her happiness, letting in a cold blast of air.

She heard the gate open and glanced out of the window, then drew a quick breath of relief.

It was Albert.

He closed the gate carefully and stood smiling as she came down the path to him.

"How are you, darling?" he said, kissing her.

"Fine. And you? Had a good morning?"

"Splendid."

"Come and look at Elaine."

She slipped her arm through his, and they began to walk round to the lawn.

"Gerry back yet?" said Albert.

"Not yet . . . Albert . . ."

"Yes?"

"I sometimes wonder whether it would be a good thing to let Gerry have her dinner at school."

"Why, dear?"

She searched for a reason that would appeal to him.

"It's rather a rush for her to get home and back."

He considered.

"I don't think that matters," he said at last. "The change probably does her good. And I should miss her chatter at dinner, wouldn't you? Besides, it would be an added expense."

"Yes, of course."

She sighed. She hadn't really expected him to agree to the suggestion.

They had reached the pram now. Elaine was awake. She lay there, her eyes fixed on the moving branches of the pear tree above her, crooning to herself.

"Who's daddy's darling?" said Albert, bending over the pram.

Elaine gave a crow of delight, smiling up at him and holding out her arms.

"May I take her up?" said Albert.

"Yes, dear," said Grace, "she's had a lovely sleep this morning. I'm so glad, because I want her to be her best for this afternoon."

Albert lifted the warm compact little form and held it against his shoulder. Elaine gurgled with pleasure and grabbed handfuls of his hair.

"I wish we weren't going," said Grace, as she straightened the pram blankets and shook up the little pillow. "This afternoon, I mean."

"I'm sure you'll enjoy it," said Albert. "It'll be a change for you

. . . There's daddy's pet! . . . And it's nice for the children to go to a home like that. Has Gerry got a birthday present for Angela?"

"She was going to buy one on her way home from school. She took the money out of her money-box this morning." She kissed Elaine over Albert's shoulder. "Naughty girl! You mustn't pull daddy's hair like that . . . Well, I'll go and dish up. Everything's ready."

She was just taking the rabbit out of the oven when she saw Geraldine coming in at the gate. She stood motionless for a moment, bracing herself, gathering together her forces against the impact of the child's personality.

The front door was flung open and Geraldine burst into the kitchen. She was hot and breathless and looked more tubby than ever in the shapeless gym tunic.

"I'm sorry I'm late," she said. "I ran all the way. I wanted to be early to help you . . . Oh, you've set the table . . . You've put out the knife that doesn't cut properly. I'll change it . . . Look! I've changed it . . . The salt-cellar wants filling up, doesn't it? . . . I'll do it . . . Daddy doesn't like that fork, the prong's bent . . . Look! I've changed it for the other." She followed Grace into the scullery. "What are you doing?"

"I'm just going to pour the potatoes," said Grace, schooling her voice to a note of gentleness.

"Let me do it . . . Let me help . . . I'll do the greens, shall I? Let me do the greens."

There was something turbid and oppressive about the child that made Grace shrink into herself. There were days when she could hardly contain her aversion, when she could hardly force herself to give the normal kisses and embraces of family life. It was something beyond her control. She fought against it helplessly and despairingly. Her only comfort was that neither Albert nor the child guessed it. Albert, she knew, felt Gerry to be as much his child as Elaine, had almost forgotten that she was another man's daughter.

"No, I'll do it, dear."

"What have you got for Elaine? . . . Oh, fish! . . . What shall we give her to-morrow? The book says she can have liver. Shall we give her that to-morrow? Where's the blackcurrant jam? Daddy likes blackcurrant jam with rabbit."

"It's in the larder."

"I got ten out of ten for arithmetic," said Geraldine, clattering into the larder and out again. "Elaine can start adding soon on one of those things with counters on rods, can't she?"

"I suppose so, dear."

"I'll teach her when she can. Look! You've left a fin in her fish. I'll take it out. And here's another . . . I'll put the chairs at the table, shall I?"

She dragged the chairs up to the table.

Grace had a curious feeling of being bruised and battered by the child's urgency. She was silent, afraid that anything she said would betray her irritation.

"I'm not going to school this afternoon, am I, because of the party. I'll wash up for you after dinner, shall I? Then you can have a rest. You've forgotten to put the water-jug on the table. I'll get it."

The door opened and Albert entered with Elaine in his arms.

"So there's our girly," he said, smiling at Geraldine, who was placing the water-jug on the table. "Mummy's right hand!"

He lowered Elaine into the high chair, and Geraldine sprang forward, eager to help.

"I'll put her feet on the footrest . . . Oh, look! . . . She's lost a shoe again. It must be in the pram. I'll fetch it."

She ran into the garden, returning with the small red shoe.

"That's a good girl," said Albert.

"Here's her feeder? . . . May I feed her? . . . Please, mummy, may I feed her?"

"No, dear. Get on with your own dinner," said Grace.

She spoke in a gentle kindly voice. She even managed to smile as she spoke. But since Geraldine's arrival everything was spoilt. Her peace and contentment were shattered. The child's vehemence was like a hand at her throat, choking her.

Geraldine sat down and set to work on her dinner. Her heart

was full of happiness. Always, when she had been away from home, even for a short time, she had to prove to herself at once, the minute she got back, that she—belonged, that she was "Daddy's girl" . . . "Mummy's right hand" . . . "Elaine's little mother."

"Will you let me wash up all by myself after dinner, mummy?" she said.

"We'll see, dear," said Grace.

"But I must . . . I want to . . . Do let me . . . Please!"

Grace forced herself to return the amused smile that Albert sent her across the table before she said:

"Very well, dear, if you'll be careful."

Elaine seized a spoon and banged on the shelf of her chair, laughing delightedly and dribbling out a mouthful of food.

"Is she eating too quickly?" said Geraldine anxiously. "Oh, mummy, may I hold her on my knee in the car when we go to Angela's? Please may I? I'll hold her carefully."

"Very well, dear."

"Daddy, I got ten for arithmetic."

"Good! By the way, what about the present for Angela?"

Geraldine plunged from the room and returned with her school satchel.

"Look!" she said, taking a brightly coloured ball from it. "I got this for Elaine. I saw it in the shop and I *had* to buy it. I meant to get something for Angela, but I just *had* to buy this for Elaine."

"But didn't you get anything for Angela, dear?"

"No, I couldn't. I'd spent all the money on this. I *had* to buy it. I knew she'd love it. Look at her! She *does* love it."

"It was a kind thought, of course," said Albert a little uncertainly, "but you should have thought of Angela as well."

"I did think of her, but there wasn't any money left. As soon as I saw the ball, I just *had* to get it for Elaine . . . You love it, darling, don't you?"

Elaine clasped the ball to her breast, then threw it on to the floor, laughing and banging on the shelf of her chair with her spoon.

"But what are you going to do about Angela's present?" said Albert.

"I'll get something on the way there," said Grace shortly.

"It must come out of the pocket-money, I think."

"Oh, yes," agreed Geraldine eagerly. "Yes, it can. I'll do without pocket-money till it's paid for, but I wanted Elaine to have the ball. I *knew* she'd love it."

Grace picked up the ball and put it on the dresser.

"She can have it when she's finished her dinner," she said. "Now get on with your own dinner, dear."

For the first time she was putting the thought into words in her mind. I wish we hadn't adopted her. I wish we'd waited. It would be so lovely if there were just the three of us . . .

She got ready for the Vicarage party in good time, helped Geraldine get ready, then together they dressed Elaine. Elaine was in her best humour, laughing and crooning as they washed her and changed her nappies.

"Let me do it . . . Let me do it," urged Geraldine, and Grace let her, trying to master her irritation with a sense of ever-deepening despair at her heart. She would never like the child . . . However hard she tried, she would never like her.

"I did it myself, didn't I? I changed her nappies all by myself, didn't I? I did, didn't I, mummy?"

"Yes, dear."

"You only handed me the pins, and I did it myself. I was a help, wasn't I? You'll let me always do it now, won't you?"

"Not always, dear, but you can help. Give her back to me now, dear."

Geraldine handed back the baby.

"Pass me her frock, will you, dear? It's on the chair."

Geraldine looked at the little white knitted frock and her face darkened.

"She's not going to wear that, is she?" she said.

"Yes, dear," said Grace.

"But it's not her prettiest one," protested Geraldine stormily.

98

"It's not her best one. Why can't she wear the blue smocked one—the one I helped you with, the one I sewed the buttons on?"

All morning she had dreamed of showing off Elaine to the other children, Elaine wearing the little pale blue smock, and of telling them that she had sewn on the buttons herself. She wanted them all—Angela, Philip and Monica—to see what a lovely baby Elaine was, and in the white knitted frock she looked just like an ordinary baby.

"The white one's warmer," said Grace.

"But she'll have her coat. She'll be warm. It's not cold . . . Oh, she must wear the blue one. Do let her wear the blue one. She must . . . I've been thinking all the time that she'd be wearing the blue one. Why can't she? It's not cold. Please, mummy! *Please!*"

Grace gave a helpless little gesture of surrender. The child's vehemence beat down her resistance, drained her vitality.

"Very well," she said.

Geraldine glowed with pleasure.

"Oh, thank you! *Thank* you, mummy! . . . I'll get it . . . Here it is. I can fasten it up. Let me fasten it up. There! May I hold her while you put your hat on?"

"Yes."

Geraldine took the baby and held it on her knee, bending over it with a sort of brooding intensity. She gave a long deep sigh.

"Oh, mummy," she whispered, "doesn't she look *lovely*?"

Chapter Nine

Beneath a silver blue sky the garden glowed with colour—michaelmas daisies, sunflowers, dahlias, and chrysanthemums. Dark shadows stood like sentinels between drowsy splashes of sunshine, and the hush of mid-day lay over it like a spell.

Philip, leaning out of his window, felt himself to be part of the scene he was watching, knew, with a curious sense of conspiracy, that the spell lay only on the surface. For the stillness was vibrant with motion, the hush with sound. In the dim caverns of the trees life stirred silently and without ceasing. Through it all ran an excitement that seemed to reach out and lay a finger on Philip's heart. He leant farther out of the window, placing his hands on the burning sill, feeling the warmth seep down into his body. And, as he leant there, something dead in him seemed to come alive and the old mysterious sense of power possessed him.

Then slowly, almost reluctantly, he withdrew into the room and looked around it. This room was still his world . . . His attitude to his family had not changed during the year that Stephen and his stepmother had been living here. Outwardly he had accommodated himself to the life of the household, building up his defences and forging his weapons in secret. His stepmother was his chief enemy—not only because she had shattered the world in which had had been happy and secure, but because she held the key of the world in which he had taken refuge.

He gave a start as the door opened and Stephen's head came round.

"Are you ready, Pip?" he said. "It's nearly lunchtime."

"I'll be along in a minute," said Philip.

"Right!" said Stephen, and vanished.

It was difficult to quarrel with Stephen. It was difficult even to feel angry with him. He was kind and easy-going and considerate. Stephen did not dislike Philip. He thought of him with careless affection as a "queer kid", and put down the "queerness" to Philip's general delicacy—to the coughs from which he suffered most of the winter and the bouts of sickness that occasionally prostrated him. There the matter began and ended. Stephen was not introspective. He lived in the passing moment and took people as he found them.

Stephen and his father were in the hall when Philip reached it.

"Hello, Pip," said Barry. "Stephen and I thought of walking over to Dallas Wood this afternoon. I've got to see about some timber-felling there. Care to come along?"

The sunshine that poured into the hall through the open door, the touch of his father's hand on his shoulder, the lingering echoes of the mood of exaltation that had seized him upstairs, all conspired to break down his defences. That happened sometimes. He couldn't always be on his guard. The sudden rush of happiness took him by surprise, and he yielded to it.

"Yes, please," he said, with his quick nervous smile.

They entered the dining-room—a high-ceilinged room with tall narrow windows overlooking the terrace. A bowl of roses stood in the centre of the polished mahogany table. Philip gazed at it dreamily as he took his seat. The sheen of the petals, the golden stamens, the delicate green leaves were so many fresh notes in the symphony of his precarious happiness. Ann, sitting next him, threw him a fugitive glance, noticing that his face wore that look of brittle intensity it wore so often, but forbearing to let her eyes rest on him, lest they should betray her tenderness. She knew how fiercely he resented any sign of sympathy or understanding from her.

"We're going over to Dallas Wood this afternoon," said Barry as he started on his soup.

"Which of you?" said Ann.

"The boys and I."

"But they can't," said Ann; "they're going to the party at Appleton Vicarage."

"Oh, good lord!" groaned Stephen. "Is it to-day?"

"Yes. Had you forgotten?"

"Yes."

"So had I," said Philip.

"What a nuisance!" said Stephen. "Why did we let ourselves in for it?"

"I'm afraid Pip did that," smiled Barry. "Apparently they're asking all the kids who were there last summer."

"Who'll be there, Pip?" said Stephen.

The sunny dining-room seemed to fade away, and Philip saw them all as clearly as if they had been there before his eyes . . . Angela dancing across the lawn, light as thistledown, her gay mocking laughter floating like bubbles through the summer air . . . Geraldine with her round rosy face, cheeks sunburnt to the colour of ripe apricots . . . Monica, her thin face framed in her long hair, her eyes dark pools, bright with fear . . .

"Wake up, old chap," said Barry.

"Who'll be there?" said Stephen again.

"Oh . . . Angela."

"What's she like?"

"She's pretty," said Philip slowly. "She laughs at you, but she's pretty."

He realized suddenly how much he wanted to see Angela again. The memory of her voice, her laughter, her swift gay movements was like a burst of song in his heart.

"Who else?" said Stephen.

"Oh"—he roused himself—"Geraldine . . ."

"What's she like?"

"She's a nuisance. She won't leave you alone. She's—stupid."

He had a swift sense of disloyalty as he spoke, remembering the warm comfort of her arms, of her soft blurred voice under the willow tree on the day when he had made his antelope.

"She's kind," he added with something of an effort. "She's kind, but she worries you."

"Sounds a soppy lot," said Stephen in good-natured disgust. "Geraldine and Angela! Gosh! What a party!"

"I expect there'll be some others," said Philip. "Oh, and there's Monica."

"What's she like?"

Philip considered.

"I don't know. She's all right. I mean, she doesn't bother you."

"Does she live near here too?"

"I don't know. She's called Monica Patterson, but her mother's called Mrs. Deverel."

"Deverel?" said Ann thoughtfully. "Don't you remember, Barry? They're the people who've taken Rowan Cottage. We met her at the Brewsters' cocktail party. She's rather lovely."

Barry gave a short laugh.

"Yes, I remember. 'Rather' puts it mildly, my dear. And, from what one hears, her light is not hid under a bushel."

"Does that knock Dallas Wood on the head?" said Stephen.

"I don't think so," said Barry. "If we start directly after lunch, it won't take more than an hour."

"May we go round by Beeches and cross the river by the stepping-stones?"

"Not to-day."

The river at Beeches ran so shallow that it could be spanned by a row of stepping-stones. Philip had often tried to cross them. He could manage the first few, but, when he reached the middle and the water began to swirl around his feet, his courage would fail him and he would stand there, gripped by a paralysis of fear, incapable of moving any farther.

"Why not?" pleaded Stephen. "It's such fun. We did when we went to Dallas Wood last week."

"We shall have Pip with us to-day," said Barry.

He spoke shortly in order to put an end to the discussion. He was pleased that Philip was going with them, but he had no intention of rescuing a shivering child from half-way across the river.

Philip sat, suddenly tense and rigid, while waves of heat and cold chased each other through his body. They didn't want him. They'd asked him out of kindness, but they didn't want him. The whole thing was spoilt for them because he was going with them. It was as if they had cunningly lured him from his citadel, accepted his surrender, then mocked and rejected him. He seemed to be emptied of everything but hurt and humiliation, sustained only by a ferocity of childish pride that would allow no sign of it to escape him. He sat there, his small face blank and expressionless, staring out of the window. Through it he could see a swallow chasing a butterfly through the air with swift ballet-like movement. He concentrated his mind on the flight, watching it with earnest absorption . . . stiffening the muscles of his face so that they should not guess his feelings.

After lunch he went upstairs slowly, checking the impulse to run blindly for the refuge of his room. Reaching it, he turned the key in the lock and stood again at his window, looking down unseeingly at the garden. The fragile happiness that had filled him when he stood there an hour ago had vanished. His spirit was plunged in a blackness so impenetrable that the colour and fragrance, the bird-haunted shadows and the blaze of golden light could no longer find their way to it. His hands were clenched by his side, the corners of his lips deeply pursed. He would never let it happen again . . . never again let them draw him from his stronghold. And through the blackness of his spirit shone the old bleak joy in his self-sufficiency. He didn't care. They didn't want him and he didn't want them.

"Are you ready, Pip?" called Stephen from the landing. "We're just starting."

"I'm not coming," called Philip in a high-pitched nonchalant voice.

Stephen clattered downstairs.

"Pip's not coming," he said to Barry, who was standing in the hall.

"Right!" said Barry. "Let's start, then."

Funny kid, Pip, he thought. Always changing his mind. Never knowing what he wanted . . . Since his marriage his responsibility for the child had ceased to trouble him. Ann was the ideal mate, Stephen the ideal son. A man of little imagination, he felt that he was justified now in leaving Philip to others. The boy was babyish for his age and was, perhaps, for the time, better left to women. Philip's withdrawal from the family life had escaped his notice. He knew that Ann worried about him sometimes, but he reassured her by a careless: "The kid's all right. A bit of a cissie, but hell grow out of it." He was fond of Philip and unaware that he showed his preference for Stephen in all his dealings with them.

Stephen's voice floated up to Philip through the open window.

"We can go across the stepping-stones now Pip's not coming, can't we?"

"Yes," said Barry, and the two set off.

Philip turned away from the window, his childish face still wearing the set stony look. All right, let them go. He didn't want them . . . But he couldn't stay in his bedroom all afternoon. The sunshine called to him, beckoning with long golden fingers, spreading out its treasures for him temptingly. He unlocked his door and looked cautiously along the landing. No one was in sight. Slowly, on tiptoe—for he did not wish to meet his stepmother—he made his way down the staircase and across the hall. The open door framed a picture of sun-dazzled garden and distant hills. He stood for a moment, looking at it, and, as he looked, the tension of his being relaxed and he drew a long tremulous sigh. Then, swiftly and with an air of secrecy, he went across the lawn to a spinney of trees that bordered the drive. At the further end was a beech tree that he had made his special "place". Sitting at the foot of it, he could not be seen from the house or the drive or the road. The sunlight fell through the branches, making a mosaic of light and shade on the ground about him. He sat, his hands clasped round his knees, his brows drawn into a frown . . . and entered his kingdom . . .

He was prince of a country that was beset by enemies on all sides. He was brave, resourceful, and universally popular. He led his army into battle, riding a coal-black charger, but his most famous exploits had been performed alone in disguise. He went as a spy into the enemy's country . . . he leapt chasms . . . climbed precipices . . . swam raging torrents. At present the King of the Country of the North was arming against him, and he was collecting his forces to repel the attack. The situation was complicated, because the King of the South, though supposed to be his ally, was plotting against him and only waiting his chance to attack him treacherously in the rear. Philip had discovered this while on an expedition that he had undertaken alone, disguised as a pedlar, through the country of the South during which he had many times narrowly escaped death. Moreover, Philip was in love with Rosabel, the daughter of his enemy, the King of the North. She had blue eyes and soft fair curls. She danced lightly across the palace ballroom, and her laughter was gay and mocking, floating like shining bubbles through the air.

On one occasion he had gone secretly through the enemy's lines, disguised as a shepherd, to meet her and had been wounded by a chance shot. A girl who was guarding her father's sheep had taken him into her hut and nursed him back to health. She had soft brown eyes and brown hair and cheeks sunburnt to the colour of ripe apricots, but he had been irked and exasperated by her devotion and had escaped by night, his right arm still so useless that he had had to swing himself over chasms and climb up precipices with his left arm alone.

His greatest enemy was the Queen of the South. She was beautiful, with wide cheekbones and deep blue eyes, but as treacherous as a snake. She tried to discover his secret plans so that she could hand them over to his enemies. And she was the wife of his supposed ally, so that he had to meet her at palace functions, balls and reviews. She tried on him every trick that her cunning mind could devise. He was icily polite to her but never let down his guard.

To-day he was going to try, alone, to find a pass over the mountains that divided his country from the Country of the North. An old peasant had told him that the pass existed, but was too dangerous to be attempted. It meant journeying through a dense jungle, scaling the sheer side of a mountain, and swimming a crocodile-infested river, but Philip intended to try it; then, if it proved possible, to lead a chosen band of his bravest men that way as soon as war broke out with the Country of the North.

He didn't know how long he had been making his way through the jungle when the sound of music invaded his consciousness. He sat listening . . . The lovely mournful notes of the Chopin nocturne floated out through the summer air. He knew that it was his stepmother playing in the drawing-room, but the spell of it was irresistible. The lush growth of the jungle that had surrounded him faded away. He rose and—slowly, very slowly—made his way to the house. The french windows of the drawing-room were open. He could see his stepmother sitting at the grand piano, with her back to the window. Cautiously, moving without sound, he entered the room and sat on the edge of the settee, listening.

Though Ann did not turn round, she knew that he was there. She could see from the corner of her eye the slight childish figure, with open-necked shirt, grey flannel shorts and bare sandalled legs, perched there on the edge of the settee, ready to run back to the safety of the garden at the first sign of her awareness. It was strange, she thought with a little twisted smile, that, in spite of the restrictions he imposed on their intercourse and that she scrupulously observed, this child of Barry's should be nearer to her than her own son. As her fingers moved over the keys, her mind was busy with the problem of how to detain him when she stopped playing.

Suddenly she saw that his eyes were fixed on a cockatoo of red Lalique glass that she had bought in London the week before, and that had been delivered yesterday. It stood on a low-table near the settee, glowing in the sunlight.

Gradually she brought her playing to an end, letting her hands drop on to her lap.

"It's lovely, isn't it?" she said.

She spoke so softly that it might have been his own thoughts speaking.

"Yes . . ." he said.

He put out a finger to touch it, making a movement as if stroking it.

She crossed the room and, taking Waley's Chinese Poems from a bookshelf, sat down by him on the settee, turning over the pages.

"A Chinese poet wrote this about two thousand years ago," she said softly, and read:

> "Sent as a present from Annan—
> A red cockatoo.
> Coloured like the peach-tree blossom,
> Speaking with the speech of men."

His lips repeated the words silently, "Coloured like a peach-tree blossom." He still seemed unaware of her. She turned over the pages.

"Here's another one by another poet. It's called 'Vision'."

> "I will wear as my gown the red mists of sunrise,
> And as my skirt the white fringes of the clouds;
> My canopy—the dim lustre of Space;
> My chariot—six dragons mounting heavenward;
> And before the light of Time has shifted a pace
> Suddenly stand upon the World's blue rim."

She threw him a quick glance. He was gazing in front of him, his sensitive intelligent face lit up by the magic of the words.

"Do you like it?" she said.

"Yes." He glanced at the book. "Are there any more?"

She turned over the pages again.

"Here's one about a garden.

> "The red flowers hang like a heavy mist;
> The white flowers gleam like a fall of snow,
> The wandering bees cannot bear to leave them;
> The birds also come here to roost.
> In front there flows an ever-running stream;
> Beneath there is built a little flat terrace.
> The flower-branches screen my head from the sun;
> The flower-buds fail into my lap."

He listened, his delicate brows drawn together, storing the words up in his mind.

"And you'll like this one," she said, turning another page.

Then the door opened and a maid entered.

"Mrs. Brewster's on the telephone, madam. She'd like to speak to you."

Ann rose with a shrug of mingled helplessness and exasperation and went from the room. The spell was broken now. Probably he'd have gone when she got back.

Left alone, Philip seemed to wake slowly from a trance. He looked around him, realizing for the first time what had happened . . . She'd been trying to get him, to make him belong to her. She'd stolen his father and now she was trying to steal him. With a blind gesture of rage he swept the red cockatoo from the table on to the floor. It shivered into fragments. They lay on the carpet like drops of blood.

Ann came back into the room and stopped short on the threshold.

"Oh!" she gasped. "What's happened?"

Philip turned his face to her. It was white and pinched.

"I did it," he said; "I did it on purpose."

"Oh, Philip, but why?"

"Because," he began. "Because—"

His face began to work and he turned and ran from the room.

She went upstairs some minutes later and heard the sound of stifled sobbing from his room, but dared not go in. She knew that he was crying because he had killed something beautiful, because the red cockatoo would never again stand with graceful crested head a ad flame-like wings.

Barry and Stephen came in shortly afterwards, exhilarated by their walk. They told Ann of the otter they had seen in the river and the long-tailed tits' nest that Stephen had found in the wood. Then suddenly Barry noticed the empty table.

"What's happened to your red bird?" he said.

Ann smiled.

"I put it right in the way of anyone coming over to the fireplace," she said, "and Philip knocked it over . . . You warned me, didn't you?"

"I certainly did," he said, as he lit his pipe. "I told you it was madness to have the thing in the room at all, with two great boys about."

"Three," she corrected.

He laughed.

"Yes, three. Was it very valuable?"

"Oh, no."

"I remember breaking a Dresden china thing of my aunt's when I was about Pip's age. She never let me forget it."

"I'll let him forget it."

"A pity, but these things can't be helped . . . Well, I suppose it's about time the boys got ready for their party."

Chapter Ten

Monica ran lightly across the field to the cottage. Strands of gossamer laced the hedgerows, veiling the bronze leaves of briony and the vivid scarlet of rose hips. In the woods, on the other side of the lane, the ash leaves showed pale yellow against the dun brown of the oaks, and tiny cones were forming on larch and fir.

Every morning before breakfast she went to the farm to watch the cows being milked. The cowman had let her try to milk Daisy this morning, but the small eager hands had at first failed to draw any milk at all and then had squirted it wildly in every direction. They had all laughed, and even Daisy had seemed faintly amused, but they were going to let her try again to-morrow.

She entered the gate of Rowan Cottage and stopped at the hutch where her tame rabbit, Pinky, lived, to pick a lettuce leaf for him and kiss his small restless nose through the wire-netting. Then she walked slowly up the garden path to the door. It was a picturesque haphazard little garden, with cabbages and feathery carrots growing among snapdragons and asters, and a clump of phloxes in the middle of a row of runner beans. The path was bordered by overgrown straggly bushes of lavender and rosemary, and there was an ancient gnarled crab-apple tree in the middle of the tiny lawn. Monica's garden—about a yard square—was marked off by stones that she had brought in from the lane. It held a carrot, a turnip, an onion, a runner bean, a towering sunflower, a pansy, some marigolds, and a small empty space thickly planted with orange pips, apple pips and peach stones. From the crab-apple tree hung a swing that Fred had made the week after the move. The move had been the result of what Fred vaguely called an "understanding" and Babs, less vaguely, a "show-down". Reggie had vanished discreetly after the night of the Brighton escapade but there had been others. There had been Bobby, George, Richard, Bobbles, Fobs, Cinders and Cocoa . . .

Before he delivered his ultimatum, Fred had talked the matter over with Monica. He had a way of talking to Monica as if he were talking to himself. It helped him, he said, to get his thoughts straight.

"You know, Babs is all right, really," he had said. "The trouble is that she's too attractive. That and living in London. If she lived in the country with a house to look after and healthy interests—chickens, perhaps, and dogs and people calling—she wouldn't always want to be having a good time. She might take up a bit of church work. People do in the country. And there are Flower Shows and Sales of Work. The country's full of healthy interests. It would give her a fresh start. You see what I mean, don't you?"

Monica had nodded.

"Well, you know," Fred had continued, "when I took you over to Appleton last summer we passed through some little villages that looked so peaceful it made me wonder why anyone ever wanted to live in towns. I kept thinking, I believe Babs would be all right if we lived in a place like this. And you'd like it, wouldn't you?"

"Yes," Monica had said, her heart leaping at the thought of a home—a real home, not just a flat. The three of them living together in a house like other families, without Bobbles and Pobs and Cinders and the rest.

"She'd be all right in the country," said Fred, trying to persuade himself rather than Monica. "She's just one of those women who can't stand up to London."

Monica was silent. She'd have a little garden and she'd play with the children next door and she'd pick bluebells in the woods and help Babs in the house. And perhaps there'd be a puppy . . .

Fred had put the matter to his wife more uncompromisingly than that. She must agree to leave London and go to live in the country or he would start proceedings for a divorce. And Babs was frightened. Her lovely blue eyes grew bright with fear . . . She didn't want to be divorced again. She was tired of Bobbles and Pobs and Cinders and the rest. She was as eager as Fred himself for a fresh start.

"I know I've not been a good wife to you, Fred," she said. "I don't know how it is. I just can't help it."

"It's with living in London," said Fred.

"Yes, that's it," she said, clutching at the excuse.

"You'll have healthy interests in the country," he said.

"Yes," she agreed.

"You won't be so interested in—clothes and things."

"No."

"And you'll cut out the drinking, won't you, Babs? It's doing you no good."

"I know . . . Yes, Fred, I will."

"We'll make a go of it this time, won't we, darling?" he said, slipping an arm round her.

"Yes." She gave him the softness of her lips. "Yes, Fred, we will."

She was so sweet and eager and penitent that he had no doubts— or would admit no doubts—of the success of his plan.

And at first it fulfilled his highest hopes. He went to a house agent in Maybridge and found Rowan Cottage in a lane off the main road from Maybridge to Pembury. It was a brick-and-timber seventeenth century cottage, with oak-beamed rooms and small latticed windows, but it had been carefully "modernized" and was without the inconveniences usually associated with such places. Meadows stretched behind it, and in front of it—just across the lane—was a wood where golden bracken stood waist high beneath silver birches. There were only three bedrooms in the cottage—Babs' bedroom, Fred's dressing-room and a little room for Monica—so there was no room for a maid. Fred was glad of this. He wanted Babs to be responsible for the running of the household. That was to be one of the "healthy interests" that were to effect the cure. A woman from the village arrived each morning at half past nine, did the housework, cooked the lunch, then went home till the evening, when she returned to cook the dinner. Everything else was to be Babs' responsibility.

And Babs was delighted with it all. She went into the woods and came back with armfuls of autumn leaves, which she put in jars and bowls all over the cottage. She got curtains and covers of sprigged chintz for the sitting-room, a couple of large Staffordshire china dogs for her bedroom chimneypiece and a patchwork quilt. She pottered about the kitchen in a hand-smocked overall of flowered *crêpe-de-Chine*. She didn't keep chickens, but she bought a rabbit for Monica and a sheepdog puppy for herself. (She got rid of the puppy after it had chewed up three pairs of silk stockings.) She fully intended to be a good wife and mother—discreet, respectable, inconspicuous. But she couldn't be inconspicuous. She was so lovely that wherever she went people turned to stare at her. She wore "country clothes" as envisaged by the world of *haute couture*, but they weren't the sort of clothes that people actually wore in the country. They were too fashionable and they fitted her too well. They suggested a mannequin parade rather than a village street. People looked at her with interest but with a faint disapproval. And gradually she grew bored with the whole thing—the cottage, the garden, the countryside.

To Monica those first few weeks were weeks of almost unclouded happiness. She played with the family who lived next door in an ugly stucco villa called Wood View, she "helped" at the farm, she rode in the milkcart, she had a home in the background—a home and a father and a mother like other children. Almost unclouded happiness, but not quite. Something deep in her knew all the time that it couldn't last, and she savoured every lingering moment of it, storing up every detail in her memory against the inevitable end. And she saw the first signs of its approach before anyone else saw them. Her heart sank when Dr. Merrivale met them in the lane and introduced to Babs the nephew who was staying with him—a tall spruce young man with a careful moustache and a face more heavily lined than his years warranted. He looked at Babs in the way that Bobby, George and Richard and the rest had looked at her, and Babs responded with the soft invitation of her violet-blue eyes. To Monica the dream ended at that moment.

Events followed at an ever-quickening pace. There were "dates" with Captain Merrivale. There were drives in his car. He discovered to Babs a world that was in the country but not of the country—road-houses where a smart sophisticated crowd gathered every evening, cottages whose owners descended on them at weekends, bringing hampers of Fortnum and Mason provisions and, distrustful of the quiet of the countryside, cars full of noisy guests. A host of new friends attached itself to Babs. Their nicknames were different, but they were so like Bobbles and Pobs and Cinders that they might have been the same.

She lost interest in the little cottage. When Captain Merrivale returned to London she began to go there regularly to meet him, leaving the cottage after Fred had gone to catch his train in the morning and returning before he came home at night. She began to drink again—not very much, just enough to bring an added sparkle to her eyes and banish the touch of wistfulness from her manner, giving her gaiety and confidence and a star-like radiance. When Fred was away from home for a day or two on business she generally went up to London to parties in the evening. Parties were the breath of life to her . . . lights, music and laughter, casual contacts, easy familiarity, surface affection, the relaxation of all effort, the vanquishing of doubt and depression.

"Don't tell Fred, darling," she would say to Monica. "I must do something. I'd go nuts if I didn't."

And the old cloud of fear settled over Monica again. All the time when she was playing with the children next door, "helping" at the farm, exploring the wood, she was wondering how long it would last . . . Sometimes she approached the cottage draggingly, with a feeling of sick apprehension at her heart, afraid of what she would find there. She avoided Fred. He never questioned her, but she had a feeling of uneasiness, almost of guilt, when she was with him.

She entered the cottage and went to the kitchen, where she and Fred always had breakfast together. She had set the table and put the kettle on a low gas before she went out. Her mother's tray stood ready on the dresser. Babs breakfasted in bed—a nibble of toast and a pot of China tea—after Fred had gone to catch his train.

She stood listening for a moment. Yes, Fred was in the bathroom. She put the eggs in the saucepan, turned up the light under the kettle and began to make the toast.

The last piece of toast was just browning when Fred entered—a thick-set solid figure in his town suit.

"Morning, Monny," he said cheerfully. "Been out?"

"Yes. To the farm. I nearly milked Daisy."

He laughed.

"Not quite?"

"Not quite yet. I'm going to try again to-morrow."

"Good!"

"The eggs are nearly ready and the kettle's boiling."

"I'll make the tea then."

"Here's the toast."

He sat down at the table and spread out his table-napkin.

"What about milk?" he said. "Have we got plenty?"

"Yes."

"Pour yourself out dollops, then. You ought to drink a lot of milk. You're too thin. You ought to have porridge for breakfast, too. I did when I was a kid."

She smiled as she handed him his cup of tea. He was always remembering things he had had as a child and trying to make her have the same.

"I don't like porridge," she said. "There's oatmeal in the cupboard. I could make it if I wanted it."

He took the top off his egg.

"Well, I suppose it's more of a winter dish," he said, "but you oughtn't to be so pale. Have some honey, anyway. That's supposed to be nourishing. And what about cod liver oil? I used to have that when I was a kid."

"You bought me a bottle."

"Yes, I remember. I told Babs to see you took it."

At the mention of Babs a constraint fell on them. Neither could have explained it, but it always happened nowadays. They went

116

on with their breakfast in silence for some moments. She saw that a worried frown had gathered on his brow.

"And . . . I say, Mon."

"Yes?"

"You ought to be getting some schooling."

"It's the summer holidays," she said, trying to reassure him.

"No. Children are beginning to go back to school. I've seen them in the train."

"Not all of them."

"They start this week or next. I must see about somewhere for you."

"I don't want to go away," she said breathlessly.

"Oh, no," he said. "Of course you mustn't. We'll find some day place near here. Mrs.—what's her name?—over at Appleton might know of one. You're going there to a party this afternoon, aren't you?"

So much had happened since she had stayed at Appleton Vicarage that her memories of it were a little hazy, but the word "party" called up a picture of shouting children, vivacious grown-ups and the relentlessly bright pattern of nursery games . . . and she shrank into herself at the thought.

"I don't want to go," she said.

He looked at her in concern.

"But you ought to want to go, Monny. You liked the children— didn't you?—and the place?"

Monica considered . . . She had been to so many places with so many children that she couldn't quite separate them in her mind. Was it the place where Dicky had pulled her long hair or where Dorita had frightened her by stories of vampires? Was it the tall dark tumbledown house next the gasworks or the overcrowded bungalow by the sea? No—the memories became clearer—it was the long low house with roses growing over it and the table in the garden under the copper beech. It was Philip and Angela and the fat little brown girl called Geraldine.

"I needn't go, need I?" she pleaded. "They wouldn't notice."

"I think you ought to, Monny," he said gently. "They're—friends

117

of yours, aren't they? You ought to have friends. They'll be a help to you. You—you'll need friends, perhaps, more than most kids. You see—" He laid down the knife with which he was spreading butter on his toast and leant back in his chair, frowning meditatively. "I've got to talk it out with you sometime or other. I didn't mean to do it this morning, but"—her heart began to beat unevenly—"this thing hasn't quite worked out as we hoped it would, has it?"

She shook her head.

"No."

His frowning gaze was bent on his plate.

"I'm not blaming Babs. I don't think she can help it. It's just the way she's made. But—well, I'm not a young man, you know, Monny, and—"

He stopped.

"Yes?"

"Well, I want a real home and children of my own. I'd hoped that Babs . . . but she won't have children, you know."

"Yes, I know."

"And she's not much of a home-maker. It's got to come to an end sooner or later, and I'm beginning to think that sooner's better than later."

An ice-cold feeling had crept over her.

"Yes," she whispered.

He looked at her with a tautening of his rough-hewn kindly face.

"I ought to be shot, talking about it to a kid like you," he said.

"But—now listen, Monny. I'm fond of you, and I'm not going to let you down. If Babs and I part forces and I can fix it up with Babs, would you like to come with me?"

She shook her head.

"No . . ."

"Perhaps you're right," he said. "I dunno . . . Anyway, I want you to know that I shall always keep in touch with you and that I'll always be there if you need me. See?"

Her throat ached with fear.

"When—?" she began and stopped.

"I don't know. Not just yet. I'll think it over a bit longer. Sorry if I've worried you, kid, but I wanted to get it off my chest and have it out in the open. We've been sort of scared of each other lately, haven't we? Things will be easier now we know where we stand, won't they?"

"Yes."

He rose from the table.

"Well, I must get off to catch my train. Come and help me start the car."

He took her hand in his large reassuring clasp and together they went round to the garage. He started the car and held open the door for her.

"Have a run to the end of the lane," he said.

She climbed in beside him and they drove down the sunny lane to the main road. There he stopped and turned to her with a smile.

"Out you get!" he said. "And—don't worry, will you?"

"No."

"And you'll go to the party?"

"Yes."

"Babs will see to you. Taking you and fetching you, I mean. I reminded her this morning. I shan't be back till to-morrow night. Promise you won't worry?"

"Yes."

"Nothing to worry about, you know. I'll see you through . . . Well, good-bye, chicken."

"Good-bye."

She stood waving at the corner of the lane till he had vanished from sight, then turned and walked slowly back to the cottage. Nothing seemed real any more. She stopped just inside the gate and, picking a handful of lettuce leaves, thrust them through the wire of Pinky's hutch, but even Pinky didn't seem to be a real rabbit now.

She went indoors and prepared her mother's breakfast tray, then, putting on to it the letters that had come by the morning post, carried it upstairs.

Babs lay in bed. She wore an exiguous nightgown of peach-coloured silk, held up by shoulder-straps. Her cheeks were flushed with sleep, her eyes vividly blue.

"Hello, darling," she said in her sweet laughing voice. "Aren't I lazy! You are an angel to bring it up to me like this."

Babs exerted her charm even first thing in the morning, even on Monica. Or rather, she did not exert it. It flowed from her as easily and naturally as the breath left her lungs. The sun of her blandishment shone on everyone around her—on women as well as men, on people who didn't matter as much as on people who mattered. Her smile caressed Monica while she sat up, arranged her pillows and took the tray on her knees.

"Did you sleep well, darling?"

"Yes, thank you."

Babs patted the eiderdown.

"Sit down and talk to me . . . How's Pinky?"

"He's all right. I've just given him some lettuce."

"Good! Has Mrs. Partridge come yet?"

"Not yet."

"I hope her rheumatism's better. Yesterday she said that it was circling round and round inside her like a factotum."

They both laughed. Then a very faint cloud shadowed Babs' radiance.

"Was Fred talking to you downstairs?"

"Yes."

"He was talking to me last night." She leant forward and stroked Monica's hand affectionately. "Don't worry, darling. He's just got to get things off his chest sometimes, then he settles down again. I can manage him all right." She smiled. "Well, I ought to be able to by this time, oughtn't I?"

"Yes."

"When did he say he'd be back? I forgot to ask him."

"To-morrow night."

"Oh, yes . . . And you're going to a party this afternoon, aren't you?"

"I don't want to," said Monica unhappily.

"But you must, darling. Of course you must . . . The only thing

120

is—" A far-away look came into the blue eyes and the delicate brows drew together. "Well, I'd completely forgotten about it and arranged something else."

"But I don't want to go," persisted Monica. "Honestly, I don't."

"Oh, but you must go, pet," said Babs, "and I must take you there. Fred seems to have got his mind set on it. He'll be furious if he finds you haven't gone. It's no good annoying him when he's in one of his moods. It's all right . . . I shall be able to arrange something."

She took up the pile of letters and turned them over one by one, throwing those with penny stamps carelessly aside. Then she picked out an envelope addressed in a large sprawling masculine hand and began to open it, her lips curving into a little secret smile.

"Run along now, pet," she said absently.

Monica went slowly downstairs. Mrs. Partridge had arrived and was clearing away the breakfast things. She was a small scraggy woman with pointed features and a long thin nose that seemed to have a life of its own, full of eager curiosity.

" 'Ow's yer ma?" she said, as Monica entered the kitchen.

She took a morbid interest in Babs and considered that "with 'er face an' 'er goin's-on she was wasted orf the pictures." She was particularly fascinated by the wisps of silk and lace that constituted Babs' underwear and would leave her work several times during the morning to go and look at them when they were in the airing cupboard.

"She's very well, thank you," said Monica.

Mrs. Partridge emptied the tea-leaves into the rubbish-pail, a ruminative expression on her long face.

"Never thought of goin' on the fillums, as she?"

"I don't think so," said Monica.

"She could, you know, with 'er face," said Mrs. Partridge, tactfully omitting any reference to the "goin's-on."

Monica took up the tablecloth and shook it at the open door.

"Why don't she speak to the manager of the Palais de Luxe in Maybridge about it?" said Mrs. Partridge. "That's 'ow I'd start if

I wanted to go on 'em. I 'spect 'e'd put in a word for 'er. They'd only 'ave to see 'er, you know."

"She doesn't want to go on the films," said Monica.

"Go on! I bet she does!" said Mrs. Partridge, pouring soap powder lavishly into the washing-up water, working it into a lather and plunging the breakfast crockery into it. "It isn't yuman nature not to . . . Sticky stuff, this 'ere 'oney, ain't it? M'notonous sort of taste, too. Can't think what bees see in it . . . I bet if she tried she could be on the fillums to-morrow. 'Course, you're a bit of an 'andicap, but she could get you on as a child." She threw a speculative glance at Monica, who was putting the tablecloth away in a drawer. "You'd make a good child. You're not winsome, but you've got a sort of 'aunted look that's almost as good. It's not 'ard work, neither. All you've got to do is to carry on nat'ral, an' you get paid for it." She flung plates and saucers into the plate-rack in a hit-or-miss fashion. "If she went on the fillums I could be 'er dresser. I've always wanted to be a dresser to a fillum star."

Monica put the milk away in silence.

"Of course, there's 'Erb," went on Mrs. Partridge thoughtfully. "I couldn't leave 'Erb, but"—brightening—"'e could go on, too. 'Erb's winsome all right, when 'e's 'ad a bit of curl put in 'is 'air. You an' 'im could act together. Sort of little sweet'earts. What d'you think of that?"

Monica thought of 'Erb, a fat seven-year-old, with bulbous eyes, a loose mouth and a constantly running nose.

"I don't want to go on the pictures at all," she said. "Shall I dry for you?"

"Thanks, Ducks," said Mrs. Partridge. "I want to get finished early to-day. Yer ma said I could go at twelve. I've got 'Erb's Gran" (Mrs. Partridge always referred to her mother as 'Erb's Gran) "comin' over an' she's a bit easy put out. She'd be gnawin' at it all day if I wasn't there on the tick to meet 'er." She stood motionless, a dish-cloth in one hand and Fred's breakfast-cup in the other. "I keep thinkin' about yer ma. 'Ow many times as she bin divorced?"

"Once," said Monica shortly.

"Oh!" said Mrs. Partridge, obviously a little disappointed. "Still—" she added hopefully, and did not finish the sentence.

Monica heard the opening of her mother's bedroom door and went into the hall. Babs was coming downstairs. There was still that faint abstracted frown between her brows.

"Hello, darling," she said with her vague sweet smile. "I've just got to do some telephoning . . ."

She went into the little sitting-room and rang a number.

"Is that you, Peter? . . . Look, I can't come up to London to-day . . . No, it's off. . . . I forgot about a party of Monny's this afternoon. Yes, I know it's a nuisance, but I must take her . . . No, I can't . . . Fred's on his hind legs again and I've got to go carefully . . . Oh, the Jack of Clubs? . . . Just for lunch? . . . W-well, I suppose I could, but I must be back in time to take Monny over to Appleton for this party . . . About half past three, I suppose . . . Good! What time will you call? . . . Oh, blast! I can't. I shall have to see to Monny's lunch . . . Yes, Mrs. Partridge has to go early . . . No, I can't . . . Peter, darling, I'm heartbroken, but I can't help it . . . I know, it would have been heavenly." She turned to Monica, who stood in the doorway, and gave her a reassuring smile. "It's all right, pet. It just can't be helped. Don't worry . . . No, was talking to Monny . . ."

"Perhaps Mrs. Cannon—" said Monica.

Hope returned to Babs' voice.

"Listen, Peter. Monny says . . . Hold on a moment. I may be able to fix something." She turned to Monica. "Mrs. Cannon . . . Yes, she might. . ."

Mrs. Cannon was the woman who lived next door at Wood View. She had three children, and at first the two families had been on friendly terms. Monica had run in to play with Unity, Charles and Brian, and Mrs. Cannon had offered to "have" Monica whenever Babs wished to dispose of her. As far as Babs was concerned, the arrangement had worked perfectly, but Mrs. Cannon had found it less satisfactory. For Babs had no conception of the give-and-take implicit in such an arrangement. She was glad for Mrs. Cannon to "have" Monica when she wished to go out for the day, but it never occurred to her to "have" Unity, Charles and Brian in the same circumstances. When Mrs. Cannon asked her to fulfil this obviously neighbourly function her blue eyes would widen in helpless dismay.

"I'm so terribly sorry. I've got an engagement that I just can't get out of. I'm *terribly* sorry."

There had been occasions when Mrs. Cannon, determined to exact her share of the bargain, had booked a date some weeks ahead, but always when the day came Babs would make her excuses, deeply contrite but resolutely evasive.

"I can't *tell* you how sorry I am. It just went clean out of my head. I made this engagement and I simply *can't* get out of it now."

Mrs. Cannon's greeting became curt and chilly when she met Babs in the lane. Her manner to Monica changed, and Monica, acutely sensitive to changes of manner, felt less at ease with Unity, Charles and Brian. The neighbourhood began to "talk", and Monica saw the matrons of the village putting their heads together, watching her and speaking in whispers as she passed. Mrs. Cannon began to find reasons why the children could not play with Monica when she went next door, so Monica stopped going . . . But she must at all costs save Babs from having to give up her date with Captain Merrivale. Branded deeply into her childish soul was the terror of being a "nuisance", of being packed off somewhere, anywhere, because people couldn't be bothered with her any longer.

"I'll ask her," she said.

"Oh, darling, if you would!" said Babs gratefully. "I do so hate asking favours of anyone."

"Or—I could get my own lunch," suggested Monica tentatively.

"No, darling," said Babs. "That's the one thing I daren't do. I think Fred would kill me if I left you alone in the house again after . . . Well, he gets ideas into his head, you know, and he's in a bit of a mood now, anyway. No, we must try and fix something."

"If Mrs. Cannon wouldn't," said Monica, "I could try Mrs. Baxter . . . or Mrs. Grant . . . I'll find somebody to have me. I will, honestly."

"All right, darling. That's sweet of you." She took up the telephone again. "Peter? . . . It's all right . . . I think I'll be able to come. We're fixing something . . . What time will you be round? . . . Good!"

Monica went down to the gate and along the lane towards Wood View. She walked very slowly, gathering her courage, repeating the words to herself over and over again.

"Please, Mrs. Cannon, mother says would you be good enough to let me have lunch with you to-day? She has a very important engagement . . . Please, Mrs. Cannon, mother says, would you be good enough . . ."

Chapter Eleven

"I think we'll start with the treasure hunt," said Greta. "It makes them feel at home."

She was standing on the lawn under the copper beech with Mr. Hassock and Bertie Carstairs.

"The trouble with children," said Mr. Hassock, "is that, once they start feeling at home, no one else does."

"Oh, these are all fairly quiet ones," said Greta. "The ones we had last year—Geraldine and Philip and Monica—and the ones we have with us now and a few local children."

"What's happened to the present ones?" said Bertie, looking round. "It seems unnaturally quiet."

He was a tall fair young man, with a high domed forehead, curly hair and a mouth set by nature in a sulky line that was belied by the unfailing cheerfulness of his manner.

"They're resting," said Greta, "and Mrs. Sanders is working in her study and Mr. Sanders is at a committee meeting of the Maybridge Archaeological Society, so we have a clear field till it's time for me to get the children ready." She turned to Mr. Hassock. "Don't you think it would be best to have the treasure hunt first?"

The glance she threw him was thoughtful and just a little resentful. This morning, for the first time for months, Frank had become real to her again, bringing back all the old happiness and comfort, and, as she tidied her hair before lunch, she had remembered that, when first she heard of his death, she had decided to have an imaginary conversation with him each day to keep his memory fresh in her mind. Gradually she had stopped doing this, but now she decided to start again. She wanted to get back to those safe

126

and comfortable days when her whole life was so completely dedicated to his memory that no further emotional demands could be made on her. So, standing before her dressing-table, drawing her comb through her thick fair hair, she had begun one of the old imaginary conversations, telling him all she had been doing, imagining his comments and replies. And she had been dismayed to find that he answered her in Mr. Hassock's voice and with that undercurrent of ironic amusement that characterized most of Mr. Hassock's comments and that was so unlike Frank himself. She tried hard to recall Frank's own voice, but she couldn't do it. He went on talking to her in Mr. Hassock's voice, so she had brought the conversation to an abrupt close. She felt that it was outrageous of Mr. Hassock to obtrude himself on the private conversations she held with Frank, and had greeted him with chilly politeness when he arrived at the Vicarage after lunch.

"Yes," he said, "then they can spend the rest of the afternoon fighting over the treasures. It will keep them happy and occupied. Where are the treasures?"

She took a wooden box from the table.

"Here."

And then Bertie started organizing. He knew exactly where each treasure should be put and what the clues should be. His arrangements were all better than the ones she had in mind. She found it irritating and vaguely depressing and agreed with him a little peevishly. When she raised any objection, he yielded at once so gracefully that she felt ashamed and insisted on his suggestion being carried out.

She left him fixing Philip's treasure—a small jigsaw puzzle—in the fork of a tree and went over to the other side of the lawn, where Mr. Hassock was kneeling on the grass, arranging a game of clock golf.

"How are you getting on?" she said.

"Fine!" he said, looking up at her. "They'll have too much sense to play it, I expect. It's a lunatic game, but it always looks well. Gives a sort of festive air to the scene. It's evidence of goodwill, if of nothing else. Shows we've given care and thought to the entertainment of the little guests, even if the little guests refuse to be entertained . . . Bertie fixing up the treasures?"

"Yes."

He got up from the grass and gave his knees a perfunctory brush.

"You know, he's one of the most capable chaps I've ever met. He's absolutely reliable. He'd never let you down."

She gave a short amused laugh.

"There's no question of his letting me down or not letting me down."

He ignored that.

"He may be a crank in some ways, but he's a good, kind, clean-living man, and what more could you want?"

"I don't know. I haven't thought about it."

She felt that she was behaving like an archly disdainful Victorian heroine, but she wanted to stop him talking about Bertie Carstairs.

"He and I were having a talk together last night," said Mr. Hassock. "He said that you reminded him of his mother."

"Well, as I never met his mother, I don't know whether that's a compliment or not."

"He only just remembers her, of course—she died when he was a child, and his aunt brought him up—but he said that she was beautiful and clever and saintly."

"She must have had a job being all three," said Greta with a touch of acerbity. She was silent for some moments, then said, "What was your mother like?"

He considered.

"She was a very good mimic and an extravagant housewife. She taught us the names of the stars and birds and flowers, but, as they were all names she'd made up for them herself, they weren't much use in later life. She could make excellent whistles and bows and arrows. She could imitate the notes of birds so exactly that you couldn't believe it wasn't the creatures themselves, and she could invent the most lurid blood-and-thunder stories I've ever come across."

"She sounds rather fun."

"My father was a parson, and in some ways she was a liability to him. I mean, she'd wash her hair on Sunday morning and sit in the Vicarage garden to dry it where all the people going to church could see her from the road."

"Did your father mind very much?"

"Well, he was proud of her hair, but he thought that Sunday wasn't the right day to display it. She said that she always felt happy on Sundays and feeling happy made her want to wash her hair."

She laughed. It occurred to him that it was the first time he had heard her laugh.

"In many ways, of course," he continued, "she was an asset to him. When she set her mind to it, she could get anyone to do anything, and that was a great help to him in the parish."

"Yes . . ." said Greta thoughtfully. "I sometimes think I ought to do more in the parish than I do."

"You don't do much, do you?"

"I do the altar flowers sometimes. I did last week-end."

"Oh, was it you? You made them look very nice, but you left bits of leaves and stalks on the altar."

"Did I? I'm sorry . . . I broke one or two at the last minute after I'd put them there, to make them shorter. I'd done them on the harmonium, looking down at them, and they look different when you put them on the altar and look up at them."

"We need more helpers for the Young People's Club, you know."

"Oh . . . What night does it meet?"

"Tuesdays and Thursdays."

"Do you go to it?"

"On Thursdays."

She considered.

"Tuesday's a bit difficult for me. Olivia's serial for *Passing Hours* has to be finished by Wednesday, and we're generally working late on Tuesdays."

Bertie Carstairs approached. He looked spruce and fresh and golden in the sunshine.

"Will you come and see if you approve of the treasure hunt

arrangements, Miss Rossiter?" he said. "I've got them all in place now."

She flushed slightly under his gaze and turned uncertainly to Mr. Hassock, but Mr. Hassock was kneeling on the grass again, absorbed in the clock golf.

The two set off across the lawn towards the copper beech.

"May I call you Greta?" said Bertie.

"Yes, if you like," said Greta.

"And you'll call me Bertie, won't you?"

"Y-yes," said Greta.

"My family call me Bobo, but perhaps you'd rather come to that gradually?"

"Yes," said Greta, wondering how one came to Bobo gradually. Bertie looked satisfied. He had passed the first milestone. He had drawn up his plan of progress and the first milestone was Christian names. The second was the Rules of Health and the third was the actual proposal. He had reached the first milestone with a good many girls, but most of them had jibbed at the second, and he had never yet reached the third.

"Look!" he said. "I've hidden the clues in the shrubbery and the treasures are all nearby, well within reach of the little people. I think that's all right, isn't it?"

"Yes," said Greta, wishing that he wouldn't call children "little people".

And then Mrs. Sanders came out on to the lawn.

She gazed round at the preparations in surprise.

"What's all this?" she said.

"We're getting ready for the party," said Bertie.

"What party?" said Mrs. Sanders. She looked reproachfully at Greta. "Why didn't you tell me we were having a party, dear?"

"I did," said Greta. "It's Angela's birthday, you know, and we're having a children's party. I told you this morning."

Mrs. Sanders looked round the garden.

"Where are the children?" she said.

"Ours are resting," said Greta, "and the guests haven't come yet."

"Well, we must get it organized, mustn't we?" said Mrs. Sanders briskly. "What a good thing I've finished my poem in time! Now what about the arrangements?"

"Mr. Carstairs has kindly arranged the treasure hunt," said Greta, "and Mr. Hassock is fixing up the clock golf."

"Treasure hunt?" said Mrs. Sanders. "What are the treasures?"

"Paintboxes, crayons, puzzles and little outfits and things."

"Paltry!" said Mrs. Sanders. "The girls must have jewellery—fetch my jewel-case, Greta—and the boys must have trains and cricket bats."

"They'd be a bit difficult to hide," said Mr. Hassock.

"Nonsense!" said Mrs. Sanders, "and I don't approve of games like clock golf for children. They disappoint the losers. We must have games where everyone can win." Her gaze swept the garden, and Greta realized with relief that her mind had now left the treasure hunt. "Where's the band?"

"Band?"

"Yes. The band. One must always have a band at a garden party. Didn't you order a band?"

"Well . . . no."

"Ring someone up and order a band," said Mrs. Sanders majestically. "And there ought to be a Punch and Judy show. Haven't you got a Punch and Judy show?"

"No."

They watched her helplessly, half relieved, half dismayed as each idea was discarded for a fresh one.

"What about a play, then? The end of the lawn under the copper beech makes an ideal stage. Couldn't the children get up scenes from *Midsummer Night's Dream*?"

"I don't think so, dear," said Greta. "There's hardly time to arrange anything of that sort now."

"But why didn't you consult me about all this before, Greta? Why bring all these troubles and difficulties to me now at the last minute? What about one of those horse things that go round? Children love those. You see them in fairs."

"They're rather large, Mrs. Sanders," said Bertie.

"There are quite small ones," said Mrs. Sanders firmly. "Quite small ones, turned by hand. I remember that some years ago a gardener left us and purchased one and made it his career. He had red hair and a broken nose. It would probably be doing the man a good turn if we could get in touch with him and hire his machine." She paused and added thoughtfully, "Or I could recite . . ."

Greta was obviously wilting and Bertie was edging his way towards the gate, but Mr. Hassock came boldly to the rescue.

"I hope it's not a very inopportune request, Mrs. Sanders," he said, "but I'm not sure how the first verse in that last poem of yours should go . . . I mean, which words should be emphasized to bring out the meaning behind it."

Greta threw him a glance of unwilling admiration. Whatever else Mrs. Sanders forgot, she never forgot her poems.

"Come! Let us go where we shall be undisturbed," she said with a commanding gesture, and led him to the kitchen garden, where her voice could be heard upraised in passionate declamation.

"Well, I'll go and see to the children," said Greta, drawing a deep sigh. "Perhaps you'd be good enough to finish the game that Mr. Hassock was setting out."

"Right you are, Greta!" said Bertie, using the name a little self-consciously.

He made his way across the lawn, wondering how soon to begin on the Rules of Health and which to introduce first. He felt most strongly, perhaps, on early morning exercises, but raw vegetables ran them pretty close.

When the children came down on to the lawn, wearing their party frocks, Mrs. Sanders was still pacing the kitchen garden with Mr. Hassock . . . The words "truth" and "ruth" . . . "love" and "dove" . . . "fight" and "right" rang out with clarion clearness. Seeing Greta, she left Mr. Hassock and joined her.

"You know, dear," she said. "I've decided against a dictaphone. The sound of one's own voice is almost too stimulating. It carries one away. It impedes the process of concentration." She looked at the children running about the lawn. "How pretty they look in those frocks!" She glanced down at her own dress—a fairly innocuous garment of blue silk, in which she had made no alteration beyond cutting the sleeves off at the elbows yesterday in the heat of midday. "Ought I to change? Perhaps"—uncertainly—"I have changed. Did I put this on this morning when I got up?"

"Yes," said Greta, "and it looks very nice. I shouldn't change it."

"I bought rather a pretty shawl the other day," said Mrs. Sanders. "I could put that on, just to brighten it up, but I'm not sure where it is. I'll look for it if it gets chilly after tea . . . I hope you've provided a good tea."

"I think so," smiled Greta. "We've got jellies and trifles and fruit salad and chocolate biscuits and cake."

"Kaiser-schmarran!" said Mrs. Sanders with a sudden burst of inspiration. "I had it somewhere once and it was delicious. We must have *Kaiser-schmarran.*" She was silent for a moment, then said reflectively: "I remember now. I caught it in something and I gave it away . . . Look, dear. Is that someone arriving?"

A car, driven by a uniformed chauffeur, had drawn up at the Vicarage gate, and two boys were descending from it—one small, thin and dark, the other tall, sturdy and fair.

"It's Philip," said Greta, "and the other must be his stepbrother."

The two boys crossed the lawn to Mrs. Sanders, and Philip introduced Stephen with an air of punctilious formality. Angela had danced up to the group.

"Many happy returns of the day," said Philip, handing her a small packet. "It's from both of us with our best wishes."

Angela opened it, and the other children ran up to cluster round her—the twins with their arms round each other's waists, Jaqueline, her mouth a round O of excitement, Trevor, with his attendant in the background, peering over Jaqueline's shoulder.

"Oh, it's lovely!" she said, drawing out a string of corals. "Thank you. *Thank* you!"

A faint flush had crept into Philip's cheeks.

"I'm glad you like it," he said.

"Oh, I love it," said Angela, fastening it round her neck, but she was looking at Stephen, her eyes bright and challenging, her lips compressed into a demure, provocative smile.

"Come along," she cried suddenly. She was still looking at Stephen. "Come along, and I'll show you my other presents."

Mr. Hassock laid a hand on her shoulder.

"Hold hard," he said. "Here are some more guests."

Another car—a small shabby one—had stopped at the gate, and from it descended a woman holding a baby, and a little girl with a round rosy face and earnest brown eyes.

"It's Geraldine," said Greta.

"I didn't know we'd ever had anyone as small as that," said Mrs. Sanders. "How interesting!"

"No, it's the little girl who was here," said Greta. "That's her baby sister. Mrs. Mortimer said that she could get a friend to motor her over, but she couldn't leave the baby, so we said bring the baby too."

"Did we?" said Mrs. Sanders. "I wonder . . . I'd rather like to have some baby prattle in *Barren Heritage*."

"This one's too young to prattle, I'm afraid," said Greta. "Oh, good afternoon, Mrs. Mortimer."

"Good afternoon," said Grace in her soft low voice.

She stood there, holding the baby, looking shy and ill at ease in her rather badly cut tweed suit. "It was good of you to let me bring Elaine."

"Show them her," said Geraldine urgently. "I want them to see her." She looked at Philip, but Philip wasn't interested. His eyes were still fixed on Angela. "Look at her, Philip." Philip threw Elaine a glance of cold contempt: "Look! Let them look, Mummy. I helped make her dress. I sewed the buttons on. I did, didn't I, Mummy?"

"Don't get so excited, dear," said Grace gently, sitting down in the deck-chair that Greta moved forward for her.

"What a pet!" said Greta, holding out a finger for Elaine to grasp.

"Does it prattle?" said Mrs. Sanders.

"Not yet," said Grace in some surprise.

"Perhaps not," said Mrs. Sanders. "I had a child of my own, of course, but one's apt to forget the stages."

"Many happy returns of the day, Angela," said Geraldine, giving her a small box.

"Oh, thank you," said Angela, taking out a silver bracelet.

She fastened it on her wrist and danced across the lawn, skimming the grass lightly, holding up her arm, so that the bracelet shone on the sunlight.

Other children were arriving: a little girl with tight pigtails and a little boy with curls and a flat, honey-coloured face, accompanied by a nursemaid. The nursemaid had a small firm mouth beneath large blue glasses and led a bull-terrier on a chain.

"Now don't forget 'please' and 'thank you'," she said to her charges, "and use your handkerchiefs and try and drink quietly and remember you're little ladies and gentlemen."

With that she tweaked the little girl's frock, straightened the little boy's collar and, ignoring the grown-ups, departed with the bull-terrier. The little boy looked after her and began to cry. They all clustered round, trying to comfort him . . . Angela was still dancing about the lawn. Stephen was watching her with undisguised admiration, Philip with a dark impassive gaze.

"Come along," called Mr. Hassock. "We'll have the treasure hunt now."

"Wait a minute," said Greta, "Someone else is coming."

Another car, driven by a tall young man, had stopped at the gate. A woman and a little girl got out and crossed the lawn to the group by the copper beech.

"It's Monica," said someone, but no one was looking at Monica.

They were all looking at the woman. Her beauty threw a sudden stillness over the scene. Even Angela stopped dancing about and stared at her open-mouthed, seeing not Monica's mother but Angela herself. That's what I shall be like . . . That's how I shall look . . . That's how I shall walk . . . I shall wear a black suit with lace at my throat like that, and I shall have a black hat with a feather that curls under my chin.

Babs made her way up to Mrs. Sanders, her lips curved into their faint unhappy smile.

"It's Mrs. Sanders, isn't it? How do you do? It's so kind of you to ask Monny . . . What time shall I call for her?"

"About seven," said Greta.

"Oh, but won't you stay?" said Mrs. Sanders eagerly.

She wanted to capture this glamorous creature and pin her for ever on the pages of *Tangled Webs*.

"It's sweet of you," said Babs, and the unhappiness of her smile seemed to deepen. "I'd simply love to, but I'm afraid I have an engagement . . . And I must go now, or I shall be late. Goodbye and thank you so much."

She drifted back to the car, got in beside the young man, waved a white-gloved hand in their direction and vanished among the trees.

With her going a spell seemed to be lifted. Everyone began to talk and move about again. Angela walked slowly across the lawn, a faint unhappy smile on her lips.

"Get ready for the treasure hunt," called Mr. Hassock.

Monica wandered uncertainly towards the shrubbery. She had had lunch with Mrs. Cannon. Though Mrs. Cannon's mouth had tightened when she delivered the message, she made no demur. She had, indeed, been very kind to Monica during the meal, but Monica had been glad when it was over. Babs and Captain Merrivale had returned from the Jack of Spades soon after lunch and were now on their way to a *Thé Dansant* at the Green Lizard.

She looked about her without much interest, seeing Philip and Geraldine and Angela and several children whom she did not know. The Gosport children were there, but they had evidently forgotten her, and she was too shy to speak to them. Instinctively she made for the thickest shadows of the bushes, trying to efface herself as far as possible. Angela flitted by. She wasn't pretending to be Babs any longer. She was too much excited by her presents and the knowledge that it was her birthday to pretend at all. She was just an ordinary excited little girl.

"Have you found your clue yet, Monny?"

"No."

"Everyone but you's brought me a present," she said, and vanished round the corner of the shrubbery.

Monica wandered on. She'd never thought of a birthday present. But it didn't matter. It was only part of a game of make-believe. It didn't matter as Babs and Fred and what was going to happen mattered . . .

"Found your clue, darling?" said Greta.

"No."

"I'll help you look."

Suddenly Monica stood still. Angela was coming back through the shrubbery, and with her was a boy—tall, blue-eyed, fair-haired. She drew nearer to Greta.

"Who's that?" she whispered.

"Stephen," said Greta carelessly. "Philip's brother. You remember Philip, don't you?"

"Stephen . . ." said Monica.

"Yes, dear. Look! Here's your clue in the laurel bush."

Geraldine parted the hanging branches of the willow tree. The twins were sitting there on the grass. They stared at her, solemn and unsmiling. On the ground by them was a cardboard box.

"What are you doing?" said Geraldine.

"It's our house," they whispered.

Geraldine looked at the box.

"What's that?"

"It's our frig."

"Is that all the furniture you've got?"

They nodded.

"Don't you want any more?"

They shook their heads.

She stepped back on to the lawn and looked round for Philip.

Jaqueline was passing. She had a long thin pale face and rather a superior expression. Her leghorn hat was trimmed with imitation buttercups.

"I always have to wear a hat in the sun," she explained importantly. "I'm delicate."

Mrs. Sanders and Grace sat on deck-chairs under the copper beech. Elaine lay gurgling peacefully on an improvised bed of cushions between them. Grace watched the children with lazy interest.

"How many of these children are staying with you?" she said.

Mrs. Sanders considered. She always found it difficult to distinguish children from other children. She could generally recognize Angela, but the rest eluded her.

"Oh . . . several," she said vaguely.

Trevor passed with his attendant.

"That's one of them," she said triumphantly. "He's been here quite a long time."

"Are his people abroad?" said Grace.

Mrs. Sanders was silent while confused impressions of Anglo-Indians, film stars, actresses, and convicts flitted through her mind.

"We don't divulge their little histories," she said at last with dignity.

"Of course not," said Grace humbly. "I oughtn't to have asked." She looked round again. "It's a lovely party."

"Yes," agreed Mrs. Sanders. "I ordered a band, but there seems to have been some hitch about it."

Geraldine came up to them, dragging Philip by the hand. She flung herself on the ground by Elaine.

"Do look at her, Philip," she said. "You didn't see her properly when she came. Isn't she lovely! I can nearly bath her myself, can't I, mummy? . . . Smile at me, darling . . . Do look, Philip. She's smiling. You can see her teeth."

Philip stood glowering. He wasn't looking at Elaine. He was looking at Stephen and Angela, who stood together at the other end of the lawn, showing each other their "treasures". They were both laughing at something Angela had just said.

Geraldine stood up, pushing her hair out of her eyes.

"She'll begin to walk soon, and then she'll go to school with me. She'll go to school with me when she's five, won't she, mummy? You'll go to school with me, won't you, darling?"

Trevor approached them, followed by his attendant, and advanced upon Geraldine with a purposeful look in his eye.

"Let him push you over, dear," said the attendant anxiously. "He likes pushing people over. He won't hurt you." She turned to Grace and Mrs. Sanders. "Checking his impulses causes a state of mental disharmony, and a state of mental disharmony retards his progress. I think he's improved quite a lot lately."

Trevor's onslaught had knocked Geraldine on to the grass. He approached Philip, but something in Philip's face evidently made him change his mind and he wandered off among the crowd with his attendant in his wake.

"Oh, there you are, dear," said Greta, coming up to them and helping Geraldine to her feet. "I think we'll have tea now. Will you just come, dear, and see if you approve of everything?"

Mrs. Sanders accompanied Greta to the house.

"We haven't made any bread and butter," said Greta. "Just a few scones."

"Quite right . . . You know I've been trying to find words for it, but it's very difficult."

"For what, dear?"

"Her face . . . I've forgotten the name."

"Mrs. Deverel," said Greta, who was skilled in following the twists and turns of her employer's mind.

"Probably . . . I want Dulcina in *Tangled Webs* to look like her. One can say 'blue eyes and dark hair', but somehow it doesn't quite convey the impression. 'Flower-like' is a good adjective, but I've used it rather a lot lately."

They had entered the dining-room and stood looking at the laden table.

"Do you like the centrepiece?" said Greta. "I brought that galleon down from the schoolroom and filled it with crackers."

"Yes," said Mrs. Sanders. "I think perhaps you can give a better impression of beauty without describing the actual features."

"And—look—I made those 'poached eggs on toast' with apricots and whipped cream and sponge cakes. They look rather nice, don't they?"

"Homer never described Helen of Troy," said Mrs. Sanders.

"You are listening, dear, aren't you? I didn't put out any jam, because, with all the other sweet things, I didn't think they'd want it."

"He just described the effect she had on people when she came out on to the battlements . . . the same effect, I suppose, that that woman had when she came into the garden this afternoon."

"We've got a reserve store of jellies and things downstairs, but I really think this will be enough."

"On the other hand, I do feel that *description* is my strong point. My power over *words*, I mean."

Greta sighed.

"You haven't listened to anything I've said, have you?"

Mrs. Sanders brought herself back to reality and looked at the table.

"Yes, dear," she said. "I think you've arranged the whole thing beautifully, but I'm still a little disappointed about the band."

The children surged in to tea, laughing, chattering and pushing each other. Trevor pushed with the best and shouted with laughter when he himself was pushed. They all sat down and began to eat. The twins sat side by side, talking to each other in whispers, nodding or smiling or shaking their heads when addressed by the others.

Jaqueline raised her voice in shrill pride.

"I'm not allowed to eat fruit or sweet things. I'm on a diet."

Mealtimes were the high lights of Jaqueline's life. There she attained an importance that she enjoyed at no other time.

"I'm delicate," she said proudly to the flat-faced little boy who was sitting next her.

The flat-faced little boy had by this time lost his shyness.

"I don't care," he shouted. "*Be* delicate if you want to. It doesn't matter to me."

It struck him suddenly that he had said something very witty, and he began to laugh loudly.

"Now don't get silly, dear," said Greta. She patted Jaqueline's shoulder. "Poor little girl! And she's so good about it."

Jaqueline smiled complacently and nibbled her dry toast with an air of suffering nobly borne.

Bertie hovered about the table, offering iced cakes and chocolate biscuits to the children conscientiously, but with a rather worried air.

"I know it's a birthday party," he said to Greta, "but I think it's a pity to let them eat food like this, even so. There's no nourishment in it."

"What should one eat?" said Greta vaguely.

A rapt look came into his face. He was approaching the second milestone and decided to make a rush at it.

"I begin the day, of course, with physical exercises, the juice of a lemon, then for breakfast I have some lemon juice with, perhaps, some lettuce and raw cabbage. It's not at all monotonous. You can vary it with sultanas and grated cheese. Occasionally I have a cup of weak China tea half an hour after that, but I always avoid drinking liquids with an actual meal, except of course in the case of lemon juice. For lunch I generally have steamed fish with steamed or raw vegetables followed by raw fruit, and for tea brown bread and honey or another cup of weak China tea. For dinner I have the same as for lunch, varied sometimes by a little milk pudding made of unpolished rice." He paused. Greta made no comment, and he continued: "You'll find that a diet like that stimulates the mind and heightens the faculties. Well, look at me. I'm always on top of my form."

"Yes," agreed Greta bleakly. "You do seem to be."

She looked round for escape and found it in the flat-faced little boy, who had suddenly begun to rub chocolate biscuits over his cheeks and forehead, shouting: "I'm a Red Indian! Look at me! I'm a Red Indian!"

"Don't do that, darling," said Greta. "Nice little boys don't. Now we shall have to wash you, shan't we?"

He might be a good, kind, clean-living man, she thought, as she led the flat-faced little boy away to be washed, but it would be like living on a mountain-top in an east wind.

"I'm going to blow out the candles now," said Angela.

"Let Elaine watch," said Geraldine. "Hold her up, Mummy. Let her watch."

"There!" said Angela. "They're out! Now I'm going to cut it."

"You can't do it yourself, darling."

"Let Stephen do it, then. I want Stephen to do it . . ."

The Vicar entered and went round the table, greeting everyone, his thin ascetic face wearing its usual expression of mechanical benevolence. He had allowed himself exactly ten minutes for this attendance at his little daughter's party. He entered the dining-room at half past four, enquired after everyone's relations, patted heads, pulled a cracker, ate a fragment of birthday cake, made a few jokes, asked the riddle about "a-bun-dance" on the table, at which the flat-faced little boy laughed immoderately, and departed with his purposeful unhurried tread at four forty exactly.

Mrs. Sanders had presided over the table for a few minutes, and had then returned to her study, where, still wearing a paper cap, she was seated at her desk trying to pin down on to paper the elusive impression of Mrs. Deverel's beauty, jotting down a list of phrases and adjectives, beginning with "flower-like" and ending with "enravishing" and including "daughter of the Gods", "serpent of the Nile", and "La bells dame sans merci."

The children swarmed out into the garden and the games began, hide-and-seek, oranges and lemons, nuts in May. The more adventurous spirits left the games and began climbing trees. The little girl with tight pigtails found a trowel and a plant pot and began making mud pies in the rose-bed, fetching water from the bird-bath in the trowel. On all sides was uproar and confusion. The party had settled down into a definite success. Trevor, tiring of pushing people over, climbed into the raintub and stood, completely immersed in the water, grinning happily over the edge. "No, don't stop him," said his nurse, waving off a rush of would-be rescuers. "He must do whatever he feels like doing. It's part of the

142

treatment. I'll take him in and dry him as soon as he wants to come out."

Greta assembled the children on the lawn.

"Now, for the next game," she said, "I want you all to choose partners. Will every little boy choose a little girl for a partner?"

Monica was standing in the shadow of the shrubbery. She seemed to be watching a scene in which she herself had no part. Suddenly she saw Stephen walking across the lawn to her.

"Will you be my partner?" he said.

She gazed at him in sudden panic. He was a being from another world—a world of light and radiance. He could know nothing of the world in which she lived. Obscurely she felt that contact with her would soil and degrade him.

"No," she said, shrinking back. "No, *no!*"

Angela came running up to them.

"I want you to be my partner, Stephen," she said. "Come along."

He went back with her to the others.

Suddenly Philip barred their way.

"I asked you first," he said to Angela. There was an hysterical note in his voice. "I asked you first."

Angela raised her eyebrows disdainfully.

"I didn't hear you."

"You did hear me. You did. You did."

"Oh, shut up, Philip," said Stephen.

"You shan't be her partner. I asked her. You—you take everything. You—"

His voice choked.

"Well, I did hear, then," said Angela, "and I wouldn't have you for my partner for anything. You're a stupid silly baby, that's what you are."

To his horror, Philip felt the tears starting to his eyes. A small crowd gathered round and began to jeer at him.

"He's a baby!"

"He's going to cry!"

"Cry-baby!"

"Cry-baby!"

The thin childish voices were like flails cutting into his flesh. He turned and ran from them, pursued by the sing-song: "Cry-baby! Cry-baby!" and plunged beneath the branches of the willow. The tent-like space was empty except for the twins' "frig". He flung himself down, his face hidden in the grass.

He knew that Geraldine was there beside him, though he did not hear her come.

"Oh, Philip . . ." she began.

He interrupted with a quick, fierce whisper.

"Don't talk," he said. "Don't talk."

He wanted the comfort of her presence, but he knew that whatever she said would spoil it.

Parents and nurses began to arrive to take the children home. Barry and Albert stood together on the lawn watching the children.

"My little girl was here last summer," said Albert.

"My boy was here then, too," said Barry.

"We were a little anxious," said Albert. "You see, Geraldine's an adopted child, and my wife was having a baby. We were afraid that Gerry would be jealous, but everything turned out all right. She's as fond of the baby as if they were sisters."

"It was rather a ticklish time for us, too," said Barry with a smile. "I was marrying again, and my wife had a son of her own. We were afraid that he'd resent it—a new home and a new father, you know—but he's settled down so well that he seems as much my son as Philip is."

"These things always sort themselves out," said Albert philosophically.

"Yes," agreed Barry. "I suppose that children are more adaptable than we realize."

"They live in the present," said Albert.

"Lucky little blighters!" smiled Barry. Stephen ran up to them. "Where's Philip, Stephen?"

"Miss Rossiter's gone to find him."

Greta could be seen leading Philip and Geraldine towards them. Philip's face was white, his eyes ringed by shadows.

"The kid gets overdone," said Barry. "Running about in the hot sun and a lot of rich food."

"Come along, Gerry dear. Mummy and Elaine are in the car waiting for us. Have you said goodbye to Mrs. Sanders and thanked her?"

"Yes."

All the little guests had gone now except Monica. She stood by the front door, her eyes fixed anxiously on the gate, while Greta cleared up the debris on the lawn. Mrs. Sanders was still in her study. She had just added "sylph-like" to the list of adjectives and crossed out "Serpent of the Nile", substituting "dark lady of the Sonnets" and putting a question-mark after it because it suddenly occurred to her that dark lady had been no better than she should be.

"Your mother did say she'd call for you, didn't she, dear?" said Greta.

"Yes," said Monica.

"Do you think she can have forgotten?"

"She might have done," admitted Monica.

"Perhaps I'd better ring her up," said Greta, as she went into the house, carrying an armful of "treasure" paper wrappings.

"She's sending someone," she said, when she returned. "They should be here quite soon now."

Quarter of an hour later Monica was driving down the road with Captain Merrivale.

"I'm frightfully sorry," he said. "We got back about seven, but the party went clean out of our heads. Babs couldn't have come, anyway. She's not exactly squiffy, but—well, she wouldn't have passed muster in a Vicarage drawing-room. No good trying to hide it from you, is it? As I said, she's not really squiffy, but—well, I expect you know. I'll just drop you at the gate. No use my coming in again. You'll get her to bed, won't you?"

"Yes."

"Sure you can manage?"

"Yes."

They drove on in silence through the gathering dusk. Monica sat gazing in front of her, her small face pale and resolute.

Chapter Twelve

Philip walked slowly along the road from the village—a lanky over-grown boy of fourteen, with straight untidy hair and dark eyes deep-set in a pale narrow face. The bluish shadows under his eyes and in the hollows of his temples gave him an air of fragility, but there was stubbornness in the set of the long sensitive mouth and a suggestion of defiance in the carriage of his head.

He and Stephen had come home from school yesterday, and this morning Stephen and his father had set off directly after breakfast for a day's fishing. Philip was used to that now. He had learnt to hide—even from himself—the resentment that still rankled at his heart. Let them go, he would say to himself with his twisted one-sided smile. He didn't want them. He was happy by himself . . . And, till quite lately, he had been happy by himself. His imaginary world had been so real that the actual world around him mattered little. Leading his armies to victory, performing fantastic deeds of valour against his foes, circumventing the ruses of the Queen of the South, winning the love of Rosabel . . . he could give a hundred twists to the familiar story. Then gradually he had lost interest in the saga and, instead, had begun to identify himself with the hero of every story he read. As Kenneth of Scotland, he went to the Holy Land in disguise to fight for Richard Cœur de Lion; as Hereward the Wake, he led his outlaws and defied the tyrant; as Odysseus, he evaded the wiles of Circe (she had wide cheekbones and deep-blue eyes) and freed her victims.

On the surface he still accommodated himself to the routine of home and school. At school he went his quiet self-contained way, doing his work well enough to escape notice, accepting his position as a "rabbit" without rancour or even interest, neither popular nor unpopular with his schoolfellows. Stephen, of course, was outstandingly popular, and their worlds lay so far apart that in school they had few dealings with each other. Stephen still retained the attitude of amused tolerance that he had adopted towards Philip at the beginning of their relationship, and lately Philip had begun to counter this by a sort of mocking politeness. Stephen was a little slow-witted. It wasn't difficult to show him up and make him look foolish. The only drawback was that Stephen didn't much mind whether he looked foolish or not. Lazily good-natured, he was as ready to laugh at himself as at anyone else. The pleasure Philip got from scoring off him was a limited one. And that, too, was obscurely a grievance . . . Against all this his dream world had been an inviolate defence.

It was only lately that it had begun to fail him. For, with adolescence and the fading of his dream world, had come a new longing for friendship. The self-sufficiency in which he had taken such a savage pride no longer upheld him. Feelings of loneliness assailed him even when he was in a crowd—chiefly, perhaps, when he was in a crowd. There was in him a consciousness that he was unlike the others and a secret longing to be like them. Every now and then he would make desperate efforts to "mix", pretending an interest in things that did not interest him, ingratiating himself abjectly . . . then, when the attempt failed, flaunting his "difference" with angry defiance, determined to affront where he had failed to please. His dream world had not, of course, really vanished. It had only shifted its focus. Instead of heroes, warriors, princes, he imagined some ideal friend who would share his enthusiasms, someone in whom he could confide his secret thoughts and feelings, to whom he could show the poems that he had lately begun to write and that he kept locked in the drawer of the writing-table in his bedroom.

He walked very slowly up the drive . . . Daffodils grew thickly in the grass beneath the trees, looking like strange and beautiful sea creatures floating on the green waves. As he stood watching them, happiness, deep and satisfying, seemed to flow from them into his heart. He turned his eyes from them reluctantly and entered the hall. After the garden—filled with sunshine and the song of birds—it seemed cool and silent . . . He remembered suddenly that to-day he and his stepmother would be alone together. That often happened, of course, but always it brought to him a mingled excitement and apprehension, a gathering together of his forces to resist her power, a secret craven longing to yield. For she was still the Queen of the South in his eyes. That much of his dream world remained. That and Rosabel, for Rosabel still seemed more real to him than Angela herself.

As he stood there, his stepmother came suddenly into the hall from the pantry, carrying a gardening basket and a pair of scissors.

"I'm going to cut some daffodils for the house, Pip," she said. "Come and help me."

She spoke casually, as if taking his acquiescence for granted. He had lived here in the house with her ever since her marriage to Barry, always on the fringe of the family life, prepared to flee to his fortress, to bolt and bar himself within it, at the first suggestion of intimacy. She had long ago learnt that it was only by taking him for granted, pretending not to notice him, that she could prevent the quick, fierce donning of his armour.

He took the basket and they went down the drive and across the grass verge to where the daffodils grew beneath the trees.

"I like the single ones best," she said, as she bent down to cut the blooms. "I think I like all single flowers best—daffodils, Canterbury bells and asters and all the rest of them. There's something rather fussy and overdressed about the double ones . . . This is lovely, isn't it?" She held up a bloom that was almost white. "Like the ghost of a daffodil . . . Come over here, Pip, and I'll get some of the ones with yellow centres." He moved with her further into the belt of trees. "I used to go and stay with my grandmother at Easter when I was a little girl, and there were wild daffodils growing on the slopes of the valley. We used to take our tea there when it was warm and have it under a blackthorn hedge. The hedge was covered with white blossom. It looked like snow. We used to pick bunches of the wild daffodils to take home with us."

His face was alight with interest . . . He saw the picture she painted and forgot for the moment that it was she who was painting it.

"I used to pick just two from each clump," she went on. "I thought of the clumps as families and I wanted them all to have a relation to keep them company when I got them home . . . and I find myself still doing it." His thin face flickered into a half-smile. She looked at her watch. "Oh, dear! I must hurry. I've got the Pollitts coming to lunch."

"The Pollitts?"

"Yes. Mrs. Pollitt and Ralph. You haven't met them yet, have you? They've taken Kenworth Towers. Ralph's about your age. You'll help me with them, won't you? It's a nuisance that they had to come to-day when Stephen and your father are out, but it was the only day they could manage." She laid the blooms she had cut in the basket. "There! I think I've got enough. I want to put them in that old Delft soup tureen on the chest in the hall."

Philip carried the basket indoors and went up to his bedroom. A feeling of excitement was mounting in him. Perhaps this boy was the friend he was waiting for, the friend who would—understand, who would take from him the feeling of being different, of being shut out of the casual easy commerce of boyhood. He washed his hands, brushed his hair and stood looking round the room. Perhaps Ralph would like the same books as he liked . . . He would show him the little figure of the Dancing Faun that he had bought with his Christmas money last Christmas, and the print of Durer's St. George that he had found in the little second-hand bookshop in Maybridge last holidays. Perhaps they would put his new record—Debussy's "Sirènes Nocturne"—on the gramophone. Already his loneliness seemed to be a thing of the past. Perhaps Ralph, too, had been lonely. Behind the surge of excitement lay the sick feeling of apprehension that assailed him before even the most trivial encounter. His heart was thumping in his thin chest as he went downstairs.

Mrs. Pollitt and her son were already in the library with Ann. Mrs. Pollitt was a tall fair woman, trim and compact in a dark tailored suit. Her eyebrows were plucked into an expression of mild surprise, and the reddened outlines of her lips emphasized their slightly petulant curves. Diamonds sparkled opulently but discreetly on hat, coat lapel and wrist-watch. Her pale blue eyes wandered appraisingly over her hostess and the room.

Ralph was a sturdy well-made boy, with a faint line of down on his upper lip and dark hair sleeked back by brilliantine. Both chin and forehead receded slightly, and his nose followed the semi-circular line of his profile, but the general impression he gave was one of good looks and intelligence. Ann introduced them, and the two boys greeted each other, Ralph in an easy man-of-the-world fashion, Philip with a jerkiness that betrayed his secret agitation. The visitor's assurance made him feel gauche and childish, but his hero-worship was ready to be fired even by that.

Ann stood at the table, mixing the drinks.

"Take Ralph out and show him the garden, Philip," she said.

Mrs. Pollitt's eyes rested on Philip with their look of slightly weary criticism.

"What a delicate-looking boy!" she said as the door closed on them.

Philip flushed. He hated being called "delicate-looking". He walked with Ralph out of the front door into the pale, clear sunshine.

"You've got a nice place here," said Ralph condescendingly.

He had an abrupt high-pitched voice—the sort of voice that seems to say the last word there is to say on every subject.

"Yes, it's rather nice, isn't it?" said Philip, trying in vain to imitate both voice and manner.

He led the visitor round the house to a spot from which the daffodils could be seen stretching like a sea of gold beneath the trees. A slight breeze had arisen, and they seemed to be bowing to each other in a stately minuet.

"They look rather jolly there, don't they?" he said.

"Yes, but one gets a bit tired of them," said Ralph. "Everyone's got them all over the place at this time of the year. Daffs to the right of one, daffs to the left of one. Personally, I think there's something a bit bilious about the things. They always make me feel as if I'd had a surfeit of boiled eggs."

He was, of course, repeating someone else's words—probably his father's. Probably the crisp, clipped accents were his father's, too.

"Y-yes," said Philip, torn between his loyalty to some mysterious power and his blind longing for this boy's friendship.

They wandered across the lawn to the swimming pool.

"Decent little pool," commented Ralph. "Just the right size. Ours is a bit too big. How d'you like living here?"

"I like it," said Philip.

"All right in the summer, of course. Pretty deadly in the winter, I should think. Not that we shall be here much in the winter. We shall probably go to Madeira this winter. Last winter we went to the South of France. Ever been there?"

"No."

"It was great. I had several little flutters at the Casino—through my father, of course."

"You mean—gambling?" said Philip.

Ralph threw him a glance of amused contempt.

"If you like to put it that way," he said.

Again the colour flooded Philip's pale cheeks. Despairingly he wondered why everyone in the world except himself was poised and assured and self-possessed.

"Mavis Dyson was staying at the same hotel as us in Monte," went on Ralph. "She's a wonderful actress. Have you ever seen her?"

"I don't know," said Philip. "We went to London last Christmas to see *Treasure Island*. She wasn't in that, was she?"

"Good lord, no!" said Ralph with a short laugh. "She's a revue actress. She never acts in straight plays. She was in that last thing at the Palladium. Ran away with the show." He glanced up at the house. "Which is your room?"

"That one," said Philip, pointing. "Would you like to see it?"

"Thanks."

They went indoors and up to Philip's room. Ralph stood there, looking round. Politeness evidently forbade comment. It was clear that neither the Dancing Faun nor Durer's St. George meant anything to him, that he would not want to hear Debussy's "Sirènes Nocturne" played on the gramophone.

"What's your school like at games?" he said. "Anyone really good?"

Philip began to burrow in his drawers, trying to find snapshots of school teams. It turned out that Ralph was not much of an athlete, but that he took a keen academic interest in the world of sport. He knew all the outstanding names in the international field, could recite past records, speculate on future chances. And Philip, seeing the hopes of this friendship slipping away, began to clutch at it with feverish intensity. If Ralph wouldn't enter his world, he must enter Ralph's. The unbridled desire to please that alternated with the aggressive desire to displease had him in its clutches. He must prove to Ralph that he wasn't—different. He flung himself wildly into a discussion of the various merits of sportsmen he had never heard of, confusing cricket with tennis, footballers with boxers, aping Ralph's manner, getting himself each moment deeper and deeper into the quagmire. Ralph brought the discussion to an abrupt close with a shrug of his shoulders and a disdainful smile.

"What sort of a crowd lives round here?" he said. "We've only just come to the Towers, you know. They all seem a bit dim. I'm going to tea with those people at Appleton Vicarage this afternoon. The woman's a writer. Do you know them?"

"Yes."

"There's a kid. Well, I suppose she's about our age, really. I met her last week. Rather pretty."

"Rosabel," said Philip, then he bit his lip, and the colour flooded his face. "I mean Angela."

Ralph gave a short laugh.

"Got a crush on her?" he said.

To Philip's relief, the luncheon bell sounded, and they went downstairs. Philip lagged behind his guest. He knew that he had been weighed in the balance and found wanting. The shame of the outcast, the misery of the despised, lay heavy at his heart. His hands were trembling as he took up his knife and fork.

Mrs. Pollitt's conversation was not unlike her son's. She discussed the latest "shows" in London and the attractions of the Riviera, and was at pains to let her hostess know, casually and without ostentation, that her husband had ample means with which to provide these diversions. Ralph displayed perfect manners, paying deferential attention to Ann, taking his due part—no less, no more—in the conversation. Philip was silent. "Something's upset him," thought Ann, "but it's no use worrying. Things upset him all the time. It's the way he's made. If one let oneself worry about it, one would never stop, but I wish he'd let me help." She sighed to herself. She had almost given up hope of winning Philip's friendship. She had worked hard, and in the process had come to love and understand him, but she felt herself no nearer him than she had been at first. Perhaps part of the trouble was that she understood him too well. He sensed her understanding and resisted it, because to surrender would be a violation of his integrity. The old resentment against her for marrying his father had died. The battle lay now between the two of them.

"A Mediterranean cruise is enjoyable, of course," Mrs. Pollitt was saying, "but one meets such a mixed lot on them these days— even in the first class. Do you remember that woman, Ralph, who thought that Pompeii was the name of an opera?"

Ralph laughed.

"Yes. And the one who thought that caviare was a wine!"

The guests took their departure soon after they had had coffee.

"Ralph's going over to tea to Appleton Vicarage," said Mrs. Pollitt as she entered her gleaming Daimler. "Two engagements in one day. Quite dissipated for the country!"

Ann and Philip stood at the front door, watching the Daimler till it vanished into the road. Then they turned back together into the hall. Ann stopped by the library door, and he lingered with her as if unwilling to leave her.

"I wish these bookshelves weren't so high," she said, "or that Stephen hadn't broken the ladder. I was trying to get *Nicholas*

Nickleby down this morning, but it's just an inch or two beyond me. It's my favourite Dickens, and I want to re-read it."

He entered the room.

"Where is it?"

"There," she pointed. "I believe I could reach it if . . ."

She put a hand on his shoulder to steady herself, stood on tiptoe and took down the book. Then, just for a few moments, she left her hand on his shoulder, and he stood there motionless, his face turned away.

"Oh well," she said lightly, removing her hand, "I mustn't start it till after tea. I've got dozens of letters to write first."

She turned to the writing-desk and he went quickly from the room. His heart was beating unevenly. The longing for a friend that Ralph had failed to satisfy still tormented him—inflamed now by the eagerness of expectancy and by disappointment—and, in the moment when he had felt Ann's hand resting on his shoulder, he had taken a sudden and momentous decision. He would at long last accept her offer of friendship. He would open the gates of his fortress to her and let her in. And with the decision a sense of glad release came to him, as though he had been freed from some intolerable burden.

He closed the door of his bedroom and leaned out of the window. Above the daffodils a group of hawthorn trees was bursting into leaf, vividly green against the blue sky. A blackbird's song rang out with startling clearness. From the distance came the soft cooing of the wood-pigeons . . . The old sense of power swept through him and, taking a piece of paper from the drawer in his writing-table, he sat down and began to write. It was a poem that he had begun to write a few days ago and abandoned because he could not continue it. Now suddenly the words seemed to come pouring out of their own accord so quickly that he could hardly keep pace with them. Then he stopped and read it over, altering a word here and there. Putting down his pencil, he sat gazing into space. An ice-cold feeling of excitement gripped him and there was a sense of constriction at his throat. Yes, he'd do it. He'd do it now . . .

He took the paper to Ann's bedroom, placed it carefully in the centre of her dressing-table, and went down to the garden to the grass verge that skirted the drive. There he stood in the sea of daffodils, leaning against the tree-trunk. The feeling that Stephen called a "dentist pain" gripped his chest. Perhaps she was reading it now. Perhaps she had read it. He looked up at the house . . . and his heart leapt. Yes, there she was, standing at her dressing-table. He could see her clearly through the window. Perhaps she would come out to find him and talk of it. Perhaps she would wait till they met at tea-time. Sick with nervousness, he covered his face with his hands . . . When he looked up she had gone. She must have found it and read it. It seemed somehow the most momentous thing that had ever happened to him.

Clouds were gathering over the sun, and the wind struck chilly through his cotton shirt. He went very slowly towards the house. The sound of the stable clock striking four floated through the air. He entered the drawing-room by the french window. A housemaid was setting the tea-tray on a low table by the fireplace. Sitting down on the settee, he rested his elbows on his knees, fixing his eyes on the ground. Every nerve in his body seemed rigid with suspense.

"Cook's made some macaroons, Master Philip," said the housemaid encouragingly.

He threw her his strained half-smile.

"Thanks," he said.

"Master Stephen's the one for them, isn't he? You'd better make the most of them before he gets back."

He swallowed and, with an effort, smiled again.

She went out, closing the door. Funny boy, Master Philip, but somehow you couldn't help liking him.

He heard light footsteps along the hall, and Ann entered.

"There you are!" she said. "I don't know what time Stephen and your father will be back. Probably not till dark."

She put his tea-cup on the table near him. He raised it to his lips, then put it down again untasted. His throat was so tight that he could not swallow.

"I was glad to see the back of the Pollitts, weren't you?" she said lightly. "Have a sandwich?"

He took one and put it on his saucer. When would she say something?

"What have you been doing this afternoon? Did you go for a walk?"

"No."

She looked at him. He was miles away from her again. She thought that she understood. His pride, of course, regretted the moment of surrender, when she had put her hand on his shoulder and he had let it rest there, and he was doing all in his power to show her that it had meant nothing to him. She responded . . . talking in a distant, matter-of-fact way about the new neighbours, anxious not to seem to presume on his moment of weakness.

Then she remembered the paper she had found lying on the landing on the floor just outside his room. His door and window were open and it must have been blown off his writing-table by the wind. She had picked it up and, before she realized what she was doing, read it. It was a poem of four verses, describing the daffodils beneath the trees. Though crude and childish, it had an odd haunting beauty, and a vein of genuine inspiration ran through it. She had read it with a smile that was half proud, half tender. He was the stuff of which poets are made . . . But it occurred to her how angry he would be if he knew she had read it. The door and window of her own room at the end of the passage were open, and the wind might have carried it further down the passage, even down the back stairs where one of the servants might have found and read it. She must replace it at once on the table in his room and hope that he would never find out that it had come her way. She entered his room, put the paper on his table and went out, closing the door.

"You aren't eating anything, Philip," she said. "Don't you feel hungry?"

He shook his head. So this was her answer—this cold rejection of his overture. Or perhaps she had found the poem so worthless that she did not want to speak of it. His humiliation was like a physical oppression, sending waves of nausea through him.

She looked at him uncertainly, sensing something of his distress.

"I've got a whole fortnight's socks to mend," she said. "You wouldn't care to read *Nicholas* to me while I do it?"

Once or twice she had persuaded him to read aloud to her while she did her household mending. It had seemed to bring them nearer to each other, though he always tried to show her afterwards that their relations were unchanged.

"No," he said in a choking voice.

He made a muttered excuse and went up to his room. And there he found what seemed to him the last and unbearable affront. Not only had she, by her silence, scorned his gift, but she had not even wished to keep it. She had brought it here and put it on his writing-table. It was as if she had flung it back into his face.

And suddenly he knew that he could not stay a moment longer in a house where he would have to see and speak to her every day. He had often made vague plans for running away. In the early days of his father's marriage he had planned several times to run away and come back rich and famous. The return had, of course, been an essential part of the scheme. He had always lacked courage to carry out the plan, but now he sat down to think out the details. He would walk as far as he could and then he would get lifts. He would go to London and find a job of some kind there. Boys of fourteen did find jobs. He would sell his watch and his fountain-pen, and the money he got from them would keep him till he found a job.

He put his watch and his fountain-pen into his pocket and set off down the drive.

Chapter Thirteen

He walked along the Penbury Road, past the two next villages, then struck into the woods, meaning to take a short cut to the main London road, where, with luck, a lorry driver would give him a lift. But already something of his courage was ebbing from him. The wood seemed to hold menace in its shadowy depth, and the silence, as he penetrated farther into it, took on a personality of its own, becoming something evil and hostile, lurking there, watching him, biding its time . . . Even the pleasant grassy paths that wound among the trees conspired against him, and after walking for a quarter of an hour he found himself back at the point from which he had started. Panic leapt at him, but he mastered it and, leaving the paths, set off again, pushing his way through the bracken in a direct line, as he thought, to the main road, in order to make up for the time he had lost. The sky darkened, and a dull roll of thunder sounded in the distance. Raindrops rustled in the trees over his head.

Surrendering to his fear, he began to run, crashing blindly through the undergrowth as if pursued. The brambles, tearing at him as he went by, seemed like living creatures, and, when he fell headlong, tripped up by the projecting root of a tree, he lay there for some moments, his face hidden in his hands, too terrified to move. Then, scrambling to his feet, he brushed the dust from his clothes and went on . . . more and more slowly as the pain in his ankle increased, till at last he felt that he could go no farther. Sitting down, he took off his shoe and sock and examined his foot. It was swollen and inflamed, so swollen that he could not put on his shoe again. He limped along, holding his shoe in his hand, but at each step the pain increased.

The rain had become a steady downpour, and the rolls of thunder grew nearer as if they were closing in on him. Suddenly he heard the hooting of cars and realized that he was approaching the main road. He made his way to it with difficulty, dragging himself through the low railings that bordered the wood. Then he began to limp along the grass verge till at last he sank down on to the ground, holding his foot in his hand, bending over it, rocking to and fro. Red-hot stabs of pain were shooting up his leg. The sky grew black above him. There was a vivid flash of lightning and a sharp reverberating clap of thunder. The rain was coming down now like a solid sheet of water. He crawled to the hedge and sat in its shelter, surrendering himself to an apathy of despair. He didn't even wonder what to do next because there wasn't anything he could do next. He could only sit there, rain-drenched, pain-racked.

Suddenly a car drew up at the roadside.

"What's the trouble?" said the driver.

Philip raised a white, dripping face.

"I think I've hurt my foot."

The man looked at him in a worried fashion. He was a short man, with kind grey eyes under thick eyebrows, a prominent nose and a raggy moustache.

"Where do you live?"

"Penbury."

"That's pretty well out of my way," said the man, "and I'm on the minutes. Look here, Appleton Vicarage is just at the end of the road. Shall I drop you there and let them fix up the doings for you?"

Philip looked round him . . . Yes, of course. He hadn't recognized it, but it was the road that led to the Vicarage. There at the corner was the little general shop, where they used to spend their pocket money on Saturdays, and the Vicarage was just round the bend. Dully, he wondered if something in him had meant to come here all the time.

"Thanks."

The man got out and helped him into the car.

"Steady! That's the way! There you are! Sorry I can't play the Good Samaritan to the tune of wine and oil and the rest of it, but I think they'll fix you up all right at the Vicarage."

An hour later Philip was lying on the settee in the Vicarage drawing-room, dried, cleaned, wearing an old dressing-gown of the Vicar's. The doctor had bandaged his ankle and his father had been informed of the accident by telephone. Philip, now bitterly ashamed both of his exploit and its failure, was relieved that no explanation of it need be given. He had been for a walk in the wood and had fallen and sprained his ankle there. That was all that need be said.

Greta was hovering about him in a faintly abstracted fashion.

"It's all rather unfortunate," she said. "The Vicar's got the new Bishop here, and can't be disturbed, and Mrs. Sanders is very busy with an instalment of her serial that has to catch to-night's post."

"And I expect you're busy too," said Philip apologetically.

"Well, Mrs. Sanders has got a dictaphone now. It only arrived yesterday, but, when she gets accustomed to it, it will save us both a lot of time."

She stood for a moment gazing into space, and Philip looked round the room. The Vicarage drawing-room had a detached impersonal air, like a drawing-room in an Ideal Home Exhibition. The Vicar and his wife lived in their respective studies, and the drawing-room was used only on formal occasions. There was something dispirited about it, as if it had lost heart from lack of encouragement. The writing-table seemed to be mutely imploring someone to write at it, the chintz-covered armchairs seemed to be mutely imploring someone to sit on them, the polished brass ash-trays seemed to be mutely imploring someone to drop ash on them.

Greta moved vaguely across the room, shook up a cushion that seemed to have sagged from sheer despair and straightened a photograph that depicted Mrs. Sanders poised on a rustic bridge, wearing a fancy dress that was vaguely suggestive of Lady Macbeth but that was meant to represent Spring. The years had brought little change to Greta. She was still doggedly convinced that her life's fulfilment lay in her devotion to Olivia and the children and Frank's memory, though each year the conviction required a few more arguments to bolster it up. She had refused Bertie Carstairs three times and he had finally married a thin tall girl with an underhung jaw, who kept an Arts and Crafts shop in Maybridge and who shared his views on raw vegetables and unpolished rice.

Greta had been relieved by the marriage and yet, to her surprise, it seemed to leave her life rather empty. Mr. Hassock had been appointed to a curacy in the East End of London and wrote to her about four times a year. She had received a letter from him this morning and was feeling a little unsettled. His letters always had an unsettling effect on her. Sometimes she felt that she ought to tell him to stop writing, but she could never quite bring herself to do it.

Philip moved his head to look out of the window. The storm was over now, and the sun shone down on the garden, turning the plants into tiny sparkling chandeliers. The garden was as he remembered it, except that the table under the copper beech had gone and a small summer-house had been built just beyond the lawn.

"Here's Angela," said Greta, and Angela entered, followed by Ralph Pollitt.

Angela had grown into a tall, slender girl, her grace and delicate beauty enhanced rather than impaired by adolescence. When Philip arrived, soaked and exhausted, she had fluttered about him excitedly, but, with the coming of the doctor, had become bored and had taken Ralph out into the garden. Now that the doctor had gone and the centre of the stage was once more free, she had returned.

"Poor darling Philip!" she said. "How are you now?"

She bent over him solicitously but sent a sidelong glance to Ralph as she spoke.

Ralph had taken his stand on the hearthrug, hands in pockets.

"Funny thing, running into you here!" he said in his clear clipped accents. "You are a chump to go and get yourself mucked up like this."

"Yes," agreed Philip.

Angela laid her hand lightly on his forehead and stroked back his hair. She was rewarded by the sudden tremor that ran through his frame and the flush that crept into his pale cheeks.

"Poor Philip!" she said again, throwing another glance at Ralph from under curling lashes, determined to wrest some sign of jealousy from him.

Philip turned his head to the window again and saw a girl coming out of the summer-house, carrying an armful of toys. She was small and thin, with dark hair and dark eyes.

"That's—that's—what was her name?" he said.

"Monica," said Angela. "She was here with you, wasn't she?"

"Yes. Why is she here now?"

"We're very glad to have her," said Greta. "She's a great help with the children."

"Her parents are being divorced or something," said Angela carelessly.

"But—they've been divorced," said Philip. "She told us so."

"Another lot, probably," said Ralph with a short laugh.

"How long holidays have you got, Ralph?" said Greta in the brisk, light voice that she used when a change in the conversation seemed advisable. She wanted to protect Monica from their curiosity as well as to prevent any possible development of the subject of divorce. The child was so shy and quiet and helpful that Greta's original prejudice against her had vanished. She still "knew things", of course, but Greta had learnt that she did not communicate her knowledge to the others, and in any case most children of fourteen "knew things" nowadays so it didn't matter.

"The usual month," said Ralph. "We shan't spend all of it at home, of course. We shall be going up to town for part of it to see a few shows."

Monica paused at the door, hesitating. She wanted to ask Miss Rossiter for a button to supply a golliwog's missing eye, but she was too shy to go into the room while the others were there. When she saw heads turning in her direction she lost courage and went quickly upstairs with her armful of toys. She would put the toys away, then she would fetch the books that the children had left in the summerhouse. After that she would help amuse the children till bedtime, and then she would tidy the toy cupboards and do some of the mending. So deep was her distrust of life that she had learnt to hem herself in by a succession of little duties, so that she need not look beyond them, need not see the dark forces that lay always beyond whatever she happened to be doing.

She had been desperately unhappy when she heard that she was to be sent back to Appleton Vicarage.

"It won't be for long, darling," Babs had said. "I must just get settled in this job, then I'll send for you. It won't be as bad as it was last time, you know, dear, because you'll be a sort of paying guest. Well"—with her soft low laugh—"not exactly paying, because the nursemaid's away on holiday and you're going to help with the children and not pay at all. I'll send for you the minute I can." She was silent for a moment or two, then continued: "I know things haven't been easy for you, pet, but everything's going to be different now. Fred was right. I hadn't enough to do. Now I've got a job—well, you'll see. We'll be as happy as sandboys, the two of us."

Fred had divorced Babs last year, and the "job" was that of hostess in a hotel on the South Coast. She had been there for ten days now.

Perhaps she'll send for me to-morrow, thought Monica, as she stooped to pick up a pink rabbit that she had dropped on the top step. Or perhaps the next day . . .

She opened the nursery door. Four children were having tea at the nursery table with a stout, elderly nurse.

'That's a good girl!" said the nurse. "They left some books out there, too, didn't they?"

"Yes," said Monica. "I'm going to fetch them."

"Will you read to us after tea, Monny?" said a little girl with red hair, a snub nose, and a smile that revealed wide gaps between a few surviving first teeth.

"Yes," said Monica.

She put the toys into the toy cupboard and went downstairs

again and out to the summer-house. From the summer-house she saw a car draw up at the front door. She recognized the boy who got out of it. It was Stephen. She had met him at Angela's birthday party. She shrank back into the doorway of the summer-house, so that he should not see her in the casual glance he swept round the garden before he followed his father into the house.

"Well, you are a young jackass, aren't you?" said Barry, smiling down at his son. "How did it happen?"

"I don't know," said Philip. "I fell."

"I'm so sorry that neither the Vicar nor Mrs. Sanders can see you," said Greta, "but the Bishop's with the Vicar and Mrs. Sanders is busy."

"That's quite all right," said Barry. "I'm most grateful for all you've done and I don't want to give any more trouble than I need. I've got the car outside and I'll just pack the kid into it. I'd better have a word with the doctor first. May I use your 'phone?"

"Yes, certainly. Do you mind using the one by the kitchen door? I don't want to disturb Mrs. Sanders or the Vicar. It's this way."

They went out of the room, and Angela stood, her eyes bright with mischief, looking at the three boys. Then, with instinctive skill, she began to "play" them, flattering first one, then another, pitting them against each other, laughing, teasing. As she did it, she was both herself and someone else—someone who watched admiringly, appraising every word and movement. She acted more for the benefit of the unseen watcher who was herself than for the schoolboys she was cajoling so expertly.

Suddenly, through the half-open door, Stephen saw Monica crossing the hall towards the staircase with an armful of books. He started up and went into the hall.

"Let me take those for you."

She drew back.

"Oh, no . . ."

He smiled and took them from her arms.

"You were here before, weren't you?" he said.

She nodded, her eyes fixed on his face.

"I remember you," he said.

"I remember you, too," she said in a small breathless voice. "Where are you taking them?"

"Upstairs to the schoolroom."

"Right!"

As she went up the staircase with him, everything round her seemed to shine with a light that was brighter even than the sunshine, and the dark, menacing forces seemed to retreat to an infinite distance.

Angela was growing bored. Stephen had left them and Philip had become silent and sulky.

"Oh, come along," she said to Ralph. "Let's go to the playroom and have a game of ping-pong."

Left alone, Philip leant back on the settee, closing his eyes. His ankle was throbbing and his head ached unbearably. The cushion was hard and uncomfortable, and his throat was dry with thirst. Suddenly he remembered the plump, dark little girl who would not have left him alone as all these other people did, who would have shaken up his cushion and brought him a drink of water.

Greta came back into the room.

"Your father's going to carry you to the car, Philip," she said. "We're just waiting till the Bishop's gone. He's going now."

"What was the other one called?" said Philip.

"The other what, dear?" said Greta absently.

"The other girl. When we were here the first time. And at Angela's birthday party."

"Oh, Geraldine."

"Yes. Where is she?"

"She lives in Minster Road. Just outside Maybridge. One of those new roads beyond the station."

"Oh, yes. We never go into that part. Does she go to school in Maybridge?"

"No, she goes to a boarding-school. Oh, dear! That reminds me. I must write to her father. He wants us to take the other little girl, Elaine, next month, while his wife goes into hospital for an operation, but I'm afraid we can't manage it. It all depends on a provisional booking." There was the sound of voices in the distance, and Greta sprang to her feet. "The Bishop's going. I'll just close the door." Footsteps came down the passage and stopped in the hall.

"You'll be taking the chair at the meeting, I suppose?" said the Bishop.

"Oh, yes, my lord," said the Vicar. "I went over the agenda with the secretary last night."

Suddenly a shrill and passionate voice rang out from the closed door behind the Bishop.

"Give me back the letters. I wrote them when I was little more than a child. Are they to darken my whole life? I have paid for my sin a thousandfold. I will sell my last jewel, pour out the last drop of my heart's blood, to get those proofs of my guilt back into my hands and destroy them, as I wish to God I could destroy you." The speaker stopped abruptly and cleared her throat. The Bishop threw a glance of startled enquiry at his host.

"My wife," said the Vicar with a somewhat constrained smile. "She writes, you know. She has recently acquired a dictaphone and she is apt to raise her voice, I think, more than the instrument actually requires. She is not, as yet, quite accustomed to it."

"I see," said the Bishop, his fascinated gaze still fixed on the door. No further sound came from it but the rustling of papers.

"Well . . ." said the Vicar, turning to the front door.

But the Bishop still lingered hopefully. The rustling of papers stopped and was replaced by the sound of the opening and shutting of several drawers in succession.

"Did she—get the letters?" said the Bishop, turning to follow his host.

"I'm not sure, my lord," said the Vicar. "My wife has not discussed that particular story with me."

They walked together down the drive to the gate where the Bishop's car was waiting.

"Would you like me to send you a copy of the agenda, my lord?" said the Vicar.

"Yes," said the Bishop absently. "What is it going to be called?"

"Called, my lord?"

"Your wife's story."

"Oh . . . I believe that particular story is to be called *Gilded Pinnacles*."

The Bishop stopped and took a note-book and pencil from his pocket.

"I'll just make a note of it," he said. "I should rather like to read it when it comes out."

Chapter Fourteen

Geraldine placed a foot in the centre of each paving-stone, carefully avoiding the joints. It was one of the taboos of her childhood, and, despite her fourteen years, she still half unconsciously observed it.

She was short for her age, but her features were losing their nebulous outline and giving promise of beauty. There was even a suggestion of grace in the plumpness that now caused her acute humiliation and had earned her the nickname of Fatty at school.

She was going to meet Albert on his way home from work. She had done this ever since she was a little girl, waiting at the corner of the road till she saw the neat dark figure with bowler hat, rolled umbrella and attaché-case, then running to meet him . . . Yes, there he was, walking with his usual short brisk steps but a little more quickly than usual. The worried frown cleared from his brow when he saw her, and he stood for a moment as he used to stand when she was small enough to run into his arms and be swung up into the air. She ran to him now, linking her arm in his, and together they began to walk homewards along the tree-bordered suburban road.

"How's mummy?" said Albert anxiously.

"I think she's better," said Geraldine. "She doesn't seem so tired to-day. I made her rest after lunch. She wanted to get Elaine ready for the party, but I wouldn't let her. I got Elaine ready myself."

"Good girl! We hope that after the operation mummy will be better than she's ever been, but we must take very great care of her just now."

"I know," said Geraldine, then, after a pause, "Have you heard yet if they can take Elaine at the Vicarage?"

"Not yet. It depends on some people who made a provisional booking for their little boy and who've gone abroad for a week or two. If they don't decide to send the little boy, Elaine will be able to go there. We should hear this week. Were there any letters by the midday post?"

"No."

Gerry thought of Elaine playing in the Vicarage garden, hiding under the weeping-willow, sitting at the table under the copper beech, doing her lessons, reading the *Blue Fairy Book* on the nursery window-seat, going for picnics in the wood with Miss Rossiter . . . Oddly she imagined Philip and Monica and Angela there too, just as they had been seven years ago.

"You'd like her to go there, wouldn't you, dear?" said Albert.

"Yes."

It was strange how important it was to her that Elaine should go to the Vicarage. The shared memories would make Elaine belong to her more securely, and it was the most important thing in the world to her that Elaine should belong to her securely.

Albert's voice broke in on her dreams.

"And what's my girly been doing to-day?"

Geraldine returned to the present.

"I helped mummy in the morning, then I did the diary for yesterday."

Albert and Geraldine kept the Weather and Events Diary together now. Geraldine was as interested in it as he was. They would discuss the entry together and then Geraldine would make it in her neat childish handwriting.

"What did you put, dear?"

"Well, you said we ought to put 'Death of Robert Bridges', so I put that."

"Quite right, dear. I think that the passing of any great figure in literature should be noted."

"And I put 'Princess Elizabeth's Fourth Birthday.' Was that all right?"

He smiled.

"Yes, dear. Quite all right."

"And I put 'Pear tree in garden in bloom. Picked speedwell in field.' I wasn't sure whether that was important enough, but I put it."

"Yes, dear. It was a very happy thought."

"And the weather was cold and showery, wasn't it?"

"Yes, dear. Definitely."

"I wrote it very carefully."

"I'm sure you did, dear."

He looked down at her proudly. Everything Geraldine did, she did as carefully as possible. Though slow, she was earnest, conscientious and wholly reliable. You could depend on her to do anything she undertook to do. People sometimes said that she had no sense of humour, but that did not trouble Albert, because he had no sense of humour himself.

"For to-day's event," he went on, "I think we must have the signing of the Three Power Naval Treaty. It's a very important event indeed. You see, Great Britain, the United States and Japan have agreed to restrict their building of warships, and that should considerably lessen the possibility of war in the future."

"Yes," said Geraldine vaguely, "and what about the weather? It's been windy and showery, hasn't it?"

"Yes, but warmer."

"I looked up to-day's weather last year," said Geraldine, "and it was quite different. Mild and sunny."

"Now that's very interesting," said Albert. "It shows how useful the diary is for checking up, doesn't it? Did you have any time for the reading, darling?"

"Yes. After lunch, when mummy and Elaine were resting. I read the last chapter of *Oliver Twist* and crossed it off the list."

"Good!"

It gave Albert a deep happiness to watch Geraldine's progress. Her school reports were excellent (he had sent her to the best boarding-school he could afford, because he believed in the cultural atmosphere of a boarding-school) and her list of Books Read and Places Seen was growing rapidly. She absorbed knowledge with the same earnestness and conscientiousness with which she did everything else. It was difficult for him to realize that she was not his own child. He loved Elaine—a harum-scarum little monkey—but he felt that it was Geraldine who was his real daughter.

"*Henry Esmond*'s next," she said. "I'll start that to-morrow. It's got forty-two chapters, so, if I read two chapters a day, I'll have finished it in about five weeks."

"Splendid! . . . You know, Gerry, I'd meant to take you to the British Museum these holidays, but I'm afraid I shan't be able to with mummy being ill."

"It would have finished the page," said Geraldine a little regretfully, "There's just room for it under the Tower of London."

" Well, we'll manage it next holidays, perhaps," said Albert. "Did you take Elaine to the party?"

"Yes . . ."

Geraldine thought of the moment when she left Elaine at the party, dancing about with a crowd of other small boys and girls, too much excited even to say good-bye, and with the memory a heavy depression came over her spirit.

"I don't think that other children are good for Elaine," she said slowly.

"Don't you, dear?" said Albert, surprised.

"No . . . They over-excite her. They make her silly. I've often noticed it."

"Perhaps you're right," said Albert.

He had a greater respect for Geraldine's opinion than he would have admitted. He felt, vaguely, that the education she was receiving, her growing lists of Books Read and Places Seen gave her, despite her youth, a wisdom that he could never attain.

"Yes . . . you may be right."

"We don't want her to grow up—frivolous," said Geraldine, after searching a moment for the word, "and other children seem to make her like that."

"I see what you mean," said Albert a little uncertainly.

They had reached the house now, and Grace came to the gate to meet them. She looked thin and worn, but she greeted Albert with her usual smile of welcome.

172

"What sort of day, darling?" he said tenderly as he kissed her.

"Not bad," she said. "The wood's come for your trellis."

He had finished the garage-playroom, and the girls used it frequently in the evenings and at the week-ends. He was now making a trellis to fit round the little bay-window and had grown a white jasmine from a cutting to tram over it.

"Splendid! I'll start this evening."

"I'll make the tea now, shall I?" said Geraldine. "Then I must fetch Elaine back from the party, mustn't I? She oughtn't to be out after her bedtime."

"There's no need for you to fetch Elaine, Gerry," said Grace. "Mrs. Sellars says she'll fetch her. She has to fetch Tony, anyway." She spoke a little shortly but with the schooled kindness with which she always addressed Geraldine. She had given up trying to conquer her dislike of the child, but all her efforts were bent on hiding it.

A tight look had come over Geraldine's face—a look that only came there when she was thwarted in her dealings with Elaine.

"I want to fetch her . . . I must fetch her . . . Please let me . . . *Please.*"

"But why?" said Grace.

"I want to. I don't want anyone else to. You let me take her there. You must let me fetch her back . . . You *must.*"

Albert put an arm on his wife's shoulder.

"Why not, darling? Gerry only wants to help."

Grace looked from one to the other in silence. This sultry possessive love of Geraldine's for Elaine frightened her, but Albert saw no harm in it. Perhaps it was her secret dislike of the child that made her resent it. Anyway, she was too tired to fight.

"Very well," she said.

"And may I put her to bed when I've brought her back? May I? Please let me . . . *Please!*"

"She can put herself to bed, dear."

"No, I don't want her to. I want to put her to bed. Please do let me."

Grace repeated her weary little gesture of acquiescence.

"Very well."

They went into the dining-room and Geraldine brought in the tea. The room looked more than ever overcrowded now. More and more specimens of Albert's handiwork had crept into it with the years . . . another bookcase here, another occasional table there, a highly ornamental paper-rack, a still more ornamental firescreen.

"And has Gerry been helping you to-day, dear?" said Albert, as the three sat round the little table.

"Yes," said Grace. "She did the shopping and the dusting and helped me with the cooking."

"I made the scones, didn't I?" said Gerry.

"Yes, dear."

The familiar feeling of compunction stirred at Grace's heart. The child was so good and capable. She worked so hard in the little house. She was so anxious to please. She tried again to overcome the feeling of shrinking and repugnance that she always had when she was with her and of which she was so bitterly ashamed.

"She's been a very great help," she added. "I don't know what I should do without her."

"I'll wash up after tea, and then I'll fetch Elaine," said Geraldine happily.

After tea Grace and Albert wandered into the little garden. Wallflowers and forget-me-nots were coming into bloom. The tulips were in bud. Cascades of aubretia—glowing red and purple—poured over the tiny rockery. The pear tree in the corner of the lawn wore its fall of blossom like a bridal veil. They sat down on the rustic seat that Albert had made the year they came to the house. Sitting there, her hand in Albert's, Grace surrendered to a dreamy happiness. Now that Gerry was no longer there, she could relax, could let peace and contentment flow into her soul.

"Gerry's a good girl," said Albert.

Grace stirred uneasily. She didn't want to talk about Gerry.

"You must finish the trellis while I'm away," she said.

"Yes." He looked round the garden in silence, then said, "I think you were right about the arbour."

174

She caught the wistfulness in his tone and smiled. Secretly he still wanted to make his arbour.

"I think I was," she said gently.

He drew her head on to his shoulder.

"You aren't frightened, are you, darling?" he said.

"No," she said. "No . . . It will soon be over."

"Yes, doctors are so clever nowadays. We shall sit here in a month's time and look back to to-day and think how silly we were to worry."

"We aren't worrying."

"No, of course not. And there's nothing to worry about as far as the children are concerned. Gerry will be back at school, and Elaine will be at the Vicarage."

"If they can have her."

"I expect they can. And I can look after myself all right. I expect I shall spend most of my time outside the hospital waiting for them to let me in . . . We'll bring down the camp-bed and you can lie on it in the garden when you come home again. I know you hate me asking you, darling, but—has the pain been bad to-day?"

"No. I've hardly had it at all."

"I'm so glad. I was thinking about you all day . . . As soon as I turned the bend in the road and saw Gerry, I tried to tell from her face what sort of a day you'd had."

"Could you tell from her face?"

"Yes." He looked at the house. "I ought to be helping her with the washing-up."

"No, it's all right. She's finished. I think she's upstairs getting ready to fetch Elaine."

Geraldine was standing in front of her dressing-table, looking at her reflection in the mirror, her brows drawn into a frown. The changes in her developing body worried and puzzled her, though she accepted Grace's somewhat confused explanations without comment or query. What disconcerted her most was the swelling of her breasts . . . They were large and round under her thin woollen jumper. She pulled the jumper this way and that, trying to hide them. She hunched up her shoulders and stooped, in the hope of making them less conspicuous. She slipped her handkerchief between them, spreading it out to fill the gap between them . . . Then the striking of the clock in the hall told her that it was time to fetch Elaine and, putting her handkerchief into her pocket again, she took up her hat and coat and set off at a run.

Her heart thrilled with pride as her eyes fell on Elaine. How sweet she looked with her tawny curls and blue eyes! The white silk frock, with its blue smocking, was crumpled and stained with chocolate, but, in spite of that, she outshone all the other little girls. She was prettier, daintier, more alive. Beneath the pride there stirred a dull ache of disappointment. For, instead of running to greet her, Elaine just waved to her carelessly across the room and continued to giggle and scuffle with a group of little guests.

Geraldine stood there uncertainly in the doorway—a short fat schoolgirl in navy blue hat and coat, her heavy brows drawn together in a scowl.

"Have you come for Elaine?" said the hostess.

"Yes, please," said Geraldine.

Elaine, seeing her departure imminent, began to "get silly" . . . pulling faces, showing off, contorting her small body into ridiculous postures, speaking in a high squeaky voice. The others crowded round her. Cascades of childish laughter filled the air . . . Geraldine watched with grave unsmiling face.

"I'll get her," said the hostess. "They're all a bit over-excited."

Mothers and nurses were arriving, and the guests were being pushed into hats, coats and gloves. Then, suddenly sobered, they remembered maternal injunctions.

"Good-bye. Thank you for having me."

"Thank you for a lovely party."

Geraldine and Elaine set off with a small band of children and mothers. Elaine's mood of excitement still upheld her. She ran ahead with the other children, scuffling, giggling, interspersing challenges and defiances with reminiscences of the party.

"I found my treasure in the treasure hunt before anyone else," she said, her voice high-pitched and unsteady with laughter.

"Oo, Elaine! You didn't!"

"I did."

"Oo, you didn't!" chorused the other children.

"I did. I did," cried Elaine; "and I was first in the musical chairs and first in the egg-and-spoon race."

"Oo, you weren't!"

"I was," laughed Elaine, "and I brought carrots out of a hat like the conjurer."

"You didn't. We all tried and we couldn't."

"I could," said Elaine, her voice fading away into giggles. "And I turned a handkerchief into coloured paper like he did."

"You didn't."

"I did. If you say I didn't again, David John, I'll push you into the ditch."

"You didn't."

"Oo! She's pushed David John into the ditch!"

"Elaine!"

"I didn't. There isn't any water in, anyway. He fell himself." David John climbed out of the ditch and sat on the bank laughing helplessly. The girl who was his mother pulled him to his feet and brushed the dust from his coat. She, too, was laughing. Only Geraldine was grave.

"They've all gone quite mad, haven't they?"

"They always do after a party."

"Now come along, children, and try to be sensible."

"How's your mother, Gerry?"

"She's better to-day, thank you."

"When is she going into hospital?"

"In about a fortnight."

"What's going to happen to Elaine?"

"I think she's going to Appleton Vicarage, where I went when mummy had her."

"Oh, yes. The wife writes, doesn't she?"

"Wonderful stuff. It has to be seen to be believed."

They had reached the cross-roads now and the groups split up, going their various ways.

Geraldine and Elaine walked together down a road over which chestnut trees were just unfolding soft green fingers. Elaine, her wildness gone, slipped her hand into Geraldine's and walked along with her, taking short dancing steps, chattering about the party. Peace descended again on Geraldine's spirit. It had been torment to share Elaine with those silly giggling children. But now she belonged to her again . . . to her alone.

"I told them you'd helped to make my frock, Gerry," said Elaine, throwing Geraldine a soft calculating glance from her blue eyes. She was little more than a baby, but she had learnt to propitiate Geraldine, to ward off the dark brooding moods that sometimes seized her, to satisfy the hunger that seemed at times to feed on her childish soul . . . It was like throwing tit-bits to a monster that would otherwise have devoured her.

"Did you, darling?" said Geraldine, her voice tremulous with happiness.

"And I told them what lovely stories you told me when you put me to bed."

Geraldine's spirits soared upward. She didn't care whether "they" knew that she had made the frock or told lovely stories to Elaine at bedtime. What she did care about was that Elaine had thought about her at the party, that the impression of indifference given by that careless wave of the hand had been a wrong one.

To herself Elaine was saying: Well, I might have said it. I said a lot of things. I can't be sure I *didn't* say it. You forget what you've said . . .

Albert was at the gate waiting for them. He walked up to the door, the two children on either side of him, holding a hand of each.

"Mummy's resting," he said. "She had a little attack of pain while you were out. Not a bad one, but I thought she'd better rest. Gerry will put you to bed, Elly darling, and mummy will come and see you when she's better. Did you have a nice party?"

"Lovely!" said Elaine, beginning to hop upstairs on one leg, holding on to the banisters. "And it's going to be my birthday soon and mummy said I could choose what I liked to do on it, and I'm going to have a party. I'm going to have"—a hop accompanied each name—"Tony . . . and Diane . . . and David John . . . and Judy . . . and Douglas . . . and Pamela and—"

"Run along now, darling, and don't make a noise," said Albert, watching the two with a smile as they disappeared round the bend of the staircase.

With deft loving movements, Geraldine took off the little garments, washed the hot sticky face and hands, brushed out the silky curls and slipped on the crisp white nightgown.

"God bless mummy and daddy and Gerry." Again the blue eyes shot a quick calculating glance at Geraldine's grave face. "Bless Gerry heaps and *heaps.*"

She snuggled down between the sheets. Geraldine knelt by the bed, her eyes fixed on the small delicate face.

"Read to me, Gerry. Read me a story from my comic. It's on the chest of drawers."

"Elly, darling, you didn't find your treasure first or win the games or do those conjuring tricks, did you?"

"No."

"Why did you say you did? It's wicked to tell stories."

"But, Gerry, it wasn't stories. It was just fun."

"Stories are never fun, Elly. Even in fun you must never tell stories. And, Elly . . ."

"Yes?"

"You did push David John into the ditch, didn't you?"

"No, I didn't. Yes, I did . . . I don't know."

"I saw you do it. It makes me terribly unhappy when you tell stories. You're sorry, aren't you, Elly?"

"Yes . . . no . . . I don't think I did push him . . . It doesn't matter."

There was a tired fretful note in the childish voice.

"It does matter, Elly. It matters more than anything else in the world to tell stories. You'll never do it again, will you? Will you promise?"

"Yes."

"Say it. Say, 'I promise Gerry never to tell stories again.' "

"I promise Gerry never to tell stories again."

"That's all right, darling. And if ever you break it, you'll tell me, won't you?"

"Yes . . . It was a lovely party, wasn't it?" Elaine sat up in bed, her eyes shining with excitement. "I'm going to have a party on my birthday. I'm going to have everyone who was there this afternoon. I'm going to have Tony and Diana and David John and—"

"Elly . . ."

"Yes?"

"Listen . . . Don't have a party on your birthday. If you don't have a party I'll do just what you like all day. I'll play with you and read to you and—do just what you want me to do. I promise I will if you'll promise not to have a party."

The childish lips pouted.

"Mummy said I could choose what I liked for my birthday."

"Choose me, Elly," pleaded Geraldine. "Elly, do choose me. Don't choose a party. I'll be your slave all day long, if you'll promise not to choose a party. We'll have such fun—just the two of us. We'll play all the games you like. Will you?"

The urgency in the voice seemed to beat down the child's resistance.

"All right," she said listlessly.

"You've promised, haven't you?"

"Yes."

"Oh, Elly, you darling! I'll buy you that doll you wanted. I'll spend all the money I've got on presents for you. We'll have a lovely birthday cake with candles on and we'll have games and dress up and act . . . and I'll lend you my new paint-box and you can paint in any of my books you want to . . . You'll like it better than a party, won't you? . . . won't you, Elly?"

"Y-yes . . . Will you read to me now, Gerry? Out of my comic?" Generally Geraldine discouraged reading from the comic, because she wanted Elaine to get on quickly with the list of Children's Best Books, but she went now without demur and fetched the comic from the chest of drawers. Then she put it on the chair and flung herself again on the floor by the bed, drawing the little figure into her arms.

"Oh, Elly," she said in a choking voice, "I do love you so . . . You do love me, don't you? . . . Say you love me."

The child threw her arms round Geraldine's neck in an access of genuine affection.

"Yes, I do. I do . . . I do love you, Gerry."

Chapter Fifteen

Downstairs Albert stood in the little sitting-room, reading a letter that had come by the evening's post.

"They can't take her at the Vicarage," he said.

Grace lay on the sofa, her eyes closed. The attack of pain had passed, leaving her exhausted. Her cheekbones stood out sharply over her sunken cheeks.

"I wonder . . ." said Albert thoughtfully.

"Yes?"

The word seemed to be dragged from her by an effort.

"I don't want to worry you about it now, darling, but—I wondered if the best thing wouldn't be to send her to boarding-school. Just for the term, anyway. And, if she settles, she might stay there. You'll have to take things easy for a long time after the operation. Do you think it would be a good plan?"

"Perhaps."

"We could afford it now I've had that rise. And, with Gerry, she wouldn't feel homesick."

Grace sat up, shocked out of her lethargy. Her eyes were bright, and she spoke in a quick breathless voice.

"Not with Gerry! Not to Gerry's school! She can go to boarding-school, but not with Gerry."

He stared at her.

"But why not, dear?"

"Gerry's bad for her."

He could hardly believe that he had heard the words aright.

"*Gerry! Bad* for her!"

She put up a thin hand and pushed back the hair that was falling into her eyes.

"I've never talked to you about it before. I didn't think it would be any use, but—Gerry *is* bad for her. She worries her. She makes her sly and deceitful."

He still couldn't believe that he had heard her aright.

"Gerry! Gerry make her *sly!* Why, darling, Gerry's the most conscientious little person possible."

"I know. That's why she makes her sly." She lay back again on her cushions. "I know you won't believe it."

He was silent for a few moments, then said:

"I'll do what you think best. I'm sure you're mistaken, but—well, we'll say another boarding-school. I'll go and tell Gerry about it now, shall I? She ought to be the first person to know what we've decided. I'll say that we want Elaine to learn to be independent . . . Are you quite comfortable, darling?"

"Yes, thank you."

He went slowly upstairs.

"Gerry!"

Gerry came out of Elaine's room.

"I've read to her and tucked her up," she said. "She'll soon go off to sleep now."

"Come into your bedroom a moment, dear. I want to speak to you."

They sat down side by side on the little bed with "Gerry" carved on the headpiece.

"Now listen, darling. They can't have Elaine at the Vicarage, after all, so mummy and I have decided to send her away to boarding-school."

Geraldine's face shone as if a lamp had been lit behind it.

"Oh, yes!" she said eagerly.

"But—not St. Julian's, dear."

The light died away, leaving her face so pale and empty that it might have been carved in stone. She sat for a moment without moving, then:

"Not St. Julian's?" she said in a whisper.

"No, dear. You see, we want her to grow up to be independent. We . . ."

His voice trailed away. For the first time in his dealings with the child he felt out of his depths and, curiously, a little afraid. He was dimly aware of something beyond his understanding, something dark and twisted and tormented in the immature childish body. She's only a little girl, he reassured himself. I'm imagining it. She's always been so good and obedient. She'll do as she's told if I explain.

"You see, dear, if you're always there to help her, she'll never learn to stand on her own feet. And she'd be a responsibility to you. It's much better that you should go to different schools."

She wasn't listening to him or looking at him. She was staring in front of her, her face still set and stony.

"She must come to St. Julian's with me. I'd rather she died than didn't come to St. Julian's with me."

Her voice was low and even, but something in it sent a chill through him.

"*Gerry!*"

She turned her eyes to him. There was a blank empty look in them.

"I'll go wherever you send her," she said slowly. "You can't stop me. I'll just go. I don't care what you do to me. I'll just go wherever you send her. If you fetch me away I'll go back and back and back. I won't let you take her from me. I won't let anyone take her from me."

"Listen, Gerry—" he began.

But she didn't listen. He repeated his arguments and she waited till he had finished then repeated stonily:

"I won't let you take her from me. I'll go wherever she goes."

He went downstairs to the sitting-room. Grace lay there where he had left her, her eyes closed, her face a pallid mask.

He sat by her and took one of her hands. Though he would not have admitted it, he felt shaken by the scene upstairs. To himself he was saying: It would be unkind to separate them. Poor little Gerry was so upset at the thought . . . But he knew in his heart that lie had met something so strong, so ruthless, that he had quailed before it.

"I—I thought perhaps we'd better reconsider it, dear," he said. "Poor little Gerry was so distressed at the thought of Elaine's going to a different school that I promised to talk it over with you again."

Grace opened her eyes, fixed them on him for a few moments, then closed them again.

"It's all right," she said. "I don't mind what you do."

"You'll agree to Elaine's going to St. Julian?"

"Yes. The harm's probably done already."

He looked at her uncomprehendingly.

"Harm? What harm?"

She did not answer, and he said solicitously:

"Darling, I don't want to do anything against your wishes."

"It's all right."

"May I tell Gerry, then?"

"Yes."

He bent over her and kissed her.

"Grace . . . do you really feel that we oughtn't to do this?"

"It's all right."

"Another thing that's occurred to me"—he was anxious to justify himself—"was that, if she goes to St. Julian's, they'll make a reduction in the fees. They do for sisters."

She smiled at him, pressing his hand in hers.

"It's all right, Albert. Don't worry."

"I'll go and tell her, then. She was—rather wrought up, poor little thing!"

Geraldine was standing half-way upstairs, waiting . . . Her face seemed to have shrunk. There was a pinched drawn look about it. It's absurd, he told himself uneasily. She's only a child. She can't—care as much as that. It's some trick of the light and shade that makes her look like that.

"It's all right, Gerry," he said cheerfully, taking her back into her bedroom. "Mummy says it will be all right for Elaine to go to St. Julian's."

Life leapt into her face, but there was still the shadow of anxiety in the dark eyes.

"Will you write the letter to St. Julian's now?" she said in a voice that broke into short gasps as if she were breathless from running. "Then I'll go out and post it. Something might happen to stop you if you don't write it now. Please write it now."

He smiled reassuringly.

"Very well," he said; "then we'll do the entry in the Weather and Events Diary, shall we? I'll have it all ready."

He drew a sigh of relief as he spoke. Everything was normal again. She'd been a bit upset, but it was all right now. She was his little girl again, his Gerry.

She had almost reached the pillarbox when she saw the tall thin boy cycling slowly down the road, and he was almost level with her before she saw that it was Philip. He dismounted and stood looking at her, with a defensive frown on his face.

"Hello," he said.

"Hello."

He didn't quite know what had brought him here, but ever since he had sprained his ankle and had lain on the settee at the Vicarage with throbbing head and aching foot the vision had remained with him—the vision of a gentle, consoling, ministering presence—and he had decided on a sudden impulse to find the road in which she lived. He hadn't meant to go to her house or try to see her. He hadn't meant to do anything but cycle slowly down the road, to look at the house and, perhaps, catch a glimpse of her in the garden or through one of the windows.

Stephen and his father had gone into the woods shooting, and he was once more spending the day alone with his stepmother. Their relations had settled down to normal again—Philip hiding behind his defences, Ann so anxious not to invade his privacy or force his confidence that she, too, seemed to be hiding behind her defences. On the afternoon of his ill-fated flight from home she had been worried about the poem that she had put on his writing-table. He might wonder how it had come to be in just that place,

186

might even suspect her of prying about his room. So the next morning, as he lay on the settee, his bandaged foot on a cushion, she had said carelessly: "Oh, Philip, I found a piece of paper on the landing outside your room yesterday and I put it on your writing-table. I thought it might have been blown from there. I don't know whether it was anything you wanted."

He had thrown her a bright guarded glance.

"Oh, yes," he had said casually. "Some old thing I'd copied out from somewhere. Thanks."

And he had felt a fierce relief that he had not, after all, delivered himself into her hands, that he had kept inviolate that aloneness, that singleness of soul that had become the pivot of his being. But his loneliness persisted, and the memory of Geraldine—warm, loving, consoling—continued to haunt him. He found himself searching for an excuse to visit Minster Road, and, consulting the local map, discovered that it might by a slight stretch be regarded as a short cut from Maybridge Public Library to Penbury Road. He felt that just to see her, just to know where she lived, would assuage something of the disquiet that possessed his spirit. And here she was, walking sedately along the road, hatless and coatless, holding a letter in her hand.

"I've just been to Maybridge Public Library," he said, pointing to the books on his carrier. "I'm taking a short cut home."

"I'm going to the post," she said.

There was a new deep note in her voice that vaguely offended him. He began to walk by her side, wheeling his cycle.

"Mummy's going to have an operation—"

"I'm sorry," he muttered with perfunctory sympathy.

"—and so Elaine's going to boarding-school with me. She's my little sister. She was at Angela's birthday party. She was quite a baby then. Do you remember her?"

"Yes."

"I haven't seen you since then, have I?"

"No."

"We wanted to send her to the Vicarage, but they couldn't have her . . . Have you been there lately?"

"I was there about three weeks ago. I—I went for a walk in the wood and sprained my ankle and—and went there."

"I'm sorry about your ankle."

"It's all right now, thanks."

"Was Angela there?"

"Yes. And Monica."

"Why was Monica there?"

"I've forgotten."

They were talking in a desultory stilted fashion, each aware of an undercurrent of constraint. He threw furtive glances at her, noticing the swelling mounds of her breasts beneath her jumper, the new lustre of her dark eyes, turning his gaze away from her again in revulsion. She shouldn't have been like this. She should have been small and soft and gentle. He was aware of a sickening sense of disappointment. She shouldn't have been like this.

The conversation dragged on. "Do you like your school?" . . . "When do you go back?" . . . "What games do you play at school?" He answered sullenly in monosyllables, regretful of having come, miserably anxious to get away.

They stood uncertainly at the pillarbox.

"I'll be going now," said Philip.

"Won't you come to tea?" said Geraldine. "I mean, it's after tea-time now, but some other day."

"Thanks," he muttered ungraciously.

"Come on Saturday. I'll ask mummy. It'll be all right."

"I—I can't on Saturday."

"Why not?" she persisted.

"We've got people coming over for the week-end."

"Who?"

"Some friends of my father's."

"They won't mind if you go out to tea. What time are they coming?"

"By the six-thirty."

"You could be back by then."

"There are—things to do before they come."

"There's your father and mother and Stephen to see to them."

He turned on her with rising exasperation. She was different from his memories of her, yet he knew now, despairingly, that she had always been like this. He felt angry and cheated.

"I don't want to come," he said shortly. He saw the hurt in her eyes and went on, taking a savage delight in punishing her, "You won't leave people alone. You go on and on . . . You were always like that. That was why I hated you."

She caught her breath.

"Why are you being so horrid?" she said. "I thought you were going to be nice. You came because you wanted me. You must have done."

The colour flamed into his face.

"I didn't," he said, stammering with anger. "I didn't."

Then he mounted his bicycle and rode off. She stood and watched him till he was out of sight. He didn't look back. She dropped the letter into the pillarbox and still stood there, her eyes fixed on the point where he had turned into the main road. For a moment she thought that she was going to cry, but she gulped back her tears and began to walk slowly down the road towards home and the Diary of Weather and Events.

Chapter Sixteen

When Monica woke, sunshine was pouring into the little bedroom, shining on the polished surface of the chest of drawers, the glass top of the dressing-table and the porcelain hand-basin. Sitting up in bed and looking out of the window she saw the blue shimmering line of the sea against the sky.

She had never slept in a bedroom like this before, never had a bedroom that belonged to herself entirely and that wasn't cluttered up with other people's possessions. She did not, of course, presume on the relationship. She treated it with diffidence, even with something of apology, careful always to make no demands on it. Everything she had was packed neatly away in the drawers. To leave even a book or a work-case about would seem to her in some way to partake of the insolence that brings Nemesis in its train. Even her bedroom slippers she was careful to keep so far under the bed that no one, opening the door, would see them. Every morning she packed sponge, flannel and toothbrush into her sponge-bag and put it into the small cupboard that hung over the hand-basin.

When she was not in it the little room showed no signs of occupation at all. That was the sop she threw to the Cerberus of Fate that seemed always to be lurking in the shadows, ready to spring out at her. "I'm hardly here at all really," she seemed to be saying, "so please don't turn me out." She knew, of course, that she was only here while Babs was hostess of the hotel and as long as no one else needed the room. Shyly, timidly, she existed on the fringe of it, staking no claim, hoping only not to be noticed.

She lay there for a few minutes, luxuriating in the comfort of the bed and the warm sunshine. Then she began to think about Stephen. She started every day by thinking about Stephen . . . going over in her mind every moment of their meeting at the Vicarage, when he and his father had come to fetch Philip home. He had carried the books up to the schoolroom for her and had helped her put them into the shelves. Then he had taken up her copy of *Uncle Remus* and had stood looking at the fly-leaf, on which was written: Monica Patterson, on her fifth birthday, with love from her father. June 2nd, 1921—all that remained to her of the father she hardly remembered.

"They're grand yarns, aren't they?" he said. "I knew them almost by heart when I was a kid."

He had put the book with the others in the shelves and turned to her with a smile.

"I expect you've had about enough of this place by now, haven't you?" he had said.

She had said nothing, because she could think of nothing to say.

"I mean, you'll be glad to get home," he said.

She had a sudden vision of what he meant by "home" . . . Friendly rooms, littered with people's belongings . . . a tennis-court . . . deck-chairs stacked in a corner of the verandah . . . a place where people laughed and teased each other and quarrelled, but always ended by laughing.

"Yes," she said, because she must make some reply.

He threw her a quick glance, as if sensing something of the world—dark and formless—in which she wandered.

"Perhaps . . ." he began, then stopped. "Look," he went on. "Come over and see us sometime. You'd like my mother."

For a moment she could not speak, then:

"Thank you," she said, "but I think I shall be going home quite soon now."

And the next day there had come a letter from Babs, arranging for Monica to join her at the hotel.

He had said so little—the conversation had lasted only a minute or two—but what remained with her was the memory of a deep kindliness and a new pride. Because Stephen had looked at her like that, spoken to her like that, she could never be quite as she had been before.

She got out of bed, washed and dressed, giving her reflection a final critical survey in the mirror—the pale oval face and the straight dark hair, hanging in two long plaits . . . the washed-out cotton frock that was too small for her, pulling across her small immature breasts and scarcely reaching her knees . . . the long slender bare legs and worn-out sandals. Then, having removed every trace of her presence from the room, as a criminal might have removed the evidences of his crime, she went down the passage to her mother's room.

If Monica's bedroom showed a total lack of personality, her mother's showed an excess of it. Dresses were flung over chairs, shoes lay anyhow about the floor; the dressing-table was littered with expensive toilet jars and bottles; a pale blue satin dressing-gown trailed over the end of the bed; one blue satin fur-lined mule lay beneath it, the other was in the fender. Babs stood at the dressing-table, giving deft swift last-minute touches to her hair. She wore a tailored dress of fine grey jersey cloth with a short coat to match. She turned and smiled at Monica as she entered.

"Hello, darling," she said, "had a good night?"

"Yes, thank you," said Monica.

She went over to the window and stood looking out . . . The hotel garden ran down to the edge of the cliff and beyond that was the shimmering expanse of the sea. A liner—tiny, toy-like—could be seen on the far horizon. The white sails of the fishing-boats were like fallen petals.

"Look at me, darling," said Babs; "have I got too much make-up on for this blasted hostess job?"

Monica turned her gaze to her mother's face. The bright morning sunshine showed its beauty slightly—very slightly—blurred. Still lovely, it had on it the first faint signs of the slow process of coarsening. The once exquisite lines of cheek and jaw sagged a little. A hint of bravado—almost of brazenness—had replaced the lazy laughter of the blue eyes. But only a critical observer would have noticed this, and Monica was no critical observer.

"You look beautiful," she said simply.

Babs laughed, then drew her brows into a frown as she considered her daughter.

"I ought to buy you some clothes, oughtn't I, darling?" she said with sudden compunction. She glanced down at the grey dress. "I oughtn't to have bought this. It was a model and cost the earth, and I didn't really need it. I wish I could stop spending money . . . I don't actually seem to spend it. It just goes. I never have any. Fred's allowance hardly keeps me in hats, and this job hardly keeps me in shoes. It makes life so complicated." She came to the window and put her arm across Monica's shoulder. "You like the place, don't you, pet?"

"Yes."

Babs shrugged.

"It would be all right if it weren't for the bitch who runs it. Manageress!" She gave a short scornful laugh. "Slave-driver's what she ought to be called."

"She's been nice to me," said Monica timidly.

"Oh, she's as cunning as the devil. She can turn on the blarney when she wants to. Of course, the whole thing is only temporary." She went back to the dressing-table and considered her reflection, running a finger over her smooth plucked eyebrows, then continued casually, "I might marry again . . ."

Monica wheeled round from the window with a catch of her breath. Whenever one began to feel—safe, some dark threatening shape would appear in the distance.

"Oh, no one in particular," said Babs, answering the question in her daughter's eyes. "I could marry anyone I wanted to, you know. Peter let me down pretty badly. He said that when Fred divorced me he'd get his wife to divorce him, and then he said she wouldn't. Maybe she wouldn't, but it seemed a bit fishy to me. Anyway, you couldn't see him for dust, once Fred started the suit." She unstopped a bottle and drew a brush of red varnish carefully over each nail. "What about Major Elliott? Would you like him for a stepfather?"

Monica, who had begun to put the room to rights, stopped and stood motionless, holding the lace-trimmed *crêpe-de-Chine* nightdress that she was folding.

Major Elliott . . . tall, lean, hatchet-faced . . . mahogany complexion . . . rasping voice . . . long mouth . . . hooked nose . . . general air of wealth and authority.

"He hasn't actually proposed," went on Babs, without waiting for an answer, "but he's gone as near as he could without actually saying the words. I'd only have to raise my little finger." Again she paused to examine her reflection. "Tell me, darling, do you think this lipstick's too purple? It's a new kind. It ought to be all right. It cost enough."

"It's lovely," said Monica, throwing it a cursory glance between hanging up the dressing-gown and turning back the bedclothes.

"There's old Mr. Ferguson, of course . . . He's very attentive and rolling in money, but"—the gay laugh rang out again—"I don't think it's marriage *he's* after."

A faint shudder ran through Monica's frame. Old Mr. Ferguson, small and wizened . . . face crossed and recrossed by innumerable tiny lines . . . sagging red-rimmed eyelids . . . shining bald head with fringe of thin white hair, tufts of white hair on the receding chin . . . pale blue eyes, leering and bleary . . . hands like claws.

"No, ducky, it's all right," laughed Babs. "Don't look so scared. I wouldn't inflict him on you—or myself. He might be useful, though. We must be nice to him. We must be nice to everyone. That's the devil of it, isn't it? . . . No, I couldn't stand it for long." There was a short silence, then she went on: "Monny, I'd love to start again. Start fresh, I mean, without debts and bills. I'd love to be a real mother to you and buy you lovely clothes and give you a lovely time and send you to a good school. You know"—the old air of wistfulness came over the lovely face—"I've never really had a chance."

The colour flamed into Monica's cheeks and receded, leaving them very pale. She went over to her mother.

"You mustn't feel like that—about me, I mean. I love you. I'll always love you. I don't want—things. I want just you and me.

You mustn't ever bother about me. That's the only thing I couldn't bear, for you to bother about me."

Babs wheeled round to her, laughing.

"You are a pet," she said. "I can't be as bad as people make out, or you wouldn't be as nice as you are . . . And now, I suppose, we ought to go down to breakfast."

She replaced the tops on the toilet jars, humming a jaunty little air. She felt pleased with herself. Monny was so grateful that she felt as if she'd actually done all the things she'd spoken of—given her lovely clothes and a lovely time and sent her to a good school. A warm feeling of complacency possessed her. Monny was a dear, well worth all the sacrifices one made for her. She put her arm round Monica's shoulders.

"Come along, darling," she said, and together they went down the corridor towards the lift.

Beach Hotel had been converted—and well converted—from a rambling old house on the cliffs. It was about three miles distant from the seaside town of Seaborough and drew its clients from the ranks of the quiet, the respectable, and, inevitably, the moneyed, for visitors were expected to pay heavily for its atmosphere of unobtrusive comfort. Down in Seaborough the Grand and the Metropole might flaunt their *thés dansant* and dinner dances with spotlights and flood-lighting and American bars. The Beach Hotel was only too glad for them to attract the less desirable of the visitors and leave the long spreading house on the cliff to the "best people", who went there year after year with unfailing regularity.

Babs had acted her part efficiently at the interview, displaying a quiet well-bred charm, but during the three weeks since she had joined the staff as hostess relations between her and the manageress had become more and more strained. Babs' friends seemed always to be staying at the Grand or the Metropole and they would invade the Beach Hotel in noisy crowds, filling the sedate little bar or bearing her off to the more congenial atmosphere of their own hotels.

The table assigned to her and Monica was a small round table in a corner of the dining-room behind the door. In the opposite corner sat Miss Chesham, the manageress. She was a woman of about fifty, with well-dressed grey hair and a pale regular-featured face. She looked capable, tired, kind and a little disdainful. There was a weary keenness in the hazel eyes. In one quick glance they would see everything that could be seen, then move on casually as if they had noticed nothing. The one quick glance she sent Babs and Monica as they entered the dining-room took in the new expensive grey toilette, the elaborateness of the make-up, the child's washed-out frock and shabby sandals.

"Good morning, Mrs. Deverel," she said. "Good morning, Monica." She gathered up her letters and went towards the door, stopping at their table to say, "Perhaps you'll look in at my office when you've finished breakfast, Mrs. Deverel, and we can discuss the plans for the day."

"Plans for the day!" groaned Babs when the door had closed on her. "I'd like just a moment to myself sometimes." Her volatile spirits had sunk. She pushed her plate from her. "This place takes one's appetite away."

Two old ladies entered, smiled a greeting at her as they passed, and went to their table by the window. They were two widowed twin sisters, short, fat and exactly alike. They dressed and did their hair in the same fashion and spent every minute of every day in each other's company. Both had pleasant wedge-like faces with thin beaky noses and chins that faded almost imperceptibly into their necks. They spent every summer—with car, chauffeur and lady's maid—at the Beach Hotel.

"Well, that finishes it," said Babs. "How can one be expected to eat in this Chamber of Horrors? I think I've got into the wrong place; don't you, darling?"

"Perhaps," said Monica uncertainly.

"I ought to be at a hotel like the Grand or the Metropole. I could hostess one of those all right. I'm wasted in a museum like this. Toots said so last night. He's staying at the Grand, you know, and I asked him to try to get me a job there. He said he'd try but didn't seem to think it could be done. I don't know why . . ." She took up a piece of toast then put it down again untasted.

"Do eat something," pleaded Monica. "You're getting so thin."
Babs laughed.

"Yes, Duggy called me a walking skeleton last night. I can only eat in the right surroundings. I've always been like that. This mausoleum is getting me down . . . Good lord!"

Lady Miriam Endersleigh was entering the dining-room. She was a tall elderly woman with untidy grey hair, a cadaverous face, pouched eyes and a bewildered, almost distraught expression. The effect of her well-cut coat and skirt was spoilt by a fussy evening blouse and collection of ill-assorted jewellery.

Lady Miriam Endersleigh was what is known as "simple" and had been bequeathed by her brother, together with a considerable amount of other property, to her eldest nephew, a peer who was well known in sporting and political circles. Each summer he deposited his "heirloom" (as he called her) at the Beach Hotel for several months, giving himself and his family a welcome respite from her.

The poor lady's eccentricities were harmless enough, consisting chiefly in a continual recital of the events of her childhood, the only part of her life that seemed to have made any impression on her, but she had a shrill monotonous voice and a habit of fidgeting with her jewellery that could in time wear down the strongest nerves.

She took her seat now at the table next the twins' and her penetrating voice filled the room.

"Kippers . . . they're really herrings, aren't they? . . . Or are they mackerel? We used to find mussels in the rocks when we were children, but we weren't allowed to eat them because there was always an R in the month."

Babs rose from the table.

'I can't stand any more of this, Monny. Come along."

Monica left her egg half eaten and followed her mother into the hall.

The receptionist handed her a small sheaf of envelopes.

"Your mail, Mrs. Deverel."

Babs lit a cigarette and stood turning them over.

"Bills," she said carelessly. "I can't face them this morning."

She tore them up and threw them into the waste-paper basket without opening them.

A gardener crossed the hall with a basket of flowers—tulips, polyanthus, lilies-of-the-valley, and sprays of lilac and cherry blossom.

"You'll be doing the flowers this morning, won't you, Mrs. Deverel?" he said.

"Yes, I suppose so," said Babs. "Put them in the flower-room."

Guests were pouring from the lift and staircase and making their way to the dining-room.

"Hello, Monica."

"Hello."

The children were friendly and ready to accept Monica with the freemasonry of childhood, but Monica avoided them with the old instinctive shrinking. She was still a child without the right to childhood.

Major Elliott stopped to speak to Babs in the hall, and old Mr. Ferguson joined them. A young man with a high forehead, aquiline nose and small girlish mouth, who had arrived last night, came up and hovered on the outskirts of the group, obviously eager to make himself part of it.

The office door opened and Miss Chesham came out.

"Could you spare me a moment, Mrs. Deverel?" she said.

She went back to the office, and Babs made a little *moue* at the door before she obeyed the summons.

"Her master's voice," she said with a ripple of laughter.

The flower-room was a small pantry just beyond the green baize door that shut off the kitchen regions. A sink with taps ran along the wall at one side, and on a table in the middle were the bowls and vases waiting to be filled and the flowers that the gardener had brought in. There Babs and Monica set to work as soon as Miss Chesham had gone over with Babs the mild forms of amusement that constituted the Saturday night attractions at the Beach Hotel.

"Ping-pong!" said Babs bitterly, ramming a handful of lilies-of-the-valley into a vase. "What does she think I am? A nursery-maid?"

Then the page called her to the telephone, and Monica was left to arrange the flowers alone.

The window of the room opened on to the garden, and as she worked she could see people sitting on deck-chairs in the shade of the trees or standing about in groups, discussing their plans for the day. Two games of tennis were already in progress. Some children were playing with a nondescript puppy, laughing at its antics, running round the lawn, throwing sticks for it. At the other side of the hotel people would be going down the wooden staircase to the beach. A feeling of peace filled her heart. Her hands moved slowly and dreamily among the flowers. And the thought of Stephen—never far away—came so near that he seemed to be in the room with her, part of the colour and warmth and fragrance. She put long sprays of lilac into a tall cut-glass vase with lingering touches that were almost a caress, burying her face in the sweet-smelling blooms. The shorter sprays she put into squat bowls with the tulips, and the lilies-of-the-valley into little vases by themselves. The room seemed to fade away as she withdrew into her memories . . . There had been a lilac tree by the Vicarage gate and beneath it lilies-of-the-valley had spread like a green carpet.

The door opened and Babs came in. Her eyes were starry with excitement, her lips curved into a happy smile.

"That was Duggie," she said. "He wants to come along and take me over to the Grand for a drink. I said, 'Take me anywhere out of this god-forsaken hole' . . . Oh, darling, you've done them beautifully. You're a clever little thing. Look! Duggie's going up to London on Thursday by car, and I'm going to take my free day then and go with him. I want a new evening dress."

"But—" began Monica and stopped.

"That thing I bought last week?" said Babs. She gave a gay breathless laugh. "It's got 'Seaborough' written all over it. I was crazy to buy it. It cost the earth, too, didn't it? Look, pet. Clothes are a sort of investment. You've got to be turned out well, if you mean to get anywhere. This job might lead to anything, but I must have the right clothes. You do see, don't you?"

"Yes," said Monica.

"I'll go to Madam Roche. She always lets me have things on tick. And I'll get some clothes for you. I really will, darling. I know you need them. There must be places where I can get them on tick . . . We're going to have lunch at the Berkeley, and go to a dance in the evening. I deserve a break, don't I, pet? I've worked like a nigger in this damned hole . . . Now let me give you a hand." Absently she took up a handful of polyanthus and put them down again. "I'm in the wrong place here, you know. It doesn't give me scope. It's too stuffy. Now in a place like the Grand . . ."

The door opened, and a young man entered. He wore grey flannel trousers and a rather horsey sports jacket. A well-formed mouth and chin under a tip-tilted nose and small close-set eyes made it appear as if the wrong halves of two faces had been put together. An air of genial good-fellowship encompassed him. He was obviously many years younger than Babs.

"Duggie darling!" cried Babs. "You haven't wasted much time."

"Time," said Duggie, "was not given us to waste." He looked at the flower-strewn table. "You needn't go on messing about with this muck, need you? All the crowd's there waiting for you."

"Oh, Duggie, how marvellous! And if anyone ever needed a drink it's me now . . . Monny, sweet, you can finish them, can't you? You're wonderful at this job. Much better than I am. You know where they all go, don't you?"

"Yes, these for the hall, and these for the dining-room, and the others for the lounge."

"Isn't she clever, Duggie? I won't be away long, darling. I'll just have a drink with the crowd and fly back. After all, I'm entitled to a break in the middle of the morning. Even a kitchen-maid's allowed her elevenses."

"Come along and stop talking," laughed Duggie. "I've got the car. You won't need a hat. 'Bye, kid."

Later in the morning, when Miss Chesham looked into the flower-room, Monica was putting the last touches to the rows of bowls and vases. Miss Chesham stood for a moment in the doorway, watching the small pale face, framed by the dark hanging plaits, bending absorbedly over the flowers. Her eyes travelled down the slender body in the tight cotton frock to the shabby sandals.

"Where's your mother, dear?" she said, advancing into the room. She spoke kindly. Beneath her shell of rather chilly aloofness she was a tender-hearted woman, and the air of neglect about the child filled her with mingled compassion and anger. Fear had leapt into Monica's dark eyes.

"She's just gone out," she said breathlessly. "She won't be away long. She's only just gone out for a minute or two."

"I see." Miss Chesham sat down on the chair at the table. "Do you know if she's made arrangements for the ping-pong tournament to-night?"

"I think so . . . Yes, I think she has."

"There's the bridge to be arranged, too. I suppose she's got it in hand?"

"Yes . . . Yes, I'm sure she has."

"Did anyone bring you milk or something at eleven?"

"No . . . I—I don't want any."

"Come to my office. There's some milk there, and I have some chocolate biscuits."

"No . . . No, thank you . . . Honestly, I don't want anything." She recoiled from this woman's kindness, because with it, she knew, went condemnation of her mother. That sort of kindness came her way too often. It hurt her far more than any unkindness could have done. She took up a heavy stone jar filled with cherry blossom.

"You're not going to carry that by yourself?" said Miss Chesham.

"Yes It's easy . . . I'm strong."

"Let me give you a hand."

"No . . . No, please . . . Please let me."

The child's distress at the thought of failing to carry out her mother's duties was pitiful. Miss Chesham shrugged and returned to her office. One couldn't do anything for her. Her pride and loyalty formed an impassable gulf, cutting her off from any help one might have given her.

When she had carried the last vase to its place on the last dining-room table Monica went to the notice-board. There was a list of entrants for the ping-pong tournament and a list of people who wanted to play bridge. She hesitated for a few moments, then unpinned the list of bridge players and took it to her mother's bedroom. On the writing-table was a small stack of empty name cards. She could at least copy out the names ready to be put on the bridge-tables. She had an unhappy suspicion that her mother had given no thought either to the ping-pong tournament or to the bridge. She sat down and began to copy the names in her neat schoolgirl handwriting.

Babs did not return till shortly before lunch. Duggie dropped her at the front door, and she entered the lounge alone. She looked flushed and bright-eyed. Monica, sitting on the window-seat with a bound volume of *Chambers's Journal* that she had found in the bookshelves, looked up with a smile that was wary and constrained. Babs hadn't had too much to drink, but she'd had quite enough. She waved to Monica and crossed the room to where Major Elliott sat at a table alone. He rose as she approached.

"Have a drink, Mrs. Deverel?"

She laughed—a gay harsh edgy laugh that set Monica's heart beating rapidly.

"Don't you think I've had enough?" she said, sitting down with him.

"Certainly not . . . What's it to be? Gin?"

"Thanks. I think it's gin I've been having—mostly. My memory is almost as mixed as my drinks."

He ordered her a gin . . . then another . . . then another. Her laughter grew more frequent. Her voice grew louder as she talked to him. Monica heard the words: "If it wasn't for the kid, of course . . . The kid's always been a millstone round my neck." She wasn't hurt. It had never occurred to her to look on herself as anything but a millstone round her mother's neck. The room began to fill as people came in for lunch. Monica pretended to be absorbed in her book, but she was aware—aware acutely and in every nerve—of all that affected the lovely figure in grey sitting at the table with

Major Elliott. She caught the wink that Major Elliott sent a man who passed the table. Child as she was, she had noticed a subtle difference in the way men treated her mother now, compared with the way they used to treat her. They still flocked round her, but there was a touch of amused contempt in their manner nowadays. A group near Monica talked in lowered voices. "Poor kid," she heard and "Dreadful woman." Words like that didn't make her angry any longer. She had learnt to refuse them admittance to her mind. Looking at Babs, she felt a burning protective tenderness, as if she were the adult and Babs the child.

"Sorry I was in the dumps this morning, darling," said Babs, as they sat down at their table for lunch. "I'm on top of the world now. I had a marvellous time with the crowd, and I'm going out for a drive with Major Elliott this afternoon."

"The—the ping-pong tournament?" said Monica tentatively.

"I'll be back in time to see about that," said Babs. "We shan't be out long . . . Look, darling . . ."

"Yes?"

"Will you be an angel and do something for me this afternoon?"

"Of course."

"Well, nearly everything I've got needs pressing and brushing and you might run over the collars and things with the cleaning stuff. You know where everything is, don't you?"

"Yes."

"And when you've done that, get out into the sunshine, dear. I want my baby to enjoy being here and have a good time."

Miss Chesham came up to their table.

"You've got the arrangements in hand for this evening, haven't you, Mrs. Deverel?"

"Oh, yes," said Babs. "There's no need for you to worry about that, Miss Chesham. It's my job, after all, isn't it?"

There was a subtle insolence in voice and manner, and Miss Chesham passed on with heightened colour.

Babs laughed.

"That was naughty of me, wasn't it? But, you know, darling, if you don't stand up to people they don't think anything of you. It doesn't pay to make a doormat of yourself. Duggie said that this morning . . . He's bringing the crowd along this evening to cheer me up. I'll wear the black velvet, I think. The hem wants a stitch. I caught my heel in it the last time I wore it. You'll see to it, will you, sweetheart?"

"Yes, of course," said Monica eagerly.

She didn't finish the various job that Babs had given her till half past three. Then she went downstairs and out into the garden at the front of the hotel. It was empty. Everyone was on the beach or touring the countryside in cars. She was walking towards a group of deck-chairs under a tree when she found Mr. Ferguson beside her. The rheumy, red-rimmed eyes leered at her.

"And what's the little lady going to do this afternoon?" he said.

"I don't know."

"What about clock golf? Would the little lady take pity on an old man and give him a game?"

She walked with him towards the clock golf, trying to conquer her aversion. The sunlight pricked out the white hairs on his chin. There was spittle at the corners of the wrinkled sunken mouth. His eyes wandered over her, noticing the grace of the slender childish figure in the skimpy cotton frock. It was the grace of immaturity, but Mr. Ferguson took a perverted delight in immaturity.

"Do you know, my dear," he said in his rasping tremulous voice, "you're going to be as lovely as your mother?"

She did not answer.

The clock golf course was on the blind side of the house, cut off from the cliff by a wall and from the garden by a clump of trees.

"Have you ever played before?" he said.

She shook her head. There had been clock golf at Angela's birthday party—the first time she had seen Stephen—but she hadn't played.

He chuckled.

"Then you must let the old man teach you. You might be the old man's grand-daughter, you know. He'd be very proud to have a pretty little grand-daughter like you . . . Now here's the club and

204

here's the ball. Stand here, my dear. Hold the club like this . . . No, you're not quite in the right position. Bend over your club so . . ."

The claw-like hands moved about her, furtively fingering the soft young breasts.

"No, you're standing too stiffly. Let grandpa show you . . ."

His hands moved with lingering relish down the long slender thighs. "That's better. Now—"

Monica stood upright. If it hadn't been for Stephen, she would have endured it in silent misery, but, because of Stephen, she couldn't. She threw Mr. Ferguson a glance that, despite the beating of her heart, was cool and assured.

"Please don't touch me any more," she said. "I don't like it."

He gave a chuckle of mingled chagrin and amusement. She put down her golf club and walked back to the hotel. He followed her, whistling between his teeth, then went towards the beach, grinning to himself.

Miss Chesham was in the hall when Monica reached it.

"Monica," she said, "has that old man been annoying you? Because, if he has, I'll pack him off here and now."

"No," said Monica quickly. "No . . . It's all right."

Her heart was pounding in her chest as she ran up to her bedroom.

The "crowd" arrived early. There were only half a dozen, but they seemed to fill the small sedate bar that opened from the lounge. Their voices and laughter seemed to fill the whole hotel.

Lady Miriam entered the lounge, dressed in a trailing evening dress of faded purple, a diamond tiara set askew on a bird's-nest erection of hair. She took her place on a low settee with the twins.

"I think someone must be having a party," she said. "There's a lot of noise. I remember my brother's twenty-first birthday party. They had beef roasted whole and fireworks and a bonfire. I was only child at the time, and I thought it was the Judgement Day."

The twins sat on either side of her, their kind placid wedge-like faces turned to her, listening. A fresh burst of laughter came from the bar. Babs stood in the open doorway, a glass in her hand, surrounded by the "crowd". Her black velvet dress, cunningly moulded to dispense with shoulder-straps, showed off the milky whiteness of her skin and the supple grace of her figure. Her eyes were fixed on the trio who sat on the settee, and she was giving an imitation of them that was evidently excruciatingly funny to her companions. Her eyes flashed into the wildness of Lady Miriam's . . . her chin receded to the angle of the twins'.

Miss Chesham came out of her office and took in the scene with a tightening of her lips. Then the dinner-gong sounded.

"Oh, darling," said Babs, coming up to Monica, "do you mind terribly? I just can't squeeze another seat in at our table. I didn't know that Archie was coming. He turned up at the last minute."

"No," said Monica. "I am rather tired. I'll go to bed now."

"Yes, pet. It'll do you good. I'll try to get something sent up to you." She laughed. "Do look at the Chestnut's face! That's all the thanks I get for bringing custom to her lousy hotel . . . Well, good night, darling. Sleep well."

It was after midnight when Babs came into Monica's bedroom and sat on her bed.

"Are you awake, pet?"

Monica awoke gradually, then sat up with a quick movement of alarm.

"Is anything the matter?" she said.

Moonlight poured through the window on to the slightly—only very slightly—dishevelled figure of Mrs. Deverel.

"No, darling. The crowd's gone and I felt too wide awake to go to bed, so I thought I'd come and have a chat with you."

Monica's gaze searched the figure for the well-known signs. They were all there—the feverish sparkle of the blue eyes, the heightened colour, the whisky-laden breath, the slow deliberation of the slightly blurred speech.

"I've been talking to Archie," she said. "He says I'm wasted here. A shop's the place for me. A shop of my own. Somewhere to give me scope for my gifts. I have got gifts, you know, darling. I've got wonderful taste. Everyone says so. And I've got charm. I could make my fortune in a shop. I might marry, too. I could marry *and* run a shop. Lots of women do."

"You mean—Major Elliott?" said Monica, her eyes dilated by anxiety.

"Not exactly, darling. I thought of him. I know I thought of him. I discussed it with him just now before I came up to bed. I said, 'Why beat about the bush? You're a man of the world, and I'm a woman of the world.' Well, I am, darling, aren't I? I said, 'I need a husband. You need a wife. Don't you think we could make it?' And do you know what he said, darling? He said, 'Nothing doing, my dear.' " She gave a tipsy giggle. " 'Nothing doing, my dear.' Just like that. Frank, but hardly chivalrous . . . That's what I said to him. I said, 'Frank, but hardly chivalrous.' I think he felt rather small. I can be very crushing when I like, you know, darling. 'Frank,' I said, 'but hardly chivalrous' . . . It's just as well, on the whole, because marriage hampers a woman. I've been married twice and I know. Both my husbands hampered me. No, a shop's the thing. A dress shop or a hat shop. Where I won't be hemmed in and bullied as I am here. I should never have come here. It was a great mistake. Listen, darling. Archie knows a man who's staying at the Grand who's got pots and pots of money, and he doesn't see why he shouldn't set me up in a shop. He's going to suggest it to him. As a business proposition, of course. Only as a business proposition. I wouldn't agree to anything but a business proposition . . ."

Monica swallowed. Her throat was dry.

"You mean—you mean, you'll give up this job?"

Again the tipsy giggle floated out into the moonlit room.

"Darling, it's given me up . . . The old bitch gave me the sack just after dinner."

Chapter Seventeen

Greta and Mr. Hassock were sitting side by side on one of the wooden seats of the London terminus. It was the end of July, and waves of eagerly chattering schoolchildren surged past at intervals with the parents who had just met them.

"It's—strange, meeting you like this," said Greta.

He smiled.

"It's not so strange, really. You told me in your letter that you were coming up to meet the children, and I thought it would be a good opportunity to get a word with you."

"They're hardly children now," said Greta. "Angela and Geraldine are seventeen."

"Are you meeting both of them?"

"Yes . . . They both break up to-day, and I told Mrs. Mortimer that I'd collect the three—Angela and Geraldine and Elaine—and save her the trouble of coming up to London. Angela and Geraldine are both leaving school. It's odd how the years fly by, isn't it? It seems no time at all since they were all children at Appleton Vicarage."

She felt nervous and embarrassed and was talking for the sake of talking. The sight of his tall untidy figure waiting for her at the station entrance had given her a shock, and she had not yet got over it.

He looked at her under his bushy eyebrows. She had obviously made no attempts at self-embellishment for this journey to London. She wore the tweed suit and rather shapeless felt hat that she always wore in the country. Her face—kindly, earnest, sincere—was without make-up. Her hair was beginning to turn grey, and there was a faintly spinsterish air about her.

"I've been offered the living of St. Mark's Maybridge," he said abruptly.

"Oh . . " She was startled. "Are you going to accept it?"

"I think so." There was a silence, then he said, "It doesn't seem quite the right place to propose, but—will you marry me?"

She was so surprised that at first she could only stare in front of her as if she had not heard him.

"I didn't want to rush you," he went on. "I wanted to give Bertie and the others a chance."

"The others?"

"There were others, weren't there? I've kept track of you, you know."

She remembered a cheerful sandy man with pince-nez and prominent eyes who had attached himself to her on all the parish outings, and a dark mournful man with a drooping moustache and pendulous cheeks who had proposed to her while she was doing the Harvest Festival decorations.

"Yes . . . I suppose so, but I never took them seriously."

A train let off steam shrilly in the distance. When the sound died away she found that he was talking about her fiancé.

"I realize," he was saying, "that I was very unsympathetic about him. I appreciate that you could never care for me in just the same way, but, if you could care for me at all—"

"I—I don't actually remember him very clearly now," she admitted. "You were right about that."

In front of them a small boy in a grey flannel suit ran into the outstretched arms of a tall fair girl, scattering an attaché-case, a miniature cricket bat and a stamp album in his flight.

"I'm sorry I'm late, darling," panted the girl.

"I thought you hadn't come," he half sobbed, clinging to her.

Mr. Hassock got up and retrieved the loose stamps that lay around them.

"Thank you so much," said the girl. There were tears in her

eyes. "It's the first time he's been away from me, and it's so lovely to get him back."

They disappeared together towards the station entrance.

"I couldn't ask you to marry me while I was working in the East End," said Mr. Hassock. "There were five of us in the Clergy House, and we weren't expected to marry, anyway, but now—" He stopped and cleared his throat. Surprisingly, he looked and sounded nervous. "Well, shall we take it as settled?"

"Oh, no!" gasped Greta. "No . . . not settled!"

"Look!" said Mr. Hassock. "Would you like me to lead up to it more gradually? Actually I didn't mean to rush into it like this. I meant only to pave the way this morning, but when I saw you I suddenly decided to get it over. That sounds a bit casual, but I'm not casual about it; I'm deeply in earnest."

He was in earnest. For the first time, she saw his eyes without the teasing quizzical light.

"I didn't realize how much I cared for you till after I'd left Appleton," he went on. "Then I began to realize it more and more. I found myself thinking of you continually."

"I—I thought of you, too," admitted Greta.

A schoolgirl, blonde and massive, passed the seat with a companion who was obviously an earnest copy of her friend.

"I had it out with her in the dorm, this morning," the massive one was saying in a ringing authoritative voice. "I said: 'Look here, Honor, we don't want to have the same trouble over the hockey next term that we've had over the cricket. Are you going to pull your weight with the team or aren't you? That's the question.'"

"Yes," said the other with a not very successful imitation of the ringing authoritative voice. "That's certainly the question. What did she say?"

Their voices died away in the clatter of an approaching luggage truck as they made their way towards the station restaurant.

Mr. Hassock leant forward, his elbows on his knees.

"If you don't care for me and never could care for me—"

"Oh, it's not that," said Greta, "so much as Olivia."

"Olivia?"

"I can't think what she'd do without me . . . what any of them would do without me."

The ghost of the old twinkle returned to his eyes.

"People do get on without one, you know. It's always a bit of a shock, but they do."

"I know . . ." She hesitated, then went on: "I *do* like you. I always have done in my heart."

He smiled.

"Well, it's a good place to start from," he said. "Will you like living at St. Mark's Vicarage?"

"No, no!" she protested. "It's not settled. I haven't said . . . I mean, I must have time to think it over, to break it to Olivia. I—I can't let people down."

He smiled again.

"When will you give me your answer definitely?"

"In a week. That's not too long, is it?"

"Yes. I'll come to Appleton for it to-morrow . . . By the way, I think I ought to tell you that my name's Theodosius. I go by the name of Theo, but my real name was the skeleton in my cupboard throughout my childhood. I was terrified of the other boys finding out about it. I pretended that it was Theodore, and that was bad enough."

"I—rather like Theodosius," said Greta.

"Good! Then I'll catch the ten-thirty to-morrow morning and come straight to the Vicarage. You can tell Mrs. Sanders to-night."

"Oh, dear!" said Greta. "She mightn't be in the mood to be told. Sometimes you can tell her things over and over again, and she just doesn't take in a word."

"Let me tell her, then."

"Oh, no," said Greta.

The rut she had lived in all these years seemed suddenly so warm and comfortable and—safe, that the thought of leaving it filled her with panic. The unknown held veiled terrors at which she dared not even look. Olivia . . . the children . . . She couldn't face a life of alien duties in which they had no part.

211

"Of course I can't marry you," she said. "I'm mad to think of it."

He put his hand on hers and closed it in a firm grip . . . and at his touch her terror faded and a new deep happiness possessed her.

After a moment or two she glanced at the clock.

"Angela's train's almost due," she said. "I must go."

He rose.

"I won't stay now," he said. "I'll be at Appleton to-morrow morning."

Schoolgirls in neat grey coats and neat grey felt hats were already streaming out of the train when Greta reached the platform. Angela was easily recognized, even in the distance. There was something in the angle of the grey felt hat and the set of the smooth shining curls that gave the slender figure an air of sophistication lacking in the others.

The lovely face clouded over at sight of Greta.

"I asked you not to come," she said a little peevishly.

"But, Angela, I wrote and told you I was meeting the train."

Girls passed them in groups, chattering, greeting parents, waving farewells.

"I wrote to you after I got your letter," said Angela. "I told you not to meet me. Good heavens! As if a girl of seventeen can't make her way across London and get into the train for Appleton without a nursemaid in attendance! I'm not a child."

"And I'm not a nursemaid," said Greta somewhat tartly. "Your letter hadn't come when I left home. Anyway, it's a rule of the school that pupils must be met."

"Pupils!" echoed Angela with an ironic laugh, putting up a hand to pat the golden curls.

"Well, now I'm here," said Greta, "what about your things? Your trunk went in advance, I suppose. Where's your hockey-stick?"

"Hockey-stick!" said Angela, shuddering. "I left it there. I really wasn't going to go about London branded by a hockey-stick."

"You're not going to go about London, surely," said Greta mildly.

"Well, the train to Appleton doesn't go till three-fifteen, and, you see . . ."

Her voice trailed away, and her blue eyes roved round speculatively as if looking for someone. As they approached the barrier, Greta realized whom the blue eyes had been looking for. Ralph Pollitt stood just beyond the barrier, obviously waiting for her. He wore a well-cut overcoat of rather a large check design, suède shoes and hogskin gloves. The dark moustache was small but definitely beyond the chrysalis stage. His man-about-town air sat upon him easily. A smile lit up his face as his eyes fell upon Angela and faded as they passed on to Greta.

"There you are!" he said. "This is grand! How are you, Miss Rossiter?"

"Miss Rossiter happened to come along," said Angela airily. "She had some shopping or something to do in town and I expect she has lots more things to do, haven't you, Miss Rossiter? We'll meet you at Victoria in time for the train. Where did you think of having lunch, Ralph?"

"I thought perhaps the Savoy?" he suggested.

"Can I go there in this ghastly outfit?" said Angela with a groan.

"It looks pretty good to me," smiled Ralph, then, with something of conscious nobility, "Won't you come along too, Miss Rossiter?"

"No, thank you," said Greta. "Angela, do you think you ought to go? Does your mother know?"

She was beginning to feel that life as Mrs. Hassock might present fewer difficulties than life as Olivia's factotum.

"What has she got to do with it?" said Angela, raising her eyebrows.

"Angela! Your mother naturally takes an interest in your doings."

Behind the smiling child's face a sudden bitterness flickered, vanishing almost as soon as it appeared.

"Does she?" said Angela lightly. "She's been a long time showing it!"

"*Angela!*" said Greta in helpless reproach.

"You needn't worry, Miss Rossiter," said Ralph. "I'll take care of her and have her at the station in time for the train. If you'd rather she didn't go to the Savoy, I could take her to a quieter place."

"I want to go to the Savoy," said Angela firmly.

"I had lunch there yesterday," said Ralph, "and I ran into Stephen. He'd come up to see about some agricultural implement or other and was staying the night there. Regular old farmer, you know, Stephen, these days. He was going to wander round here himself this morning to meet Philip's train and see if he'd like to go to a show."

"Philip?"

"Yes, Philip gets in from Marlborough some time this morning. The whole place is lousy with schools, isn't it?"

"Yes. Ghastly. Let's clear off before the thing turns into a jamboree. Geraldine and Elaine are somewhere in the offing, I believe."

She wanted to get her hand in with Ralph before she started on Stephen and Philip. She always felt her weapons slightly rusty after a term at school. Beyond the music master—a small short-sighted man who suffered from chilblains—and a few odds and ends of brothers on visiting days, she got little practice.

"We'll meet you in time for the train, Miss Rossiter."

"Oh, dear!" said Greta, conquering a rising inclination to get flustered. "I don't know whether you ought to . . ."

"Hello! There's old Stephen," said Ralph, and Stephen joined the group, greeting them in his easy pleasant fashion. His eyes rested admiringly on Angela, and as she returned his smile the colour in her cheeks grew deeper and her eyes sparkled. Life was going to be fun now that she'd left school.

"Did you find your pitchfork or whatever it was?" said Ralph.

"It was a four-wheeled tractor, and I got a beauty, thanks," said Stephen. "By the way, what's happening to the world of high finance while you dally here?"

"Oh, working for the old man has its points," said Ralph. "I can take a holiday when I want one. I'm carrying Angela off to the Savoy for lunch." He grinned. "Sorry, old man. The party can't be enlarged. I've only booked a table for two."

"I won't grudge it you," said Stephen. He smiled at Angela. "There will be other days; other luncheons."

Angela threw him a challenging glance from under dark lashes.

"I take it that's a definite engagement?" she said.

"Of course," said Stephen.

"Oh dear!" said Greta again. "Look! There are Geraldine and Elaine. I told them to wait by the bookstall."

The group moved over to where Geraldine and Elaine stood by the bookstall, both wearing the heavy navy blue overcoats and hats that were their school uniform. An air of depression hung over the two. Elaine—now a tall thin child—looked pale, and peaked. Geraldine's face was sallow and a little sulky. They brightened as the group approached, but only with the artificial brightness that pays tribute to the social conventions. Angela and Ralph, both in high spirits, talked animatedly, rallying Geraldine on the end of her schooldays, teasing Elaine about the dreary waste of rules and arithmetic that still lay ahead of her, while Greta stood in the background. A stream of schoolgirls in green coats and skirts issued from a nearly platform, to be claimed by parents. One of them was a slender dark girl, who was met by a thick-set burly man. He took her suitcase and began to steer her through the crowd with a hand on her elbow.

"Why, I believe—" said Greta uncertainly. "Wait a minute. I must go and see."

She crossed the platform and approached the two.

"Monica!" she said.

Monica turned with a start.

"Miss Rossiter! . . . This is Mr. Deverel, my stepfather. This is Miss Rossiter, Fred."

"How d'you do," said Fred, putting down the suitcase and shaking hands with Greta.

"I lost touch with you, Monica dear," said Greta. "I didn't know you'd gone away to school."

"Yes, she's been at boarding-school for two years now," said Fred. "This is the last day of the last term, isn't it, Mon?"

"You're all leaving school to-day," said Greta. "There are Angela and Geraldine over there, dear. Won't you come and speak to them?"

Monica looked at the group by the bookstall. Stephen was smiling down at Angela. He was bareheaded, and his fairness seemed to shine in the dingy station surroundings. She recognized him with a leap of her heart, then the old paralysis of shyness seized her.

"No, thank you," she said; "we haven't time, have we, Fred?"

"Perhaps not," said Fred.

"Well, I won't worry you if you're in a hurry," said Greta. "I know it's difficult to get away from these young people. They chatter so. How's your mother, dear?"

"She's very well, thank you," said Monica. "We ought to be going, oughtn't we, Fred?"

"Right, my dear," said Fred, taking up the suitcase and raising his hat in farewell.

Greta made her way slowly back to the bookstall. When she reached it she found Geraldine and Elaine standing there alone in sombre silence.

"Angela and Ralph have gone to lunch," explained Geraldine, "and Stephen's gone to meet Philip's train."

Greta sighed.

"Oh, well," she said, "let's have something to eat in the station restaurant."

Greta, with Geraldine and Elaine, was on the platform three-quarters of an hour before the train was due to start. Lunch at the station restaurant had been an unsatisfactory meal. Both the fish and the suet pudding had been soggy and tepid, and neither Geraldine nor Elaine had responded to Greta's attempts at conversation. Asked what she was going to do now that she had left school, Geraldine had replied shortly that her father had obtained a post for her at the Maybridge Public Library. Asked if she would miss Geraldine next term, Elaine had replied that she was leaving the boarding-school and going to Maybridge High School, so she would still be with Gerry. After that they relapsed into silence . . . As soon as

216

they reached Victoria, Greta had bought an evening paper for herself, a *Strand Magazine* for Geraldine and a schoolgirls' magazine for Elaine, and the three sat on the bench reading them.

Stephen and Philip were the next to arrive. They had had lunch together and gone to a news cinema instead of a matinée, because Philip, though he did not admit this to Stephen, wanted to go home by the same train as Angela. He was pale and lanky and over-grown, looking much less mature for his age than the other two boys. There was a gleam of excitement in his dark eyes and his manner was absent, as if his thoughts were elsewhere. At the beginning of the term he had sent a poem to a new literary journal and it had been accepted. The copy of the journal containing his poem had arrived yesterday and was in his pocket now. He had told no one and he intended to show it to no one—except Angela. He felt as he had felt in the days when he had lived in his dream world and had performed prodigious feats of valour for Rosabel. Always, when he had been absent from Angela for any length of time, she slipped back into Rosabel.

Stephen had ordered champagne for lunch and after his second glass Philip had had a roseate picture of himself and Angela wandering together in a world of enchantment—of mystery, poetry and romance. He was disconcerted to find Geraldine there, sitting with Miss Rossiter on the station seat. Geraldine didn't fit into his dream world, and he was relieved that she made no claims on him. She greeted him shortly, then returned to her magazine. Stephen took his seat by Greta and began to talk to her. His manner, kindly and affable, vaguely depressed her. It was the manner used by well-intentioned and nicely-brought-up young men to elderly and unattractive females. They discussed the weather, the political situation, the tennis club concert, the forthcoming production of *She Stoops to Conquer*, by the Maybridge Amateur Dramatic Society, and the new by-pass that was being made between Maybridge and Penbury. Geraldine and Elaine sat reading their papers.

Philip paced the platform. Occasionally he would put his hand into his pocket to touch the folded copy of *The Helicon*, and then the dingy station would vanish altogether and his spirit would be caught up in a rush of happiness.

Then Ralph and Angela arrived. Greta gave a gasp of dismay when her eyes fell on Angela. The little monkey must have had a whole outfit of make-up in her bag. Her cheeks were rouged and powdered, her mouth outlined in scarlet, her eyes shadowed, her brows pencilled.

"Well, we've had a grand time," said Ralph heartily. "Eaten our heads off and talked our heads off . . . and now I've got to run back to the office. I promised the old man I'd look in and fix a few things before it closed."

When he had gone, Angela stood irresolute. They had made room for her on the seat, but she didn't want to sit with them and talk about the silly ordinary things they were sure to talk about. She felt wildly excited, but beneath the excitement was an undercurrent of depression, growing stronger every minute. When she wrote to Ralph asking him to meet her and take her out to lunch, the picture she had had in her mind was very different from what had actually taken place. She had purchased her make-up secretly and carefully. She had meant to look poised and smart and sophisticated, and she had looked, she knew, like a schoolgirl lunching with an elder brother. Women with well-dressed hair, expensive furs and fashionable hats had sat all around her. She had meant to look like one of them, but, in spite of the twists she had given the grey felt hat, and the carnations that Ralph had bought for her, she hadn't done. She had felt overawed by the atmosphere of the place and had been at a loss more times during the meal than she cared to recall.

Ralph's manner, too, now that she thought it over, had been far from satisfactory. There had been a hint of patronage, even of kindly amusement, in it. He had treated her as a schoolgirl, ordering lemonade for her, though the women at the other tables were drinking wine. "Eaten our heads off" . . . the sort of thing one would say of a schoolgirl's meal. Poised and beautiful women of the world didn't eat their heads off, and she had wanted to be a poised and beautiful woman of the world.

"Sit down, dear, and tell us about it," said Greta.

Philip strolled up to them.

"No, I don't want to sit down," said Angela peevishly. "I've been sitting down at lunch and in the taxi. I'd rather walk about."

She found herself pacing the platform with Philip. He was talking, but she didn't listen to what he was saying. She would put the hateful school uniform into the jumble sale sack first thing to-morrow morning. She would buy some new clothes. Black . . . the woman at the next table had worn black . . . a hat with a little veil coming over her eyes . . . and a fur coat. She must have a fur coat, but how could she get one? It was no use talking to mother and it was no use talking to Miss Rossiter. They just didn't understand.

"Here it is," said Philip, taking a paper from his pocket and handing it to her.

She didn't know what he'd been talking about, but she saw a poem called "Trees at Night", signed Philip Shenstone. It began, "Slowly the moon climbs the ladder of the fir tree."

She handed it back to him.

"Did you write it?"

"Yes."

Tensely, he awaited her comment, but, before she had time to speak, Greta called from the seat:

"Here's the train. Come along."

They found an empty carriage and all got into it. As the sense of anti-climax increased, Angela's depression was turning to angry irritation. For years she had looked forward to this day—the day of leaving school and entering the adult world—and everything had gone wrong with it. Ralph had treated her as a child, Philip had burbled on and on about his own affairs, showing her a stupid poem she couldn't make head or tail of, as though he were unaware of the new allure of her rouged cheeks and reddened lips, and Stephen had attached himself to Miss Rossiter, as if the two of them were alone together on a desert island. She had taken for granted that this day would be the beginning of a life of excitement and gaiety—parties, dances, theatres. And now, for the first time, she began to wonder how she was to find this life in Appleton, a village in which the Flower Show was the highlight of the whole year, with a father so immersed in committee work as to be dead to all human contacts, and a mother who was the laughing-stock of the neighbourhood. Her lips tightened as she remembered the deep humiliations she had suffered from that bizarre figure in her childhood, remembered how she had joined in the other children's mockery with a sickening sense of treachery at her heart, how she had decided, even then, to make of herself a figure so radiant, so perfect, that the grotesqueness of that other figure could cast no shadow on it.

Philip waited in an anguish of suspense for some sign from her. He remembered how he had suffered this same torment when he had tried to show one of his poems to Ann, but this would be different. He found himself looking at Geraldine as if for reassurance, but Geraldine sat with a stony face, looking out of the window. He dared not look at Angela.

"Like to see the evening paper, Stephen?" said Greta. "There's not much in it. An account of the meeting of the World Economic Conference and an article on the Polish Corridor."

"Oh, yes," said Stephen, taking the paper. "Hitler seems to be casting his eyes on it, doesn't he?"

"Well, he wants to come to some arrangement," said Greta; "but he says quite definitely that he wouldn't think of going to war over it."

Stephen glanced through the paper and handed it to Angela. Angela sat holding it unopened on her knee.

"Pass it to Philip, dear, if you don't want to read it," said Greta.

The disappointments and disillusionment of the day seemed to boil over as Angela threw the paper to Philip.

"Philip doesn't want to read newspapers," she said. "He only likes moons climbing ladders and dreams like pale children lost in a forest and the birth pains of a grey and weary dawn."

She quoted the words with an intensity of childish spite.

Philip took the paper in silence and opened it. Angela looked at him, noticing the tight lines of his mouth, and compunction flooded her heart. She was tired and unhappy and—sorry that she had been unkind. His hand was on the seat by her and she slipped hers over it. He did not respond or move his hand. The train sped on through the familiar countryside. Geraldine, Elaine, Philip and Angela sat in silence. Only Stephen continued with dogged gallantry to entertain Greta with a laboured account of the news-reel that he and Philip had seen that afternoon.

Chapter Eighteen

'Look, there's Daisy," said Fred, guiding Monica through the crowded restaurant, "at that table over there."

Fred's wife was a short, stout woman, with a round soft dimpled face, china-blue eyes and golden hair. She wore a pale-blue two-piece, with a large collar of hare fur, and a pale-blue hat with too much trimming on it. As her eyes fell upon Monica her mouth broadened into a smile. It was a smile of rich and mellow kindliness, of warm, generous, all-embracing good-humour.

Fred had married Daisy three years ago. They lived in Wimbledon in a house called Homeleigh and had a fat little boy two years old and a fat little girl of three months. Daisy had been a barmaid at one of the hotels in the Midlands where Fred put up regularly on his business trips. Fred wanted an affectionate, uncritical wife, a comfortable home and children, and Daisy had given him all three. On her part, she had loved Fred for years, and his proposal had seemed to come straight out of one of the novelettes that she read so avidly in her leisure moments. She couldn't believe it at first. She couldn't believe it till she found herself snugly ensconced in Homeleigh, with a three-piece suite in the lounge, a refectory table in the dining-room and a refrigerator in the kitchen. In order to prove her gratitude, she had produced the babies on which Fred had set his heart without delay, and the babies themselves, blue-eyed, golden-haired, were part of the fairy-tale.

Fred's marriage had done little to alter his attitude to Monica. He still considered her one of his chief responsibilities, and Daisy, rather surprisingly, agreed with this view.

After leaving Beach Hotel, Babs and Monica had spent several weeks in a boarding-house in Pimlico, then Babs had obtained a job as "hostess" in a dance-hall in the region of the Old Kent Road. From this Fred had rescued them—or, rather, had rescued Monica, for Babs, who was fast losing her old standards, enjoyed the tinselly glitter of the life, the music and lights and laughter, the free, and easy *camaraderie*. He had entered Monica as a pupil in a good day school in London and had found Babs a job with a good-class florist in the neighbourhood of Bond Street. But Babs, after a month or two, drifted back to the dance-hall, then, after an interlude as receptionist to a doctor of dubious reputation in Kensington, became in turn the manageress of an equally dubious hotel, assistant in a cut-price dress shop and again "hostess" in a dance-hall.

Fred rescued her at intervals from the straits into which all these jobs seemed to lead. He found her, generally, deeply in debt, for money still melted like snow through her long white fingers. He found, too, that the money he allowed her for Monica's school fees were not being paid to the school. Monica herself was pale and thin, trying to do her homework in the evenings and at the same time to instil some sort of order into the makeshift background of Babs' life. So he consulted a scholastic agent, who recommended a boarding-school in Surrey, and there Monica was sent with the arrangement that Fred should pay her school fees direct to the head-mistress. Babs was glad to be relieved of the child, for it happened that a possible "protector" had just appeared on the horizon. He lacked youth, breeding and education, but he did not lack money, and Babs was prepared, as she cheerfully put it, to "take him as she found him". The presence of Monica hampered the development of the affair, and Babs agreed readily enough to the boarding-school project.

Life at the boarding-school had for Monica, as always, a curious quality of unreality. She did her work conscientiously, but made few friends. Some holidays she spent with Fred and some with Babs. The "protector" faded away, but another took his place then faded away in his turn. Babs drifted from job to shady job, from "protector" to shady "protector", finding her chief comfort in drink, living always in the passing moment with a courage that could face anything but boredom.

"Come on, love," said Daisy, smiling affectionately as Monica approached. "Come and have something to eat. You look as if you could do with it."

Monica's answering smile held in it the anxiety that was always there when her thoughts were with Babs. After greeting Daisy and asking after the children, she turned to Fred.

"You did say that Babs was all right, didn't you?" she said.

"Yes, yes, but I thought it would be nice to have a little talk with you before I took you home. She told you she'd moved from the old address, didn't she?"

"Yes."

"I'd like to have asked her to have lunch with us," said Fred, with rather unconvincing heartiness, "but I thought she'd probably rather wait to have you to herself."

Babs had only met Daisy once (Fred had asked her to Homeleigh in the naïve hope that friendship with Daisy would arrest her downward course), but the meeting had not been a success. Babs had been immensely amused by the Wimbledon *ménage*. There had been covert mockery in her voice, and her eyes had danced with mischief throughout the visit. Daisy, aware of the mockery and the mischief, had been silent and sulky, and Fred had not repeated the experiment.

"Daisy and I wanted to have a little talk with you first," he added.

"Things—*are* all right, aren't they?" said Monica.

"Oh, yes . . . She's got a job in this hat shop and it seems to be a success so far. More or less."

The waiter came to their table, and Fred gave the order.

"Celebration, isn't it, Monny—leaving school? Salmon . . . What about that? Salmon and Peche Melba. Daisy and I will have lager. What about cider for you?"

"Lovely!" said Monica, trying to still the anxiety at her heart and to respond to the note of festivity that Fred evidently wished to introduce into the occasion.

"Why did Babs leave the place we were in last holidays?" she said when the waiter had gone.

"Oh, some sort of row with the landlady," said Fred evasively.

Monica was silent. She could see the scene as well as if she had been there . . . Babs tipsily abusive, her voice rising higher and higher . . .

"Don't you worry, love," said Daisy. "Everything'll turn out all right. What Fred and me would like would be for you to come to us."

"Monny knows that," put in Fred.

"It's—good of you," said Monica, "but I must stay with Babs."

"She may find things easier now she's got you with her permanent," said Daisy. She sounded unconvinced and unconvincing, but continued on a note of determined optimism. "One never knows what's round the corner, does one?"

"One thing we ought to talk about, Monny," said Fred, "is what you're going to do now you've left school."

"I must get some sort of job," said Monica.

"Why not take a secretarial course?" suggested Daisy. "I've always thought they must be interesting. Typing and suchlike."

"Yes, I'd like that."

"Good!" said Fred. "I'll fix it up for you. I'll have a talk with your mother about it when I take you home."

"I oughtn't to let you do so much for me, Fred."

Fred's rough-hewn face softened into a smile.

"We'd like to do more than you let us," he said, "but you always know we're here for you to fall back on when you need us, don't you?"

"Yes . . ."

After lunch Daisy went to do some shopping, arranging to meet Fred for tea, and Fred and Monica set off in a taxi for Babs' address.

It turned out to be a drab little house in Golders Green. Babs had a sitting-room and a bedroom, and another bedroom had been reserved for Monica.

Babs came to the door to meet them, and Monica flung herself into the outstretched arms, then stood back to look at her. Babs was painfully thin, her cheeks sunken but brightly rouged, her hair carefully dressed but with a harsh metallic glint. She wore a black pleated skirt and a black chiffon blouse. Under the chiffon her neck-bones stood out like knives.

"Well, darling," she said gaily, "isn't this lovely! Come along in, both of you."

It was a dispirited little room—dingy tapestry curtains at the windows, lustreless furniture and a threadbare carpet. There was a fan of stained discoloured paper in the empty firegrate and a vase of faded artificial flowers on the chimneypiece. Fred had noticed that of late Babs had grown more and more indifferent to her surroundings.

"Which is Monny's room?" he said. "I'll carry her bag in."

"Here it is," said Babs, opening a door. "It's a dear little room, isn't it, darling?"

"It's lovely," said Monica eagerly.

Fred looked round the room in silence. It was frowsty and airless, the walls stained, the mirror spotted, the counterpane soiled, the carpet grey with dust.

"Let's get some air into it," he said, throwing the window open. "Now, Monny, suppose you unpack while I have a talk with Babs."

He followed Babs into the sitting-room. She watched him with dancing eyes as his gaze went speculatively round the room and finally came to rest on her.

"I know what's in your mind, Fred," she said. "You needn't worry. I'm leading a comparatively blameless life at the moment. The last one married a barmaid and went out to Canada. How's Daisy, by the way?"

"Quite well, thank you."

"Good. You needn't look at the bookcase. There aren't any bottles behind the books this time. I've not been really drunk for some time, and I'm doing quite well at my job. Probably the calm before the storm, but we must be thankful for small mercies, mustn't we?"

226

The brittle gaiety of her tone brought a lightening of his heavy features.

"Sit down and have a cigarette, Fred."

He sat down on the ramshackle sofa, which shifted under his weight.

"You're too thin, Babs."

"I know I am."

"You ought to eat more."

"I'm never hungry. You can't eat if you aren't hungry. But you didn't come here to talk about me, did you?"

"No . . . Monny's left school now."

"I know."

"She wants to take a secretarial course."

"Splendid!"

"I'll make arrangements at the nearest decent place, and she can go there every day from here."

"Yes, that'll be lovely."

"Babs, you'll be careful, won't you?"

"Why shouldn't I be? I'm fond of Monny."

"I know you are, but she's only a child. Babs, there's one thing I want you to promise me."

"What?"

"I don't want you to take her into public houses. You did last holidays, and it's not good for her."

Babs laughed.

"One can acquire a lot of wisdom in public houses, you know, Fred."

"And a lot of other things as well. Will you promise?"

"Yes."

"Good!"

"You'd have made a wonderful children's nannie, you know, Fred."

Her voice was light and gay, but he noticed the restlessness of her thin, nervous frame. She leant back in her seat, then sat up jerkily. Her long fingers pulled incessantly at the worn covering of the armchair.

He rose slowly.

"I'll be going now."

"Stay and have tea with us."

"No, thanks. I'm meeting Daisy."

There was a flash of mocking laughter in her eyes.

"I certainly mustn't keep you, then."

"You'll remember your promise, won't you, Babs?"

"Of course. On my honour and cross my throat."

"What are you going to do this evening? Would you like me to get you tickets for some show?"

"No, thanks. I think a nice quiet evening would be best. We shall have lots to talk about."

"As you like . . . I'll be looking you up again soon. Take care of yourself and Monny."

"Yes, I will. You're—good, Fred. Perhaps you're too good. Perhaps if you hadn't been so good I shouldn't have been so bad.

I don't know, I should probably have been bad anyway. I'll call Monny to say good-bye to you."

After tea the two sat in the little sitting-room and Babs lay back in the armchair, smiling at Monica.

"It's lovely to have you, darling," she said. "Now, tell me everything about last term."

"I told you nearly everything in my letters."

Babs thought of those long, closely-written sheets that arrived every Monday morning and that she seldom read.

"Tell me again, darling. I forget . . . and, anyway, it's different reading a thing and being told a thing, isn't it?"

Monica began to talk as she only talked to Babs, losing her shyness and inarticulateness, telling her all that had happened during the term, but the signs of Babs' restlessness grew more and more apparent. She drummed her fingers on the arm of her chair, she yawned, she looked at the clock, she got up and moved about the room, touching things, altering their position, putting them back to where they had been before. Monica's recital died away.

"It's all right, pet," Babs said, sitting down again in the armchair. "I'm loving it. It's just that I get stiff sitting. Do go on, darling.

What were you telling me about? The play you did last term . . .
Midsummer Night's Dream, wasn't it?"

"No. *The Antigone*."

"Yes, of course. What did they wear? Who took the parts? Do
tell me, darling." She lit a cigarette, drew a few puffs, stubbed it
out and lit another. "I want to know all about it. What was the
stage like?"

"They had black curtains at the back," said Monica, "and an
altar in the middle, and—"

"Look, darling," said Babs, rising abruptly from her chair, "there's
a place near here where we might just go for an hour or two. I've
been going there in the evenings lately. It's not exactly a pub." She
paused and went on: "Well, I suppose it is, in a way, but it's quite
a nice atmosphere. It's at the end of the large block of flats, and
there's a couple of men who live in the flats and generally go there
about this time. They're two brothers who married two sisters. I
haven't met the sisters yet, because they've been away, but they
were coming back to-day, and I expect they'll be there to-night.
They're nice people, and you ought to meet nice people, you know."

She had sat down again as she spoke, but her fingers were not
still for a second, interlocking, dancing on the arm of her chair
pulling at the chair-covering. Her eyes were as restless as her fingers,
darting about the room with swift bright sliding glances. She leapt
to her feet with an air of relief. "Come on, pet. Put on your coat."

"Wouldn't you rather—just go by yourself?" said Monica.

Babs gave a shrill, empty laugh.

"No, darling, I'd hate to leave you here alone your first evening.
Come along. We'll have a jolly time. Much better for us than sitting
in this stuffy place. Does one good to get out, you know. Gives
me the blues to stay in all evening."

The pub was a very ordinary pub at the corner of the block of
flats. The brothers were already in the bar when Babs and Monica
entered—two prosperous-looking men, very much alike, with sleek
dark hair, dark moustaches, and rather expressionless faces, wearing
well-cut evening suits. They seemed a little taken aback at seeing
Babs.

"I thought you said you wouldn't be coming along to-night," said one.

"Oh, I managed it, after all," said Babs gaily. Her excitement had increased with every step since leaving the house. "Knew you two couldn't get along without me. This is Monny, my little girl. Isn't she sweet? She's just seventeen. Well, where's your gallantry? Don't I look much too young to have a daughter of seventeen? Which of you is going to say it first?" They smiled constrainedly and she gave a high-pitched laugh as she continued: "This is Denis, Monny, and this is Bob. I don't know their surnames. They may have told me, but I've forgotten. I haven't a surname mind. I'll have a gin, and Monny will have a lemonade, won't you, darling? Her stepfather's been reading me a lecture this afternoon. Made me promise not to bring the child up on strong drink." She looked round the crowded, brightly lit scene, and her gay, empty laugh rang out again. "Oh, no, I wouldn't desert you. I don't desert my friends. I've got a boy-on-the-burning-deck complex where my friends are concerned.

Monica had taken her lemonade over to a table by the wall. She sat there, watching Babs anxiously as she babbled on. The men's responses to her sallies were sheepish and unwilling. Her laughter rang out again and again.

"What's the matter with you boys to-night? You aren't your own bright selves, are you? Have the girls come back?"

"Yes, they came back this afternoon," said Denis. "They're joining us here for a drink and then we're all going on to a show."

"Oh, good!" said Babs. "Well, here's to it! I'm looking forward to meeting the girls."

And then the "girls" entered—two tall handsome women, one dark and the other fair, dressed with expensive simplicity and carrying an air of well-bred assurance. Ignoring Babs, they joined their husbands at the bar.

"We haven't long, Denis. Just a quick one."

The four stood in a self-contained group that obviously excluded Babs.

"Well, introduce me," said Babs shrilly.

"I'm sorry," said Bob. "This is Mrs?"

"Oh, Babs will do," said Babs. "I'm Babs to everyone. The boys have told me all about you, my dears. I've been longing to meet you."

But the group had closed again, excluding her.

Monica watched from her table, pleading silently . . . Oh, come away. Do come away. Leave them . . . But Babs couldn't leave them. Her shrill voice, her shrill laugh, rang out, as she addressed first one then another of the four, rallying, teasing, challenging. Each responded shortly, with perfunctory courtesy, then proceeded once more to ignore her. She stood there, glass in hand, outside the group, raddled, haggard, with sunken cheeks, her dyed hair now a little dishevelled, her eyes glinting feverishly. Again and again she returned to the attack. She tried to elbow her way into the group, but, wherever she stood, a shoulder was turned on her, a conversation started in which she could have no part.

The noise and closeness of the smoke-laden, drink-laden atmosphere had made Monica's head ache, but she had thought only for Babs. She caught the glances of amusement exchanged by the bystanders, and her heart was torn by love and pity as she watched. Oh, stop, darling . . . Do stop . . . Don't you see that they don't want you? Why don't you stop?

Chapter Nineteen

"Well now, I suppose the girlies will want to unpack," said Albert, drawing his chair back from the table.

"We'll help you wash the tea-things first," said Geraldine.

"No, dear," said Grace. "I'll see to that."

"I'll do it," said Albert.

Grace had been much better since her operation, but Albert still did all he could to spare her exertion. Whatever Albert's wife had been like, he would have done all he could to spare her exertion. A healthy wife would have been wasted on Albert.

"I'll do it," said Grace firmly. "I know you've got a lot to do."

"Well, I could finish the arbour," said Albert. "It only needs the last half-dozen pieces of wood to finish it."

"You and your arbour!" smiled Grace.

She had yielded at last on the subject of the arbour, and for the last few weeks Albert had spent all his spare time erecting an elaborate arch of rusticwork at the corner of the garden path.

"Well, then, mummy will wash up," he said, "and I'll finish the arbour and the girlies can unpack and then we'll all meet together for a good talk."

Geraldine and Elaine went upstairs, and Albert helped his wife carry the tea-things into the kitchen.

"It's good to have them back, isn't it, dear?" he said as he placed the laden tray on the kitchen table.

"Yes," said Grace. She put the tea-cosy into the drawer in the dresser. "They're very quiet. They've hardly spoken since I met them at the station."

"I believe I've done all the talking," said Albert with a smile, stacking the used plates and cups on the draining-board. "I know how they feel, though. Too excited to talk. And I expect they're tired, too. Probably they didn't sleep much last night. And, of course, it's rather a solemn occasion for Gerry—leaving school and setting out into the world."

"Y-yes," said Grace, pausing with her hand on the hot-water tap. "You know . . . I sometimes think it would have been better to have let Elaine stay on at St. Julian's."

"Not without Gerry," said Albert, putting the sugar away in the cupboard. "They're so devoted to each other, and Gerry's such a good influence on her. With Elaine at Maybridge High School and Gerry working at Maybridge Public Library, they can still have their evenings together. And Gerry can help her with her homework, I must say I'm looking forward to having both our chickens in the nest for a little . . . Sure you wouldn't like me to dry for you, dear?"

"Quite sure," said Grace. "Run along to your arbour."

He smiled and went out to his carpentry shed to get his tools. He walked rather slowly . . . Of late he had begun to walk rather slowly. On his way home from the office he now made a habit of stopping several times to admire the view of the Parish Church spire against the sky. He had been a little worried by the feeling of breathlessness that came over him more and more frequently, and the curious pain that seemed to be located in the region of his chest. Without mentioning the matter to anyone, he had made an appointment to see his doctor to-morrow afternoon. A touch of indigestion, he told himself, which a box of pills would soon put right. Still—there was just the possibility that the doctor would order him to rest, and Albert wanted to finish his arbour before anyone ordered him to rest. There were only half a dozen pieces to put up and he would do it to-night, quietly and slowly.

Upstairs in Elaine's bedroom Geraldine and Elaine were alone together for the first time since the moment when they had met in the passage at St. Julian's just before breakfast this morning, and Geraldine had looked at Elaine and said in a voice of horror,

"Elaine!" . . . and Elaine had realized that she knew. Then the breakfast bell had rung and everything since then had been hurry and bustle. Now Geraldine closed the door and stood facing Elaine across the little blue and white bedroom, with the teddy bear that Geraldine had given her for her third birthday sitting on the chest of drawers and Fra Angelico's Annunciation, framed by Albert, hanging over the bed.

"Elaine," said Geraldine, "is it true?"

Elaine stood there, sulky, defiant, but with a hint of tears behind the sulkiness.

"Who told you?" she said.

"It doesn't matter who told me."

"It does. They all promised not to tell you. It was Netty Oldham. I know it was. She's a sneak."

"That's better than being a cheat."

Elaine dropped her eyes before Geraldine's accusing gaze.

"It was only arithmetic," she muttered.

"Why did you do it, Elaine?"

"I was bad at arithmetic and you kept wanting me to be good at it. You kept on and on about it. And you were pleased when I got good marks."

"Elaine! As if I wanted you to cheat! I've always told you that truth was the only important thing."

There was a silence, broken by the sounds of the washing of crockery from the kitchen and of hammerstrokes from the garden.

"How did you get the answers?" said Geraldine.

"I knew that Miss Walker had a book with answers and I went to her room one Sunday when I had a cold and everyone else was at church and copied them all out."

"Elaine, I can hardly believe it."

"She didn't find out till the end of term because she just corrected the answers without looking at the working, and then the last week she started looking at the working and she—made me tell her."

"What did she say?"

"She said that I was leaving anyway, so she wouldn't tell the

Head. I think she didn't want the Head to know that she hadn't been looking at the working when she corrected them . . . Gerry, I always tried to get them out without cheating. I did work . . . I worked hard to get them like they were in the answers, but I couldn't always and you were cross when I got bad marks and pleased when I got good ones." There was another silence broken now by no sound of washing-up or hammerstrokes. "She called me a cheat and a liar." The childish voice faltered. "She called it me in front of everyone."

"Elaine, have you ever cheated at other things beside arithmetic?"

"Sometimes. When I wanted you to be pleased . . . when—"

Suddenly Elaine sat down on the bed and began to cry. Life had held a nightmare quality ever since that day last week when Miss Walker had begun to question her about her arithmetic answers. The growing fear and shame, the terror of exposure, the sick humiliation of the moment when she had stood up before the whole form to be pointed out by Miss Walker as an example of cowardice and dishonour. For the last few nights she had not slept, and she had eaten only with an effort.

Geraldine ran across the room and gathered the small sobbing figure into her arms.

"Oh, darling! . . . Don't cry . . . Don't worry any more . . . It's all right now . . . You're with Gerry . . ." Elaine clung to her, shaken by sobs.

"Don't cry, darling. You're with Gerry. You've got Gerry . . . It's all right now. You won't do it again. It's all over."

Elaine sat up, her face stained and swollen, her head throbbing. There was the salt taste of tears in her mouth.

"It isn't over," she gulped. "Daddy will be terribly upset."

Geraldine sat gazing in front of her. She was trembling, and her heart was beating unevenly. The touch of the childish arms clinging to her, the childish head resting on her breast, the utter abandonment of childish love and trust . . . filled her with an emotion so intense that it was almost more than she could bear. It was as if some deep ever-ravening hunger had been—temporarily, at any rate—appeased.

"Will it be on your report?" she said.

"No. She found out after the reports were done, and I don't think she wanted the Head to know. Gerry, daddy will mind terribly."

Geraldine spoke slowly, still looking in front of her.

"We won't tell mummy or daddy," she said.

"Oh, Gerry!"

Relief leapt in Elaine's heart, like sunshine breaking through the clouds. When she found that Gerry knew, she had taken for granted that her parents would be told of it. And now . . .

"Oh, Gerry!" she said again, her voice high-pitched with relief gratitude and the aftermath of sobs. "But—they'll see I've been crying."

"No, they won't," said Geraldine cheerfully. "Let me bathe your face in cold water and then I'll do your hair. We can say you're starting a cold. Look! We'll put a pretty frock on. Come along, darling."

Lovingly she washed the tear-stained face, brushed out the silky curls and drew off the dark school uniform, putting on a pale blue frock of artificial silk.

"There's my little girl," she said. "Now, it's going to be our secret, darling, and no one else will ever know. And I'll help you . . . You gave way to temptation, didn't you, darling, but now we know your weakness we'll fight it between us. When you're at Maybridge High School we'll have the evenings together. We can arrange your work, and I'll be there to help you do it properly." Her voice ran on eagerly and she planned their life together . . .

Elaine turned away and stood motionless. The feeling of happiness had gone quite suddenly. It was as if the sun had been hidden not by a cloud, but by the walls of a prison that Gerry's words were building, brick by brick. She was ashamed of feeling like this about Gerry, whom she loved, but she couldn't help it. Shut up alone with Gerry in a dark stifling prison . . . Panic swept over her. She wheeled round again to face Geraldine.

"Gerry, I want them to know," she said breathlessly. "I want mummy and daddy to know."

"No, darling," said Geraldine. "I know how you feel. You want to make a clean breast of it and start again, but you needn't feel like that. It's enough that I know. You see, one can be selfish even in wanting to do right. It would make them so unhappy, and you don't want to make them unhappy, do you?"

"No."

"So it will be just our secret. Come along now, darling. Let's go down."

Geraldine's arm round Elaine's shoulder, Elaine's arm round Geraldine's waist, the two went down the narrow staircase to the sitting-room.

Grace rose from the settee as they entered.

"I'm just snatching a rest," she said. "We're going to celebrate by a chicken for supper—it was daddy's idea—so I must be getting busy soon. Come into the garden to daddy."

They went into the garden to Albert. He lay at the foot of his finished arbour, the hammer still in his hand, a look of faint surprise on his face. He had died quite peacefully after driving in the last nail.

Chapter Twenty

Monica leant back in the corner of the railway carriage, absently watching trees, fields, houses, telegraph poles flash past the window.

It was four years since she had left school and joined Babs in the dingy rooms at Golders Green. They had been, for Monica, years of fear and anxiety; for Babs, years of swift disintegration. Her craving for drink had become so insatiable and unashamed that she had long ago given up the attempt to find or keep the jobs that had once been an outlet for her driving restlessness. Monica had begun the training in secretarial work, but it had never been completed, and she had found it impossible to hold any post for long. The constant series of crises at home put any ordered routine out of the question. There were days when she dared not leave Babs for a moment. There were scenes of public humiliation . . . tipsy quarrels with landladies and fellow tenants . . . summary ejections from boardinghouses and rooms. The sordid love affairs continued—at first furtively, then openly. "I can still attract men, you know, darling, and I'm rather amusing when I'm tight."

It had racked Monica's spirit to watch the gradual coarsening of all that had once been fine and lovely. She had fought desperately and unavailingly against it, blaming herself for the failures, gathering together her forces after each for a fresh effort, upheld by a flame of love and pity that nothing could dim. And at last Fred had delivered his ultimatum.

"You must go into a home and take a treatment, Babs," he had said, "or I'll stop your allowance. It isn't fair on Monny."

Babs, caught in one of her intermittent states of sobriety, had been unexpectedly docile.

"I know," she had said. "I'll try—I will try—if you don't think it's too late."

"No," he said. "I've been to Linden Lodge—it's one of the best places, I believe—and talked it over with them. They've had the most astounding cures."

" 'Astounding'," Babs had said with a flicker of laughter, "will certainly be the word."

She had kept her promise, making her preparations with the ghost of her old gay insouciance.

"I will try, Monny darling," she said with her thin tinkling laugh. "It'll be lovely if they make me good, won't it? I can't imagine myself good, can you? Somehow, it wouldn't be me. Fred called it a nursing-home, but I suppose it's really an inebriates' home, isn't it? . . . I'll take the black evening dress. It seems more suitable than the gold one. Or perhaps inebriates don't dress for dinner. I think it's so unkind to call it inebriated. It's so hard to say it when you are it. I'll buy a new dressing-gown, I think. Something bright to cheer me up. You'll think of me, pet, won't you, being uninebriated. It's sure to be a lousy process. I'd like to take a few bottles of gin with me to help me through it, but I suppose they wouldn't let me."

Monica and Fred had taken her to Linden Lodge yesterday and left her, chattering vivaciously, upheld by the old jaunty courage, in the clean, bare, white-painted reception room. Monica's heart contracted at the memory.

She had gone back with Fred to spend the night at Homeleigh, and they had discussed the situation when Daisy was putting the children to bed (there were now three blue-eyed golden-haired babies).

"There's quite a good chance of a cure, you know," Fred had said rather uncertainly.

"I know . . . I can't even try to thank you," Monica had said.

He was silent for some moments, smoking his pipe and gazing in front of him, then he said:

"I loved your mother, Monny. I loved her in a way I could never love anyone else. I think you know that."

"Yes."

She had wanted to stay near Babs during the "cure", but the doctor had dissuaded her, and the letter from Greta had arrived just as she was wondering how to fill in the time during the weeks of Babs' treatment.

Greta was now Mrs. Hassock, busy with her own home and the parish affairs of St. Mark's, but she could not rid herself of a feeling of responsibility for Appleton Vicarage, and Mrs. Sanders magnificently ignored all other claims on her ex-secretary's time and interest. She had engaged a succession of secretaries since Greta married, none of whom stayed longer than a few weeks, and it happened that just now the nursery governess had gone home to nurse her mother through an illness.

It will be only for a few weeks, I think [wrote Greta], *but if you'd come along and give us a hand we'd be so grateful. It will just be a case of helping nurse with the children (we're going to let lessons slide) and helping Mrs. Sanders if she needs you. With the dictaphone, of course, there's not so much to do as there was in the old days, but she's planning an historical novel, and there are occasional references to be looked up.*

Monica, after discussing the matter with Fred, had agreed to go, and now the well-known landmarks were flashing by. She watched them dreamily, surrendering to an unfamiliar sensation of peace. It was strange to be able to relax like this, to be rid of the heart-rack of anxiety that she had known for so long; strange not to be wondering each moment if Babs were coming to some harm. Babs was safe—for the time, at any rate—in the cold white sanctuary of Linden Lodge. Freed from that ever-present preoccupation, Monica could turn her mind to the future. With the eager resilience of youth, she imagined a Babs restored to health of mind and body—the Babs whom she remembered faintly from her childhood—imagined the pleasant country home that they would share. She would get some work, of course. In the last years she had had many shortlived jobs, and the one she had liked best had been that of nursery governess to two children. It was a small enclosed world in which she felt safe and happy. The shyness and the distrust of life that had eaten so deeply into her soul did not hamper her there. She would try to find a post of that kind. A daily post with children in the country. Babs looking after the house and garden . . . knowing the neighbours . . . tea in the garden . . . walks in the woods . . . music on the wireless . . . long talks together . . . Just the two of them, like other girls with their mothers.

For a moment the picture was there like a light at the end of a tunnel, then it vanished and refused to come again. Life had given her so little that she couldn't really believe that it would ever give her this.

The train slid into Appleton station. She took her suitcase from the rack and stepped on to the platform. Nothing seemed to have changed since the last time she was there. A row of milkcans still stood by the station entrance, and the penny-in-the-slot machine was still out of order. Even the porter was the same—a little older, a little stouter, but as slow and deliberate as he had been seven years ago.

"Yes," he said, contemplating her suitcase thoughtfully, "I can take it up to the Vicarage for you, but mebbe not till after tea. Mebbe not till later. I got to stay here till the four-thirty comes in. 'Less old Somers turns up. Old Somers might take it up for you. Or one of the children. They hangs round here, coming back from school. I might send one o' them along. Or I might bring it up myself, but mebbe not till teatime. Mebbe not till later . . ."

She walked slowly along the lane to the Vicarage. The woods bordered the lane on either side, and here and there the oak trees met overhead. Beneath them, the delicate green lacework of the bracken stretched as far as she could see. A gate into the wood stood open, and, glancing down the broad shady ride, she saw three figures on horseback. The middle one was Angela, the others Stephen and Ralph Pollitt . . . Gripped by shyness, she hurried past the gate, turning her head away so that they should not recognize her.

She passed under the lilac tree and went up the drive to the Vicarage door. It was open, and there was no one in sight. After hesitating a moment, she entered and made her way upstairs to the schoolroom. Greta was sitting at the table in her hat and coat, making notes on a sheet of writing-paper. Greta looked younger and prettier, and there was a new air of assurance about her. She ran her home and parish with admired efficiency and was deeply happy in her marriage.

"Oh, there you are, dear," she said, as Monica entered. "I meant to meet your train, but I've been so busy getting things to rights here. This historical novel of Mrs. Sanders' has kept me rather on the run, because she needs a good deal of research. Actually and in strictest confidence, my dear, she doesn't know much history and she won't keep to what she does know, and I can't help thinking that it's a pity she launched into it at all. However, I'll just tell you about things very quickly, because I have to dash off to a G.F.S. meeting and I'm going to be late already. The children have taken their tea into the wood with nurse, and they won't be back till bedtime."

"How many children are there?"

"Four. Meg's parents are in India and an aunt took charge of her, but she finds the child rather a nuisance so sent her to us. Then there's Richard. His people have gone abroad for an indefinite period. I rather suspect that the father's in some sort of trouble. Someone from Scotland Yard came last week, asking questions about him . . . Then there's Penelope. Her parents are being divorced and neither of them wants her at present. Little Pamela was brought by her grandmother. I fancy that she's illegitimate, though she didn't actually say so. None of them wants the children home for the holidays, so it makes it a full-time job for us. It's good of you to come."

"I was glad to," said Monica.

"Angela ought to help, of course, but she won't. She won't help with the children or her mother's writing. I'm afraid she's selfish. When I think of the days when I did practically everything for the children and all Mrs. Sanders' secretarial work as well—!"

"She must have been upset when you told her you were going," said Monica.

Greta smiled a little wryly as she thought of that interview. She had passed sleepless nights bracing herself for it, preparing herself to face reproaches, tears, entreaties, and the actual interview had been almost incredibly short and simple.

"Olivia," she had said in a trembling voice, "would you mind very much if I left you? I'm going to marry Mr. Hassock."

"No, dear, that's quite all right," Olivia had said absently, without raising her eyes from the manuscript she was working on. "You'll train someone else before you go, won't you? . . . Will you look up 'ecstasy' in the Thesaurus, dear, and find another word for it? I've used it three times in this paragraph. No, four."

Greta gave Monica a brief account of the interview, and Monica smiled her slow shy smile.

"It's rather like Mrs. Jellaby, isn't it?" she said. " 'I've engaged a boy, and there's no more to be said.' "

"Actually, of course," said Greta, "she's never really taken in the fact that I've gone, and she still expects me to be about the place all day, which makes it a little difficult for me . . . I've made one or two notes about the work she's doing now. It might help you, but I'm afraid it won't, because she doesn't seem quite sure herself what she's doing." She rose and drew on her gloves. "And now I must fly. I want to escape before she catches me again. Come and see me if you have time, won't you, dear? I could find you something to do in the parish, but I'm afraid you won't have time for that . . . By the way, do you remember Geraldine Mortimer?"

Monica considered . . . A plump little girl with a round earnest face . . . a tense urgent little girl . . . a rather uncomfortable little girl.

"Yes."

"She's in our parish, you know—St. Mark's—and I find her most helpful. She takes the elder girls in Sunday School. Poor child! Her father died suddenly the day she left school. She's a great stand-by to her mother and sister. I don't know what they'd do without her. She's a librarian at Maybridge Public Library and doing very well there . . . Good-bye, dear. I'll run round and see how you're getting on in a day or so . . . Oh, if Mrs. Sanders wants to know anything more about Charles the Second, it's no use going to the Library, because I've got every book there is on him from every library within reach and they're all somewhere in the study. I've tried to weed out her anachronisms, but it isn't any use. She just puts them back again. Well, good-bye once more, dear. Oh, your bedroom's the one next the nursery. Now I'll creep down the back stairs, so that she can't catch me."

When Monica reached her bedroom she found that her suitcase had arrived. She unpacked the children's books that she had brought with her and took them along the passage to the schoolroom. Standing by the bookcase, she turned over the pages of *Uncle Remus*, remembering how Stephen had once stood there with her and said: "They're grand yarns, aren't they? I knew them almost by heart when I was a kid."

Then the door opened suddenly, and she turned to find Stephen in the room. He looked tall and handsome in his riding clothes.

"There you are!" he said. "I heard you were coming, so I thought I'd look in and say 'how-d'-you-do.' "

"That was kind of you," she said, trying to still the tumult of her spirit.

He perched on the edge of the table, swinging his legs and smiling at her.

"Not a bit. It's—seven years since the last time I saw you, isn't it?"

"Yes . . . Seven years."

He thought how little she had altered. She was not much taller. She was certainly no fatter. Her pale oval face was still framed in straight dark hair. It had hung in two plaits seven years ago. Now it was drawn into a coil on the nape of her neck. She wore a dark skirt and a plain white blouse. Her wrists were still thin and fragile, like an over-grown child's.

"It's many happy returns of the day and congratulations this time, isn't it?" he said.

Her eyes widened in surprise.

"Well, isn't it?" he said. "You were twenty-one last month, weren't you?"

"How did you know?"

He laughed and pointed to the book she held in her hand.

"I've got a good memory and I can do sums. It has the date of your fifth birthday in, you know. Look!" He put his hand into his pocket and brought out a small leather case. "It's not much of a thing, but there it is, with 'Many happy returns of the day.' "

She took the case and opened it. There was a brooch—three pearls on a thin gold bar. She turned away, unable to speak for a moment. Her twenty-first birthday had passed unnoticed. Babs was only just beginning to recover from one of her worst outbreaks, and Fred never remembered birthdays.

"Don't expect me ever to remember birthdays, kid," he had said, "because I can't. I've tried, and I've given it up."

In any case the youngest baby was ill at the time, and he had had thought for nothing else.

"I expect you had heaps of exciting presents, didn't you?" said Stephen.

She smiled at him unsteadily.

"No, I haven't had anything but this. It's so kind of you . . . I don't know what to say."

There were light footsteps in the passage outside, and Angela entered. She wore jodhpurs and a thin silk blouse with a velvet cap, perched askew on her soft fair curls. There was about her a radiance of health and vitality and joy of living.

"Hello, Monny," she said. "It was sweet of you to come and hold the fort. I'm the villain of the piece, of course. I ought to, but I just won't. I suppose Greta's told you I'm selfish. I am. I cling to my selfishness as a drowning man clings to a spar. Without it life in this house wouldn't be worth living." She looked at the case that Monica held in her hand and took her seat by Stephen on the table. "Does she like it?"

He nodded, smiling.

"Angela helped me choose it," he said to Monica.

"He wanted to get an awful thing with M on," said Angela.

For a moment Monica regretted the awful thing with M on, then happiness swept over her again.

"And . . . oh, dear, aren't I awful!" went on Angela. "I meant to get you something myself as well. I did, didn't I, Stephen? You remember, I said so. A handbag or something. And then it went clean out of my head. Things do go clean out of my head. I shouldn't be my mother's daughter, I suppose, if they didn't."

Stephen slipped an arm round her shoulders.

"Let's count it from both of us," he said.

"Yes. May we, Monny?"

"Oh, yes . . . It's so lovely. I can't tell you how I love it."

"Did you have a dance on your twenty-first?" said Angela.

"No."

"I did. It was wonderful. And I was wonderful, wasn't I, Stephen? White chiffon, Monny, very full, floating like cloud all round me. And gold shoes and a gold fillet in my hair. Philip wrote a poem to me. Don't tell him I told you or he'd kill me. I couldn't understand a word of it."

"You remember Philip, don't you?" said Stephen to Monica.

"Yes. He'd sprained his ankle the last time I was here."

"Yes, I remember. The young chump! He's just finished his third year at Oxford now, and he's on holiday with a friend in the Tyrol. He's brainy, you know. He's had quite a lot of his stuff published."

"No one can understand it," said Angela. "That's why he gets away with it. Like the Emperor's New Clothes. No one dare say they don't understand it in case someone else does."

"No, it's good stuff" said Stephen seriously. "I'm not highbrow myself—"

"No one thought you were, darling," said Angela. "You needn't try to break it gently. But you can survey and that's much more useful." She turned to Angela. "Stephen's working for his Final Examination. He's going to be a surveyor. He knows all about optical squares and offsets and test gauges and chain angles and things, don't you, Stephen?" She jumped down from the table and took the case from Monica's hands. "Let me put it on for you." Deftly she pinned the brooch at the neck of Monica's blouse. "There! It looks lovely. I wish you'd been here for my dance, Monny. Gerry came, but she sulked all the time."

246

"I think it's just her manner," said Stephen.

"If anyone murdered you, you'd say it was just their manner," said Angela. "It's horrible that it's over. I wish I could be twenty-one every week. It was the loveliest dance. Everything went right with it, even to mother's not being there. She meant to go to it till the last minute. She'd evolved a marvellous costume. A mixture of the Princess from *Swan Lake* and the Ugly Sister from *Cinderella*. You can imagine it, can't you, Monny? Then, at the last minute, she discovered that James the Second was Charles the Second's brother, not his son, so she had to stay at home to replan the whole book in the light of the discovery." Her gay chatter filled the room like bird-song. She had taken her seat on the table again next Stephen. They both watched her—Stephen with undisguised tenderness, Monica with wistful admiration. "Father came, of course. One eye on the clock and the other on the right people. He said all the right things to all the right people in the right tone of voice, taking just the right time for it. He might just have well sent a gramophone record. Greta was my real support. She did everything and saw to everything. She chaperoned and catered and lady's-maided and worked till she was fit to drop. Greta's got a bulldog grip. Once she takes hold of a thing she never lets go till it's through."

"Hi!" called a voice from the garden.

Angela leapt down from the table and went to the window.

"Right!" she called. "We're just coming." She turned to Stephen. "It's Ralph. He's got the tennis net fixed up, and he's champing to start. I've got to change, but I won't be a minute . . . Make a fourth, Monny?"

Monica shook her head.

"I can't. I'm sorry."

"Well, I'll fly and change. 'Bye, Monny. See you later. Don't let mother get you down."

She blew Monica a kiss and vanished.

"She's—lovely, isn't she?" said Monica, as the door closed. Stephen turned his eyes to her with a smile.

"Very lovely indeed."

There was a silence, then Monica said:

"You're in love with her, aren't you?"

"Yes."

"Are you—is she going to marry you?"

The corners of his long mouth deepened to seriousness.

"I hope so," he said. "I'm going to ask her this morning. Wish me luck, won't you?"

"Yes . . . Yes, of course I wish you luck."

"Gret-ah!"

Mrs. Sanders' voice filled the house like the distant echo of a storm.

Stephen and Monica looked at each other in startled silence.

"Gret-*ah*!"

Beneath the imperiousness was a certain wild appeal.

"I'd better go," said Monica.

Mrs. Sanders was standing at the foot of the stairs. Her hair was in disarray and there was the familiar smudge of ink across her forehead. She wore a dress of the "coat frock" variety that buttoned up the front and that showed strange little loops where the wrong buttons met the wrong holes.

"Where's Greta?" she demanded.

"She had to go a G.F.S. meeting," said Monica, descending the stairs.

Mrs. Sanders raised her hand to her head.

"I remember now. You're Muriel, aren't you?"

"Monica."

"Monica?" Mrs. Sanders appeared to give the name deep consideration. "Didn't I say 'Monica'? I thought I had done . . . Well, anyway, come into the study now, Muriel dear. I want you to do something for me."

Monica followed Mrs. Sanders into the study and stood for a moment in the doorway looking round in silent dismay. Books covered floor, chairs and sofa. Even the fender was full of them. Some were closed, some open. One had a shoehorn thrust into it to mark a place. Another was hung over the wall-bracket of the electric light evidently for the same purpose.

"Listen, dear," said Mrs. Sanders. "I want the exact details of the marriage ceremony at Gretna Green in Charles the Second's time. It's sure to be in one of those books. I've started looking, but I can't spare the time to go through all of them. I'm just drawing up the plan of the book, and I've got an elopement in the first chapter, and I must have the correct detail. Correct detail is important in a historical novel."

"I—I don't think that Gretna Green elopements existed in Charles the Second's time," said Monica.

"Oh, nonsense, Muriel!" said Mrs. Sanders. "There have always been Gretna Green elopements in historical novels. I've never read one without it. The whole plot generally revolves round it."

There was a new note of peevishness in Mrs. Sanders' voice. Something of her serene detachment had deserted her since she had decided to write a historical novel. It had been a momentous decision and she had not taken it without long and serious cogitation. She had not tired of her novelettes. It was the public that had tired of them. Slowly, surely, incredibly, her sales had shrunk. For some time she had refused to acknowledge it, but it had at last reached a point where neither she nor her publisher could ignore it any longer. And it was at this point that she had decided to write an historical novel. She had thrown herself into the idea with enthusiasm. The enthusiasm had faded . . . had revived . . . had faded again.

"I'm suffering the birth pangs," she would say grandiloquently, "of a new career."

But she was irked and irritated by the fidelity to fact and detail that such a work entailed, and periods of deep depression would alternate with outbursts of fretfulness against the various historical personages whose lives refused to comply with the formula of her novelettes.

"Now, come along, Muriel," she said briskly. "We'll go through the books together. You start over there by the fireplace and I'll start by the window. You can take in the sofa and I'll take in the armchair. If there's an index in any of them, look up Gretna Green."

"But—" began Monica uncertainly.

"Now don't start chattering, dear," said Mrs. Sanders. "I find it so distracting."

For some moments they turned over pages in silence, then suddenly Mrs. Sanders shut the book that she was consulting and flung it away from her.

"It's no good," she said. "I can't get on terms with Charles the Second. He doesn't *mean* anything. There's no *grandeur* about him, and I must have grandeur." She gazed into the distance and gradually a light began to shine through the gloom of her ink-stained countenance.

"Henry the Eighth!" she cried. "I could get on terms with him. He has grandeur . . . A little adjustment here and there, a little glossing over of the cruder episodes. He had seven wives, didn't he?"

"Six, I think," said Monica.

"Oh, yes. I always confuse him with the man going to St. Ives. Six . . . Four chapters to each. I see the whole pattern of the book already. Grandeur and romance . . . Collect all those books together, Muriel dear, and take them back to the library and get me out all the books there are on Henry the Eighth."

Monica stacked the books as neatly as she could against the wall. Mrs. Sanders was sitting at her writing-desk, her head in her hands.

"You may go now, dear," she said. "I must be alone. I must concentrate . . . I'm trying to think of a title . . . 'A Royal Lover' . . . 'Shattered Dreams' . . . 'Tangled Skeins' . . . 'Twisting Paths' . . . 'Fallen Idols' . . ."

Monica went upstairs and began to look into the bedrooms to find out which belonged to which children, so as to be able to help them when they came back from the wood . . . Yes, this was Meg's room. There was a framed photograph on the chest of drawers of a pretty, rather wistful-looking young woman, inscribed, "Mummy, with dear love to Meg." The mother in India who had left her in a sister's charge . . . and the sister had found her rather a nuisance and had sent her to Appleton Vicarage. She went to the window and stood, looking down at the garden. Stephen and Angela stood by the gate, talking. I wonder if he's asking her to marry him, thought Monica. I wonder if she will. I hope she will. I hope she'll make him happy. He deserves to be happy more than anyone else in the world. He's so kind . . . Then her thoughts went to Babs—Babs, with her ravaged haunted face, in the bare white prison of Linden Lodge—and she felt guilty at having forgotten her even for a moment.

"Darling," Stephen was saying, "you don't know how happy you've made me."

Angela laughed.

"You do talk in *clichés*, don't you, Stephen?" she said. "Mother's heroes always say that when they've laid their heart at the heroine's feet and she's picked it up."

"It may be a *cliché*, but I mean it . . . Angela, why mayn't we tell people?"

"Because I don't want people to know yet," said Angela. "I want it to be a secret between us—just for a bit. You promised, Stephen."

"I know."

"Promise again. Say, 'I swear it.'"

"I swear it," he said reluctantly; "but—we are engaged, aren't we, darling? You are going to marry me?"

"Of course. I've said so, haven't I?"

"You do love me?"

"Yes, I do . . . I do, Stephen."

"Kiss me again."

"Not here!" She laughed. "They can see us from the road and from all the windows in the house. Be good, darling. We've got the rest of our lives for kissing each other."

"When can we tell people?"

"Oh, soon," she said vaguely. She looked up at him with a coaxing smile and put her hands on the lapels of his coat. "I want it to belong to the two of us for a bit. Just something of it will be spoilt when other people know. Let's have it for a secret just for a day or two, Stephen. Be nice to me about it. It's only because I love you so."

He kissed her on the lips.

"*Stephen!* They'll see."

"Let them."

She freed herself and ran indoors.

As she passed the study door she heard her mother's deep voice . . . "'Warped Webs' . . . 'Darkening Skies' . . . 'Clouds at Sunset'."

As soon as she reached her bedroom the telephone rang, and she took up the receiver from the little table by her bed.

"Hello."

Ralph's clear penetrating voice answered.

"That you, darling?"

"Yes."

"Has Stephen gone?"

"Yes."

"I've been in hell, thinking of you and him together."

"Why shouldn't we be?"

"He's so damned good-looking. But, darling, it is me you're going to marry, isn't it?"

"Of course."

"When can we tell people?"

"Not yet. I want it to be a secret between us just for a bit longer. You promised."

"I know. I'm finding it damned hard to keep."

"If you don't keep it I'll never speak to you again. Be nice to me, Ralph. It's just that"—her eyes were dancing, her lips curved into a smile of mischievous enjoyment—"just something of it will be spoilt when other people know. It's because I love you so."

"Darling!"

The clear penetrating voice was hoarse with emotion.

"I must fly now. Good-bye."

"Good-bye, loveliest."

She put back the receiver and took up a letter that lay by it on the table. It was from Philip, and was, for him, unusually straightforward and to the point.

Up here among the mountains you seem nearer to me than when I'm at home. I can't give you any of the things you ought to have, Angela, but could you ever care enough to wait for me? Do I mean anything to you at all? Will you tell me when you write? I can't bear the uncertainty.

She thought of the letter she had written and posted last night. In it she had told him that she needed time to get used to the idea of an engagement. She assured him that she loved him, but said that the "understanding" must remain a secret for the present.

She went out on to the landing. An exhilarating sense of adventure and danger possessed her, giving everything around her a new and heightened significance, investing even the narrow Vicarage corridor and the mop that a housemaid had left there with an air of mystery and romance.

A door at the end of the corridor opened, and Monica came out.

"Hello, Monny," said Angela. "What are you doing?"

"Just exploring," said Monica. "That's Meg's room."

But Angela was not interested in the flotsam and jetsam of child life that was cast up on the shores of the Vicarage. She stood there, smiling to herself.

"You know, Monny," she said, "I've spent my life trying not to be my mother's daughter, but I'm beginning to suspect that I am, after all."

Chapter Twenty-One

Monica approached the counter behind which Geraldine sat in official isolation, flanked on one side by a bowl of marigolds and on the other by a filing cabinet.

"Hello, Gerry."

Geraldine stared at her for a moment.

"Why, it's Monica!"

The warm kindliness of her smile dispelled Monica's shyness.

"Yes. I've come to help at the Vicarage."

"Of course. I remember now. Greta told me you were coming. It's splendid of you."

"No, I was glad to come. I was—at a sort of loose end. My mother's gone into a nursing home and—"

"Nothing serious, I hope?"

"Oh, no. She—she needed a rest. It's just a rest cure, but she'll be there for some time."

She looked at Geraldine with interest. She had not seen her since the day four years ago when she had caught a fleeting glimpse of her on Paddington station. She was still short and plump. Her mouth was large and full, her eyes soft and velvety behind the horn-rimmed spectacles. An air of kindliness and efficiency radiated from her.

"I've brought some books back," went on Monica, opening her attaché-case.

"Thanks," said Geraldine, taking the books. "Not fined, for a wonder. How are things at the Vicarage?"

"All right."

"What's Angela doing with herself these days?"

"She's out riding with Stephen this morning," said Monica absently. She was wondering if Stephen had proposed yesterday. The engagement had not been announced. Perhaps he's proposing now, she thought. Just now—this very minute when I'm standing here with Geraldine.

Geraldine's mouth had tightened. She disapproved of Angela.

"She would be . . . Philip's in the Tyrol, you know."

"Yes. Stephen told me."

Geraldine hesitated, then took her handbag from a shelf under the counter and brought out a picture postcard.

"I had this from him."

It was a picture of Lake Scin with Mount Tofane in the background. On it was written: "*Having a wonderful holiday here. Best wishes. Philip.*" It was the first time Philip had written to her, but she knew by now every turn and twist of the erratic handwriting. She had read it a hundred times since it had arrived.

"It looks lovely," said Monica. She glanced round the library. "This must be an interesting job."

"Yes, it is," said Geraldine. "I was lucky to get it. I had to have a job near home when my father died. I have my mother and Elaine to look after now."

Her thoughts went back to the day when Albert had been found lying at the foot of his arbour, and she remembered with a familiar feeling of guilt the stab of exultation that had shot through her before she had time to stop it. She's mine altogether now . . . Mine . . . Mine . . . She had explained it away to herself over and over again, translating it into a determination to carry on Albert's work, shoulder his responsibilities, but she couldn't quite convince herself. She had loved the earnest conscientious little man who had been her foster-father, but something in her had been glad when he died, and the knowledge still made her deeply ashamed.

Greta approached the counter, a book under her arm. She looked well-groomed and smart in a tailored suit and a becoming hat.

"Well, Monica, how are things going?"

"Quite well," said Monica, "but Mrs. Sanders has decided not to do Charles the Second, after all. She's decided to do Henry the Eighth, and she wants the books changed."

"Oh, dear!" said Greta. "I knew there'd be nothing but trouble once she got this historical idea into her head. She'll never settle. As Theo says, she'll just *flit* from age to age. Oh, well, it can't be helped. She's got plenty of tickets because she uses the whole household's. I'll go round with you, dear, and help you choose some." She handed her book to Geraldine. "Theo's sent back the Thomas Aquinas and he wants Bede's *Ecclesiastical History*. I'll go and see if it's in the shelves. Come along, Monica. We'll see to yours first."

The two went round to the historical section, and Greta pulled out half a dozen books dealing with the reign of Henry the Eighth.

"There you are, dear; though, honestly, it's not worth while taking much trouble over it, because she'll probably have changed her mind again before you get back."

Grace and Elaine were having tea in the little sitting-room. The evening was turning chilly and they had lit the fire. Grace sat in the armchair, and Elaine on a footstool at her feet. The tea was laid on a low table on the hearthrug. There was about the two of them a suggestion of enclosed but precarious happiness. Every now and then one of them would steal a furtive glance at the clock, to see how much time they had left before Geraldine came home.

"Would it be terribly greedy of me to eat the last of those little cakes?" said Elaine. "They are lovely, aren't they? Where did they come from?"

Elaine was small and slight for her fourteen years. Her chestnut hair hung loose about her shoulders, shading the oval face and grey-blue eyes. The body in the navy blue skirt and white blouse was still a child's body. There was a delicate fragile air about her.

"Gerry made them last night."

At the mention of Geraldine a constraint entered the atmosphere, and they seemed to draw closer together as if in defence against some common foe. The thought of Geraldine always did that to them, and neither of them could have explained why. Elaine finished the little cake in silence, then moved the table to one side and rested her head on her mother's knee.

"Mother . . ."

"Yes, darling?"

"I want to leave school when I've passed School Cert, and learn typing or something and get a job. I don't want to go to college."

"Gerry wants you to, dear."

"I know."

"And she does so much for us."

"I know." Her head jerked up mutinously. "But I'm not clever. I don't even want to be clever. I hate school."

Her school days at Maybridge High School had not been happy ones. The presence of Geraldine—anxious, loving, self-sacrificing— in the background had cast a shadow over them. Geraldine supervising her work, her friendships, her interests, exacting with loving insistence at the end of each day a full account of the day's doings—an account that, as the years went on, became more and more full of little lies and evasions. And tugging against the resentment was her love for Geraldine, a love that had its roots deep in her childhood and that had grown up maimed and tormented.

"Well, let's not worry about it now, darling," said Grace.

"All right . . . Mother, we are going up to London on Saturday, aren't we?"

She spoke in an eager whisper as if afraid of being overheard.

"Yes, darling. We'll go up by the eleven thirty."

"May we have lunch at Fuller's?"

"Yes."

"And then—we *are* going to *Me and My Girl*, aren't we?"

"Yes."

They had done this several times on Saturdays lately—gone up to London after Geraldine had left for the Library, had lunch, gone to a matinee, and been back at home before Geraldine returned from work. They had made no mention of their "jaunt" and Geraldine had never suspected it. Neither could have put into words the instinct that made them keep it a secret from her. The conspiracy had been tacit and slightly shamefaced. But the days stood out in the memories of both of them—golden days, full of happiness and a delicious sense of adventure.

Elaine lifted her head and looked at her mother, eyes alight with excitement.

"Won't it be fun! Just you and me! Let's shop-gaze down Bond Street first, shall we? We shall have time. Let's buy you a hat."

Grace laughed.

"No, darling. I don't need a hat and, anyway, I couldn't buy one in Bond Street."

Elaine clasped her hands round her knees. Her vivid little face sparkled with pleasure.

"Well, *something*. Let's go into a shop together and buy something. Even if it's only a hairnet or hairpins."

"All right. Hairpins," said Grace.

Elaine gave a chuckle of amusement.

"It'll be a lovely day, won't it?"

"Yes," said Grace.

She leant back in her chair and let her eyes wander round the room at all the things that Albert had made—the bookshelves, the writing-desk, the little table, the chair with PAX 1918 on the back. Suddenly Albert seemed to be there in the room with them, and her world was complete once more.

Then through the silence came the sound of Geraldine's key in the lock. The two roused themselves with a start, and into both their faces flashed a look of rather comical and quite unconscious guilt.

Geraldine entered the room, bringing with her the atmosphere of briskness that she always seemed to bring with her wherever she went. Her arms were full of parcels, and she stood in the doorway smiling at them affectionately.

"How are you, darlings?" she said. "Had tea?"

"Yes, dear," said Grace. "We thought it best not to wait."

"Of course," said Geraldine, coming into the room. "I hate you waiting for me. Besides, if Elaine's had her tea she can start right away with her homework, can't you, darling?"

258

The smile she turned on Elaine was full of pride and tenderness. Elaine sprang to her feet, and Grace straightened her drooping figure in her chair. The contented lassitude that had enclosed them had been shattered by the first note of Geraldine's voice.

"I'll get your tea," said Elaine.

"No, don't bother, Elly."

"Yes, I will."

Elaine put the used tea-things on to the tray and carried it from the room.

Geraldine sat down on the settee and laid her parcels by her, "Tired, dear?" she said to Grace.

"No, thank you."

Geraldine never noticed Grace's lack of response. So entirely did Elaine fill the forefront of her life that Grace only existed for her as a vague gentle figure in the background. She was not, in any case, perceptive, and she had always put down Grace's quietness and air of indifference to her general ill-health.

"I've had quite an amusing afternoon," said Geraldine. "Monica Patterson came in. She's that girl who was at the Vicarage with me, you know, when Elaine was born, and she's come to give a hand there now. Mrs. Sanders was going to write a novel about Charles the Second, and she's changed to Henry the Eighth overnight."

Her laughter rang out. She was feeling even more cheerful than usual this evening (and she always loved this moment of homecoming) because the thought of Philip's postcard was like a warm glow in her heart. Grace gave a constrained smile. She had never considered Mrs. Sanders amusing.

"Now look, darling," said Geraldine, opening one of the parcels. "I've got this sock wool for you from Miss Cambridge. She belongs to a sort of society that knits socks for fishermen, and I thought it would be so nice for you to join. This will make four pairs, and when you've finished them I'll take it back and get you some more. It will help to occupy your time."

Grace looked at the wool without enthusiasm. The trouble was that she didn't want her time occupied. She was quite content to have her time unoccupied . . . She loved to potter aimlessly about the house and garden. She could lie for hours on the sofa in a state between waking and sleeping. Effort of any kind exhausted her. But Geraldine, of course, couldn't understand this. Ever since Albert's death she had considered it her duty to try to find fresh interests for Grace. In some way this eased the secret feeling of compunction she always had towards Albert, compensated for that swift shameful stab of joy that had seized her unawares when she saw him lying there at the foot of the arbour.

"And I met Mrs. Foxton and her sister in Maybridge in the lunch hour," went on Geraldine. "I asked them to come in next Sunday evening."

Dismay flashed into Grace's face. She was terrified of strangers.

"But I don't know them," she said.

"I know, but you'll like them when you do get to know them. You ought to know more people, dear. It would be good for you. It's only a question of making an effort . . . They have a little discussion group that meets every other Thursday, and they said they'd be glad for you to join it."

"I don't want to join it, dear," said Grace.

She drew nearer the fire as she spoke. Despite Geraldine's brightness, the room seemed to have grown colder since she entered it.

Elaine brought in the tea-tray and put it on the table by Geraldine.

"Thank you, dear," said Geraldine, smiling at her. "What is it to-night? Latin Unseen, Algebra, French Translation and the History essay, isn't it?"

"Yes."

The light that had shone in Elaine a few moments ago had gone out. She looked listless and sulky.

"We must really tackle your Latin seriously, you know, darling," said Geraldine, as she poured out her tea. "I think an hour a day next holidays would help, wouldn't it?"

"Yes."

"I could set you some work each morning and correct it in the evening, couldn't I?"

"Yes."

Geraldine laughed.

"Don't sound so depressed. We must get you into college, you know. Look! I've brought you a present." She opened one of the parcels that lay by her and took out a book. "I got it at Smith's in the lunch hour. It's the story of the Aeneid. A lot of the unseens are taken from Vergil, you know, and it does so help to have a clear idea of the story in your mind."

"Thank you very much," said Elaine, sitting down and turning over the pages of the book.

She would have liked it if Gerry hadn't made a lesson book of it. As it was, it joined the dead weight of the things that Gerry expected of her . . .

"And I got a little guide to the Shakespeare country out of the Library," said Geraldine, taking a small book from her handbag and giving a rather self-conscious laugh. "I know it's terribly early to think about next summer's holiday, but it's fun to plan it, isn't it? We could read it together in the evenings. I think the Shakespeare country would be grand, don't you, mother?"

"Yes," said Grace.

She avoided Elaine's eye as she spoke. Those summer holidays that Geraldine planned so exhaustively, on which she spent her money so lavishly, organizing little expeditions each day . . . and every year they longed guiltily to slip away together and have a lazy effortless holiday, just the two of them.

"Oh, and I've got a little present for you, too, mother," she said, opening the last parcel and taking out a small box. "It's two packs of patience cards and a little book with twenty different games. I thought it would give you something to do in the evenings when Elly and I are busy with her homework. Some of them are for two players. You and I could play them after Elaine's gone to bed."

Grace turned over the pages of the book. Useless to tell Geraldine that she didn't like patience. She'd told her so a hundred times already.

"Well, this won't do," said Geraldine, rising briskly to her feet and carrying the tray to the door. "I'll go and take my things off and then we'll tackle the French, shall we, dear?"

Again she turned the proud loving smile on Elly. Elly must do well in her exams, go to college, qualify for a good career, whatever sacrifice it meant. Only the best was good enough for Elly.

As soon as the door had closed on her Elaine put down her book and knelt by her mother's chair.

"Saturday?" she whispered.

"Saturday."

"Let's go by an earlier train. Let's go the *minute* Gerry's out of the house. Let's have coffee somewhere. Let's make it a real treat."

"Very well, darling."

"Let's buy lots and *lots* of hairpins."

Grace took the small shining face between her hands.

"All right. We'll even buy a hairnet."

"Two hairnets!"

"Yes."

Laughing, Elaine hid her face on her mother's knee. Then she raised it.

"Let's have a Charlotte Russe at Fuller's. I'll stand you one out of my pocket-money."

"No, I'll stand you one."

"Don't you hope the one-man-band comes when we're in the pit queue?"

"Yes."

"And the one that cuts out paper patterns?"

"Yes."

"And the one that imitates Harry Lauder?"

"Yes."

"We could catch the nine-forty—"

The door had opened suddenly.

"Catch the nine-forty where?" said Geraldine, entering.

"To London," said Elaine.

Her face had gone set and sullen.

"We thought of going up to London on Saturday," said Grace quietly.

Geraldine sat down and drew her brows together thoughtfully.

"Saturday . . ." she said. "Yes, I think I could get off. They always let me change my free day if I want to."

They looked at her helplessly. It never occurred to Geraldine that she was not a welcome third on all their outings.

"What are the plans?" she said.

Elaine answered reluctantly, her eyes on the ground.

"We were going to have lunch at Fuller's and then go to *Me and My Girl*."

Geraldine considered.

"Fuller's, darling? That's a little extravagant, isn't it? We ought to be saving for your college fees now, you know, so we mustn't be extravagant. We could take sandwiches and eat them in the park or, if it's wet, in the station. It saves quite a lot, doesn't it?"

"Yes."

"And why start so early?"

"We wanted to shop-gaze."

Geraldine laughed.

"Shop-gaze? Oh, darling, that *is* a waste of time. If one has anything definite to buy, it's different, but you haven't, have you? It would be much better to spend the morning finishing your homework and then you could go with a clear mind . . . Did you say *Me and My Girl*?"

"Yes."

"Quite amusing, I believe, but not really worth while. Do you know, I think *Twelfth Night* is on at the Old Vic and that's one of your set books for next year, so you certainly ought to see it. Shall we fix on that? Will that be all right, Mother?"

"Yes," said Grace.

She was too tired to fight or even argue. Always, after a few minutes of Geraldine, she was too tired to fight or even argue.

"You'd like that, wouldn't you, Elly?"

"Yes," muttered Elaine.

A dreary meal of sandwiches . . . *Twelfth Night*, with Gerry giving her lessons on Shakespeare in the intervals . . . all the fun and adventure gone from the day.

"That's all settled then," said Geraldine brightly. "We'll go up on Saturday and have a really lovely time. And now you ought to start your homework, dear. Come into the dining-room and I'll get you settled."

They went from the room, but Elaine turned at the door and ran back to her mother.

"The Saturday after?" she whispered.

Grace nodded reassuringly.

"Yes. The Saturday after."

Then she leant back in her chair, gazing at the fire. There was a strange new feeling of desperation at her heart. It can't go on, she thought. I shall have to do something to stop it.

There came the sound of a knock at the front door. Geraldine, who was hearing Elaine's French verbs, went to answer it. A boy of about sixteen stood there—a tall lanky boy of sixteen with untidy hair and a pleasant ingenuous expression. He was one of the Ropers, who lived next door, and he had lately begun to attach himself to Elaine whenever possible. Geraldine looked at him coldly.

"What do you want, Terence?"

Terry looked taken aback. He hadn't seen Geraldine return and he had thought that it was one of the nights when she stayed late at the Library.

"Is Elaine in?"

"Yes, but she's busy. What do you want?"

"I—I wanted to swop stamps."

"You can't. She's doing her homework."

"May I come in later?"

"No. She'll have no time. Good night."

She closed the door on him abruptly.

"Who was it, Geraldine?" said Grace, as Geraldine entered the sitting-room.

"It was Terence Roper," said Geraldine.

There was a high colour in her face and her lips were tight.

"What did he want?"

"He said he wanted to swop stamps with Elaine." She closed the door. "I don't want Elaine to have anything to do with him or any of them. They aren't the sort of friends she ought to have. They're second-rate."

"Elaine likes Terry," said Grace. "She must have friends."

"There are the Middletons. They're very nice children. Sensible, quiet and well-behaved."

"I don't think that Elaine likes sensible, quiet and well-behaved children."

"Of course she won't," said Geraldine a little tartly, "if she's allowed to associate with people like the Ropers."

Grace was silent. If Geraldine had not set her face so venomously against the friendship between Elaine and Terry Roper, it would not have taken on the element of secrecy that it now held. She knew (though Elaine did not know that she knew) that Elaine had gone to the pictures with him on the afternoon when Geraldine thought she was at the Maybridge Museum.

The telephone bell rang, and Geraldine went to answer it. She returned a few minutes later, smiling to herself.

"That was Monica," she said. "Mrs. Sanders has decided not to write the book on Henry the Eighth, after all. She's going to write one on Boadicea, and she insisted on Monica's ringing me up to see if we have any books on her in the library. As far as I know we have some, but she'll probably have decided on King Canute or Queen Victoria by to-morrow."

Grace didn't answer. She hadn't been listening. I shall have to do something to stop it, she was saying to herself.

Chapter Twenty-Two

Ann stood on the terrace of Penbury Lodge, looking out over the garden. A morning mist, milky and tenuous, still lingered there, hiding among the bushes, drifting like a ghost across the open spaces. Through it glowed the fire of the roses, the leaping flames of dahlias and michaelmas daisies.

Barry strolled round the side of the house and joined her, pipe in mouth.

"It's going to be hot," he said.

"Yes. We're lucky. We've never had the garden-party as late in the year as this before."

"All set for it, I see."

At the end of the lawn the servants were putting out small tables and groups of chairs. A gardener was mowing the grass paths. Another one was taking a last survey of the borders, hoe in hand.

She nodded.

"All the years I've been here it's never once been wet for the garden-party."

"Yes, that's the tradition," said Barry. "My mother used to say it never rained on that day. She seemed to think that it was one of the laws of nature."

"It does seem to be. Barry . . ."

"Yes?"

"Do you remember when we stood just like this fourteen years ago, when Philip was coming back from Appleton Vicarage? I was so afraid."

"And there was no need to be. I told you at the time. He's—an odd chap, but he's all right. I think this trip in the Tyrol has improved him. Taken him out of himself."

Her smile was tinged with a faint irony.

"I don't think anything could do that. And there's nothing he'd hate more."

"Well," said Barry indulgently, "all writers are a bit self-centred and he seems to be settling down into a writer." He paused and added, for he found Philip's work quite incomprehensible, "A writer of sorts, anyway. He gets his stuff published and that's pretty good for a boy of his age."

Philip came up the steps from the garden. He wore a yellow scarf with a green golfing jacket and puce-coloured corduroy trousers. He had returned from the Tyrol last night and was still mentally in the transitional stage between home and holidays, trying to feel his way back into the manner of cynical detachment that was his ordinary attitude to his family. His costume was intended to assist his efforts. For a long time now he had aimed at striking a note in dress, speech and manner that would class him among "cissies" and "Bohemians". Once this had had the desired effect of shocking his family circle, but they had now grown so used to it that they accepted it with amused, if slightly rueful, resignation, and he sometimes felt it hardly worth the trouble.

"You're not going to appear in that costume this afternoon, I hope, Philip?" said Ann.

"If you aren't careful," said Philip, "I shall appear in my Tyrolean peasant's outfit."

He had defended his fortress against Ann so resolutely and so blindly that it had been a long time before he had realized that defence was unnecessary because she was already inside it, but the sympathy between them was so deep that it could be ignored on the surface, and his manner to her was the same manner of cynical detachment that he showed to the others.

"We've got the loud-speaker fixed up in the oak tree over there," said Barry. "I understand there is appropriate music on the B.B.C. programmes."

"*The Merry Widow*, I hope," said Philip. "Such a sweet tune and so much in keeping with the atmosphere of the occasion."

"Well, I like it myself," said Barry, with the indulgent smile he always accorded to Philip's vagaries.

A gardener came up the steps.

"Shall we put the trestle tables in the usual place, madam? I thought perhaps with it bein' later in the year the other side of the lawn might be better, because of the shadow of the cedar tree. It falls over this end about four o'clock."

"Yes, of course," said Ann. "I think the other side, don't you, Barry?"

He nodded.

"Yes, the other side," said Ann.

The gardener touched his cap and went down the steps. Ann looked at her watch. "I oughtn't to be idling here, there's such a lot to see to."

"Don't wear yourself out before it starts," said Barry.

"Why do you have the thing at all?" said Philip.

"What d'you mean—why do we have the thing at all?" said Barry.

"Well, you ask the same people every year and they have to ask you back and you all find it a nuisance and expense and are glad when it's over. It's like the savage ritual dance of some primitive tribe. Why go on with it?"

Barry laughed.

"My dear boy, one can't let the social side of things go."

"Why not?"

Ann slipped her arm through Philip's. It was rather a daring gesture, but he did not repulse her.

"Don't be tiresome, Philip. You haven't told us anything about your holiday yet. Did you go to Vienna?"

"Just for the last four days."

"Did you hear any opera?"

"Yes. *Don Giovanni* and *William Tell*."

"Lucky boy!"

Stephen came out of the french windows and strolled across the terrace to them. At once Philip moved away, as he always did when the four of them were together, standing in deliberate isolation, leaning over the parapet.

"A grand day, after all," said Stephen.

"I knew it would be," said Barry. "There was a red sunset last night. The place might have been on fire."

"Looked pretty good, didn't it?" said Stephen, throwing a glance at the house. "I saw it from Halcomb Hill."

"It's the red brick with the trees round it," said Barry. "I used to get a kick out of it at sunset even when I was a kid. I used to think it was like something out of a story, like—"

"A strawberry jelly on a lace d'oyley," said Philip. "It was a pretty good joke to build this terrace with a stone balustrade."

Because he knew that his father and Stephen loved the place, he always tried to hide his own love for it under a covering of mockery.

"Your great-great-grandfather did that," said Barry. "People couldn't leave their places alone in his time. Originally the ground just sloped away to the tennis-court. By the way, Stephen, got the tennis fixed up?"

"More or less," said Stephen. "I know pretty well who's going to play." He glanced across at Philip. "You going to play, Pip?"

Philip shuddered.

"Heaven forbid!"

Stephen grinned.

"You are a young jackass," he said.

"Well, I'll go and finish unpacking," said Philip and turned to go indoors.

In his bedroom he looked round at the open suitcases and the welter of packing that littered the floor, then, sitting down at his writing-desk, took Angela's letter from his pocket and read it again. As he read it, he came to a sudden decision. He would ask her to marry him this afternoon at the garden-party.

There was a knock at the door, and Stephen entered.

"How are you getting on?" he said. "Can I give you a hand with anything?"

"No, thanks," said Philip, slipping the letter back into his pocket.

"The chaos looks worse than it is. It's what is known as the darkest hour before the dawn."

An attaché-case lay open on the floor, disgorging its contents all round.

"May I look at these?" said Stephen, bending down to pick up some picture postcards.

"Yes . . . and I've got some sketches here that Westering did." He burrowed among the papers. "Here they are. They're pretty good, aren't they?" He stood by Stephen looking down at the sketches. "That's part of the Ampezzo valley. You can see the Cristallo group of mountains. And here's the Antelao. You can see the snow slopes at the back of the summit and the splintered buttresses that strike down towards Borco and Vodo."

Stephen looked at the views, sucking his pipe.

"It's grand scenery," he said.

"The colour's indescribable."

"I'd like to try some climbing out there one of these days. Where exactly did you go?"

Philip took a map from the confusion of papers in his attaché-case and began to trace the route he had followed, describing the holiday day by day, incident by incident. Stephen listened with interest, asking questions, making comments.

Suddenly Philip turned and went to the window, standing there with his back to the room. He knew that when he did not resent friendliness, as he frequently did, he was apt to respond to it with overmuch eagerness, but Stephen's interest had touched him, and the need to confide in someone was irresistible.

"Stephen . . ."

"Yes?"

"I don't want you to tell anyone, but—I'm going to ask Angela to marry me."

Stephen's face went blank. His hand tightened over a picture of the Auronzo valley.

"I know, of course," went on Philip, "that we shall have to wait years before we can get married, but, if she cares enough, and I think she does care enough—"

He turned round. Stephen had stood up.

"Wish me luck," said Philip, "and—"

But Stephen had muttered something inaudible and gone from the room.

The garden-party was in full swing. The day's promise had been fulfilled, and the sun shone down from a clear blue sky flecked by sleepy white clouds. Figures in white flannels and tennis frocks darted to and fro on the tennis-courts, while their elders strolled about the garden or sat in deck-chairs watching the games. The strains of the *Rosen Kavalier* waltz floated down from the oak tree, and over all was an atmosphere of decorous enjoyment and well-being.

Angela looked radiant in a dress of white organdie and a wide-brimmed leghorn hat with black velvet ribbons tied under her chin. Having had to choose between tennis and the white organdie, she had chosen the white organdie. She was escorted by a tall angular youth, called Cedric Horsham, whose father, a wealthy baronet, had lately come to live in Maybridge. She gave him her whole attention, throwing him provocative glances from under her dark curling lashes, aware of the other three—Stephen, Ralph and Philip—hovering in the background, each waiting his opportunity to claim her. After her first bright impersonal smile of greeting, she had ignored all three.

It was Stephen who managed at last to waylay her, snatching a moment when Cedric had been dispatched by an old lady to fetch her lorgnettes from the pocket of her car.

"Angela, I must speak to you."

"Not now, Stephen," she said, looking round for escape.

"It's something important!' he said. "Something's happened that I must tell you about."

"Please, Stephen!"

"I won't worry you, and I won't keep you for more than five minutes, but I must speak to you."

She yielded to his urgency with a shrug.

"Very well."

"Come into the summer-house. I don't want anyone to disturb us. No, darling, I've promised you that I'm not going to worry you, but there's something I must talk to you about."

Reluctantly she accompanied him to the summer-house. It was a small tumble-down affair that Barry's grandfather had built when he brought home his bride. She used to sit there on summer afternoons, doing her needlework, and the two of them used to have tea there. It had been a bright new toy in those days—with curtains at the windows, gay cushions on the chairs and a tea-cloth of Madeira work that she had brought home from her honeymoon. Now it wore a sad decrepit air—a prey to damp and dust and slow decay.

"I hate these places," said Angela a little peevishly. "All earwigs and spiders' webs and mould. They smell like graves. I can't think why people ever had them."

"Listen, Angela," said Stephen. "Did you know that Philip was in love with you?"

She turned a slow wondering gaze on him.

"Philip?"

"Well, he is," said Stephen. "He's in love with you and he's going to propose to you this afternoon. I want you to let me tell him—about us. I didn't tell him because I'd promised you not to, but now I must tell him. It would be cruel to let him go on without knowing. I feel the greatest bounder on earth for not having told him at once, but I'd promised."

She smiled at him alluringly from under the shade of the broad-brimmed hat.

"He's just a silly boy," she said.

"Then may I tell him?"

"Tell him what?"

"That we're engaged."

"You take a lot for granted, darling," she said. "I'm terribly fond of you—you're one of the best friends I have—but did I ever say we were engaged?"

"You know you did."

She wrinkled her brows as if in thought.

"You proposed to me, and I wanted time to think it over, didn't I?"

"Don't tease me, darling. You told me you loved me and you promised to marry me. You do love me, don't you?" He took her in his arms and sank his voice almost to a whisper. "Tell me you love me."

"Be careful of my hat."

"Take the damn' thing off." He untied the ribbons. "There! Now tell me you love me."

She relaxed in his arms.

"Of course I do, Stephen."

"Say 'I love you'."

"I love you." She gave a sudden start. "What was that?"

"What was what?"

"I thought I heard someone."

"No more red herrings. You didn't hear anyone."

"I did."

"Well, never mind if you did. Angela, darling . . ."

Philip walked blindly away from the summer-house. He had gone there in search of Angela, his footsteps falling silently on the moss-grown path, and the sound of voices had brought him to a standstill. Only gradually did the meaning of what he heard penetrate his senses, then he turned and walked back along the path to the lawn. He stood there irresolute, shrinking into the shade of the trees, afraid that someone might speak to him. Strains of the *Teddy Bears' Picnic* floated out from the oak tree. A group of people near him was discussing the local horse show.

"Rotten jumping. Pretty low standard all round. Nothing like as good as last year."

Another group was discussing the political situation.

"The blighter's asking for their colonies back now. It's outrageous."

"Fantastic."

"Oh, we shall probably have to come to some compromise. They say that Halifax is going out to see him personally about it."

Philip felt that he couldn't stay another moment among the chattering crowd. He made a movement to return to the house, then stopped. He couldn't go back to the room where he had told Stephen, and Stephen, listening with treachery in his heart, had planned to forestall him.

Skirting the lawn, he went out by the wide iron gates and began to walk quickly down the road.

He didn't know where he was going, till he found himself at the end of Minster Road.

Chapter Twenty-Three

"But, darling," said Mrs. Sanders, looking up from the sea of papers that surrounded her, "do you mean to say that you're actually engaged to three people at once?"

"Four, counting Cedric," said Angela with modest pride. "I'm as good as engaged to Cedric."

"But, my dear!" said Mrs. Sanders. She was torn between the consternation natural to a mother who discovers her daughter to be engaged to four people at once and half a dozen ideas that presented themselves simultaneously for using the situation in a story. Not Boadicea, of course. One couldn't have Boadicea engaged to four people at once. But she had begun to think that she must have a modern novel on hand at the same time as Boadicea. She found an undiluted historical atmosphere thwarting and depresssing.

"Four!" she ejaculated again, and the sea of papers covering floor and chairs around her seemed to rise in waves of sympathetic horror.

"Counting Cedric," said Angela complacently.

She had moved a jam tart and a dressing-jacket in order to sit on the armchair. Her blue and white check gingham frock made her look like a little girl, and she wore a fillet of blue ribbon round her hair.

"But how did it happen?" said Mrs. Sanders, pushing a pile of papers away from her with a despairing gesture.

When Angela entered she had been Boadicea delivering an impassioned speech to her followers, and she felt that she would never again, after this interruption, get back to the same pitch of inspired fervour.

"Well, you see," said Angela, "I like Stephen and I like Ralph, and Philip wrote me a beautiful letter, so I wrote a beautiful letter back. Philip doesn't really come into it. I was only trying to be kind to him, but I didn't know whether I wanted to marry Stephen or Ralph, and I didn't want to let either of them go till I'd made up my mind. And, of course, Cedric complicated things."

"Cedric?"

"He's got a yacht and he'll have a title when his father dies, and I've always wanted a yacht and a title. But he says his chief hobby is bird-watching, and I couldn't stand a bird-watching husband, so I've decided to let him go, and I've finally fixed on Ralph."

"Why, dear?" said Mrs. Sanders faintly.

"Well, Stephen's so nice and he'd want me to be nice, too, and I'd find it such a bore. He's got no malice in him, and I like a touch of malice. He's better-looking than Ralph, of course, but one can't have everything and—anyway, I've thought it over and I'm going to marry Ralph."

Mrs. Sanders considered.

"What will you do about the others?" she said at last.

"Oh, I'll tell them it was a misunderstanding. Most things are misunderstandings when you come to think of them."

Mrs. Sanders looked round her in a bewildered fashion. Then she remembered that she had had no breakfast, and reaching out her hand for the jam tart, began to nibble it in an abstracted fashion.

"Well, Angela," she said in a judicial tone as she nibbled, "I don't pretend to approve. It isn't—"

There was a knock at the door. Mrs. Sanders sighed. Not that it really mattered. Her Boadicea atmosphere was ruined, anyway.

"Come in."

Monica entered.

"I've just come to say good-bye, Mrs. Sanders," she said. "I'm going by the twelve forty-five."

"Going?" said Mrs. Sanders in majestic displeasure. "Why? Where?"

"I'm going home," said Monica. "I only came to replace Miss Gregson, you know, and she comes back to-day."

"Why did no one tell me?" said Mrs. Sanders pathetically.

"We did tell you," said Angela. "You never listen."

"I do listen," said Mrs. Sanders with dignity, "but my mind is full of more important things. One can hardly carry the whole field of British history in one's mind and remember every unimportant domestic detail as well." She looked at Monica. This gentle shadowy child was useful. She did things without being asked. She was quiet. She never broke threads. Half-unconsciously, Mrs. Sanders had come to rely on her. Having finished the jam tart she took a half-eaten banana from a drawer and consumed it absent-mindedly as she talked.

"But, Muriel dear," she said, "surely your parents are in India. Why should you go home?"

"Monica's parents aren't in India," said Angela. "Her mother's in a nursing home with a nervous breakdown, and that's why she could come."

"A nervous breakdown?" said Mrs. Sanders bitterly. "I feel or the verge of one myself. Have they cured her?"

"Y-yes," said Monica. The letter from Linden Lodge had been rather non-committal. "She's coming home to-day and I want to be there when she comes."

Mrs. Sanders looked at Angela.

"Have I got a secretary, Angela?"

"No," said Angela. "You didn't like the last one, so you decided to manage with odds and ends—Miss Gregson and Greta and whoever else could be drawn into your net."

"Will you stay with me as my secretary, Muriel?" said Mrs. Sanders graciously.

Monica shook her head.

"I'm sorry. I must go home."

Mrs. Sanders' gaze travelled speculatively to her daughter.

"What do you do with your time, Angela? Surely it isn't fully occupied."

"I'm afraid it is," said Angela. "It's very fully occupied."

"Have you ever helped me?" said Mrs. Sanders, honestly trying to remember.

"No," said Angela simply.

Mrs. Sanders dismissed the whole subject with an expansive gesture.

"Get me a secretary," she said shortly. "As much like Muriel as possible." She put the banana skin in the wastepaper basket and turned to her desk. "And now I'm afraid I can't waste any more time. I don't know why you had to come, either of you. You've broken threads that are essential to the story and that I may never be able to pick up again."

It was two o'clock when Monica reached the small flat in Chelsea that Fred had taken for her and Babs. It was in a quiet side street of vaguely Regency aspect. Its door was painted geranium red, and the window-boxes were planted with geraniums. Nearly all the doors of the street were brightly painted and the splashes of colour against the mellow brickwork and grey pavements gave an air of gaiety and Bohemianism. Graceful balustrades of wrought-iron flanked the steps up to the front doors, and over each was a fanlight of exquisite tracery.

Fred was in the flat to welcome her—large and rather portentous-looking.

"Daisy's been over once or twice to see to things," he said. "We didn't want you to be worried by it. I think it's all ship-shape now."

Monica stood and looked round the small cheerful room, with its white paint, Regency striped curtains and chair-covers, crystal doorplates and handles, and drew in her breath.

"Fred, it's lovely," she said.

"It's not bad, is it?" said Fred, relaxing the tension of his expression. "It's the sort of place she'll like, I think, don't you? I wanted to give her a good start. It might—set her back to come to a place that wasn't up to standard. I didn't want a splashy sort of place. They aren't good for her. I think it's quite a success, isn't it?"

"Yes," she said, trying to control the trembling of her lips. "Fred—"

"Yes?"

She hardly dared say it.

"Do you think they really have cured her?"

"I don't see why not." He spoke rather aggressively as if beating down the arguments of an unseen opponent. "They *have* done some wonderful cures."

"You haven't seen her?"

He shook his head.

"Best not, you know, while the thing was going on. They said so . . . Daisy was sorry not to come to meet you, Monny, but she's expecting her baby next month, and she can't run about as she used to. In any case, she and Babs don't hit it off. She sent her love."

"Thank you . . . Fred, it *is* a lovely place."

"Come and see the rest of it. Here are the bedrooms."

The bedrooms were charming. Monica's had a patchwork quilt and a little Georgian dressing-table. Babs' had a dressing-table skirted in apricot taffeta with a bed coverlet to match. There were curtains of frilled net at the windows.

"But, Fred," she gasped, "how much does it cost?"

"Oh, not much," he said evasively. "I didn't want to take any chances. I wanted her to start off happy." He went to the window. "There seem to be some nice people living about. She might make some nice friends."

"When is she coming?"

"She'll be ready at four. I'm going to fetch her."

"Shall I come with you?"

"No, you stay here, Monny. I've thought it out. I want her to find you here with the flat. It'll make it seem like home to her. It won't be like coming to a strange place if she finds you here."

"I must get a job as soon as things are settled."

"We can talk about that later. Listen, Mon, I'll pay you her allowance, but don't let her have any money, will you?"

Monica's heart sank.

"Very well," she said.

He didn't really believe that she was cured.

He looked rather wistfully round the room.

"She ought to be happy. Looking after it, I mean. There are books and the wireless and if she gets to know nice people . . . I've got in some magazines and things for her to read. We'll take out a library subscription for her. The great thing is to occupy her mind. I suppose—I suppose she wouldn't care to take up some sort of social work?"

"I don't think so," said Monica, torn between tears and laughter.

He took out his watch.

"Well, I'll be getting along," he said.

Left alone in the flat, Monica wandered restlessly from room to room. Her anxiety was like a physical oppression. She stood looking at the bedroom that was to be her mother's, dainty and spotless, waiting for—what? She tried to throw her thoughts into the future, then drew them back, shrinking from what she might find there. For reassurance, she put her hand up to the brooch that she wore at her throat, the three pearls on the gold bar that Stephen had given her. She saw him again, sitting on the schoolroom table with Angela, and comfort flooded her soul. Perhaps he was engaged to Angela now. No engagement had been announced, but perhaps they were keeping it secret for the present. Suddenly she heard the opening of the front door and footsteps on the staircase . . . and her heart ached with love as the sweet laughing voice floated up to her.

"Fred, it's all too charming! How *did* you find it?"

Then the door opened, and Babs entered. She was pale and thin, but the ravaged look had gone from her face and the feverish glint from her eyes. There was about her a new look of health and vitality.

"Monny, darling!" she said, holding out her arms.

Monica flung herself into them, and, to her horror, burst into tears.

"Oh, darling . . . darling . . . I'm nearly crying myself. It's lovely to be back with you."

Fred stood watching them, happy, awkward and self-conscious. There was a knock at the door and he went to take a tea-tray from the landlady.

"Here we are!" he said, returning with it and speaking with overdone heartiness in order to hide his embarrassment. "A cup of tea will do you both good."

Babs sat down in the easy-chair and, drawing off her gloves, looked round the room. There still hung about her the gay careless charm that had always been inseparable from her. She was completely at her ease.

"Fred, it's *too* delightful. How did you do it? When I heard that you were getting a flat I had visions of fumed oak and aspidistras. Surely"—with a sudden mocking light in her eyes—"Daisy had no part in this?" She put her hand on his knee in sudden penitence. "I'm sorry. I'm so grateful to you, Fred, but I don't know how to say it, and I can't help teasing you."

"It's all right," he said. "I understand. It's funny how I did choose it. I kept a-looking at flats and somehow they weren't you, and then I saw this and—well, it *was* you. I don't know how I knew. I suppose because I've known you so long."

She was touched.

"Tell me about Daisy. When's the baby coming?"

"Next month. She's as fit as a flea."

"Good! And how are the other children?"

He began to tell her about them, his large face beaming with ingenuous paternal pride. Babs listened with an expression of interest that grew rather fixed and strained as he recounted the escapades of Tony, the comical sayings of Sally. She's trying so hard to be good, thought Monica, and her heart yearned over her.

"And now we ought to talk about plans, I suppose," said Babs, when he stopped for breath. She looked at him with the faintly mocking light in her eyes. "What are you going to do with me?"

"Well," said Fred, "I—we thought that you'd be happy just looking after the flat and—and reading and going about a bit. There seem to be some quite nice people round."

"And I'm going to get a job," said Monica.

"I'll get a job, too," said Babs. "I feel I might tire rather soon of reading and going about—even with nice people . . . Monny and I will both have jobs and make lots of money and have a nice housekeeper to look after us—the sort you find in books who bullies and adores you—and we'll knit jumpers in the evenings and go to Prom concerts on Saturdays and to Bournemouth for our summer holidays with—just very occasionally—a Cook's tour to the Chateaux of the Loire and a Mediterranean cruise."

Fred smiled and rose slowly to his feet.

"Well, I must be going now . . . What are you going to do tomorrow?"

"I'll buy some clothes," said Babs. "I must have some new clothes. You can't make a fresh start in old clothes. I must have some clothes that don't know about me. This suit, for instance"—she glanced down at the black tailored suit she had on—"has seen me at my worst. Or almost at my worst. I feel slightly embarrassed by it. It probably feels slightly embarrassed by me. We hold painful memories for each other. Some of my clothes, of course, react differently. I have a yellow evening dress that used to egg me on, and a powder blue one that always tried to hold me back. It's never forgiven me for making a public exhibition of it and it never will. No, I don't think one can start the New Adam on the Old Adam's wardrobe."

"I'll give Monny a cheque before I go," said Fred.

Babs caught the glance exchanged between them and gave a twisted smile.

"You can trust me with money, Fred," she said. "I may be extravagant, but I won't buy gin and whisky with it."

"I'm sorry, Babs," he said. "I only want to make things easy for you. Well, I'll be off now. I'll give you a ring first thing tomorrow."

When he had gone Babs made room for Monica on the settee beside her.

"Happy, darling?"

"Yes, terribly."

"We *are* going to be happy. You look very sweet. That's a new – brooch, isn't it?"

Monica put up her hand to it.

"Yes. Stephen gave it to me for a twenty-first birthday present."

"Oh, dear! And I forgot, didn't I?" said Babs ruefully. "I'll buy you something really lovely to make up for it . . . Who is Stephen, darling?"

"He's Philip's brother. Philip was at Appleton Vicarage with me when we were children."

"Oh, that grim place! Darling, does Stephen like you? Bring him to see me. Bring him to tea. You can do it quite safely now. I'll just sit behind a tea-table and talk about the weather and the Royal Academy."

"Oh, no," smiled Monica. "There's nothing like that. I mean, he's going to marry Angela."

"I'm rather glad. I don't know who she is, but I feel sure that they're suitable to each other. Stephen and Angela. You've only to say the names to know that it's one of those marriages that are made in heaven. And I want you with me for a bit longer."

She slipped an arm round Monica, drawing her head on to her shoulder, and they sat there in silence. Dusk fell, sharpening the delicate outlines of the lovely face, deepening the shadows beneath the blue eyes, emphasizing the beauty of bone and structure that nothing could destroy.

"I can't help baiting Fred," said Babs suddenly, "but he's got more than a heart of gold. He's solid gold all through, isn't he? . . . Isn't it odd how bad people so often have good people attached to them to clear up the mess? Such a waste of time and energy, but life seems to encourage waste of every kind."

"You aren't bad," said Monica indignantly.

"Darling!" said Babs. "We're going to be terribly happy together, aren't we? And you needn't worry about me. I never want to touch the stuff now. Honestly I don't."

Chapter Twenty-Four

Let's sit down a moment and get our bearings," said Philip. "I expect you'll be glad of a rest. I've dragged you up hill and down dale."

"I'm not tired," said Geraldine, "but it would be rather nice to sit down."

They sat down on the crest of the hill, and Philip took the map from his pocket and spread it out on the grass. Beneath them, wooded slopes swept down to a little village in the valley. Chimneys, a church spire and an oast house could be glimpsed among the trees. The sudden barking of a dog rose sharply from a farm on the hillside.

Geraldine wore a short tweed skirt and a yellow blouse. Her cheeks were glowing with air and exercise.

"Do you see that farm over there, Philip?" she said. "It's just like a toy farm I once had. Every one of those cows in that field came out of my box."

Philip grunted, his head bent over the map.

"Yes, I see where we are," he said. "If we go down into the valley we can get either the bus or the train back into Maybridge. We've covered a pretty good stretch. That's where we got off the bus . . . There's Crown Hill . . . That's where we met the old man who showed us a snapshot of his pig—Queenie, wasn't it called?"

"Yes, and all the time he was talking about it, before he took out the snapshot, I thought he was talking about his wife."

They both laughed.

"This is where we had tea . . . at a cottage on the village green."

"It was a tea, wasn't it?"

"Well, we didn't leave much."

"I was ravenous."

"And this is where we are now. We've covered about sixteen miles. I hope you aren't whacked."

"No. I'm tired, but it's a nice lazy sort of tired." She lay back on the grass. "It's almost the last day of the summer, isn't it? It's nice to think we've used it all up and haven't wasted any."

It was the third Saturday afternoon that she had spent with Philip. Her thoughts went back to the evening—the evening, she knew, of the Penbury garden-party—when he had arrived at the house in Minster Road, looking white and shaken. The visit was unprecedented and the excuse he made for it—some question of the possible issue of a library ticket for a friend who was coming to stay with him—seemed trivial and unconvincing. He did not tell her what the trouble was, and the visit lasted only a short time, but before he went he asked her to come to a concert with him in Maybridge the next Saturday afternoon. She went, had tea with him in the town afterwards, and arranged to go with him the next Saturday to a film at the local cinema. And for this Saturday he had suggested a walk.

Geraldine was glad to fill up her free time by outside interest, for she was alone now in the little house in Minster Road. A fortnight ago, giving as the reason a slight attack of flu from which Elaine was recovering, Grace had suddenly announced that she and Elaine were going for a holiday to Cousin Milly's at Bexhill. Cousin Milly was a distant cousin of Grace's, with whom, till now, communication had been limited to a yearly exchange of Christmas cards. The arrangement had been made with no reference to Geraldine, and Geraldine had been so hurt and mystified that her protests lacked coherence and decision.

"But why didn't you tell me?" she had said. "I could have arranged to take the fortnight off and come with you. And what about Elaine's work?"

"That doesn't matter," Grace had said shortly.

About Grace was a strange new determination, all the more difficult to combat because it was as vague and gentle as Grace herself. To all Geraldine's protests and questions she returned evasive answers, and the two of them had set off for Bexhill, leaving Geraldine still hurt and bewildered. Grace had only written once since she went away—a short note announcing her arrival—and Elaine had not written at all. Geraldine was lonely in the little house, and whenever she thought of Grace and Elaine the hurt feeling twisted in her heart like a knife. Only when she was with Philip could she forget it. Why hadn't they told her when Cousin Milly's invitation arrived? Why hadn't they consulted her? If they wanted a holiday, why hadn't they discussed the matter with her? They could have gone somewhere more interesting than Cousin Milly's and had a pleasant holiday together. She answered all her own questions. They knew that the Library was understaffed and that she was busy and they didn't want to worry her. They hadn't suggested her joining them because they didn't want to encroach on her own holiday and wanted to spare her expense. It was because they loved her that they had told her nothing of it. She would not admit that they did not want her, but sometimes the shadow of the knowledge fell over her spirit, turning it cold and dark. So she had thrown herself eagerly into this friendship with Philip, and to-day, outstretched in the sunshine with Philip at her side, a happiness as nearly perfect as happiness can be seemed to possess her.

"We ought to be moving," said Philip at last, folding up the map. Then he took a packet of cigarettes from his pocket and drew out the last remaining one. "Oh, blast! Only one left," he said, lighting it from the cigarette end he took from his mouth. "I'll get some more in the village."

"You smoke a lot, Philip."

"Do I?"

"Yes. I sometimes think you smoke too much."

He made no answer.

"How many do you smoke a day?"

"Does that matter?"

The tightness of his smile was a danger signal, but Geraldine had always been blind to danger signals.

"Well, I think it does," she persisted. "It's a drug, after all. It can't be good for the nerves, smoking almost incessantly as you do, and you're a bit nervy to start with, aren't you?"

He stood up and put the map into his pocket.

"Shall we go now?" he said.

A cloud had come over the sun, and a faint chill invaded the air. They began to walk slowly down the hillside. Both were unused to long walks and both were tired. The long day in each other's company had drawn them nearer together, but in the very nearness was a danger.

"I saw Angela out with Ralph Pollitt yesterday," she said. "Do you know when they're going to be married?"

"No."

His thoughts went back to the evening of the garden-party. He had not returned to Penbury till all the guests had gone. Then Stephen had told him that he was engaged to Angela.

"I couldn't tell you before because I'd promised, but I got her to let me off my promise this afternoon. I'm sorry, Philip."

Philip had lain awake all night, consumed by the old sick hatred of Stephen, and the next day they had heard of her engagement to Ralph Pollitt.

"Philip . . ."

"Yes?"

"Were you in love with Angela?"

"Do you mind if we don't discuss it?" he said.

They walked on in silence till they reached the outskirts of the village. Then Philip, ashamed of his boorishness, said:

"I'm going over to see Westering on Wednesday. He's had some of the snaps he took in the Tyrol developed and he wants to show them to me."

"You like him, don't you?"

"Yes."

"Is he your greatest friend?"

"I don't think I have a greatest friend."

"You know a lot of people round Maybridge, don't you? I saw you passing the Library on Thursday. Where were you going then?"

Suddenly he had the same sensation that he had had with her in his childhood—the sensation of being fingered by small plump hands whose touch set every nerve a-quiver.

"I don't remember," he said curtly.

The train was in the station when they reached it, and they had a carriage to themselves. Geraldine felt dully unhappy, but, having once begun to probe, she couldn't stop. A kind of desperation drove her. She was going back to the empty house, and the thought of it seemed to raise again the spectre of insecurity that had haunted her ever since she could remember. At all costs she must cling to the only thing that now belonged to her.

"Philip . . ."

"Yes?"

His tone showed his irritation. This friendship was failing him, as everything failed him. He wouldn't ask her to come out with him again. She drained and exhausted him.

"Do tell me something about your writing. You haven't told me anything."

"Haven't I?"

"What are you writing now?"

He looked at her, marvelling how she could go on questioning him in face of his obvious reluctance to answer. The soft brown eyes met his with anxious loving confidence. He forced himself to reply.

"A short story."

"What about? Do tell me what it's about."

His precarious self-control gave way, and he turned on her, his face tight with anger.

"Oh, for heaven's sake, leave me alone!"

She stared at him, her cheeks pale, her eyes blank with dismay.

"I'm sorry," he muttered.

The train slid into Maybridge station. He opened the carriage door and they got out. She was still very pale. They walked past the barrier into the street.

"I irritate you, don't I, Philip?" she said humbly. "I wish I didn't. What did I say that specially irritated you?"

He stopped short.

"I've got to go round by the post office," he said, "so I'll leave you here. Good-bye."

He walked quickly away without looking back. He was ashamed of himself but aware that he could not have stayed with her another moment without giving rein again to his exasperation. His irritation faded when he had gone some distance, and the thought of the unhappy bewildered look in her brown eyes began to pull at his heart. He hesitated, then, Oh, it's no good, he thought with a shrug. It would all happen over again . . . and continued doggedly on his way.

Geraldine walked slowly down Minster Road. The day with Philip was spoilt, and she didn't know what had spoilt it. Determinedly she tried to throw off the thought of it, turning her thoughts to Elaine and Grace. They hadn't said when they were returning home, but, to cheer herself, she imagined that they might have come home that afternoon while she was out. Letters often went astray, and Grace was always a little vague about her arrangements. Perhaps she would open the front door and hear Elaine's, "Hello, Gerry! Is that you?" They would be unpacking, their things all over the place. Elaine would be chattering excitedly about the holiday. Her mind went to the future. She would take Elaine abroad—to Paris Brussels, Vienna, Rome . . . They would go first to Rome . . . trace out the ruins of the Forum, see the Pantheon and Colosseum . . . Tivoli and the villa of Hadrian . . . the Temple of the Sibyl standing aloft on its soaring cliff . . . Frascati and the ruins of Tusculum.

There was a dreamy far-away look in her eyes as the pictures formed themselves in her mind. Elaine must have every advantage that it was possible to give her. Each month she put something aside towards the "nest egg" of savings that she was making for those important formative years while Elaine was at college. And Cousin Milly would be useful now that they had got in touch with her. Grace could stay with her while she and Elaine took their trips abroad. Still determinedly keeping her thoughts from Philip, she opened the gate and looked up at the windows. No, the windows were still shut. They hadn't come back yet. Or—her hopes rose again—perhaps they had just come back and were still upstairs taking then things off. She put her key in the lock and opened the front door, then stood for a moment listening. No, they hadn't come. There is no mistaking the silence of an empty house. She closed the door then picked up a letter that must have arrived by the afternoon's post. It was from Grace. Perhaps it would tell her when to expect them home.

If they came on Monday she must take her lunch-hour for shopping and getting in household supplies. She would have a special supper for them—a sort of celebration. She opened the envelope and took out the letter, glancing over it as she opened it. Then, because her knees felt suddenly unsteady, she went into the dining-room and sat down at the table, spreading out the letter in front of her.

Dear Geraldine,

It's very hard to tell you this, but we aren't coming back. Were going to live here with Cousin Milly. She turned the first floor of her house into a flat, you know, and the tenant's leaving and we're going to take it. There are two bedrooms and Elaine can go to the school here. We want to be on our own—the two of us. I know you've meant well and we're grateful for all you've done, but we haven't been happy with you. I expect you'll be going into rooms or taking a small flat of your own. This flat is furnished, so you can have what you want of the furniture, except just one or two of the things Albert made.

She raised her eyes from the letter and stared in front of her, noticing dully how a spider was beginning to weave its web in a corner of the chimneypiece. It ran down the thread, fixed it on to the wood, then started another. Resolutely she forced her mind to go over the past months, the past years, seeing with suddenly clarified vision a hundred instances of their avoidance of her. Her mind sheered away from them, but she forced it back. The pain was like the pain of a dead limb awakening to life. I ought to have noticed . . . I should have noticed if I'd let myself . . .

Dusk gathered. The last lingering rays of the sun fell on the corner cupboard that Albert had planned on his honeymoon and made immediately on his return, illuminating the Gothic lettering of the intertwined A and G . . . Then it faded and the shadows closed over the room. And still she sat there, staring in front of her.

Chapter Twenty-Five

Let's think what we'd do if there was no one in the world but you and me," said Bobby.

He was a solemn sturdy freckled little boy of five, and Monica was taking him home through the park. She taught him every morning and took him into Kensington Gardens every afternoon. On some days they went further afield to do shopping for his mother.

She had had the job now for a month and was happy in it, as she was always happy in the enclosed world of childhood. It was a world in which one lived from day to day, in which one need not always be summoning one's courage to meet the unknown.

"Starting from here, do you mean?" she said. "Just where we are now?"

"Yes."

"I'd pick a bunch of tulips from that bed. I could pick as many as I liked because there'd be no one to stop me. What would you do first?"

"I'd go to that toy shop that we were looking at yesterday and I'd take the engine and the aeroplane."

"How would you get to it? The shop, I mean."

"I'd go by bus."

"You couldn't," she objected. "There wouldn't be any bus-drivers."

He chuckled.

"I'd drive a bus myself. Could I drive a bus myself, do you think?"

"I don't think so."

"I'd walk then. Is it a very long way? Is it too far to walk?"

"Yes, it is."

He thought deeply, wrinkling his brow. Then:

"I'd be magic," he said triumphantly. "I'd be so magic that I could go anywhere I wanted to just by thinking of it."

"Do you mean, all over the world?"

"Yes." A grin spread slowly over his face. "That makes it exciting, doesn't it? I'm not going to have the toy shop for my turn. I'm going to the country where the Red Indians are, so that I can watch them doing a war dance."

"But they wouldn't be there," Monica reminded him, "because there'd be no one in the world but you and me."

Again he chuckled.

"I keep forgetting that. I think I'll have the toy shop, after all. But I'll take everything that's in it. Every single thing."

"How will you get them home?"

"I'll magic them home."

They had reached the high block of flats where he lived now, and Monica handed him over to his mother. Then she set off homeward. She walked slowly, the familiar cloud of foreboding settling over her spirit. Babs had said that she would not be home till late to-night, giving no explanation except that she was meeting some friends. Things were not going well with Babs. There was the old feverish glint in her eyes, and there had been lately one or two of the old terrifying scenes. Babs had been contrite and apologetic afterwards.

"I'm so sorry, darling. I just had a little break-out. They said there were bound to be ups and downs, you know. Actually, I think that a little break-out does me good occasionally. And I don't really drink these days. I just have a drink now and then when I'm with friends. I never keep any in the house."

But only that morning Monica had found a bottle of whisky hidden at the back of Babs' wardrobe.

She slackened her pace as she approached the street in Bayswater where their flat was. They had moved once or twice since Fred had settled them in the Chelsea flat. They had had their present one for a month now. It was bare and rather makeshift, but it was clean, and Monica had brightened it up by new cushion covers and curtains.

Reaching the door, she opened her bag to take out her key, then looked up at the man who was approaching from the other direction. It was Stephen. The colour flamed into her cheeks.

"Stephen!"'

He smiled.

"I'm sorry. I didn't mean to give you a shock."

Her heart was knocking against her ribs.

"Oh, no," she said unsteadily, "but—do come in. We live here."

"I know. I was coming to see you. I had a message from Mrs. Hassock. She gave me your address."

She opened the door and he followed her up the dark staircase to the flat on the first floor. She threw open the door of the sitting-room, wondering if Babs had, after all, returned. It was empty.

"Do sit down," she said.

"Thanks . . . I'll get the message over first, shall I? Mrs. Sanders' secretary has left at a moment's notice, because, I suppose, she couldn't stay the course, and Mrs. Sanders is insisting that Muriel—she calls you Muriel, doesn't she?—must return. She says that Muriel is the only secretary who doesn't irritate her."

"But I wasn't really her secretary," said Monica.

"Everyone who sets foot in the Vicarage in any capacity whatsoever is Mrs. Sanders' secretary," said Stephen. "She even had the Bishop looking out references for her the last time he was there. Anyway, I happened to meet Mrs. Hassock in Maybridge and she said that she was going to write to you to ask if you could spare a week or two to cope with things, so I said that I was coming to London myself to-day in any case and I'd look you up and ask you."

He wondered if the excuse sounded to her as thin as it really was.

"I'm afraid I can't," she said. "I have a job here and—I don't want to leave my mother . . . You'll stay and have some tea, won't you? I was just going to get my own. I'm sorry my mother's not in."

She talked quickly, unsteadily, trying to cover her confusion. She still felt dazed by his sudden appearance.

"Yes, I'd love to." He spoke in a tone of gentle reassurance. "Let me give a hand."

"Thanks. The kitchen's just here."

In the kitchen she put a tray on the table and began to set cups on it.

"What can I do?" he said. "Where's the milk? In the frig?"

"Yes. How's everyone at Penbury?"

"All right. Philip's back at Oxford—he's having a fourth year there, you know."

"And"—she wanted to say "Angela", but couldn't—"Geraldine?" she substituted.

"She's got a librarian's job somewhere in the Midlands. Her mother and sister have gone to live with a relation somewhere, and they've sold the house in Minster Road."

"And"—she had to say it, bending her head over the tray so that he should not see her face—"Angela?"

"Angela turned me down," he said. "Didn't you see her engagement to Ralph Pollitt in the paper?"

"No . . . I don't often look at engagements."

Her mind was a turmoil of anger, compassion and a wild relief that she would not recognize.

"The kettle's boiling," he said.

They carried the tea-tray into the sitting-room and he talked, to put her at her ease, of local Maybridge doings and the more outstanding vagaries of Mrs. Sanders. She listened, surrendering to the peace of his presence. Whatever happens to me afterwards, she thought, I shall always have this to remember. Then, encouraged by his gentle questioning, she began to tell him something of her own life—her childhood, the places where she had lived, the job she had now. Babs was in the background of the story—the mother, loving and beloved. He listened, interested and a little puzzled. It didn't make sense. It was like a code written in cypher of which the key was missing.

"Your mother's delicate, isn't she?" he said tentatively.

"Yes," she said, and the glow that had transformed her faded as she spoke.

He sensed her embarrassment and turned to the shelves where she kept her books.

"You've still got *Uncle Remus*," he said, smiling, then began to look at the others,

"They're a dreadful mixture," she said. "I'm afraid my education is mostly gaps."

"Good!" he said. "I like gaps."

Then they sat on the settee and talked. They talked about nothing in particular, but beneath the trivialities of their words the bond of sympathy between them grew stronger. It was just as he was telling her about his mother's French poodle who had taken to hunting in the woods that the door opened and Babs stood in the doorway. Her hat was awry and her hair disordered. She was gloriously, outrageously drunk. She lurched forward and caught hold of a chair. Stephen looked at her. So this was the key to the cypher . . .

"Who's your visitor, Monny?" said Babs, the words slurring into each other. "When the cat's away the mice will play, eh?"

Stephen had laid a hand protectively on Monica's arm. Babs turned on him, her face suffused with anger.

"Keep your filthy hands off my girl, you drunken beast," she said thickly.

"Please go, Stephen," said Monica, not taking her eyes from Babs.

"But—"

"*Please.*"

He hesitated a moment then went from the room.

It was an hour later when Monica left Babs, sleeping heavily and noisily in bed, and returned to the sitting-room. The room was in darkness, but the street light showed Stephen standing by the window.

"Stephen! I thought you'd gone."

"I did go. Then I came back. The door was ajar . . . Monica, will you marry me?"

She shrank back.

"No!"

"That was the first thing you ever said to me. 'No, no!' . . . Just like that. I'd asked you to be my partner at Angela's birthday party. Do you remember?"

"Yes."

"Why won't you marry me?"

"You've seen why."

"Is that the only reason?"

She turned her head away.

"Angela . . ."

"Angela's a fever in the blood, Monny. I've worked it out of my system more quickly than I thought I should. I came here to-day because I knew I loved you. I didn't mean to rush you like this, but after to-night I couldn't go away without telling you."

"I can't marry you."

"We could get someone to look after her."

"I shall never leave her."

"I'll wait—"

"*No.*"

"We'll look after her together. She can live with us."

She shook her head.

"Never that . . . It isn't any use, Stephen. I love you, but it isn't any use. I shall never leave her. Never."

Her face was pale and set. He knew that her resolve was inflexible. He put his arms out to hold her, but she drew back.

"Please go," she said.

She stood at the window and watched him till he had vanished into the darkness.

She left Babs still asleep when she went to work the next morning, but on her return found her lying on the settee in the sitting-room.

"Hello, Monny. Have you had tea?"

"Yes, I had it with Bobby. His mother had some people in for bridge."

"Come and talk to me, darling," said Babs, making room for

Monica on the settee. "Tell me. I was terribly, terribly drunk last night, wasn't I?"

"Don't think about it," said Monica, laying a hand on her arm.

Babs frowned.

"I must think about it. I want to think about it. Who was the young man who was with you?"

"Stephen."

"Stephen . . . I remember. He gave you your brooch, didn't he? The one you're wearing now."

"Yes."

"And he's going to marry Angela."

"No. Angela turned him down."

"Did she?" Babs smiled ruefully. "And I said that when he came to tea I'd sit behind the tea-table and talk about the Royal Academy. I'm afraid I didn't, did I?"

"Darling, don't think about it."

"I couldn't have done, anyway, because I haven't been to the Royal Academy for years. I used to find the portraits so depressing. They all had the same look of imbecile highmindedness."

Monica smiled.

"How are you feeling now?"

"I've got the foulest headache, but I'm seeing things clearly. For the first time for years I'm seeing things clearly."

"What do you mean by that?"

"Nothing in particular. Let's have a nice evening, darling. Let's put on the gramophone. Let's have that record you used to like when you were a little girl. What was it? The *March of the Tin Soldiers*, wasn't it?"

"Yes."

"I know it's among those records. I saw it the other day. Put it on, darling."

They sat together in the firelight as the dusk deepened round them. The gramophone record played itself out and they did not replace it. Monica sat on the hearthrug at Babs' feet. Babs' fingers rested lightly on her hair.

"What are you thinking of, Monny?"

"I'm thinking that I love you."

"You're thinking that you'll never leave me, aren't you?"

"You know I'll never leave you."

"It's time we went to bed."

Babs stood up and Monica rose slowly to her feet.

"Good night, darling."

"Is your head better?"

"No," smiled Babs.

"Take something to make you sleep."

Babs held Monica's face between her hands and kissed it.

"Yes, darling. I'll take something to make me sleep."

Chapter Twenty-Six

Geraldine sat in her small bed-sitting-room . . . It was a pleasant enough little room, with an easy-chair, a divan bed, curtains of fresh printed linen at the windows and a blue chenille cloth on the round table in the middle, but she found it difficult to occupy her time when her working hours were over. There were books, of course, and the wireless and walks, but a black unbearable loneliness seemed always to be lying in wait for her. She had made few friends since coming to the town. There was in her a new sensitiveness, born of bitter hurt and disappointment, that made her chary of forming friendships. Where once she would have thrust herself into the centre of a group, blind to any signs that she was not welcome, she withdrew now into herself, waiting for some signs from the others. Elaine and Grace had spurned her love. Philip had spurned her friendship. And—in that illuminating flash of vision that had come to her as she read Grace's letter—she had known why they had done so. The defence that she had built up against the dark fear of her childhood—the fear of not "belonging" anywhere—had crumbled to the ground.

The family who owned the house where she lived consisted of a Mr. and Mrs. Pelham and their three children. They had been delighted to find a tenant as quiet and considerate as Geraldine and had welcomed her into the midst of their family life, giving her a general invitation to join them whenever she wished. And at first she had taken advantage of the invitation in her old impetuous fashion. She had gone there every evening to sit in the bright cosy room that was sitting-room, dining-room and nursery combined. She had bathed the baby. She had helped the eldest child with her homework. She had advised the mother on her housekeeping and the management of her children. She had bought a new lampshade for the living-room, a new mat for the hall, a new saucepan for the kitchen and a new coat for the baby. And she had noticed—it was the first time it had ever happened—the first faint, almost imperceptible, signs that they were beginning to tire of her, beginning half unconsciously to resent her advice and her gifts. Since then she had stayed upstairs in the evening, waiting to be asked down to the living-room. And they had not asked her . . .

So she sat now in the pleasant, rather bare little room, trying to read a novel that she had brought back with her from the library, and fighting an overwhelming longing to go downstairs and join the family below. The longing was so strong as to be almost a physical compulsion. All she had to do was to go down the staircase, knock at the door . . . and she would be in the warm lighted room at the heart of the family life. They would ask her in, and she would sit in the armchair by the fireplace, perhaps with the baby on her knee. She glanced at the clock. It was just about the baby's bathtime. Mrs. Pelham would be bathing it and the other children would be playing about the room. Mr. Pelham would be sitting reading the evening paper or helping with the baby's bath. The room would be full of chatter and laughter and splashing. In her loneliness she craved for it as a drug addict craves for his drug.

A gust of laughter floated up the stairs and an excited shout that she recognized as the baby's. The fight was all the more difficult because it was so new. The forces on her side were weak and inexpert, the forces against her strong and practised. She looked at the clock again and wondered how to get through the hours till bedtime. She might go out for a walk, but the streets, too, were full of happy groups of people who had no need of her. Then she heard the sound of footsteps on the stairs, and her heart leapt. One of the children coming to invite her down to join them . . . There was a knock at her door.

"Come in."

Dicky Pelham burst into the room, threw two letters on to the table, with a "Two letters for you, Miss Mortimer," and plunged downstairs again, shouting, as he went, in continuation of the interrupted game. The top letter was in Elaine's handwriting. She opened it slowly and read it. It was a stilted little letter—rather shy and quite impersonal—recounting baldly the day-by-day events of the past week, but Geraldine, starved for affection, read affection into it and her eyes filled with tears as she read it.

The other letter was from Philip.

Dear Geraldine,

I've got your address from the Library. I wonder if you'd care to come up to London next Saturday? If you would, we might meet for lunch and go to a show afterwards.

Yours,

Philip.

She put her head down on the blue chenille tablecloth and began to cry.

He was waiting for her in the foyer of the restaurant when she arrived. There was constraint on both sides in their greeting. He had regretted the letter as soon as he had posted it. He could not understand the impulse that had made him suggest a renewal of a friendship that had always irked and irritated him. It was as if some mysterious compulsion, beyond his comprehension or control, always drove him back to her. And yet he had never met her without a gradual uprising of exasperation, ending always in a resolution to see no more of her.

They took their seats at the table, and he ordered cocktails, gathering his forces together to resist the impact of her personality. But there was a new timidity in her. It was some time before he realized that, instead of having to resist her, he was himself trying to break down a barrier that hid her from him. They talked desultorily about Maybridge and Penbury and his family.

"Our great news is that Stephen and Monica are to be married next month," he said.

"How lovely! . . . Her mother's death was so tragic, wasn't it?"

"Yes. It was an accident, of course. The sleeping stuff was rather strong, and she took a double dose by mistake."

"I suppose she'll be married from your house?"

"Yes . . . If war comes Stephen will be called up at once. He's in the Terriers. He's dragged me into it too. And the old man's champing to join his old regiment, and Ann's deep in the V.A.D."

There was a silence, and his thoughts went back to his last interview with Barry. He had met him by chance in the village, and the two of them had walked home together through the park.

"You're in your last year at Oxford, aren't you, Pip?" Barry had said. "What are your plans for when you come down—always supposing that we aren't at war by then?"

"I'd like to get a job on some paper," Philip had said vaguely.

"You haven't forgotten that Penbury will be yours when I'm gone, have you?" Barry had said.

"Surely Stephen will have that," Philip had said with an ironic edge to his voice. "It seems only suitable."

"Listen, Pip," Barry had said slowly. "I'm fond of Stephen, as you know, but you're my son, and I want my son to have Penbury when I die. Let Stephen run it for you if you like, but I want it to be yours."

Then Ann, crossing the park from the stile in the lane, had joined them and no more had been said. But, though Philip had made a number of cynical comments on the scene in his mind, the memory still sent a wave of happiness through his heart whenever he thought of it.

"You don't really think there's going to be war, do you?" said Geraldine.

"No. Hitler's out to get all he can by the threat of war, but he won't risk losing everything he's got by actually going to war. He'll carry on his bluff to the last minute, I've no doubt, but he'll call off then. At any rate, that's my opinion and the opinion of most of the Germans I've met. The old man and Stephen take it much more seriously, but I think they're wrong."

They discussed the books they had read recently, the people around them, and both were aware of a slackening of the tension that had always till now made them faintly ill at ease in each other's company. There was a new understanding, tenuous and indefinable, between them.

"I expect you miss your mother and sister, don't you?" he said.

"Yes . . . I do."

Pity caught him unawares, but the idea of pathos in connection with Geraldine was so strange that he refused to admit it.

Soon, to his surprise, he found himself telling her about a play that he was planning to write. She listened to him in silence. So careful was she to seem to exact no confidence, to make no invasion on his privacy, that it was as if she carried in her hands a precious and fragile vessel that a single false step might shatter into fragments. He told her more than he had meant to tell her, talking in the end as much to himself as to her. Then he looked at his watch.

"What show would you like to see?" he said.

"I don't mind."

"Let's not go to a show, then," he said. "Let's go and sit in the park."

They sat in the park and the hours fled quickly by. Both were a little shy of the new relationship, afraid to trust it, fearful that a casual word might destroy it, but it seemed to grow deeper as the afternoon wore on. Once he gave his quick twisted smile and said:

"I think life must be mellowing us. We've been together all afternoon and haven't quarrelled yet."

He saw her off at the station.

"Are you free every Saturday?" he said.

"Yes."

"Well, may I come over and see you some Saturday? Or would it be a nuisance?"

"No . . . it wouldn't be a nuisance."

Chapter Twenty-Seven

The three—Philip, Geraldine and Monica—stood at the window of the Vicarage schoolroom, looking down at their children, who were playing on the lawn. Sally had Geraldine's soft brown eyes, but there was something of Philip in the long sensitive mouth and the quick turn of the small dark head. Bill was fair and grey-eyed and sturdy like Stephen. There was little of Monica in him.

It was 1945, and the V bombs were still falling on London. Philip and Geraldine had decided to motor down to see Sally, and had rung up Monica to ask her to go with them to visit her small son. It happened to be her free day at the hospital where she worked, and Philip and Geraldine had driven round to call for her on their way.

Philip and Geraldine had brought their daughter to Appleton Vicarage early in 1941 when Philip went overseas with his regiment and Geraldine was driving an ambulance for the Civil Defence. Philip was now out of the army, learning slowly and painfully to manipulate the artificial right arm with which he had recently been fitted, and preparing to take up a job in the Ministry of Information. Grace had died the year before, and Elaine had married Terence Roper. Geraldine was fond of Elaine, but her love for Philip was the mainspring of her life and nothing else was quite real to her.

Monica leant out of the window, watching her son push a horse on wheels round the side of the lawn. Geraldine had promised to run her over to Penbury before they started for home. She wanted to show Ann the letter from Stephen that had reached her the day before. Stephen was somewhere in Italy. He wrote short but cheerful letters. Popular with both the men and his fellow officers, Stephen found a certain satisfaction in army life that Philip had failed to find. Penbury Lodge was a military hospital and Ann worked there as a V.A.D. Barry was with his old regiment in India.

"Greta looks older," said Geraldine suddenly, as Greta crossed the lawn with a teddy bear under her arm.

Mr. Hassock was an army chaplain in Italy, and Greta was once more installed at Appleton Vicarage, helping to cope with six little evacuees and picking up the somewhat frayed and tangled threads of her work as Mrs. Sanders' secretary.

A car drew up at the gate of the Vicarage and there was the sound of voices as Angela got out with her three children—two fairylike little girls and a sturdy little boy. Ralph was in the Air Force, and Angela was living with her mother-in-law at Kenworth Towers.

"She's as lovely as ever, isn't she?" said Monica.

Certainly neither child-bearing nor life with her mother-in-law had dimmed anything of Angela's radiance. But the restlessness had gone from it. She wore now a look of settled matronly efficiency, of rosy contentment. Angela alone had undertaken no war work. Her children absorbed all her time and thoughts. Her passion of maternal devotion had surprised even herself.

"I'm going to have dozens of them," she said. "I always thought that children were a nuisance, but they're fun when they're your own."

She saw the three at the window and waved to them.

"What are you doing up there?" she said.

"Exploring old haunts," said Philip. "Checking up old memories. Making sure that the piece I bit out of the table is still missing, and that the mark's still on the carpet where you threw the ink-bottle on to the floor."

"We'll come down in a moment," said Geraldine.

Mrs. Sanders issued from the front door in a garment that looked as if it had been fashioned (as it probably had) from an old evening-dress and a new overall. She embraced Angela and looked vaguely at her grandchildren, whom she seldom recognized. "Which are yours, dear?" she would say to Angela, then in a tone of faint surprise, as they were pointed out, "Oh, those!" She was still inky and dishevelled, but something of her old magnificence had gone. She wore a slightly—very slightly—defeated air. The historical novel (she had finally settled on the Gunpowder Plot) had been a failure, and no one seemed now to want her colourful novels of passion and romance. Ignoring this, she still continued to turn them out with the old feverish haste, working till the early hours of the morning forgetting meals, nibbling biscuits and fruit at her desk, while the piles of completed manuscripts slowly accumulated in the cellar among odds and ends of disused pieces of furniture. She was like something wound up that couldn't stop.

Mr. Sanders joined the group on the lawn, patting his grandchildren's heads, giving Angela his bland paternal smile. About him, too, hung a faint air of defeat.

In these days of stark reality and human need, he felt, obscurely, at a loss. He could conduct meetings, draw up agenda, guide the course of committee meetings with firm unerring hand, preach sermons whose literary and intellectual quality was undeniable, but something more was being demanded of him that he couldn't give. He wasn't even sure what it was . . . His religion had become formal and arid with the years. The light and warmth that had once inspired it had died for lack of tending. There were times when he was deeply unhappy, but, like his wife, like something wound up that could not stop, he went on performing actions that had become meaningless, hurrying from appointment to appointment, drawing up motions, imposing order and discipline on the proceedings of every organization he had dealings with, firmly repressing everything that savoured of "irregularity". But fewer and fewer people seemed to care for these things. He was like an actor in a puppet show in which the audience had lost interest.

Mechanically he drew out his watch.

"Well, well," he said, "I mustn't waste any more time. I have my sermon to write. Sermons and Sundays wait for no man."

As if in self-justification, he had begun to give far more time and thought to his sermons. They had become so abstruse, so packed with erudition, that few of his parishioners could understand them. He was seldom asked to preach outside his own church now.

The three watched his brisk purposeful progress from the lawn to the front door.

"Angela said that when she was very small she thought he was God," said Monica. "She was furious with him for letting the bears eat the children who called Elisha 'Baldhead'. When he said he wasn't God, she didn't believe him. She thought he was trying to get out of it."

They laughed, then turned to watch the children again.

"How like Stephen Bill is, Monny!" said Geraldine.

"Yes. He's like him in everything."

"Stephen's on good terms with the war, isn't he?" said Philip. "I could never find anything to say to it, but Stephen seems to get on with it all right."

"Yes, I think he does," said Monica with a smile.

All day and every day she sent out her thoughts and prayers to Stephen, but, in spite of her ceaseless anxiety, she carried a conviction at her heart that he would return to her in safety.

Philip took out his cigarette-case from his pocket, and using his artificial hand, clumsily and with difficulty, extracted a cigarette. Geraldine turned away, the muscles of her face growing tight. It still cost her an effort to watch his fumbling as if she did not notice it, to refrain from offering the helping touch that would have performed the action for him.

"And Sally's like Gerry," said Monica.

"Ridiculously," agreed Philip, taking out his lighter.

There was a pause, then Geraldine said:

"There used to be a table under the copper beech. We used to do lessons there."

"Philip made a plasticine deer," said Monica dreamily.

"Yes . . . I remember."

"It was different for us," said Monica. "We were older than our babies and we were here because they didn't want us at home."

"It did something to us, didn't it?" said Geraldine. "I felt I'd been robbed, so I had to grab things for myself with both hands to make up. Philip felt that he'd been robbed, too, but he took it differently. He said: 'All right. If I can't have that, I won't have anything', didn't you, Philip?"

He smiled. "I suppose so . . ." He turned to Monica. "What did it do to you?"

"It made me frightened," said Monica slowly. "All my life I was frightened till I met Stephen. Then I stopped being frightened."

"And Angela? She wasn't much better off than we were."

"No," agreed Geraldine. "She found out that she didn't mean anything to either her father or her mother and so she began to build up a glamorous figure of herself and worship it as a sort of make-weight. But it wasn't real. It's her children who've made her real."

"She worked the poison out of her system by child-bearing," said Philip. "Well, I suppose it's as good a way as any."

They looked down at the lawn again, where Angela sat on a rug, playing with her baby.

"Come down!" she called. "Let's show off our children to each other."

"We're just coming."

But they still stood there, as if unwilling to break some spell. A droning sound filled the air, and, looking up, they saw a formation of Spitfires passing over the house. They passed slowly and serenely, like silver birds against the blue sky.

THE END

Lightning Source UK Ltd.
Milton Keynes UK
UKOW04f0343010917
308374UK00001B/128/P

9 781509 8595